THE EDGE OF DAWN

TOR BOOKS BY MELINDA SNODGRASS

The Edge of Ruin
The Edge of Reason
The Edge of Dawn

THE EDGE OF DAWN

Melinda Snodgrass

A TOM DOHERTY ASSOCIATES BOOK
New York

THE EDGE OF DAWN

A Tor Book
Published by Tom Doherty Associates, LLC
175 Fifth Avenue
New York, NY 10010

www.tor-forge.com

Tor® is a registered trademark of Tom Doherty Associates, LLC.

The Library of Congress Cataloging-in-Publication Data is available upon request.

ISBN 978-0-7653-3816-7 (hardcover)
ISBN 978-1-4668-3781-2 (e-book)

Tor books may be purchased for educational, business, or promotional use. For
information on bulk purchases, please contact the Macmillan Corporate and
Premium Sales Department at 1-800-221-7945, extension 5442,
or write to specialmarkets@macmillan.com.

First Edition: August 2015

Printed in the United States of America

0 9 8 7 6 5 4 3 2 1

For Carl,
Always in my heart,
Never far from my thoughts

Acknowledgments

This book happened because of help from a lot of people. First and foremost, my amazing agent, Kay McCauley, who kept fighting and pushing so this series would have a second chance. My editors, Stacy Hill and Miriam Weinberg, who believed in me enough to also take the chance. To my writers' workshop cohorts—M. T. Reiten, Ian Tregillis, and Sage Walker—who kept me honest and whose notes always made the book better. Also, huge thanks to Jim Moore, a world-class archaeologist, who suggested the way to disrupt a subdivision.

THE EDGE OF DAWN

Chapter

ONE

MOSI Tsosie was scared.

The family had moved their flock of sheep to BIA land near the edge of Chaco Canyon and built a hogan. Grandfather was very traditional and refused to let them use a prefab building. They did carry the logs in the bed of the pickup because trees were scarce to nonexistent out by the canyon, but the sod was cut from the earth, and the logs were chinked with that same soil, and it had five sides and a door facing east as was proper.

Mother had selected that site for summer grazing because there had been a lot of rain in western New Mexico and the grass was high. Grandfather, being traditional, had wanted to do a ceremony in the canyon near the pueblo of Wijiji. And her father, who was an excellent potter and silversmith, knew he could make a lot of money selling to the sunburned tourists who would be filling the campground.

That was all normal. What wasn't normal was her brother, Abel.

Abel was smart, really smart. He wanted to become a doctor after he finished high school. A lot of people laughed at him because Abel wouldn't even start high school until the fall, but Mosi knew he would do what he said. Abel was that kind of person.

At the end of the summer session at the boarding school at Sheep Springs, Abel had been given a computer along with everyone else at the school. The computers were fun, with colored cases instead of the usual white or black or silver. Abel's was a deep purple like a sunset after a rainstorm.

Dad was proud of Abel, so he had bought a wind-powered generator so Abel would have electricity even while they were following the flock and doing ceremonies and selling pottery and bracelets. Abel spent all his time on the computer.

But Mosi had seen the grotesque, twisted faces in the screen. Not normal people-faces of friends on Facebook, or LiveJournal. They had Internet only when they were in Gallup or Farmington, but these faces kept appearing on the screen even way out here among the canyons and the mesas. At first Mosi thought Abel might be stealing the Internet from the rangers at Chaco Canyon, but she'd snuck over to the computer and checked, and there was no signal. Which meant the faces weren't part of the white man's technology; they were spirits or witches.

They whispered to Abel late in the night when everyone else was asleep. Mosi would lie in her sleeping bag watching the shadows jump on the walls of the hogan as the fire in the potbellied stove died to embers, listening to the guttural voices and shivering.

Mother and Father were tired at night, slumbering so deeply they didn't hear the voices. When Mosi tried to tell them, they ruffled her hair and gave her a kiss and talked about what an imagination she had. Now Mosi wished she had never started telling stories. Then they might have believed her.

Mosi went with Grandfather on the morning he performed the ceremony. She had helped him gather crow feathers and tie them with yarn left over from Grandmother's weaving. Grandmother had died over the winter. Mosi suspected the ceremony was for Grandmother because Grandfather had loved her very much, but he wouldn't say. He just let Mosi help while never explaining.

They had placed the fetish in an adobe tower halfway up the cliff above the ruins of Wijiji. Navajos had built the adobe tower against the back of a large red boulder where white people wouldn't find it. Partly because they were lazy and partly because they were told by the rangers not to leave the trails, and most of them obeyed the rules.

Grandfather used his stick to help him descend the cliff. Mosi bounded ahead of him. At one point the scree shifted beneath her feet, and it was like skiing on rocks. She reached the canyon bottom, dumped pebbles out of her tennis shoes, and tried to figure out how to tell Grandfather about the faces.

The side canyon that held Wijiji faced west, and the sun was setting. Fingers of light flowed between the rocks, turning them to gold and rose. High overhead a crow rode the thermals, turning in lazy circles, the shadow of his wings sweeping across the sand and sage. The broken walls of the pueblo scratched at the indigo sky, and the stacked stone gleamed as if a fire had been lit inside the sandstone.

They began walking down the road in the center of the canyon. Dust puffed up around their feet like blown dandelion fluff. They passed a tourist in shorts, tank top, and hiking boots, thrusting two ski poles into the dirt to propel her along. Her blond braid bounced on her back, and her nose was red.

For some reason, the sight of the silly girl burning in the desert sun gave Mosi the courage to speak to Grandfather. She smoothed the sleeve of her long-sleeved shirt, averted her eyes, and said in a rush, "I think there's a skinwalker or a witch in Abel's computer. Maybe a lot of them."

Grandfather grunted and spat out a glob of phlegm into the dirt. "Skinwalkers don't use modern toys. Nor witches, for that matter."

"But I've see—"

"It's not possible."

And that ended the discussion. Sometimes being traditional wasn't such a good thing, Mosi decided.

That night the faces were whispering most intently to Abel. Mosi wondered if they knew she had tried to tell. She decided that tomorrow, when Abel went out to their latrine trench, she would take the computer, run into the desert, and throw it away.

Thinking of the latrine, Mosi realized she needed to pee. She slipped out of her sleeping bag, slid her feet into her tennis shoes, and pulled aside the blanket that covered the hogan's door. The night air brushed against her bare arms and legs and crept through the thin material of her nightgown, raising goose bumps. In just a few hours the sun would rise, and heat would once again dance above the rocks, but right now it was night in the desert and it was cold.

She went to the latrine and listened to the patter as warm pee splashed down into the trench. She wiped with a tissue and buried the paper in the dirt. Back at the hogan, she pulled aside the blanket and froze as a new scent hit her nose. The smell of woodsmoke, beans, chili, and sweat had been replaced by a sweet cloying aroma. She had smelled it often enough before. Whenever Mother butchered a lamb or a sickly sheep, or when father and Abel brought home rabbits they had trapped.

Blood.

But there were no lambs or rabbits in the hogan. Just people. The moon was rising late this night. The silver light entered the hogan and glittered in her brother's eyes. He was holding the big butcher knife their mother used to shank leg bones. It dripped blood. Mosi had only a moment to react to the sight of her grandfather, head thrown back, throat cut, before Abel lunged at her.

Mosi screamed, stumbled back, and ran. Abel was older and taller, but Mosi was quicksilver fast, and she had spent every day playing outside around the hogan and she knew the ground. Abel had spent his days in conversation with the witches and didn't.

There was a thud, the crackle of broken brush, and a string of curses from Abel. Mosi clenched her fists and ran harder until she reached the barbed-wire fence that separated the national park from the BIA land. She slipped through the wires, felt her nightgown catch on a barb and tear, along with a bit of her skin. It stung, and she felt a tiny trickle of blood.

She heard Abel's harsh breaths behind her, but not too close. She ran until the stitch in her side felt like a knife and her throat burned. Past the visitors' center. On toward the small cabins where the rangers lived. She didn't like to turn to the government men and women. They often tried to drive her father away so they could sell their own souvenirs, but it was another mile to the campground, and she wasn't sure the tourists, many cocooned in their giant RVs, would be of much help.

And the rangers had guns.

TWO

SWEAT ran in rivulets down his sides, trickling beneath the ceramic-insert body armor to pool at his waistband. The biting, throat-choking smell of an Old One overwhelmed even the cloying scent of rotting vegetation from the jungle that surrounded the Aztec ruin. Dark clouds roiled overhead, promising a drenching rain to come. Up until now, Richard Oort's experience with Mexico had been the dry Sonoran Desert south of his home in New Mexico. He had never experienced the jungles of southern Mexico. And right now he wished he wasn't there, as the high-powered bullets pinged against the body of the jeep behind which he had taken cover.

The guttural music of machine gun fire punctuated Richard's words as he spoke aloud, "There are too many damn guns in this country." Which he then amended to, "Maybe there are just too many damn guns in the whole damn world."

Not for the first time, he cursed Kenntnis for not updating his own weapon while it was still possible. If the sword had become an Uzi that could spew magic-destroying bullets, Richard would be a whole lot happier. But Kenntnis was now mindless, and the opportunity had passed.

Richard's own Lumina troops were all around him, using abandoned trucks and jeeps and fallen stones for cover as they tried to push forward through the dying jungle that enshrouded the Aztec pyramid. They were augmented with gunmen provided by Teo Santiago, the man who had brought them to this stretch of jungle south and east of Santa Cruz Xoxocotlán, a place where there was a tear in the fabric of reality, where something alien, hostile, and evil had entered the world. The only thing that could defeat it was the ancient weapon, currently carried by Richard. Unfortunately, Richard had to get close enough to the creature to touch it with the blade of the sword so it could be destroyed.

The sound of gunfire also meant that the Old One was not nearby, since modern technology didn't do well in the warped reality of a tear. The absence was good. If the creature had retreated into its own multiverse, all they had to do was fight their way to the opening, and the sword would close it, keeping the Old One from returning.

One of Uncle Teo's paramilitary men rolled into cover with Richard. His dark-skinned face was shiny with sweat, and he hugged his rifle like a kid with a teddy bear as he spat out a barrage of Spanish. Richard found the colloquial Spanish a bit hard to follow, but he could understand, and even make himself understood, in his more formal Spanish. Now the man was telling him that there was a trench seven hundred yards to the west dug by archaeologists a few years ago. It ran all the way to the temple and offered some protection from the guns of the fanatics who had spent the past two years worshiping the Old One and increasing its power with their sacrifices.

Damon Weber came racing across the open plaza, bullets whining at his heels. One must have hit his Kevlar armor, for he staggered before catching his balance. Richard's heart squeezed down tight with fear and anxiety, then Weber dove, sliding in beside him.

"Motherfucker! I'm gonna have a bruise from that one." Weber was a tall man in his late forties with faint acne scars around his eyes and jawline. His brown hair was tinged with gray at the temples, his skin tanned and leathery. "The things you get me into."

"Hey, at least this time somebody took it seriously, and gave us actual . . . oh . . . help."

"Yeah, and let's not talk about the irony of *that*."

Richard understood because the men fighting at the side of the Lumina security forces were the elite bodyguards and enforcers for Uncle Teo's massive drug cartel. Once upon a time Weber and Richard had worked together as police officers in Albuquerque, and tried to stop drug cartels.

Richard wondered if the Old One had any idea what had brought down this shit storm on its stronghold and its followers. Not that it could have changed the situation even if it did understand. Old Ones warped and disrupted the natural order. Wherever they held sway, magic worked, people went mad, and plants perished. Uncle Teo's pot fields had started to croak from the encroaching power of the Old One, so Uncle Teo had gone looking for help and come across the Lumina Web site which, in addition to listing its various business interests, made no bones about the other services the company offered. *We have the means to close rents in the fabric of the universe and destroy any creatures that may enter through those tears.*

A few years before, they wouldn't have been so forthcoming. Partly because until Richard stumbled into this secret war, Lumina didn't have a paladin who could use the sword, and because the world at large didn't know about this age-old battle between magic, religion, and superstition, and science, reason, and rationality. Now the world knew, and Lumina didn't need to hide. Of course, what the Web site didn't mention was that that power rested in a young man of very modest height, with a rather shy demeanor, armed with a sword.

Richard had taken the call from Mexico, listened to the situation, called Weber, who was then in Africa, and ordered the security chief to gather a strike team and meet him in Mexico. They had been met with armored limos at the airport and driven to the drug lord's palatial hacienda, where on the sweeping stone steps at the entrance they had been made welcome by the stoop-shouldered, gray-haired man.

Once Richard and Weber were settled with chilled glasses of horchata and beer, respectively, provided by Teo's gorgeous wife who was at least thirty years younger than himself, the old man said with absolutely no irony, "*Those government* pendejos *in Mexico City won't do shit for an honest businessman.*"

He'd also been willing to help, augmenting the Lumina troops with fifty of his own men. Now, looking at that round, sweat-drenched face of the gunman, Richard wondered how many drug rivals, policemen, and maybe innocent citizens the man had killed. *Don't think about it. Do what we came to do. Get out.*

Richard brought Weber up to speed. The older man popped up for a quick look, and ducked back down when a hail of gunfire hit the jeep. "Well, first we have to get you into the trench. Looks like a feint from the other direction is in order."

"You'll lead that?" Richard asked.

"No, I'm going to be with you."

"Don't leave it to Uncle Teo's thugs."

But Weber was already on his throat mike calling his second in command. "Wangai, we need a distraction on the left."

"How big you want it, bwana?" The woman's voice was a husky alto with a lilting accent of her native Kenya.

"Big."

"Right ho. Give me five to get things arranged."

"Copy that."

"And take care of Richard."

"I will."

"I'm right here, Wangai," Richard said, disgruntled by the unspoken implication.

"I know you are, *jumbe*. You do what Weber tells you."

Richard broke the connection. "Why does she call you bwana and me *jumbe*?"

"'Cause you rate. Bwana just means boss. *Jumbe* is chief."

"So why do I still feel like you're both treating me like I'm six years old?"

Weber just grinned at him and checked his watch. They waited, sweltering, as seconds ticked into minutes. The radio crackled back to life.

"One of Teo's madmen has a rocket launcher," Wangai said. "When you give us the word, we'll light up that pyramid."

"Archaeologists around the world are going to love us for this," Richard said.

Weber shrugged. "We'll blame the drug lord. Ready?"

"Yeah." They duck-walked to the front end of the jeep. Richard touched the hilt of the sword where it rested in a holster at the small of his back. He then hugged his assault rifle against his chest.

A wave of sound, physical in its intensity, swept past them, and the darkening landscape was lit as the dead and dying trees caught fire. Richard and Weber sprinted for the test trench as Weber panted, "You have got to get us some of those!"

Richard tucked and rolled into the trench, and grunted when his hip hit a piece of masonry in the bottom, followed by a squelch as he rolled into the mud. "Yuck."

"Yeah, heaven forfend that you end up dirty while fighting in a military action," Weber grunted.

They rushed down the trench. A shadow overhead was his only warning. Richard flung himself forward and twisted around to bring his rifle to bear. A man in ragged, mud-stained clothes was on the edge of the trench above him. Richard held down the trigger. A sharp short burst of lethal lead, and the man collapsed.

Twenty-nine. He added this man to the mental list of people he knew he had killed with malice aforethought. There had been a time when such an action left him nauseated and shaken. He hated fire-fights, but he was getting coldly efficient at them, and he wasn't sure that was a good thing. Which was why he kept the count, to remind himself this wasn't a video game. These were real lives and real deaths with real consequences. Somewhere people would mourn this man. If they were true believers or servitors of the Old Ones, he supposed he would be less sorry. The kind of humans who would turn against their own kind deserved no regret, but still, Richard never wanted to stop being affected.

They charged forward, hoping the crazies only had enough foresight for one sentry. The trench ended at a doorway in the base of the pyramid. The archaeologists had started to excavate beyond but obviously hadn't gone far. They stepped through the door but could go only a few feet before dirt, roots, and fallen stones blocked their way. They exchanged a glance.

"Ah, shucks, we don't get to go into the dark, scary interior of an Aztec pyramid and fight an alien monster," Weber said.

"No, instead we get to do a frontal assault up the outside steps of the pyramid, being resisted every step of the way by crazed cultists," Richard said.

"Yeah, awesome."

"At least we reached the pyramid." Richard cocked his head as the sound of gunfire suddenly choked off. He then experimentally pulled the trigger on his rifle. It didn't fire. "The Old One. It's here."

"Fuck. We never catch a break."

Richard set aside his rifle. It was of no use now and could be a danger with a bullet lodged in the barrel. He pulled the sword hilt from its holster. The hilt looked like a piece of gray glass formed into intricate loops and curves reminiscent of a Klein bottle. Richard made a fist with his right hand, pressed it against the base of the hilt. He drew his hand away, and a space-black blade shot through with silver light like captured stars appeared as if from inside his palm. Drawing the sword was never a subtle act. A single musical chord and the accompanying overtones shimmered in the air as the blade appeared. It was a sound that shook a person down to his core, as if he were leaning against the biggest speaker ever made.

"Well, it knows I'm here now," Richard said. His mouth felt dry.

Only a unique individual could draw the sword, an ancient weapon crafted thousands of years before. A person like Richard who possessed a rare genetic mutation. Magic had been bred into most humans by the Old Ones because it made it easier for them to feed, but Richard was a human born without a trace of magic. Right now he wished he wasn't quite so unique. Weber drew the kukri that hung at his belt. The glint on the curved blade was dulled by the overcast light, but that only added to its air of menace.

They retreated from the partially excavated room and found three raggedly dressed humans waiting. Richard lunged, rapidly tapping two of them with the flat of the sword. They screamed, collapsed, and began to convulse when the blade touched them and stripped from them the magic that was woven in their DNA. Weber had to handle the third, and his solution had to be lethal. They didn't like killing the people caught up in these tears. You never knew who were innocents and who had been willing participants, and even the willing could sometimes be salvaged once the sword had done its work. But sometimes it was unavoidable.

The rain that had held off all day finally began, a warm downpour that brought no relief from the oppressive heat. They started up the cracked stone steps of the pyramid, striking at the human servitors who tried to stop them. Richard's heart felt too big for his chest as it labored. His lungs pumped, trying to suck in enough of the bitter, sour air. They reached the top platform. A small stone pinnacle held a door into a small room. The opening between the multiverses was inside, a window on an alien world. Structures whose angles and bulk were disturbing to human eyes dotted the landscape.

Alien suns, one bloated and red, the other small and blazing white, hung on that planet's horizon. Their light spilled through the tear and stained the Earth stones red, an echo of the blood that had once flowed across them and was now flowing again.

Richard laid about himself with wide, swinging blows. Worshipers screamed and collapsed. Richard started to rush forward to reach the opening and close it, and was knocked to the stone surface by a body leaping from above. A woman had been standing on top of the building, and he hadn't spotted her.

Gotta remember to look up, he thought as she hit. The body armor helped, but he banged his left elbow hard, and his hand went numb. He couldn't keep a grip on the sword. The hilt fell from his hand and rolled away. The instant it left his hand, the blade vanished.

He managed to look to the right to see Weber struggling with a clot of eight or ten humans. A shadow fell over Richard. His assailant scrambled away, keening and crying, hiding her face in her hands and behind her long tangled and filthy hair. The Old One was just a confused image of claws and too many eyes, and it was *big*. Richard tried to roll away, to reach the hilt, but one of its segmented arms shot out, and claws dug through the body armor and into his side. Richard screamed. It felt like acid had been injected into the wound. It lifted him into the air, pulled him close like a mother embracing a toddler. Richard tried to struggle, but each movement was agony. His vision narrowed, darkness closing in at the edges. The thing was taking him to the dimensional tear.

"Damon! Help!" he called, but his voice was faint in his own ears.

Weber, beset on all sides, looked over at Richard. Richard had never seen such panic and desperation on his friend's face. "Richard!" Weber tried to break through the circle of foes but was beaten back.

A figure leaped up the final steps and onto the platform. It was Wangai. The beads in her beautiful cornrows were clashing against each other, and her chiseled features were set as if she were carved from ebony. She raced forward, scooping up the sword hilt as she passed, and she threw it unerringly to Richard. He caught it. The Old One gave an inarticulate roar and tried to paw it out of his hand with one of its claw-tipped arms, but Richard turned enough to shield it with his body. He felt more tearing as he moved, and he fought the impulse to just give up and faint. Now the creature drew back, trying to get away from Richard, but its claws were locked in the armor and his ribs. It was trying to shake him off like a person trying to fling shit off his hand. Each flick was agony, but Richard managed to get the sword drawn. Holding the hilt with both hands, he twisted until he was facing the Old One and drove the blade deep into the creature's chest.

An unearthly cry ripped at the sky, and the thing collapsed into black and bubbling sludge. The sound of gunfire erupted once more, a few explosions and a few screams as the bullets trapped in the barrels of guns detonated with unfortunate results.

"Oh, yuck," Richard said faintly as he lay in the widening pool of corruption. Then he fainted.

A pungent scent yanked him back to consciousness. Someone had broken an ammonia cap under his nose. He tried to retreat from the harsh stink, gasped in pain, and stopped moving. Weber's arms were around him, hugging him close, his head cradled on the older man's chest.

"Sorry, *jumbe*, but you must close the opening before this one's"— Wangai gestured at the black goop—"father or husband comes looking for her."

Richard wondered why Wangai thought the Old One had been female. And did Old Ones actually have genders? Richard realized he was drifting. He gathered his wandering thoughts and nodded. "Weber," he croaked as Wangai helped him to stand. "Are you okay?"

Weber climbed to his feet and clasped Richard's outstretched hand between his. "Few nicks, bites, and bruises. I'll live. I'm more worried about you. Let's get this done," he said over Richard's head to Wangai.

With Wangai supporting him on one side, and Weber, arm around his waist, supporting him on the other, they got him into the building. Richard drew the sword, placed the point of the blade at the base of the tear, and wove the blade back and forth as if stitching. The rent in reality closed. Outside the gunfire died away, and he heard the confused murmuring and cries of misery.

"Do you think Uncle Teo has a doctor on retainer?" Richard said faintly.

"Probably a good one."

"I'd like to see him . . . or her."

The last thing he remembered was his feet leaving the ground as Weber swung him up into his arms.

———◊◆◊———

Uncle Teo's physician turned out to be a dapper Frenchman who cleaned the wounds in Richard's side and stitched up the places where the claws had torn long gashes. Uncle Teo was effusive in his gratitude and offered prostitutes, fine brandy, some of his product, anything that Richard and Weber might have desired. Richard would have been amused if Lumina hadn't lost two members of the strike team. He asked Uncle Teo to pay death benefits to their families. The elderly drug lord seemed startled by the request—he had lost twelve of his men and seemed unfazed by their deaths—but he agreed to make the funds available. Then it was back to the airport, where Wangai oversaw the loading of equipment into the waiting Lumina jets.

Richard clasped Weber's forearm briefly. "You take care," he said.

Weber gave him a hug that had Richard gasping as Weber's arm came in contact with his stitches. Contrite, Weber muttered, "Sorry."

Richard's inclination would have been to lean into the embrace. Instead he used the pain as an excuse and an opportunity to step out of the hug.

"You be careful too," Weber added.

Richard nodded, then couldn't control the impulse and said, "I miss you."

"You're the one who put me in charge of overseas security," Weber pointed out.

"Yeah."

"So, let me trade with Joseph."

Was that hopefulness? Richard realized he was projecting, put aside the temptation, and gave Weber a wan smile. "I'll think about it."

Once on the plane, Richard took two pain pills and slept during the flight back to Albuquerque.

━━━◇◈◇━━━

His head of domestic security was waiting along with Estevan at the airport. Joseph Malcomb was an older African-American man with threads of gray through his black hair and a nose that had been broken more than a few times. "Wish you'd taken me," he said as Richard climbed stiffly into the car.

"It makes me feel better knowing you're here to guard my people."

"I understand, Richard, but you're too valuable to risk."

"Well, thanks, but I don't see any way around it."

"Cross needs to find us another paladin," Joseph grumbled as they left the airport.

"He's trying, but as he keeps pointing out, there are seven billion people on the planet, and he's looking for a very small needle in a very large haystack."

Richard leaned against the backseat and closed his eyes. Twenty minutes later, the seven-story Lumina building was before them. It was built on the shoulders of the Sandias, and its gleaming white-and-silver exterior was a crystal knife set against the dark blue–gray granite of the mountain. Off to the right, a tram car was just starting its ascent, heading for the restaurant on the crest. The dying rays of the sun turned it into a jeweled bead suspended from a silver string.

Joseph keyed the gate to the underground parking lot and pulled the limo into a spot between the Ferrari and the Lamborghini. Richard's predecessor had been a car fanatic, and there were seven including the limo. A strange vice for a man determined to save the world, but there was one nod to green technology. Among the cars was a Tesla.

Estevan returned to his sentry duties, Joseph to the security office, while Richard was whisked up to the sixth floor. His sister Pamela was seated on the edge of Jeannette's desk. Both his assistant and his sibling rushed him when he stepped off the elevator.

"You've got to stop playing the hero," Pamela groused.

"I've arranged for Dr. Bush to look you over," Jeannette said.

"You take too many chances," hectored Pamela.

"Jorge wants to see you," Jeannette said.

Richard raised his hands, palms out. "Stop! I don't want to see another doctor. I have to close these openings. And remind me again, who is Jorge?"

"Grenier's research assistant," Jeannette said crisply. "Sophomore at UNM, journalism student, studying new media. You inoculated him back in April."

"Right, got it." Richard headed into his office.

It had changed little over the past year and a half since Richard had been given control of the company. Despite that authority, he still considered himself to be merely a seat warmer. Kenntnis, the man who'd built Lumina, was back now, and it was just a matter of time before he would recover. Eventually. Maybe. Hopefully. It hadn't happened yet, but Richard hadn't given up. Something had to get him out of this chair and the responsibility that went with it.

Richard had moved the giant espresso machine out into reception because most of the time he didn't drink coffee, and the Steinway

Kenntnis had purchased for him stood in one corner. He had his Bösendorfer upstairs in the living quarters. He preferred the touch on his own piano. The only other change was a television. With the 24/7 news cycle, Richard wanted to know what was happening at any given moment, and having the TV on as background noise saved him from having to pop out to the web too often. Lumina's computer science division had made their system as secure as possible, but a hack was always possible.

He turned his attention to the man waiting for him. Jorge Tafoya was a very young man whose features and coloring were a throwback to his conquistador ancestors. He was standing in front of the large oval desk and tracing the whorls in its granite top with a forefinger. Richard looked up and remembered hiring the boy. As they shook hands, Richard couldn't help it, his eyes followed the muscular forearms visible because of a short-sleeved T-shirt, and up to the line of the jaw. Standing this close, Richard could smell the Old Spice mingled with a touch of sweat, and the kid had been eating salt-and-vinegar potato chips.

"Jorge, what can I do for you?"

"I think I've got one . . . an incursion, sir. I know Mr. Grenier says I'm not supposed to bother you, but he's gone to the dentist, and the Jesus Man isn't around, and I think this is really important. I didn't think it could wait." He studied Richard's face and ducked his head. "But only if you feel up to it. We heard you got hurt."

"I'm okay, show me."

Jorge laid a handful of printouts from websites and two newspaper clippings on Richard's desk. "Finding God in Everyday Tasks," read one headline. "Cutting the Lawn as an Act of Grace," read the title on a conservative website. Richard scanned the first article. It seemed a "prayerful" subdivision known as Gilead's Balm was being built in Orange County, California, funded by the reclusive right-wing billionaire Alexander Titchen.

"What do we know about this guy?" Richard asked.

"Here's the public scoop." Jorge bent over the papers, and Richard considered the whorl of black hair at the nape of the young Hispanic man's neck. He resisted reaching out to touch it. "The Titchen Group's a global investment company founded in 1938 by Henry Titchen. His son, Randolph, took over in 1963 and ran it until 1990. The company's now run by *his* son, Alexander Titchen. The old man, Henry, was a stone-cold racist. He funded a bunch of bullshit research to prove that brown, black, and yellow people are intellectually inferior to the Mighty Whitey. Randolph was a Holocaust denier, and he gave some interviews where it sounds like he believed it's America's duty to bring about World War Three in the Middle East so the prophecies of Revelation can be fulfilled and the infidels and sinners appropriately punished. Alexander seems to avoid that kind of talk, but you have to wonder if that apple fell very far from the racist tree," Jorge concluded.

"Lovely," Richard muttered. He pinched the bridge of his nose. "These so-called Christian communities aren't a new concept. A Catholic subdivision was built in Florida a few years ago. It never occurred to me they might be a front for the Old Ones."

Jorge nodded energetically. "Yeah, I felt the same way until I came to work for you guys. Now I just assume that anything associated with religion could be trouble."

"Not always. The people who actually try to follow actual Christian tenets can do good work."

"True, though our Jesus Man doesn't think much of them either. But check *this* out," he said, his voice jumping with suppressed excitement.

Jorge pulled a satellite photo out of his folder. The boy's arm skimmed across Richard's side as he reached. Richard hissed and stepped aside, but it wasn't just due to the touch on his wound. He was surprised by his arousal. It had been a long time since he'd felt this way. Richard remembered waking in Weber's arms, and the hug . . . He pushed those thoughts aside and looked down at the photo.

A number of houses were already completed, others were in various stages of construction. Roads snaked through them. There were several parks where the landscaping was merely a suggestion, and the young trees looked like bushes from this height. What it all added up to was a rune. A big one.

"You didn't bug Bob Franklin for this, did you?" Richard asked. "I don't want him in trouble with the FBI."

"No, sir, this is Google Earth." Richard looked again at the satellite photo. "Now tell me that's not a rune," Jorge said triumphantly.

"It's a rune," Richard agreed.

Jorge gave a fist pump. "*Yes*. I knew it. I knew I didn't need to run this past Grenier or Cross. So what's the plan? And could I please go with you on this one, Mr. Oort? I just really want to see your sword, you know, in action. I love the whole sword thing."

Richard felt his color rising, then realized that there was no hidden meaning to Jorge's inartful remark. He hadn't sensed Richard's interest. Wasn't responding. He just thought the sword was cool.

On the day Richard had "inoculated" Jorge, Richard explained that Jorge had to be touched by a sword as a condition of employment. The young man had been delighted and declared it the cutting edge of punk: a sword—"*totally a fantasy trope, man—but it destroys magic. I mean, how awesome is that? It's like antifantasy,*" he'd declared.

"Are you going to move in? Scope it out? I could pretend to be your . . . your . . . son . . . or something."

Amusement and annoyance struggled for primacy. Annoyance won out. "Excuse me, I'm only nine years older than you are," he said to Jorge. "I'd have to have been pretty damn precocious to be your father."

"I'm sorry, sir. You just seem a lot older, sir. Maybe it's because I'm still in school and you're . . . . my boss."

The boy looked contrite, and Richard felt like he'd kicked a puppy.

"I don't know what I'm going to do yet, Jorge," Richard said. "And these things often turn out to be dangerous. I couldn't face your parents if anything happened to you. Thank you for bringing this to my attention. If you could, tell Jeannette to send in my sister and Joseph, and send Mr. Grenier to me once he gets in."

⬦

Grenier returned to Lumina headquarters after he'd treated himself to a delightful lunch at Chez Nous, a bit of comfort after having a tooth prepared for a crown. His sense of satisfaction faded when he found a message from Jeannette waiting—he was wanted in Richard's office as soon as he got in.

He was panting as he reached the elevator bank. One of the pert girls from accounting was already in the car, and he noted her eyes darting to his shirt. He looked down and discovered a button had surrendered in its battle against his burgeoning belly and slipped free, revealing an expanse of white skin. He sucked in his gut, turned away. His prosthetic hand, courtesy of Lumina money and R&D, wasn't up to the task, and it took several tries before the gap closed. The button gave way again. He was going to have to buy new shirts. Again. Or lose weight. Neither prospect was particularly pleasant.

The elevator dropped the pert girl on five and Grenier continued to the sixth floor that held Richard's office and the conference room. As he passed Jeanette's desk, she keyed the intercom and murmured, "Mr. Grenier has arrived, sir."

"Send him in," came Richard's light tenor voice.

Grenier found Richard behind the desk, hands clasped in front of him. The boy was paler than usual, and the circles beneath his ice-blue eyes were like bruises. Joseph, standing across the expanse of granite from his boss, flipped through a sheaf of papers. The older man was frowning, and the grooves in his forehead, like furrows in dark, rich soil, deepened the longer he read.

Richard indicated the pages should be passed on to Grenier. Almost as an afterthought, Richard asked, "How's your tooth? Jorge said you were at the dentist."

Pleasure that Richard noticed and inquired was crushed by annoyance that Jorge had talked with Richard. "And why were you talking to Jorge?"

"That." Richard waved a slim hand at the papers.

Grenier began reading. He looked at the satellite photo of the subdivision. The runic shape was clear to see. Grenier's lips twisted in a sneer. It was a simplistic rune that would at best produce a tear in reality and allow one or possibly two Old Ones to enter. Alexander Titchen had always been a workmanlike sorcerer. Grenier, on the other hand, had possessed formidable powers. He had opened a *full gate* between the multiverses, and the Old Ones had poured in.

Then Richard had destroyed all his plans and his life.

The memory of a space-black blade descending toward his wrist rose up to choke him. Phantom pain danced along the nerve endings in his wrist as Grenier remembered that blade severing his hand. Even now he could feel the warm gout of blood pumping from the stump. Given Richard's nature, he had, of course, applied a tourniquet. Sometimes Grenier wished Richard had just left him to bleed out. Grenier glanced at the preternaturally handsome face of the young man behind the desk, and his high-tech prosthetic right hand reacted to the raging electrical impulses in his brain and closed into a tight fist, crushing the papers. The crackle was loud in the silent room.

"Yeah, I agree," Joseph said, misinterpreting the reason for Grenier's fist clench.

Richard's absurdly long eyelashes lifted, and he gave Grenier a piercing glance. Grenier had a feeling that Richard knew exactly the bitter, angry thoughts that had elicited the reaction, but he said nothing.

Pamela entered. Grenier offered the pages to her. She shook her head. "I've already read them."

"Does anybody want anything?" Richard asked. People shook their heads. "So, what do we do?"

Grenier settled into a chair, grateful to take his weight off his feet. "Disrupt the shape of the rune, obviously."

"We got that far already," Richard said, and his look wasn't kind. "What are they going for? Tear or full-blown gate?" he demanded, pinning Grenier with his gaze.

"A rune this big looks like gate," Grenier lied. There was a bitter pleasure to watching Richard blanch.

"Great."

"I looked for any way to claim a zoning violation, but they've got good lawyers and they dotted every *i* and crossed every *t*," Pamela offered.

"Sounds like we need some recon," Joseph said. "I can do it."

Discomfort flashed across Richard's face. "It's not exactly a place that encourages diversity," he said diplomatically.

"You can just say it, Richard. I've got a little too much melanin," Joseph said.

Richard shook his head. It wasn't clear exactly what he was negating. "I think it's got to be me. I can go in, check things out."

"You're just back. You were hurt. There are things here that need your attention," Pamela demurred.

"Look, we just got the gates closed by freeing Kenntnis. We can't afford another large incursion. I've got to deal with this."

"You'd do anything to get away from the day-to-day management of this company, strap on your weapons, polish up your badge, metaphorically speaking, and go be a hero." The heat and anger in Pamela's voice had Richard glaring. Grenier saw what was behind it. The woman was terrified for her brother.

Grenier leaned back and laced his fingers on the mound of his belly. "Not true, Pamela. He's afraid. He's going because he's worried if he gives in to the fear, he'll never go out again."

"I'm right here, I'm not on a couch, and neither one of you is a therapist," Richard snapped. A lock of white-blond hair had shaken free. Richard shoved it back angrily and continued. "And I'm not afraid."

"Then you're stupid," Pamela said.

Richard ignored her and stood up. "I'll need a house. See if I can rent something. Otherwise we'll have to buy," he said to Pamela.

"You're being an idiot," Grenier said.

"Excuse me?"

"You're just going to move in? A young, single man? A young, single man who's as pretty as you are?" Grenier scoffed. "You'll never pass muster."

"So, what?" Pamela demanded. "He needs a wife?"

"At a minimum. A quiver full of children would also be helpful, but that's probably a bridge too far."

"And who would you suggest? It's not like he has a girlfriend," Pamela snapped, and immediately looked embarrassed.

There was a woman who would have happily played that role. Angela. But she was gone, murdered by a vicious killer nurtured and protected by Grenier. Grenier felt no guilt over that, but clearly Richard did. Grenier watched the remorse wash across the boy's face. He blamed himself for her death because of course he did. His guilt complex was a lovely handle that Grenier used as often as he could.

As for Pamela, her embarrassment probably had more to do with her discomfit over Richard's bisexuality then Angela. Of all Richard's family, she had handled his sexual orientation the best. Which wasn't hard, since Richard's father had disowned him, and the other sister had fled back to Boston disturbed not only by his sexuality but also by Lumina and its function. The strict Dutch Reform church background affected both siblings and Grenier knew how to play that with the skill of a master violinist.

"Yeah, I don't exactly have a lot of ladies lined up," Richard said with a wry smile. "Would it be creepy for you to fill that role?"

Pamela looked horrified. "Absolutely! How could you even . . ." She finally caught the humorous glint in his eyes. "You're joking."

"Yes."

"I really don't have a sense of humor, do I?"

"No."

Richard pushed back the chair with a groan and stood. He glanced at Grenier. "I'll take your objections under advisement and see if I can come up with someone. Or another alternative."

Chapter THREE

GRENIER returned to his office mad as hell

at his assistant for going over his head. Of course the situation in Gilead had to be addressed. Grenier knew how dangerous these incursions could be, since two years ago *he* had been the man planning the invasion. His failure to acquire the sword for his multidimensional masters, and his subsequent alliance with Richard to avoid death at the hands of his erstwhile allies, had Grenier marked for death. So he didn't want any more gates or tears that might deliver his killer into human reality.

With an effort, he controlled his breathing, but his heart continued to hammer in a most alarming manner. Given his current weight, such agitation was not healthy. What Grenier needed was an outlet for his rage, and fortunately he had one right at hand. He keyed the intercom. "Jorge, get in here. Now."

A few moments later, the young student walked in. Grenier noted that the boy didn't bother to knock first, which added to his anger.

"You were completely out of line," Grenier snapped. "You know the protocol. You bring anything you find to me *first*. I, in consultation with Cross, determine if there's sufficient cause to disturb Richard."

The dark eyes looking down at him were contemptuous, and the chiseled planes of his face were set and hard. "You were at the dentist, Cross wasn't around, and I didn't need the Jesus Man to see this was a damn rune."

"You are my assistant. You do not go over my head for any reason."

"Look, I've been working here long enough to see this wasn't some piddly tarot card reader or End of Days nut. This was big and I knew Richard would want to see it right away. And he didn't mind," the boy added, suddenly sounding very young. "He said I could come see him anytime."

"Well, I say you can't. You work for me."

"No, I don't. You don't cut my paycheck. Richard does or, well, Lumina does, and Richard runs Lumina, so I work for him. We all know what you did to Richard, and frankly, some people can't understand why he keeps you around. But hey, it's his choice. Point is, you're only here because he lets you stay."

"He told you?" Grenier asked, fighting to pull breath into a suddenly tight chest.

"Richard? No, Julie in accounting told me."

Grenier brought to mind the young girl whose defining feature seemed to be that she talked a lot. He could not imagine Richard confiding in her. "And how did she come by this information?" An ache began deep in his gut. A sickness that came only from emotional agitation when you started to wonder what the people around you were saying about you behind your back.

"Trina told her, and I think she heard it from Estevan in security."

Who had probably heard the story from Joseph and Weber. Weber had been part of the team that entered Grenier's Virginia compound to rescue Richard, and of course he would talk to Joseph. They were both ex-military with much in common. Grenier could imagine them kicking back, drinking beer together, and talking about what an asshole he was, and how Richard had tricked and duped him. Once again pain flared in the nerves of his wrist.

Jorge was talking again. "You're always strutting around here, acting like a big shot, but you're not. You're not Reverend Mark Grenier, world-famous televangelist any longer. You're Mark Jenkins now because you jumped bail, and you're living with fake ID courtesy of Lumina. You're the guy who handles publicity and occasionally tells us what a badass sorcerer you used to be, and acts like a fucking genius when *I* find something. Not like it's hard to spot once you know what to look for. And you can't even do magic any longer because Richard took care of that," Jorge concluded triumphantly.

"Get out!" Grenier forced through stiff lips.

"Gladly."

Grenier stared at the closed door, tried to get his racing pulse to subside. He felt hollow inside. Heaving to his feet, he slid past the desk and hustled down the hall to the small ad hoc kitchen he'd set up on the fifth floor. He pulled a frozen pizza out of the small refrigerator, threw it in the microwave, and waited, quivering with anxiety until the timer dinged. Snatching it out, he started eating, gulping ravenous bites that threatened to choke him and burned the roof of his mouth.

He would leave. If they didn't appreciate the work he did here . . . well, they could see how well they did without his expertise. And Jorge's hero worship of Richard. Disgusting. He wondered how long that would last if he were to tell the young man that his hero liked boys?

Anger gave way to sober consideration. Sure, he had opened a gate, but he had failed in another of his tasks and his masters dealt with failure . . . harshly. It was only Richard and the sword that kept them at bay and Mark safe. So he couldn't leave, and the sense of confinement and lack of options once again had his heart racing.

He, who had once prayed with presidents and wielded great political, financial, spiritual, and magical power, was reduced to *this*. Taking sass from a juvenile, working for a deeply inadequate salary, living in an inferior apartment in an overgrown cow town, and being forced almost daily to face the man who had stripped him of power.

<hr />

The office seemed small with so many people present and all of them talking at the same time. Grenier hunched over a laptop resting on the closed lid of the piano. Joseph stood next to him. Richard moved to where Pamela, her nostrils pinched in disgust, stood next to a bum.

Cross wore a faded blue T-shirt with a picture of the Milky Way galaxy, an arrow, and the notation YOU ARE HERE. Long stringy brown hair hung over his shoulders. His blue jeans were adorned with various mysterious stains, and his tennis shoes had seen better days. A giant piece of chocolate cake threatened to fall off the sides of a plate.

Cross's features were a compilation of every Jesus painting, though at the moment he didn't have the beard and mustache. *The Jesus Man, as Jorge calls him*, Richard thought. Cross gestured with his fork and brushed the back of his hand across the icing, coating his knuckles. He licked away the icing and wiped what remained on his stained jeans. Pamela looked even more pained.

He drew close enough to hear Cross say, "Burn the place down. That gets rid of the rune." Cross gave an emphatic nod and jammed another giant bite of cake into his mouth.

For an instant, Richard was somewhat envious of Cross's philosophy of life. For him, every problem was a nail and he was a hammer. Richard opened his mouth to point out the myriad of flaws in the plan, but Pamela beat him to it.

"I did *not* hear you say that," she said, staring down her nose at the homeless god. "And if you actually believe that, then you are certifiably insane."

Richard clapped Cross on the shoulder. "We *are* supposed to be the good guys," he said mildly.

"You gotta break a few eggs to make an omelet," Cross said, and there was a glitter in his eyes that Richard had never seen before and that he didn't like at all. Once again he was forcibly reminded that Cross was an Old One. Just an Old One who happened to be on their side. A shiver like a single drop of ice water ran down his spine. "You call in a bomb threat and evacuate the place first," Cross said.

"And sometimes people don't heed those warnings. And you know that every plan always goes pear-shaped." Richard shook his head. "No. This topic is closed."

Pamela pulled him aside. "He won't go off on his own and do something horrible, will he?"

"No. He still obeys me."

A strange expression crossed his sister's face. "Whatever you end up doing, it won't be dangerous, will it? Not like Mexico?"

"What's this? Worry?" Richard joked, made uncomfortable by the honest emotion Pamela was displaying.

She stiffened. "You never listen."

"Sorry. I'll be careful, and since we've devolved to murder and mayhem, it's probably time—past time—for me to take control and decide just what I *am* going to do," Richard said quietly.

He then used the singer's voice, words supported on a column of air straight out of his diaphragm. "All right!" Amazingly they all shut up. "I am *not* going to bomb, burn, raze, or otherwise drop an airplane on this place. People . . . families live there. I'm more than happy to kill Old Ones, but I'm damned if I'm going to kill my own kind unless I absolutely haven't got a choice."

"Well, we've got to do *something*," Joseph said. "It's the buildings and the streets that are making this rune thingy. We've got to destroy it."

"It would just get rebuilt," Grenier said. "Titchen has the money."

"And all we'd have done is delay the problem rather than solving it," Richard added.

There was a long silence while all of them pondered the problem. Richard had a feeling Cross was still wistfully contemplating blast yields and radii. But Richard didn't need to eradicate the subdivision, he just needed to *alter* it. His brain seemed to be spinning in circles, closing down tighter and tighter until, in desperation, stupid unconnected thoughts came floating through.

Richard found himself remembering the time he'd been stuck on traffic detail when he was still a uniformed cop. It had been a late July day, the mercury was flirting with one hundred degrees, and the New Mexico sun hit his pale skin like burning needles. A new visitors' center was going up near Tingley Beach, but construction had been halted when the backhoe had hit artifacts.

"Archaeology," Richard said aloud, and blessed his subconscious.

"What?" Pamela asked.

"What the fuck?" was Cross's version of the same question.

"I gather you're thinking about seeding a site?" Grenier drawled.

Richard nodded. "Find me an archaeologist and some tribes that are native to California," he ordered Grenier.

"Better be some unscrupulous ones," Pamela muttered.

"If we force the subdivision to relocate a road, or several roads and houses, will it be enough?" Richard asked Cross.

The homeless god nodded. "These runic power sources are pretty touchy. Mess with the design, and you've got nothing but a bunch of twisty lines and traffic snarls."

"We're not likely to change a line and end up with something *worse*, are we?" Richard asked in an abundance of caution.

Cross cocked his head, a raptor's motion. "Huh, that's kind of interesting. I've never thought about that."

"Maybe you and I ought to consider that," Grenier said, and the onetime sorcerer took the onetime god's elbow.

There were certain uniforms associated with New Mexico, Richard reflected, as he watched Mike Allistaire approach. Not actual native dress, but attire that established culture. There was the New Age hippie babe in the long skirt, tank top, Birkenstock sandals, and graying hair down to her butt. There was the tough Chicano in baggy trousers, black tank top, and leather jacket with silver chains no matter the temperature. There was the Native American lawyer with black hair down to his shoulders, a beaded headband, and a Canali suit. And finally there was the grizzled cowboy.

Allistaire fit in the last category. He wore blue jeans, a plaid shirt, scuffed boots, a bandanna tied at his neck, a straw cowboy hat with an elaborate silver hatband, and his enormous watchband was formed from large chunks of turquoise. As he entered the dimness of Charlie's Back Door restaurant, he removed the hat to reveal a thatch of black hair liberally streaked with gray. His luxurious handlebar mustache was more gray than black, and his skin had the consistency of old cracked leather left too long in the sun.

He slid into the booth across from Richard and gave him a piercing blue-eyed look. "Oort?" he grunted.

"Yes. How do you do." They shook hands

"Your secretary said you needed my expertise," Allistaire said. He scanned Richard's suit jacket, tie, and shirt. "You look like a developer. You got some property you want assessed?"

"No. I have a development I need to . . . disrupt, and some of the people we contacted indicated you were the man we wanted."

His eyes narrowed. "Because I've been busted?"

"It did weigh in our decision," Richard said, and then tensed because Allistaire's body language was all too clear—he was pissed.

Their waitress arrived, fortyish and zaftig with big hair. "You gents decided?" she asked, and her eyes lingered on Allistaire.

Who was staring coldly at Richard. "Depends on if I stay to eat," he said.

"Look, eat, hear me out, and if you leave . . . well, no hard feelings, and you've had a free meal and been paid for a day's consulting."

Allistaire nodded sharply. "Sounds fair. I'll have the huevos rancheros, eggs scrambled, beans, and can I get carne adovada with that?" She nodded. "And Christmas," he added, referring to a plate that's half red chili and half green chili. "And I'll have a margarita, Silvercoin, rocks, salt, and no mixer. Just lime juice and tequila."

"And you, sir?"

"I'll also have the huevos, eggs over easy, beans and potatoes, and green chili on the side." The lips of both the waitress and Allistaire quirked in little sneers. "I have an ulcer," Richard said defensively. "And milk to drink."

She went away, and Richard began to shred his napkin into smaller and smaller bits of paper. "Okay, I seem to have mortally offended you, but you were arrested."

"Yeah, for busting up a reception at that dickwad Marvin Klein's Canyon Road gallery."

Richard knew Canyon Road, the premier art street in Santa Fe, New Mexico's capital city, but he had no idea who Marvin Klein might be. Allistaire sensed his ignorance.

"Klein? Has a seven-thousand-square-foot monstrosity on the ski road that he calls a house. Who knows how many city councilors he had to bribe to get that through permitting. Then there's the giant gallery specializing in ancient Native American artifacts, and a martini bar where the Palace restaurant used to be. That was a great restaurant, and a real historical building—it was a whorehouse back in the nineteenth century, and now it's a yuppie flesh market."

It was a seemingly inexhaustible flow of words, but Allistaire finally circled back to Klein.

"Anyway, he's a pot hunter and a grave robber, and I just wanted to make sure those asswipes in the press knew it. He bought this fourteen-hundred-acre ranch up around Abique 'cause he knew there was a pueblo on it. We'd been urging the state to buy the property so we could excavate and catalog the findings, but he beat us to it and gave the rancher enough money that the jackass just rolled over. Klein's been digging up graves for the grave goods and selling them for a fortune to Eurotrash. So I pointed it out at his fancy-ass reception."

"And got arrested," Richard finally got in.

"Yeah. *And* lost my job with the state archaeology department. Dickheads. Since then it's been contract work for me. And the economy has really tanked since all that craziness out east two years ago, so it's been damn hard to make a living."

He was referring to the gate that had opened in the countryside near Washington, D.C., a gate Richard had managed to close, but Richard didn't enlighten Allistaire to that.

"Actually, I think you're the perfect man to help me with my problem," Richard said.

Allistaire stared suspiciously at the younger man. "I'll listen, but no promises."

"I need to shift a road or a house in a subdivision that's being built in southern California. It doesn't need to be by much, and as an incentive I can tell you the people behind this subdivision are the same group behind that craziness out east." Richard comforted himself that what he'd said was seventy percent true. "Anyway, we thought maybe archaeology might offer a solution. Maybe if they found a site . . ."

The archaeologist was already shaking his head. "You don't want to seed a site. It'll never stand up. Maybe for a few weeks or months, but the fraud will be exposed. It's not as easy as throwing some pot shards and an arrowhead into the dirt. You have to find a place where the soil has been cut away, and pick the strata that would correspond with the period that would have supported that society. Also, archae-ologists look for more than a few artifacts. There needs to be evi-dence of habitation—fire pits, middens, that kind of thing. Now maybe you can fake the trash, but the fire pits are tough. We carbon-date the charcoal, so you either have to find wood from that period and burn it, or charcoal from that period and lay it in place."

Richard's gut started to hurt, and an incipient headache fluttered around the edges of his eyes. The waitress arrived with the food. The scent hit Richard's nose, bounced into the back of his throat, trav-eled to his stomach, and he gagged. Allistaire tucked into his food, alternating bites with sips of margarita. Somehow talking also oc-curred.

"What you really need . . ." *chew, swallow, gulp* ". . . is an Indian." *Chew, swallow, gulp.*

His side was hurting, he was nauseated, and the remark just hit Richard wrong. Before he could call them back, the words were out. "And what flavor would you recommend? Navajo? Arapaho? Hopi? Apache? Cherokee?"

Allistaire gestured with his fork. "Sarcasm, right?"

"Got it in one."

"Look, your plan won't work, but there's one that will. But you have to have a *Native American*"—he stressed with an eye roll for fur-ther punctuation—"partner."

"Okay, I'm listening."

"You need to use a TCP, traditional cultural property. You get an Indian, preferably more than one Indian, and he claims that a cer-tain place in this subdivision is a shrine or a sacred area. He then threatens to sue if they build on that site."

"But it's Orange County California. There won't be anything to see."

"And that's cool. Your Native American's response will be, 'No, you can't see it because white men can't see it, but we know it's there, and it's very, very sacred.'"

"What kind of thing are we talking about?"

"It can be anything. A tree, a rock, a hillside. The hot springs at Ojo Caliente are sacred to some Mexican god's granny. She's supposed to live in one of the pools."

"And this TCP thing really works?" Richard asked.

"Oh, yeah. Developers hate two things—spending money and bad press. You get a tribe suing you, and you've got both in spades."

Seeing a possible solution had done wonders for his appetite. Richard took a bite of the huevos and even added a cautious amount of green chili. "Not to be indelicate, but how do I find . . . a willing partner for this?"

Allistaire just blinked at him. "What do you think?" And he rubbed his fingers together in the universal gesture for money.

"That seems pretty . . . indelicate, and frankly rather . . . racist."

"You really are a white yuppie liberal, aren't you?" Richard started to bristle but ultimately couldn't deny the accuracy of the label. He nodded. Allistaire continued. "Look, the poorest minority group in the country are Native Americans. Average median income on the Pine Ridge Oglala Lakota reservation is between twenty-six hundred and thirty-five hundred dollars a *year*. Yeah, the casinos have helped, but the situation's pretty dire with most tribes. And I bet they could find a religious dispensation for screwing over a developer and keeping some rich whites from getting to build a couple of McMansions." He cocked his head to the side, a smile playing beneath his mustache. "In fact, it's a real Coyote move."

Coyote, the trickster who often helped humankind. Without knowing it, Allistaire had said exactly the right thing, because Kenntnis—the man . . . creature who had brought Richard into this secret war—had told Richard he had been known by many names, among them Prometheus, Lucifer, Loki, and . . . Coyote.

Chapter

FOUR

A rental car had been waiting for him at John Wayne Airport, a name that left Richard baffled and bemused. He'd made a joke about it at the Avis desk, and the clerk told him that the Burbank airport was named after Bob Hope. Richard had tried to fathom the California fascination with actors and failed.

Now he was driving up a rutted dirt road into the arid and stony mountains east and south of Anaheim toward one of the many Cahuilla reservations in central and southern California. Like in other parts of the West, the Native Americans of California had been hounded out of the fertile areas and relegated the poorest parcels of land as a grotesque booby prize.

Heat shimmers danced on the rocks, and even the gray-green chaparral looked like it was wilting in the fierce heat. Richard tried not to, but his eyes flicked down to the temperature readout on the dashboard of the Ford Impala: *117 degrees*. No wonder the struggling air conditioner was doing little to dry the damp place in the small of his back. Thinking about that area made him aware of the sword in its holster digging into his kidney.

He shifted, trying to find a more comfortable position, and grimaced when that pulled on the stitches in his side. The success of the entire mission was dependent on what happened when he reached the Cahuilla town of Tecolote. He hoped his diplomatic skills were up to the task.

Minutes crawled by, and Richard scanned the landscape for any sign of life. High in the brass-bright sky, a black speck hung like a mote in heaven's eye. It resolved into a bird. After seven years out west, he had learned to recognize vultures, and they still gave him the creeps. The car nosed over a final, rocky ridge, and he looked down on the reservation. Richard, working with his staff back in Albuquerque, had picked Tecolote because this particular group of Indians had been granted a paltry eleven and a half acres to call their own. According to their website, they had a fire truck, purchased after the community hall had burned down last fall, and forty-two people of some varying degree of kinship to each other. The desperate poverty would, he hoped, make the Cahuilla amenable to bribes.

Tecolote wasn't much different from some of the small Navajo and Pueblo reservations he had visited in New Mexico. There were a dozen or so sagging, rusting trailers, each with a satellite dish reaching toward the sky. There were a couple of houses, one built out of wood and sheets of plywood, and another out of stone. There was a pack of mangy dogs lying in the shade provided by the trailers. Whenever they gave themselves a desultory scratch, clouds of dust puffed up. There were three tiny children clad only in T-shirts playing in a cheap rubber wading pool under the watchful eye of an elderly woman who shucked corn while she sat on the steps of a trailer.

The children gaped at him. The woman stared at him with that flat, hard expression you saw in the faces of people who had been isolated due to poverty and race, and assumed every white man in a big car was bad news. It wasn't just paranoia, Richard reflected. For people like these, that was often the case.

The dogs set up a ululating chorus of bays and barks announcing his arrival, and they came racing toward the car as he pulled to a stop. They flung themselves against the doors. As their claws scrabbled at the metal, Richard pictured long scratches in the paint and reminded himself of the rental car mantra—*no curb too high.*

He couldn't tell if those lolling tongues and rows of teeth were doggie smiles or held a more sinister warning. He also knew huddling in the car wasn't going to win him any points. Richard took a deep breath, picked up his Yankees ball cap from the passenger seat, and pulled it on in the probably vain hope it would protect him from the blazing sun. He opened the door and stepped out into a blast of heat that seared his lungs and sucked the moisture from every pore as he broke out in an instant sweat. California was supposed to be so great, Richard thought. Thus far he had found it to be a hellhole.

"Down!" he ordered the lunging dogs, and amazingly all of them save the Chihuahua obeyed. The Chihuahua took a grip on the tassel of his loafer and started pulling. Richard resisted the urge to drop-kick it into the wading pool.

The door of the stone house banged open, and a man emerged, tucking his shirt into jeans washed so many times they were more white than blue. He had a barrel chest and bandy legs, and long black hair hung raggedly to his shoulders. A few more doors banged and more men arrived. The man from the stone house stood well back from him and called, "Our kids are going to school."

Allistaire had mistaken Richard for a real estate developer. Now he'd been mistaken for a truant officer. Richard wasn't sure if that was a step up or a step down. He held out a hand in a pacifying gesture. "I'm not from the government." Tension leached out of a few shoulders. "I'm a . . ." *policeman*, his mind wanted to say, but that was probably worse than a bureaucrat, and it wasn't strictly accurate any longer. He decided on brutal candor. "Look, I'm rich. I need you to do me a favor and I'll pay well for it."

Glances were exchanged all around, and the old woman on the trailer steps gave an almost imperceptible nod.

"Okay, come in," said the barrel-chested man. He turned and headed toward the stone house. "I'm Johnny Calderón," he threw back over his shoulder. "I lead this band."

"Pleased to meet you. Richard Oort."

Inside there was a window air conditioner blowing full blast. The pages of the top magazine on a stack of *Popular Mechanics* fluttered in the breeze. The front door kept opening and closing as more people drifted in. Burly men, a few sporting tattoos that indicated military service. Slim youths with hair so black it gleamed. And an old man with sunken cheeks, who settled into a chair by the cool air. No women, however, until the old woman arrived carrying a big jug of lemonade. Richard wanted to kiss her. He removed his cap and thrust it in his jacket pocket, then took out a handkerchief and mopped his face and neck.

"Hot, huh?" Calderón said as he pulled back his hair and confined it with a rubber band

"Yes, very. It's hot in New Mexico too, but not this bad."

"Huh, New Mexico." He paused. "Long way to come for a favor. Don't you have any Indians to screw over in your part of the world?"

Looking into those dark eyes, Richard realized that Johnny Calderón was a very shrewd guy. Peddling bullshit was not going to fly. Calderón grabbed a chair, spun it around, and straddled it, arms resting along the back. Nobody offered Richard a chair.

Richard cleared his throat. Knowing it forcibly displayed his nerves but unable to prevent it. "I read about your situation. How the community center burned down and there's no money to build a new one. How you're trying to buy fifty acres from your neighbors, but they're not budging on the asking price. I know unemployment is chronic." He paused and surveyed the ring of implacable faces, and hurried on. "I'm prepared to rebuild your center, buy the fifty acres, and build and staff a health clinic." Richard tilted a hand toward Calderón, physically passing the conversational ball.

"And what do we gotta do to earn all this unsolicited generosity?" Calderón asked.

"Violate your religious beliefs."

That got a reaction. People shifted, and there were even a few basso rumbles from the circle of men. Calderón shrugged. "I'm a lapsed Catholic. Not sure how that's going to help you," he said.

"Not Christian beliefs. Your traditional beliefs." There were more rumbles at that and more than a few head shakes. Richard held up a hand. "Just hear me out. I need to shift a road or a house in a subdivision that's being built down near Anaheim. I'd thought about seeding an archaeological site, but an archaeologist told me it wouldn't stand up to any kind of scrutiny."

"He's right. You can't just throw around pot shards and arrowheads. You gotta show habitation, middens, fire pits," the old toothless man said.

"How you know that, Granddad?" one of the younger men scoffed.

The old man was offended. "Worked a few digs in my time. Learned some things. You should try it."

Richard took back the conversation. "This archaeologist suggested I use TCP—

"What's that mean?" Calderón interrupted.

The old man broke in again. "Traditional cultural property."

Calderón glanced at him, then looked back to Richard. "And I repeat, what the fuck does that actually mean?"

Richard hesitated, certain he didn't want to directly quote Allistaire. "Basically, I need you to find a shrine or a sacred area in this subdivision and force a change in the design and layout."

"Why?" Suspicion made the word sharp as ice.

This time there was no hesitation. Richard knew what was at stake and he didn't hold back.

"The layout of the buildings and streets forms a rune. If it's completed, it will tear a hole in reality and allow monsters to enter our world. I intend to keep that from happening." A ring of carefully bland faces was all the response he got.

If this had been three years ago, the people in the room would have decided he was nuts, but the events in Virginia and around the world had removed that worry.

"Is this more of that crap that went on back east?" Johnny asked.

"Yes."

The man's eyes raked Richard up and down. Richard tried to stand a little taller. He knew what Calderón saw—a short man who was a little too thin and looked younger than he was.

"And you're going to handle that, huh?" Doubt and amusement laced the words.

Richard's spine stiffened and his jaw tightened. "Your help will make this easier, but with or without you I'm going to stop them."

There were more looks around the room. Then the old woman left her chair, walked over to him, and took his chin in one gnarled hand. She smelled of dust and the sweet scent of cornhusk. She turned his face from side to side. Richard allowed it "You're that boy," she finally said, "the one in the papers."

"Yes," he said simply, though he wasn't thrilled at being called a boy. He would be thirty in December.

"Make up a god," said the old woman.

A few people shifted uneasily. Calderón shook his head. "It's not good to piss off the gods."

"This made-up god won't care. The white men won't know." She pinned the listeners with a glance as fierce as a hawk's. "There are only a handful of us left. They killed us and our traditions. Let them pay." She paused and looked down into Richard's face. "Starting with this one." She released his chin and hobbled back to her chair.

After leaving Tecolote, Richard decided to check out Gilead. Driving down the twisting streets, he tried to get a sense of the shape of the magical rune formed by the streets and houses. It had been so obvious when he'd viewed the satellite photo of the subdivision, but from ground level it just seemed like winding roads lined with palm trees. He wondered what each twist and turn signified to the Old Ones who were trying to enter through this five-square-mile rune. That raised a new worry. Were the Old Ones pressing close to the boundaries of human reality able to sense the weapon nestled at his back? If yes, would they inform the human quislings who did their bidding by building this gateway?

Rays from the setting sun glinted on a glass lens. Richard frowned and realized that the palm tree was a clever fake and that it sported a CCTV camera in place of a coconut. As the son of a federal court judge and the brother of a former defense attorney, he found such intrusions on privacy disturbing. As a police officer, he loved the cameras and wished every American city was surveilled as closely as London. Though in this community, Richard had a feeling that it had less to do with preventing crime and more to do with monitoring behavior.

The last of the newly planted real and fake palm trees petered out along with the pavement. Richard negotiated the final sharp curve, and there were the three houses straggling out toward graded ground waiting for the next house to be built. Plowed-in roads formed Nazca plain–like patterns, and fire hydrants stuck up like yellow teeth from brown gums.

He stopped on the side of the bladed-in road, pushed his sunglasses up onto his forehead, and contemplated the parched landscape. A sudden breeze lifted dust into a spiral. Richard's gut clenched. Sometimes there was a change in air pressure when a rent opened. But this wasn't a tear in reality. It was just a normal wind in drought-stricken earth.

It was important that Calderón not be perceived as a pure opportunist. He and Richard had agreed the man needed to get a job with the construction company working at Gilead so he could *see* the sacred site. That meant a delay of at least a couple of days while Richard hired away one of the crew and Calderón replaced him.

Lumina had an L.A. office. Richard could work from there while they got things arranged. Realizing he had probably lingered too long, Richard put the car in gear, turned around, and headed for a freeway going north.

By the time he got off the freeway at the Wilshire Boulevard exit, he was quivering with tension. It had taken him four hours to drive the thirty-some miles between Anaheim and L.A. in bumper-to-bumper traffic. But it wasn't just the traffic that had his gut roiling. He had been to California only once before, when he'd come to neutralize a deadly enemy. The fact that enemy had been an eighteen-year-old girl, and he had turned her into a vegetable, lay heavy on his heart. He told himself there was no other choice. Half human and half Old One, Rhiana had been a formidable magical talent who had abandoned humanity and thrown in with the monsters. He still didn't feel good about it, and, to assuage his guilt, Lumina paid for Rhiana's care. Richard briefly toyed with the idea of calling her adoptive parents to see how she was doing. He shoved away the thought; he knew how she was doing. She was lying in a bed at a long-term care facility being fed through a tube and crapping into a diaper.

The need to listen to the instructions from the GPS bot-girl helped push Rhiana out of his thoughts. Even with the navigation aid, it was confusing as hell, but eventually he located the office in a ziggurat-shaped building very close to the L.A. art museums. As he drove down the ramp into the underground parking lot, the weight of the multistory building seemed to be pressing down on his head. He prayed that the Big One wouldn't hit at that instant. Earthquakes were something he found terrifying—unpredictable and they struck without warning. They were like nature's version of an Old One.

The lobby continued with the whole Babylonian Hanging Gardens motif. It was festooned with plants, their tendrils stretching up toward the central peak of the ziggurat, which was a large faceted window with thick glass. *Pyramid power.* Richard knew what Kenntnis would have said about such nonsense. The alien's scorn wasn't reserved just for traditional religions but for New Age gibberish too.

Richard found that the legacy of 9/11 had infested Los Angeles as well. The armed rent-a-cop at the desk demanded to know Richard's business before he would let him approach the elevators. Of course the security didn't extend past harassment and security theater. All Richard had to say was he was going up to Lumina Enterprises and he was waved through. It was nearly five o'clock, and he wondered if the assistant who manned the office would still be there. Like so much else with Lumina, Richard kept the L.A. office open because Kenntnis had. Maybe Kenntnis had actually used it.

He walked into the small office suite and caught sight of a slim, beautiful girl with bobbed red hair and a tiny diamond nose pierce just standing up from the reception desk and pulling on a very high-heeled sling-back shoe.

"May I help you?" She sounded both surprised and irritated.

"I'm sorry, I should have called ahead," he said as he walked forward, hand extended. "I'm Richard Oort."

She was a good five inches taller than Richard, and he gave an internal sigh. He had noticed that California grew females tall, or seemed to attract the tall ones.

"Okay," she said in that tone that indicated it was anything but.

"I'm your boss. Technically."

"Oh." She dropped back into the desk chair. "Nobody told me you were coming."

"My fault. I should have had someone call you, but this was a rather sudden trip. Do you think you can get me a hotel reservation?"

"Sure. How many nights?"

"Let's say three. My plans are, shall we say, fluid."

"Okay." She picked up the phone.

Richard was amused at her single-minded focus on the task at hand. "Do you have a name?"

"Yeah."

"Might I know it?" he prodded. Amusement was threatening to become annoyance.

"Um, okay. It's Azura—"

"No wonder you were hesitant to tell me," Richard said. "That can't really be your name."

The girl's mouth pouted, but he noted that her eyes were dancing. "Oh, okay. It's actually Amy, but Azura looks better on a publicity still. Catches the eye, you know?"

"I didn't know."

"Of course, nothing will help if you don't have the looks." She scanned his face. "Have you ever thought about acting? You're really handsome."

Richard felt a blush rising into his cheeks. "No. Never."

"Too bad. You would totally have the female casting directors creaming themselves."

"I think I'm a little a short for a leading man."

"Oh, heck no. A lot of the big stars are shrimps. Uh . . . sorry, that didn't come out exactly right."

Richard hid a smile, glad that Amy's blush now probably matched his own. "No problem. So I take it working for Lumina isn't a long-term career path?" Richard asked.

Amy/Azura made a face, which on her was very cute. "Sorry, no. There was an ad, and this was perfect because it wasn't full time, and almost nobody calls, so I have plenty of time to study lines and go to auditions. I know it's stupid. Every girl who's been in theater or was homecoming queen thinks she can make it in the movies, but I just *had* to try. Fortunately, my dad's very big on just going for it. Dream big, he always says—"

There seemed to be an inexhaustible flow of information. Richard cleared his throat. Azura/Amy wasn't stupid. She quickly said, "Oh, sorry. You probably want me to get that reservation, don't you?"

"I'd like a shower. These freeways are unbelievable."

"I'm on it."

Richard went off to explore the inner office. It was as sparse and utilitarian as the outer one. He sat down behind the desk and tried to force himself to pick up the phone and call the office back in New Mexico. Then he remembered it was past six there, and he slumped with relief. He could avoid problems and decisions for at least one night.

Amy/Azura appeared in the door. "I booked you at the Sofitel. It's just a few blocks away."

"Perfect." Richard rested his hands on the desk, levering himself to his feet. He grimaced as the stitches pulled.

"Um . . . do you want to get . . . dinner?" the girl asked.

He stared at her, noting the heightened color in her cheeks, and realized this was a not-so-subtle come-on. Beautiful? Yes. Young but not too young? Yes. Interested? No.

He shook his head. "I'm beat. I'm just going to get room service."

"Oh, okay. Rain check, then."

"I'll see you in the morning."

"Oh, so you're coming back in."

"For as long as I'm in town." He added a barb. "I hope that won't interfere with any plans."

She got it, and her jaw gave a defensive thrust. "No, sir. I'll see you tomorrow."

<hr />

The next morning, Amy/Azura was at her desk and dressed in young-woman-professional-chic. Richard recognized it because he'd seen both his sisters wearing the exact same look.

"Good morning, sir." The greeting made him feel suddenly old. "I talked to the Albuquerque office, and Jeannette forwarded a number of messages." Richard sighed as he eyed the handful of pink call-back slips Amy/Azura was holding. "Jeannette also said to remind you to inoculate me. That sounds kinky and ominous. Are we going to play doctor?" She touched the tip of her tongue to her upper lip.

"Nothing that . . ." Richard groped for a word that wouldn't encourage the girl or terrify her. "Interesting."

"Oh, too bad." She leaned back in her chair, which accentuated her cleavage, and her knees opened a few inches.

Richard decided to wait on using the sword on this problematic employee. He needed to figure out a way to explain this particular requirement of employment and also how to defuse the girl's interest. *Of course the pain inflicted by the sword might do the trick*, he thought, as he took the handful of slips from her.

"Oh, and she said to tell you to call the FBI agent first."

"Okay."

Shuffling through the slips, Richard went through the door into the inner office. He found the one from the FBI agent, and it wasn't who he expected. He frequently consulted with Bob Franklin; with Samantha, the foul-mouthed sniper; and occasionally with the director himself. But this message was from Jay Haskell.

Jay hadn't been a big fan, so Richard was a little surprised he was calling. Jay had been part of the team that assaulted Grenier's old compound the second time, when Richard had been leading the assault rather than the one needing rescue. The agent had played bullshit macho games all through that effort. It also hadn't helped that nothing had gone as planned—they'd lost one of their own during the assault, and Angela was already dead.

Richard went to the window and looked down at the river of cars flowing past on Wilshire Boulevard. He tried not to fixate on events in the past, on things he couldn't change, choices he could not undo, but sometimes the guilt and the sense of failure would rise up and crush him with the force of a falling wave. Angela was dead, and Kenntnis, his mentor, perhaps permanently impaired. Richard rested his forehead against the glass.

He glanced down at the message slip crumpled tightly in his fist. He unclenched his fingers and studied the number. It had a 505 area code. That was most of New Mexico. So what the hell was Jay doing in New Mexico? Last Richard knew, the agent had been in D.C. Had he come to New Mexico specifically to see him? He went to his desk and made the call.

"Hi, Jay, it's Richard. And what the heck are you doing in New Mexico?"

"I got transferred. Don't know why the hell you were so eager to get back out here. It's the ass end of nowhere. Place looks like the fuckin' moon."

Richard chuckled. "That was my initial reaction, but don't stay more than six months. The place gets under your skin, and you'll find you won't be able to leave."

"Yeah, just watch me. I'm gonna be leaving a dust cloud like the Road Runner in a Wile E. Coyote cartoon. Anyway, I've got a case . . ." Jay's voice trailed away. "I think it's one of yours." Richard could hear the reluctance in the man's voice.

One of yours. Words Richard had come to dread. He was glad Jay had learned and accepted enough to recognize when something was Richard's, but it felt like one more giant brick being placed on his chest. They kept clearing incursions. He'd faced down close to a dozen Old Ones, and so far the score was Richard eleven, Old Ones zero. But how long until one of them did more than just score his ribs with a claw and *actually* rather than *almost* drag him through a tear between the worlds? Sometimes Richard felt like King Canute, or Sisyphus. He decided to pick a different myth. Those two guys never succeeded in their tasks. Maybe Hercules. At least he finally completed the twelve labors.

"Tell me about it."

"Little Navajo girl. She turned up at the rangers' cabins in Chaco Canyon dressed only in her nightie. She said the witches had taken over her brother and had him kill the whole family. She had blood on the hem of her gown, and the soles of her shoes. One of the rangers said he saw a figure, it might have been a boy, staring at the cabins, but when he went out to investigate, the person was gone. Anyway, they called us. You know the FBI has jurisdiction on Indian and BIA land?"

"Yes. Go on."

"I got sent. The rangers had found some clothes that almost fit the kid, and she led us out to the hogan. Sure enough, dead family— mom, dad, granddad. She said the witches appeared to her brother in the computer he'd been given. Faces in the screen is what she said. The rangers thought she was just talking about the Internet, You- Tube, that kind of thing, but what she described reminded me of those things we saw in Virginia. So I checked it out, but it just looks like a cheap computer to me."

"Yeah, but you've been inoculated. They can't reach you. What about the brother?"

"We finally found him. Well, his body. He'd just walked off into the canyons and died of thirst and exposure."

"Lovely."

Jay cleared his throat. "So, how do we tell if this computer thing is real? And if it is, that's really scary shit. There's a crap load of computers in the world."

"We'll use Cross. He can sense magic. If the computer is the source of the tear, he'll know. And yeah, the idea that they can reach through the screens of computers . . ." It was a nightmare scenario. He continued, "I'm dealing with a potential incursion in California, but the ramifications of this are huge. I think I've got to check it out right away. Have you got the computer?"

"Yeah."

"Whatever you do, keep control over it. We don't want it affecting anybody else. And where's the girl?" Richard asked.

"With her aunt's family. Someplace called Shiprock. Why?"

"She deserves to know she was right."

"Yeah, I guess that's true."

"I'll get there as soon as I can," Richard said, and ended the call. The moment he hung up, Richard realized he'd forgotten to ask a critical question. He called Jay back.

"Yeah?"

"Who made the computer?"

"Who knows? Don't you remember the fucking world is flat now?"

"Yeah, yeah, just give me the name on the case. We can track it."

"Hang on a sec."

It was more like ten minutes, but finally Jay returned to the line. "Gaia. Ever heard of it?"

"No, but I'll check it out. Thanks for the heads-up, Jay."

"Yeah, you say that *now*, but when we're up to our asses in monsters out on the rez, I think you'll be cussing me."

"Oh, probably," he said lightly. "May I have a private number where I can reach you?"

The agent provided a cell number, and they hung up.

Shaking off the anxiety, Richard booted up a browser. He went to Google and typed in *Gaia computers*. He got an article in the *Wall Street Journal* dating from six months earlier about the attempt to place low-cost, kid-friendly computers in third-world countries and rural, poverty-stricken areas of the United States. These efforts had begun after Gaia had been purchased by Wilton Hedge Funds. More digging revealed that Wilton was managed by the Titchen Group.

Richard leaned back in his chair. "My, my, you have your tentacles everywhere, don't you?" he said aloud.

Jorge had done a cursory analysis of Titchen. It was now time to dig deep. Richard began by reading article after article on the company.

Unlike Lumina, which bankrolled high-tech, cutting-edge research into alternative energy and biotech, Titchen specialized in bankrolling mining and oil interests—very much nineteenth-century products. Which made the purchase of Gaia very out of character.

Richard dug further. Looking to see if the Titchen Group had a history of philanthropic activities, he didn't find a single other instance aside from the very creepy prayerful community, which he was trying to subvert. And they certainly weren't giving away the houses in Gilead. The investors in Titchen were making money off the subdivision.

He found himself contrasting that with Lumina. Their single largest outlay of money was to fund various charitable projects around the world. They backed organizations that built health clinics and schools, dug wells, handed out mosquito netting, provided seed stock engineered for a given area and climate, helped reclaim exhausted farm land, and so much more that Richard couldn't remember it all.

Richard found a few photos of the man, which revealed him to be tall and spare with a receding hairline and wire-rim glasses, and the brown eyes behind those lenses were calculating. Maybe Alexander had suddenly grown a conscience? But he was bankrolling a subdivision that was creating a rune. Could it be the actions of others in his company? Some kind of cabal of middle-range officers? Richard would want proof of that before he gave Alexander a pass. *Faces in the screen.* Leaning back in his chair, Richard thoughtfully tapped his front teeth with a forefinger. The whole thing was very hinky.

Another hour of digging on Titchen convinced Richard that these really weren't his kind of people. The Titchen Group had defied the boycott of South Africa during the 1980s, and the board seemed to have a number of South American and Asian dictators among their number. Titchen was also named in close to twenty lawsuits alleging that the activities of subsidiaries of the company had polluted the water and endangered the populations of poor, rural, yet resource-rich areas.

No, it didn't look like Alex had grown a conscience.

But now they were making computers available to underprivileged kids. Richard leaned back, laced his hands behind his head, and frowned at the computer screen, which displayed the logo of Titchen, an elaborate affair with birds and keys and griffins and what appeared to be a phoenix surrounded by flames. He wished he could just send Cross alone to the FBI office to look at the computer, but that was impossible. Richard could just imagine the reaction when the long-haired man in tattered jeans and a food-stained T-shirt turned up at the front door.

Richard called New Mexico. "Jeannette, where's the jet? Is it still at the John Wayne Airport?"

He heard the fast clicking of keys, then she said, "No, it's been sent to Hong Kong to pick up Dr. Chen and take him to Rochester."

"Who's Dr. Chen?" Richard asked plaintively.

"Nobel Prize–winning physicist. Eddie wants him for the sword project."

"Oh, right."

"Eddie also wants you and the sword at the Rochester research facility as soon as you can manage it."

"Yeah? Well, that's not going to happen real soon."

"What's up?"

"I need to come home for a day or two. I'll take a commercial flight."

"Call me with your itinerary and I'll have a car waiting at the Sunport."

"Thank you. You're the best. I also need Cross. Is he out back?"

"He hasn't been around for a few days," she said.

"Leave messages for him at the usual drops. Tell him to get back and wait for me at Lumina."

"Got it," Jeannette said, and hung up.

Anxiety and a nervous knot in the stomach propelled Richard to his feet, and he walked out into reception. Azura/Amy looked up.

"Would you please book me on a flight back to Albuquerque?"

"When?"

"Today."

The red hair bobbed as she nodded and bent to her computer. She gave him an odd look, but just nodded again.

Richard returned to his office. Since he was a police officer, he had the option to travel with his weapons, but it often led to questions and delays. Easier to leave the guns behind, though the thought of that made a place between his shoulders itch. Everything about Titchen was making him twitch. He shook off the feeling. Just because the man had turned up twice didn't necessarily mean anything. Coincidence was not causation. Removing his suit coat, he shrugged out of his shoulder holster holding the .40-caliber Browning. He then bent and removed the ankle holster with the Smith & Wesson .38 snubby, and placed them both in a bottom desk drawer. He felt strangely naked without the dragging weight of his weapons. He touched the hilt in its holster at the small of his back for reassurance.

Azura/Amy tapped on the door and stuck her head into the office. "I've got you booked on a direct flight out of LAX leaving at four fifty. Okay?"

"Sounds great. When should I leave for the airport?"

She pulled her cell phone out of a pocket and checked. "One thirty. I was about to get lunch. Want me to bring you something? The food at the airport is awful."

"That would be very nice, thank you. Club sandwich with avocado on wheat bread. Lemonade." Richard dug out his wallet and handed her a twenty.

While he waited for Azura/Amy to return, Richard read through his e-mail. There was a note from Eddie reminding him about Chen. Another team, researching ways to save the world's reefs, needed another $2 million. The energy division wanted an appointment to present their proposal.

"Maybe Lumina should add a cloning project," Richard muttered to the room.

The outer door opened, and Azura/Amy returned carrying a plastic sack and a to-go cup. Richard joined her in the outer office to eat. He ate quickly, constantly checking his watch. At one o'clock, he balled up the sack and tossed it away. "Well, I better get going. And we better do that . . . um . . . that inoculation." He reached into the holster at the small of his back and removed the sword hilt.

After two years at this, Richard still hadn't figured out the right approach. If he had the sword already drawn when a person entered the room, that was sort of alarming. Unless someone was really enamored of the Highlander movies, seeing your boss with a long black blade shot through with silver lights in his hand was never comforting.

The other option was to draw the blade in the person's presence, though when he pulled his hand away from the base, and the aforementioned long black blade suddenly appeared out of his hand, it was also disconcerting if not downright alarming. Azura/Amy had that whole Goth thing going, but she was a young woman, and meeting her with a sword in his hand seemed like a rather unsubtle metaphor, especially given her evident interest. Richard hoped she was going to be fascinated rather than terrified when the blade appeared.

He held up the hilt. "This is the hilt of a sword." He closed his right hand into a fist and pressed it against the base of the hilt. "When I do this"—he pulled his hand away from the hilt—"the blade appears." Azura/Amy gasped as the long blade seemed to slide from his hand.

Her eyes went wide. She clapped her hands together and breathed a single word. "Coooool."

"Now, I'm going to touch you with the flat of the blade. You will have a reaction. I can't predict how much." Richard had learned not to tell people it would hurt. That never went over well.

Amy thrust out her arm. "Go for it." As the blade was lowering toward her skin, she asked, "What's it inoculating me against?"

The strange metal touched her. She cried out and her body jerked. Richard dropped the hilt, the blade vanishing, caught her, and eased her down to the floor. She shook in his arms as a series of small convulsions took her.

"Magic," Richard said softly, answering the question, though he doubted she could hear him as the sword did its work and stripped away her ability to ever do magic or have magic used against her. Now no Old One could feed on her. If only he could do this to every human in the world, the creatures would have to retreat back to their own worlds or starve. Unfortunately, that wasn't a viable option.

As for Amy, he'd seen much worse reactions. The spasms passed after about ten minutes. He went over to the water cooler and got her a glass of water. She leaned against his shoulder, taking tiny sips.

"Wow, that hurt."

"I'm sorry. Warning people seems to only make it worse."

"What did you do?"

He explained the sword's power.

She pulled away from him. "Well, that kind of sucks. Maybe I want to be magical."

"Trust me, you don't. Bad things can feed on you then. I hope you won't quit, but I'll understand if you want to." Richard checked his watch. "And now I really need to go if I'm going to catch that plane."

She stepped back, planted her fists on her hips, and glared at him. "Okay, bub, you do not get to throw out a statement like *bad things can feed on you* and then not explain it. You are buying me dinner as partial compensation for taking my magic, and you're giving me a much better explanation than *this is an ancient and powerful weapon that removes from an individual the ability to do magic or be a conduit for magic.*"

"Amy, your mask just slipped. You are not a ditzy actress with only three brain cells to rub together. You repeated back my statement verbatim, and *partial compensation?* Really? Did you graduate from law school, or did you drop out?"

She went beet-red and rubbed her bobbed hair into a haystack. "Guilty. I dropped out a year short of graduating. I just hated it. But how did you . . . ?"

"My father's a judge and one of my sisters is a lawyer. Believe me, I know the lingo."

"You didn't . . . ?"

"Not smart enough."

"How do you know what I'm going to ask before I ask it?" Amy demanded.

"Cop."

"Oh."

"And you're right, I do owe you a fuller explanation, but not to-day. I have to get back to New Mexico." Richard headed for the door. "When I get back. I promise."

"And when will that be?"

"A couple of days, no more. I've got things here . . ." His voice died away as he contemplated the subdivision,. He would need to call Calderón and explain the situation. He hoped the man would be-lieve him and not think he was trying to renege on their agreement.

Chapter

FIVE

RICHARD rode down the final escalator at the Albuquerque Sunport to the exit. The automatic doors slid open, and a blast of dry, oven-hot air slapped him in the face. August in New Mexico. The sun glowed like a brass coin, its rays highlighting the cones of the distant extinct volcanoes. The Mercedes limo was at the curb with Joseph behind the wheel and Estevan standing next to the back passenger door. To Richard's eyes, the bulge of the shoulder rig under the young man's coat was painfully obvious.

When did I become the guy who travels in limousines and has bodyguards? Do I like it? Not sure.

Estevan grinned at him. "Hey, welcome home, Richard."

"Thanks," he said as he stepped into the car. "But it's a quick trip."

"How was the flight?" Joseph asked, glancing at him in the rear-view mirror.

"Okay. Bit of a flying cattle car, and I do wish people didn't think traveling in sweatpants or shorts was okay. I'm not asking for hat and gloves, but some of them look like they just rolled out of bed." The two men laughed, and they pulled away from the curb. "Is Cross at headquarters?"

"Wasn't there when I left, but he can turn up pretty fast," Joseph said.

"That he can," Richard said, thinking of the creature's abilities.

"Are you hungry? Shall we stop for dinner?" Joseph asked.

"I'm okay," Richard said.

This time Joseph actually looked back over his shoulder. The setting sun made his dark skin glow and brought out the gray flecks sprinkled through the black of his hair. "Okay, but I'm going to tell Franz you haven't eaten and have him fix something."

"I hate to have him cook another meal."

"That's his job, and you have a tendency to forget to eat. You can only run on nerves and adrenaline for so long."

"Yes, Papa," he murmured meekly.

"Don't try smarting back to me. I am old enough to be your father," Joseph said in the cadence of his South Carolina upbringing.

"Wish you were," Richard said under his breath, and he firmly pushed aside any thoughts of his real father.

Once back at headquarters, Richard headed upstairs. He wondered if he should call Pamela and let her know he was back for a flying visit, but then decided he'd let her have her evening. There were no lights on in the penthouse. Richard turned on a graceful torchère, revealing the treasures that casually filled the living room and found Cross waiting. This time he had a giant piece of carrot cake on a plate. He crammed in a bite and mumbled, "Hey, got your message. What's up?"

"Bad stuff," Richard said, and elaborated. Cross listened without comment, just gobbled cake.

"So you want me to check out the computer and see if there's magical shit going on?"

"Exactly."

"When do you want to do this?"

"Tonight if possible." Richard scanned the ratty figure critically. "It's probably better if we don't go in during normal business hours."

Cross shrugged. "They'll just think I'm a snitch."

"Or a homeless guy looking to use the bathroom," Richard countered. He went to a phone and called the number Jay had provided.

"Yeah?" Like many law enforcement types, Jay wasn't big on social niceties.

"It's Richard. Can we get in tonight?"

"Sure. What time is it now?"

"Little after eight," Richard answered.

"How about we meet at the office at nine thirty?"

"Works for me."

"Um . . ." Richard waited, wondering what the agent was about to add. "Which form is Cross gonna be in?" Jay asked, sounding worried.

"Homeless guy."

The relief was evident in Jay's voice. "Oh, good. I was afraid he'd look like he did in Virginia. That was . . . scary."

Richard glanced over at Cross just finishing off the cake. "Not scary tonight, just crummy."

Cross grinned, raised a middle finger toward Richard, then ostentatiously brushed cake crumbs off his T-shirt. "Hey, that works on several levels."

Richard had no sooner hung up with the FBI agent than the house phone rang. Richard answered. "Joseph stopped by and told me you needed dinner. I have a slice of quiche and a salad ready. May I bring it up?" The voice had a soft Eurotrash accent and a wealth of arrogance.

"I really don't have time—"

"I'll tell Joseph."

"Oh, God, all right," Richard snapped.

"Perhaps a little glass of white wine?"

"No. Just water."

There was a put-upon sigh, and Franz hung up.

A few moments later the elevator arrived. Franz, small and in-tense and sporting a nascent paunch, entered carrying a silver tray. In one corner there was a cut-crystal goblet. In the other a matching carafe. The plate of food was covered by a white linen napkin. Richard sat down at the small inlaid wood table, and Franz swept aside the napkin with a flourish. Presentation was important to Franz. The slice of quiche was a perfect triangle and garnished with a sprig of parsley. Next to it was a tumble of field greens and bitter herbs adorned with a few piñon nuts and mandarin orange slices. The smell of citrus and champagne dressing mingled with the scent of warm cheese, ham, and green chili. Saliva filled Richard's mouth. He hadn't realized he was hungry. But hungry or not, there was no way he was going to finish it all. The portions were gigantic.

Richard looked at the chef. "Did you think you were serving Gre-nier? I can't possibly eat all this."

"Whatever you don't finish, I will," Cross said.

"You just ate all that cake," Richard objected.

"So?"

There was nothing to do but sigh and shake his head. Cross sprawled on the sofa. While he ate, Richard contemplated the array of treasures the room contained. A Madonna and child by Caravag-gio hung on one wall between floor-to-ceiling bookcases, which held many first editions. A Mughal dagger rested on the edge of the table where he sat eating. Canopic jars that had once been in a pharaoh's tomb, and perhaps still held that pharaoh's entrails, stood on an end table. The only thing in the room that was Richard's was the Bösen-dorfer grand piano by the windows.

"You oughta put this stuff in storage. Bring in your own stuff," Cross said with uncanny perspicacity. "It's been almost two years. Stop living like a permanent houseguest."

Richard shook his head. "I can't. This is Kenntnis's place. I wouldn't feel comfortable changing a thing."

"Yeah, but I don't think Kenntnis is coming back. Oh, the body may hang around, but Kenntnis, the Kenntnis we knew, he's gone."

"That's horribly depressing," Richard said quietly, and pushed away his plate, no longer hungry.

"Hey, how do you think I feel? He found me in 923 A.D. trying to kill myself, and offered me the deal. Now he's never going to pay off." Cross's expression brightened considerably. "But you could. One touch of the sword and I'm toast."

"I'm not going to kill you. I know you; it would feel like murder. And I need you. Like tonight. You can see magic, and you're looking for more paladins. How's that coming, by the way?"

"If you haven't noticed, there are a shit load of you monkeys crawling on the surface of the planet right now, and I have to look at each and every one of them to see if any of them have your mutation. It takes a little while."

"I know, but if I die, we've got to have someone to replace me."

"We did okay with only one paladin in the twentieth century."

"What? Wait! You and Kenntnis told me there hadn't been a paladin for years."

Cross shrugged. He left the couch and snagged Richard's abandoned plate. "We lied. Also the last one came to a pretty horrible end, and we didn't want to discourage you." Cross finished off the quiche in a few quick bites. "I'll be in my box. I want to prepare. Come get me when you're ready," Cross said and left.

Richard realized he still hadn't called Calderón.

He paused in the master bedroom to shrug into a shoulder holster and slid a Browning .40 caliber into it. He reassured himself that the sword was in the holster at the small of his back. On his way back through the bedroom, he plucked a set of car keys out of a drawer of the dresser. He then chose the stairs over the elevator, feeling the need to move after hours sitting at the airport and being cramped on a plane.

He stopped at his office and rang the tribe leader.

"Hello?" The man's voice was heavy and hoarse.

"This is Richard Oort. I had an emergency and had to head back to Albuquerque."

"An emergency like realizing you didn't want to give money to some Indians?" The hoarseness was intensified, and anger snapped and whined around the edges of the words.

"No. I will be back in California in a couple of days. I give you my word."

"Yeah, that's worth exactly nothing."

Richard drew a breath, held it, and pushed down his desire to react with anger. He forced himself to assume the flat delivery that every cop learned to use when in court and was faced with a hostile defense attorney.

"A young Navajo boy went nuts and killed almost everyone in his family. Only his sister escaped. The man who built the subdivision was behind this too." It was a stretch, but Richard didn't feel that he owed Calderón more. "I'm dealing with that. You'll get your money as long as I get my sacred site."

"Okay. You've got two days. You fuck us, and I'll go to the people at the subdivision and tell them about you."

Richard almost said, *I'll be back*, but he couldn't bring himself to utter the Terminator's catchphrase. He bit back the words and said instead, "I promise I will return."

That task resolved, Richard clattered down the rest of the steps to the bottom floor. There he entered the security code on the keypad and pushed open the heavy steel door that let out on the back of the building. A large wood and cardboard crate sheltered by a battered green tarp rested against the building. The warm golden light of a Coleman lantern spilled onto the asphalt and made the mica flecks in the granite boulders at the foot of the mountain sparkle. There was also the distinctive smell of a hot dog being roasted. Cross had pulled back the curtain that served as a door. He sat on a wire spool, a wiener skewered on a toasting fork, the skin bubbling, darkening, and cracking as he turned it over the flames of a camp stove. On one side of the box was a cot with an orange crate as a bedside table.

"You're eating again?" Richard asked.

"Yeah, so sue me. You ready?"

"Yes."

Cross turned off the propane gas to the stove and crammed the entire hot dog in his mouth. "Muu unm phing?"

Richard assumed the mutter was a question as to how they were traveling. "Yes, I'm driving."

They reentered the building and took the elevator down to the parking garage. He had pulled the keys for the Ferrari. Probably not the most subtle choice, but he loved to drive both it and the Lamborghini. "You're not likely to splinter, are you?" Richard asked, a hand on the door handle of the sleek sports car.

"Nah, I'm feelin' very together right now," Cross replied.

"Okay."

The automatic gate slid open at their approach, and then they were flying down Montgomery, headed for the freeway.

⸻◇◆◇⸻

Haskell paced back and forth in front of the bank of elevators, his heels beating out a tattoo on the stone floor. He was a burly man with buzz-cut brown hair and gray that Richard didn't remember. The frown, Richard did remember. Even at this late hour, Haskell was still wearing the de facto regulation FBI uniform—cheap dark suit, narrow tie, and white shirt. He and Richard shook hands, and then Jay looked Cross up and down.

"Well, at least he doesn't look totally like a bum tonight. Maybe when they check the security footage in the morning, they won't wonder if I've gone totally nuts."

"I think you totally say totally too much," Cross said.

Jay opened his mouth to retort. Richard gave an internal sigh and held up an admonishing finger. "Don't," he said, and mustered up a glare at both of them. They rode the elevator up to Jay's office in silence.

"I pulled the computer out of the evidence room," the agent said as he opened the door for them. "I was worried it would be trashed or stolen or sold as seized property since nobody thought it was relevant to the investigation."

The laptop lay in the center of the agent's desk. The plastic case was a dark purple. Cross checked just past the threshold and stared at it. He then circled the desk like a terrier at a rat hole.

Cross touched it lightly with his fingertips. "Yeah, it's buzzing with magic. When we're done, you better zap it with the sword," he said to Richard. He opened the lid and studied the screen and the keyboard. "Nothing on the outside. Must be in the guts." Cross took a butterfly knife out of his pocket and ratcheted it open with a flick of his wrist. He then pried the back off to reveal the motherboard.

Dirty fingernails traced across the circuits. "Yeah, here it is. It's a rune, a dandy one formed by the wires and chips."

"What does that mean?" Jay asked.

"That when the kids are logged on, they ain't just talkin' to pals on Facebook or Snapchat. Something else is on the line, and eventually it starts looking back out at them." He flipped the computer back over and tilted the screen so it flashed at the two humans. "Our kind likes mirrors, but this is a tolerable substitute."

Jay dropped down into his chair. "How many of these things are out there?" he asked.

Richard shook his head. "No idea. The articles I found indicated Gaia/Titchen had been selling them cheap. Maybe even giving them away. The question is, can an Old One move from a computer infected with the rune to one without a rune? If yes, we've got a big fucking problem," Richard said, worry and weariness driving him to an uncommon burst of obscenity.

A fingernail tapped against Cross's front teeth as he considered. "That would be big magic. My guess is no, but we need to get these little time bombs swept up, melted down, and thrown away."

"And keep Gaia from making any more," Richard added. "They also need to be shut down." Richard sat down too. "Oh, they're going to love that."

"Who? What?" Jay asked.

"The officers of my company." Richard waved him off. "Never mind." Standing, Richard pulled the hilt from its holster and drew the sword. As the chord and overtones vibrated in the air, a horrifying, twisted visage floated up in the screen.

"Shit!" Jay jumped out of the chair, caught his heel on the carpet, and fell heavily against the desk. Cross grabbed up the computer and spat grotesque words in an unknown language at the face on the screen.

Even the indistinct image of the Old One was enough to set Richard's guts and knees to quivering. He lunged, tapped the computer with the tip of the sword, and it reduced itself to a black sludge that ran down Cross's hands and dripped onto the desk. The stench tore at their throats.

"Oh, gross," Jay said, gagging. "How am I going to get that stink out of my office? The damn windows don't open. And worse, how do I explain it?" he added mournfully.

"Flatulence?" Cross suggested.

"Ha-ha, very funny."

The smell drove them into the hall. Richard held out his hand. "Thanks, Jay. I owe you. Thanks for catching this."

"How bad is it? This computer thing?" he asked.

"Real bad."

The next morning, Richard woke far later than he'd intended because he'd sat up far later than he'd intended. After verifying that the Gaia computers were designed as gateways to other dimensions, Richard paced and wondered how many vicious murders had been perpetrated, how many families torn to pieces, how many children driven mad. It was a grotesque parody of first-world generosity containing a poisoned heart. The modern-day equivalent of smallpox-infected blankets being given to the Cherokees before they were marched along the Trail of Tears.

After a stingingly hot shower, he dressed and headed down to his sister's office. If Pamela hadn't had the blinds in her office drawn tight, it would have offered the same view that Richard saw from his office two floors above—the three extinct volcanoes on the edge of Albuquerque and the blue peak of Mount Taylor floating in the distance seventy miles away. Instead, the atmosphere in the room was decidedly subaqueous. Pamela even had the lights off, which left her a dim shape behind her horseshoe-shaped desk.

"About time you got up. Some of us got to work *before* eight."

"I was up until three. Cut me some slack." Richard moved toward the windows, only to be arrested by her shrill command.

"If you touch those blinds I will stab you to death with a letter opener. It's a hundred and two degrees out there—"

"Yeah, but it's a dry heat—" The words had hardly been uttered when a tube of hand cream came flying at him. Richard threw out a hand and snatched it out of the air before it could collide with the wall. He laid it back on her desk but placed it well out of her reach.

"This place has two types of weather," Pamela said, her tone bitter. "Wind that never stops blowing and leaves you wearing a grit mask, and sun that doesn't shine, it *assaults* you. Lumina has offices all over the world, but we stay here in this godforsaken—"

Richard interrupted. "Because Kenntnis was here . . ."

"Which means Albuquerque is important," they finished in concert.

"I know. I know. Though why this dusty, overgrown cow town would be important is beyond me," Pamela groused.

Richard shrugged. "He's an alien. Who knows why? And we can't ask him now," he added sadly. He shook off the mood. "But why are you sitting here in the dark?"

"Even the lights make it hotter."

"Turn up the air-conditioning."

"Then I'm too cold."

Richard threw up his hands in defeat. "Okay, let's pretend we're not siblings and try just talking." He pulled a chair closer to the desk. "But I'd like to see your face." With a put-upon sigh, Pamela conceded and snapped on the small reading lamp on her desk.

"So, why were you up until three?" she asked.

He told her about the computers, concluding, "We've got to pull back these computers and destroy them, and to do that I think we've got to buy the company, recall the computers, and shut down the assembly line."

"We're going to buy a company just to destroy it?" Pamela asked.

"Well, I suppose we could get rid of the rune on the motherboards and keep making real and safe computers. It's not a bad business model—inexpensive computers for the developing world," he said thoughtfully.

Pamela pulled her keyboard closer. "What's the name of the company?"

"Gaia. It's a subsidiary of Wilton Hedge Funds, which is a subsidiary of the Titchen Group."

"Oh, great, them again," Pamela said. "Just once, can't we come up against people who are just political and business rivals and not evil sorcerers?"

"That's not our line of work."

"Which means Titchen has probably heard of us—"

Richard immediately caught her drift. "And they won't want to sell."

"Or they'll jack up the price," Pamela said.

"We'll buy it through front companies. You handle that," Richard ordered.

"I'll look through our subsidiaries to find an appropriate front, and talk to Dagmar and Fujasaki about finding the money. It's going to be expensive. How long are you here for?"

"Not long. After I get back from Shiprock—"

Pamela interrupted. "Where?"

"Shiprock. It's between Gallup and Farmington."

"And you're going there why?"

"To tell this little girl that she was right," Richard said.

"I really don't think that's necessary."

"I do. How awful to go through life thinking you're nuts."

"You're not driving, are you?" Pamela demanded.

"Oh, God no. I've rented a helicopter. Anyway, it'll leave from the airport, bring me back, and I can catch my flight back to California." Richard checked his watch. "In fact, I need to leave for the airport in an hour."

"You're not using some rent-a-pilot?"

"No, Jerry will be flying. We just rented the machine. Do you think we should buy a helicopter?" Richard added.

"No. And you need to watch your spending."

Richard flushed at the hectoring tone. "You make it sound like I'm spending it on hookers and blow."

"You do spend a lot on your clothes."

"It's hard for me to buy off the rack, and I'm the head of Lumina. I have to maintain a certain standard . . . Why am I defending myself to you?"

"Because nobody else will criticize you."

"Well, you never missed an opportunity." It came out more resentful than he'd intended. "And by the way, everybody picks at me constantly. Making sure I eat. Making sure I sleep. Reminding me of this meeting and that meeting—"

"Oh, poor you."

They were glaring at each other, they were Yin and Yang, Richard with his silver-gilt blond hair and pale blue eyes, Pamela brown-haired and gray-eyed. She also topped him by a good three inches.

"Look, I enjoy the money, I admit it, but in terms of the company and our subsidiaries, where would you like me to start belt-tightening? Our environmental company warns me the Great Barrier Reef is dying at an alarming rate and that we may have already passed the tipping point to restore the oceans. Since a lot of the world's population depends on subsistence fishing, I divert more funds to them. Then the medical division warns me there's a chance that Ebola may become a pandemic, so I give them more money. And that's only two among dozens of divisions and subsidiaries. So tell me, Pamela, where do you want me to cut?"

"It's not my job to make those kind of decisions. You're in charge."

A weight settled on his shoulders. Richard stood, feeling very isolated. "Yeah, prevaricate. That way you don't have to commit yourself, and you can keep taking cheap shots at me."

Pamela came to her feet, leaned in, fists resting on the desktop. "What do you want from me, Richard? I've given up my law practice to work for you. I've broken with our father over you. But I can't take over for you. Kenntnis left this company to you. You have to run it or lose it."

He reared back, the final two words as tangible as a blow. "What do you mean?"

"Having Kenntnis back but not really back is causing . . . confusion. Legal and emotional. The document turning control of Lumina over to you was pretty specific. If he failed to check in in any twenty-four-hour period, the company came to you. Well, he hasn't checked in, but he's . . . present, so how does that affect your status?" She shrugged. "No one's raised it yet, but it's there, like a low-level toothache. And at least half the time you're running around the world acting like an action hero instead of paying attention to business."

"I'm the paladin. The only one we've got. No one else can close the tears in reality. Should I leave them open? Let the monsters in?"

"Nobody's saying that."

"So what are you saying?" he asked.

"I'm not sure they understand the reality. The idea that Kenntnis was . . . is an alien is hard for them. They dealt with him in his human form, and they never saw the light creature—"

"They saw the pictures," he protested.

"And pictures can be faked. He still looks like the man they dealt with."

"But his mind is gone."

"Then show them that. Let them realize it and accept that you're it. There isn't an alternative," Pamela said.

"And how do I do that? Or is that me asking you to take over for me?" he concluded with bitter sarcasm.

"No, this falls under legal advice." She came around from behind the desk and took his hands in hers. "Call a meeting of the officers. Let them interact with Kenntnis. Help them understand what happened."

Richard considered, nodded slowly. "I could bring in Eddie, have him fill them in on his efforts to reverse the damage to Kenntnis."

Pamela nodded. "That would be good. Then they would know you're not just taking advantage of your position."

"Okay. I'll do it. Just as soon as I get back from California."

"And when will that be?"

"In a few more days."

He started to leave, only to be pulled back when Pamela said, "Are you planning to see Grenier?"

"I really don't have anything to discuss with him," Richard said.

"You ruffled his feathers with this California thing. You might want to do a bit of feather smoothing while you're here."

Richard sighed and smothered the sudden flare of irritation and resentment. As if he didn't have enough to contend with, now he had to soothe the ego of a man he feared, hated, distrusted—and needed.

"Okay, I'll stop by and see him."

⟨⊰⊱⟩

He heard footfalls approaching. The quick, sharp staccato of heels on stone, and he knew at once who it was. There was nothing restful about Richard; he moved like one of those dust devils that periodically swirled and danced across the deserts and mesas of New Mexico. Grenier felt a momentary sense of pique. He hadn't been told the boss was coming home, but then anticipation replaced the feeling and he looked up as Richard swept through the door.

Richard looked well. More rested than was usual, and he'd gotten some sun. The narrow nose and high cheekbones were tinged with a bit of sunburn. That nose wrinkled as the young man took an appreciative sniff of the redolent and seductive smells of ginger, mint, lemon grass, and chili that floated though the office.

"Oh, that smells good." He paused and cocked his head, one of his little habits. "I didn't have any breakfast, and I just realized I'm hungry." Grenier suppressed the urge to hug the take-out containers to his chest and protect his lunch. Richard held up a finger in a wait-one-moment gesture and was gone with a swiftness and grace that reminded the older man of quicksilver and lightning. He returned in a few moments clutching a plate and utensils. Somehow he knew of Grenier's ad hoc kitchen, which had Grenier wondering how much else Richard knew about his habits.

Richard began scooping out Tip's famous teriyaki fried rice and added a large dollop of pad Thai and an inordinate amount of ginger beef. Grenier tried to curb his annoyance. Clearly he failed, because those ice-blue eyes, brimming with amusement, stared challengingly into his.

82

"You don't mind if I bogart part of your lunch? There's enough here for four," Richard said.

A flush swept up Grenier's cheeks. "That was cold."

"But true." Richard took a bite of noodles, chewed and swallowed. "You know, I really wish you'd grow back your beard. That many chins just aren't natural."

"Did you come here solely for the purpose of irritating and insulting me?" Grenier snapped. "But you are correct," Grenier continued. "I ordered too much food, and I would have eaten it all if you hadn't shown up."

"I think you're gorging because you lost your magic. Trying to fill the void," Richard said.

Grenier found the remark smug and condescending, and he struck back. "So says the man with daddy issues."

There was a flash of anger in the amazing blue eyes. "Okay, I'd say we're even on the exchanging-insults front," Richard said.

Grenier gave him a thin smile. "Don't try to outpsych me, Richard. Two can play that game, and I'll always win. But let's start with your statement. I did not *lose* my magic, as you so euphemistically phrased it. *You* robbed me of it, and took my hand in the process."

"You were trying to kill my father and Angela." Once again the pale cheeks were awash with color.

"The merest touch of the sword is enough to destroy a person's power," Grenier shot back. "You didn't have to cut off my damn hand!"

"You had spent the past two days having your thugs beat me up, then topped it off with *you* running electricity through my balls. At that point I wasn't feeling very charitable."

There was no good answer to that, and Grenier didn't try. Instead he voiced the question raised by Jorge. "People wonder why you let me stay here." Then he added a poisoned dart. Looking down at his desk, he shuffled papers and casually added, "It makes them question your judgment." He looked up quickly to catch Richard's reaction, and was pleased when he saw doubt cloud those eyes.

Richard shook it off and gave Grenier a challenging look. "Would you like me to kick you to the curb?"

"I'd rather you not. The Old Ones have long memories."

"Besides, you know why you're here," Richard said.

"Actually, I don't. Why do you keep me around, Richard?"

"You know how the Old Ones and human quislings work together, and you can recognize signs of those unholy alliances—"

Grenier held up an admonishing finger. "Ah, religious allusion from the newly minted atheist."

"First, it's been two years since Kenntnis and Cross showed me how the world actually worked. And sometimes you can't avoid the occasional *dear God* or *good heavens*. But back to the subject. I like to keep you where I can watch you."

"So you don't trust me?"

"Would you?"

"No," Grenier admitted, and tried to cover the emotional hurt with a rueful laugh. He decided to launch one more poisoned dart. "But you also need me here. I'm the daddy figure you cannot do without." He watched it land with bitter satisfaction, because while Richard had initiated the break, the estrangement from the man haunted him. Richard had spent his life trying to please and win the respect of his cold and distant father, and while he had come tantalizingly close when he had outplayed and defeated Grenier, ultimately Richard had failed.

Richard stood and looked down at Grenier. "Well, you're just full of little croakers today, aren't you? Pamela said you needed stroking. Looks like she was right."

"You're learning to punch above your weight."

"Not a very good allusion in your case," Richard said with a smile that extended only from the teeth out.

"Touché."

Richard checked his watch. "And I've got to go."

He walked out, and Grenier stared for a long time at the closed door.

⸻ ◇•◇•◇ ⸻

After the rather fraught conversation with Grenier, Richard returned to his office. As he emerged from the stairwell, he contemplated sneaking past his assistant, but Jeannette had her desk arranged to defeat any such maneuver. She handed him a stack of messages as he walked past. The sheaf of pink papers included the COO based in London; the CFO based in Japan; Damon Weber; Cassutt, who ran Lumina's Washington lobbying firm; and Egan, who ran human resources out of offices in Harlem in New York City.

"Do you want me to ring them for you?" Jeannette asked.

This was an ongoing dance-battle. She had slowly trained Richard to behave like a proper executive. He no longer came out to the reception area to greet visitors. He didn't make his own dinner reservations. He didn't type his own letters, which was one dictum he didn't mind. He had come to hate typing because he'd always gotten stuck typing up reports when he was a cop. Richard was a touch typist while his fellow officers were strictly hunt-and-peck, and he had been a rookie so there was no way to avoid being drafted. Since talking into a recorder made Richard feel stupid, he wrote out the letters in longhand and gave them to Jeannette to type. It wasn't the most efficient use of either of their time, but it seemed a suitable compromise.

But Jeannette hadn't won on the phone thing. "No, thank you. The day I'm unable to punch a few buttons, you need to take me out and shoot me," he said.

"Don't even joke about it," Jeannette said, and Richard could see he had really upset her.

It wasn't conscious, but Richard found his hand gripping his thigh where the bullet had torn through. Next he touched the bandage over his ribs and wondered if the claw wound was going to leave a scar.

Jeannette glared at him over the top of her reading glasses. "Look, it diminishes you when you call, and some secretary—"

Richard held up an admonishing hand. "Uh-uh, administrative assistant, please."

She threw a computer screen cleaner designed to look like a Siamese cat at him. He caught it, and began squeezing it, feeling the seeds inside crunch and slide. It did seem to be a day for people to throw things at him.

Jeannette continued. "While an administrative assistant"—she rolled her eyes—"keeps you waiting while she rings through to her boss. The assistants should do the waiting."

Richard hitched a hip onto the edge of her desk and stared down at her, fascinated.

"You're taking this seriously, aren't you?"

"Yes. With really important people, assistants try to make certain that you both come on the phone at exactly the same time." She shrugged. "It's a power thing."

"My ego isn't that big, and besides, most of the people I call work for me," he demurred.

"True, but you should let me place the call when it's anyone outside Lumina. Otherwise you'll leave the impression with that other executive's assistant that you're not powerful, a bit naïve, and probably a pushover, and she'll pass that on to her boss, which puts you at a disadvantage."

Surrender came in the form of a sigh, then he added, "Okay, I'll agree to that much." She reached for the messages, but he pulled them away. "But all of these people work for me." He went through the heavily carved wood-and-glass doors and into the office.

He settled into the chair behind the desk. Studied the colors swirling and combining like a mad creation by Jackson Pollock. He couldn't put it off any longer. With another sigh, he picked up the wireless receiver and started making calls. Cassutt wanted to host a Washington mill-and-swill and needed funds. Richard okayed it. Kenzo, the CFO, wanted to fly in from Tokyo and meet with him. The Japanese man's voice sounded grim, and Richard desperately wanted to postpone the meeting, or fob him off on Lumina's COO, Dagmar Reitlingen. Instead he reminded himself that the buck stopped with him, and he said okay. He jotted down the date on a piece of paper to give to Jeannette. He then applied himself to the stack of papers on his desk, only to be interrupted by a soft knock on the office door.

It was Joseph. "We need to leave for the airport."

Richard checked his watch. "Right." He wasn't sorry to abandon both the office and the paperwork.

SIX

IN the distance, Shiprock thrust its jagged pinnacles toward the sky as if some ancient power had placed a stone pipe organ in the middle of the desert. Richard peered through the front window of the helicopter and felt awe.

"The Navajos call it *Tse Bit' a'i*, rock with wings," Jerry, the helicopter pilot and a Desert Storm vet, called over the headphones.

Richard nodded, the beat of the chopper's rotors a thrumming in his chest. He sat in front next to Jerry, while Joseph, his dark features serene, sat behind them, a duffel bag containing a shotgun and a submachine gun at his feet. The sword hilt gouged at Richard's lower back, and he shifted in the seat.

Beyond the mass of red sandstone that dominated the space, distant peaks, blue tinted, edged the horizon in all four directions like rampart walls defending the basin. Immediately below, the scrub brush, blasted brown by summer heat, clung doggedly to the tan dirt. In the distance, Highway 491 made a black scar on the face of the desert. A red pickup, looking like a toy from this height, drove in splendid isolation. Such vastness and emptiness left Richard momentarily longing for the green of Rhode Island and the blue of its lakes and the bordering ocean. He knew he would never return home; there was nothing there to return to. But at odd times he found himself afflicted with homesickness.

"Where are we landing?" Richard asked.

"Near the senior center," Joseph answered. "There aren't a lot of choices out this way."

"Really? Looks to me like we've got hundreds of miles of choices."

"Not if you want to be anywhere close to town," Jerry said. In the west, monsoon thunderheads were building, lightning jabbing at the earth beneath. "We want to land before that hits," he added, a frown between his gray brows.

The helicopter had seemed small. Now it seemed a fragile soap bubble caught between rock and fire. A few more minutes and the town came into view. There didn't seem to be a lot of houses or trailers. What there was, was a long, wide main street lined with a multitude of fast-food restaurants, a few unidentifiable buildings, and some banks. Smaller roads snaked away into the desert, but only for a block or two. As they drew closer, more details came into focus. Virtually every car on the road or in the parking lots was a pickup truck. People looked up as the helicopter pulsed overhead.

A gust of wind made the copter yaw, and Richard grabbed for a handhold, but Jerry was unruffled and set them down in a dirt lot next to the senior citizen center. The rotors slowed and stopped. Richard pulled off the headphones and opened the cockpit door. The wind swirled into the helicopter, carrying the scent of dust, rain, and fried chicken. In the distance, the sky muttered to itself. A car, a big dust-covered Cadillac, pulled out of the center's parking lot, drove down the shoulder, and came jouncing across the dirt lot toward them. Richard slipped behind the tail of the copter and laid a hand on his gun. Only when Joseph walked forward to talk to the driver did Richard relax.

Joseph beckoned, and Richard headed to the car. "We'll leave as soon as I'm back," he said to Jerry.

The older man pointed at the threatening clouds. "Only if that lets us."

Joseph held open the door against the buffeting wind and Richard climbed in. He leaned forward across the front seats and held out his hand to the driver, a broad-shouldered man with his hair in a traditional rolled queue bound with a white cloth. He also wore a Washington Redskins baseball cap. "Hi, I'm Richard Oort."

"Wendell Benally. So, we're goin' to Henry Yazzi's?"

Richard checked his notes on his iPhone. "Yes."

"They're not in trouble, are they?"

It was an echo of what Richard had heard on the Cahuilla reservation. It depressed him to think that the arrival of a white man always meant trouble to these native peoples. "No, not at all. I'm a police officer, and we have information for Mosi Tsosie about what happened to her family."

"They all got killed by that crazy kid. What else is there to say?" Benally grunted.

"Well, we have a bit more insight into what happened. I thought she should know."

"Hmm, not how cops usually act."

There was no possible response. They drove north on the main drag of Shiprock. Past a KFC, presumably the source of the smell, a Taco Bell, a McDonald's, a Domino's Pizza, and the largest Laundromat Richard had ever seen. Most of the male population seemed to be teens and younger and over sixty. There was a wider age range among the women. Richard's impression was of sleek black hair, T-shirts, and blue jeans. Occasionally there was a flash of deep blue as an older woman in the heavy traditional velvet skirt and blouse, loaded with turquoise jewelry, flashed by.

"Was this a traditional encampment?" Richard asked, making conversation.

"Nah, it was founded in 1903 when the government built a school and agency here."

"Oh."

"And we don't call it Shiprock. We call it Naat'áanii Nééz." Richard repeated the words, trying to wrap his tongue and palate around the unfamiliar syllables. Benally gave a short laugh. "Not bad for a white eyes." He laughed again. "Now you see why they used it as a code during World War Two. My grandfather was a code talker," he added with pride. "They're almost all gone now."

"That's sad," Richard said.

Benally shrugged. "That's life."

The road took a sharp curve to the right, and they crossed over a river. A sign identified it as the San Juan. Richard could see where the river had originally flowed, hundreds of yards wider, but irrigation and drought had reduced it to a narrow blue ribbon. They crossed a modern bridge, but on the other side the traffic crossed over an old steel truss bridge. Benally turned left on Hephaestus Peak Road. They passed a police station and a run-down mission called the Power Place. At the top of the bluff, Benally turned left down a small paved road. Well, it was paved only if a person was generous. The edges had been nibbled away, and the center of the road was a collection of potholes.

They passed a corral with a pair of tired-looking horses standing head to tail and swishing flies. A trailer with nine cars and trucks in various states of disrepair parked in the dirt yard out front. Then they reached a cinder-block house painted bright blue. The tin roof was adorned with thirty or so old tires. Richard wasn't sure why. Nestled among the tires, a large, rusting swamp cooler thrummed and clanged as it tried to beat back the heat.

As in Tecolote, there were a lot of dogs, and they began caroling when he and Joseph stepped out of the car. The noise brought a heavyset woman to the front door. Richard put her in her forties. The high cheekbones of her Amerind genes struggled to be seen in a round, fat face. Her expression was tight and closed off as she watched Richard and Joseph walk toward her.

"What do you want?"

"Mrs. Yazzi?" There was a stiff nod in reply. Richard flashed his badge. "I'm here to see Mosi Tsosie." He found the name hard to say with the three *s* sounds, and he flushed with embarrassment.

"FBI said we all done with that," came the unencouraging reply.

"This is the final follow-up, and we have information that we thought would be a comfort to Mosi," Richard said. Sweat was breaking out in his armpits, and the August sun beating down on his bare head made him feel faint.

"That girl's crazy. Maybe crazy as her brother. She smashed the screen on our computer. Tried to smash the computer screens at the library."

"I may be able to help with that," Richard said.

Her face closed down even more. "We're gonna have a medicine man do a sing." The message was clear: *We* don't need *your* help, White Eyes.

"If I could just see your niece, please."

The leading edges of the clouds rolled over them, and the temperature immediately dropped twenty degrees. Lightning flared and thunder snarled overhead. The woman reluctantly stepped aside, and Richard and Joseph entered the house. The furniture was fairly new and of better quality than Richard had expected. "Your husband isn't here?"

Mrs. Yazzi shook her head. "He's on a roustabout crew out in the gas fields round Farmington. I'll get Mosi."

They waited in the living room. Joseph leaned in close. "Is your telling her she was right going to help or hurt her, sir? She can't go through life smashing computers."

Mrs. Yazzi and the girl returned before Richard could answer. She was a graceful child and seemed very tall for her age, which from the file Richard knew to be nine. Long black hair fell almost to her waist; arching eyebrows accentuated the almond shape of her dark-brown eyes, but they were wary.

She spared him only the briefest of glances before looking away. Thin wrists thrust out from the sleeves of a too-small blouse, and her blue jeans were a tad too short. She did have the new craze in tennis shoes—pink lights in the heels flashed in the storm-darkened room as she shifted from foot to foot.

"If we could talk privately," Richard requested.

"I'll be in the kitchen," the aunt said.

"Mind if I get a drink of water?" Joseph asked.

A nod of permission, and they left the room. Richard and the girl contemplated each other. Unlike other children Richard had known, she didn't speak. The silence stretched on and on. Some of that was no doubt her own nature, and the trauma she'd endured, but it was also a hallmark of her culture. His first year in New Mexico, Richard had sung in the choir at the Lutheran church. One of his fellow choir members was involved in a musical outreach program to the Pueblos and reservations, and he'd helped out for a few months. One of the performances had been at a Navajo boarding school southwest of Shiprock, a place called Sheep Springs. One of the teachers had warned them not to expect applause or comment. *"If they really like it, they may gather around and want to touch you,"* she had warned.

That had been the case. Richard had sung Mozart and Schubert lieder, his tenor voice echoing off the gym walls, while his accompanist contended with an old upright piano whose upper B wouldn't sound. Each song was met with total silence from the stone-faced audience, and he wondered what earthly relevance this music and his presence could have to these children. After he'd finished to an awkward silence, and the teacher had dismissed the students, he'd found himself surrounded by a sea of children and reaching hands. They'd ruffled and tugged at his white-blond hair, touched his hands and his face. There had been a small amount of chatter in Navajo, and then they had flowed away and vanished, emulating the summer rains on the desert outside.

Well, it was going to be up to him to start. He took a breath. "First, let me tell you how sorry I am about your family." There was the smallest twitch of the muscle at the corner of her mouth, the start of a grimace quickly suppressed. "And I want to tell you that you were right. There *were* monsters in your brother's computer, and they're what caused your brother to murder your family. I saw them." It seemed harsh, but grief calls when he'd been an active-duty cop had taught him that euphemisms actually weren't kind. People wanted truth and they wanted it unvarnished.

That shocked her into reacting. Her eyes widened, her breath quickened, and she clasped her hands and pressed the clenched fists against her belly. "No. You couldn't have. They hid from the . . ." And she used a Navajo word.

"Does that mean FBI?" She shook her head.

"Police?" Again the head shake.

Richard took another stab. "White men with badges?" This time she nodded.

"I saw the face, and I sent it away and destroyed the computer," Richard told her.

"Not crazy," she whispered, as if talking to somebody not in the room.

"No," he said firmly.

She looked up at him, not a long way since she was only about a foot shorter than Richard, then she burst into tears. His first instinct was to enfold her in a comforting hug, but there was a pride and strength to this child along with her culture that made him hesitate.

Instead, he stepped to her side and touched her lightly on the shoulder and found her arms wrapped around his waist, her face pressed against his chest, slim body shaking with sobs. He patted her back and murmured the usual platitudes.

"It's all right. Go ahead. You can cry. You're safe now."

After a few minutes she stepped back, scrubbed at her wet face with her hands, and looked around for something to wipe her streaming nose. Her arm was just coming up so she could use the sleeve when Richard pulled out his handkerchief and handed it to her. She studied the folded piece of white cotton and linen embroidered with his initials, and dabbed carefully at her cheeks and eyes.

"It's okay, you can blow your nose."

"It'll get all dirty."

"That's what it's for," he said.

She blew her nose, then stepped back and gave him a serious look. "Really, it's okay? They were just in that one computer?" Which was a very prescient question from a nine-year-old.

"No, but I'm going to take care of that. I'm going to buy them all and destroy them."

"Won't that cost a lot of money?"

Richard considered his officer's reactions and gave a rueful smile. "Yes. But it's what we have to do."

"But until you get them all, they'll still be out there and they might get me," Mosi said.

"I can make sure that won't happen, but it might be a little scary."

"Scary how?"

"I have a sword, and when I touch evil things with it they die, and when I touch people it makes them safe from the evil things."

"You're a *hatalii*."

"I'm sorry, I don't know what that means."

Mosi frowned, and Richard could almost see her weighing and evaluating words. "Singer." She considered again and added, "Medicine man."

"No. I'm just a man, and there's no magic to the sword. It's just a tool, a weapon like any other weapon."

The brows came together in another considering frown. She gave a quick, determined nod. "I'd like you to make me safe."

"All right." And he drew the sword. The overtones shimmered in the air, and the first smile he'd seen blossomed on the girl's face.

"Oh, *it's* a singer." Richard laughed. She stood on tiptoes and looked down the length of the black blade. "It's pretty."

Richard contemplated the silver flecks like captured stars in the space-dark blade and nodded. Because this was a child, he felt he needed to be fair and warn her it would hurt. He did so, and while she looked momentarily alarmed, it passed, and she stood taller and held out her arm as if for an injection. "That's okay. Grandfather said we are warrior people and warriors have to be brave. I can be brave."

"You certainly can, Mosi." Richard took a breath and laid the sword gently on her shoulder.

And gaped as she continued to stand there and stare up at him with a questioning expression that turned into alarm. "Didn't it work? Can they still get me?"

Richard tottered over to a battered La-Z-Boy recliner, the sagging seat covered with a Navajo saddle blanket, and dropped down. "Oh, Mosi," he breathed. He swept his right hand back up the length of the blade, sheathing it once more. He handed the hilt over to the girl. "You saw what I did. How I made the blade appear. Could you try to do that for me, please?"

She shrugged and took the hilt, which seemed large in her small, slender hand. She shifted it to her left hand but looked uncomfortable.

"Are you right-handed or left-handed?" Richard asked.

"Right-handed."

"Then hold it in your right hand and pull with your left. Just like you saw me do." He stood and demonstrated.

"I won't get cut?"

He held up his right-hand palm out to show the unmarked skin.

"Okay." She placed her fist against the base of the hilt and pulled. The blade appeared. Because she was small, she couldn't quite pull it fully clear of wherever the blade resided when it wasn't present, so Richard stood up, laid his hand over hers, and helped her fully draw it.

"Oh, Mosi," he said again.

"Why do you keep saying my name and in that way?"

"Because you are a very, very special girl."

The noise from the rotors made it impossible to call from the helicopter, and there was no time to return to Lumina after they landed. As it was, Richard left his gun with Joseph and ran to catch the Southwest flight back to LAX. He fidgeted during the two-hour-plus flight and tried to quiet a nervous stomach with a bag of peanuts. It was a mistake, and he ordered spicy tomato juice, thinking that seemed more like food than a soda. It was a crazy impulse, but he had them make it a Bloody Mary. It was hard to control his impatience until he reached the car, but he wanted no casual eavesdroppers to this conversation. Once in the car, he turned on his phone, adjusted his earpiece, and called Pamela.

"The Navajo girl I met today. I need to adopt her."

"Are you high?" came his sister's response.

"Ask Joseph why, and get back to me. Also, he can give you her information."

Pamela just hung up on him. Richard checked his watch as he eased onto I-405 heading north toward his hotel and discovered it resembled a parking lot. They inched forward with cars jockeying in and out of lanes searching for the lane that would move. Fifteen minutes later his phone rang. As expected, it was Pamela.

"Okay, you're not high, but this won't be easy. We're up against the Indian Child Welfare Act. You have no relationship with the child, and she has family."

"You've got to find a way. Make her my ward or something."

"This little girl is going to have some feelings about this," his sister warned.

"I'll cross that bridge when I come to it. Right now we just need to keep her safe. Can we make up a scholarship or something? We're enrolling her in our special, elite school?"

"Richard, calm down. Gold and I will figure out something, but we have to be careful. You're a twenty-nine-year-old man bringing a nine-year-old girl into your household, and you don't have a wife. If I were a prosecutor, it would have all my antennae twitching."

"Oh, Christ, I hadn't considered that. My enemies would make hay with that."

"Yes, and that's why you have lawyers. Do you want security on her?"

He thought about it for a minute and made his decision. "I know I'm taking a risk, but no. If we assign security to Shiprock, New Mexico, the bad guys might notice and wonder why. But tell Cross, he might be able to do discreet surveillance." He paused to carefully negotiate a change out of a lane that didn't appear to be moving at all. "What if you make the petition for guardianship?"

"Hmm, not a bad idea," his sister said.

"And we can always throw money at the problem. Judging by the house, the aunt could use the money."

"I don't love that idea," Pamela said. "It could easily turn into a blackmail situation."

"I know, but we have to have her under our protection. Do whatever you have to."

"Okay, we'll keep you posted. Be safe."

"I'll try."

Once he reached the Sofitel and was back in his room, Richard called Calderón. "I told you I'd be back. I'm back."

"Good, 'cause I found the spot," Johnny replied. "I was gonna drop the hammer on 'em tomorrow."

"I'd like to be there," Richard said.

"As what? The sleazy lawyer I brought in?"

"That'll work," Richard said. "And you might need somebody to back your play."

"You know anything about the law?"

"I was a cop. My sister is a lawyer, and my dad's a judge. I can talk the talk."

"Sling bullshit, you mean. Well, okay."

"What time tomorrow?"

"I'm gonna not show up in the morning, then confront the contractor at lunchtime when he's nice and pissed off. Oh, and I'll be bringing Joe."

"Who?"

"The old guy. He can do the mystic Indian shit. After that I'll call you, and you'll show up when you show up."

"How about three o'clock?" Richard suggested.

"Sounds good. Let me know if the time changes."

After they hung up, Richard paced the confines of the luxurious room. He picked up the room service menu, put it down, turned on the television and was assaulted by the news. He finally just took a shower, swallowed a Pepcid, ate a handful of Tums, and went to bed.

W HERE is he?"

The words were delivered with clipped care, partly from language differences, but mostly due to barely suppressed rage. It was four o'clock in the afternoon, and Grenier and Pamela were in a meeting. Pamela jumped up from behind her desk. Grenier heaved himself around to see who had entered the office and found himself looking at a Japanese man in his midsixties. His black hair was lightly sprinkled with gray, and his implacable expression reminded Grenier of portraits of shoguns or samurai.

"Kenzo," Pamela said, and Grenier realized this was the CFO of Lumina Enterprises, Kenzo Fujasaki. "What are you doing here?"

"I had a meeting scheduled with Richard. I am here. He is not."

"Oh, dear . . . I'm sorry . . . there must have been . . . he's away," Pamela stammered.

"I gathered that much," came the pointed rejoinder. "Jeannette said I wasn't on the schedule. I'm not clear on how to interpret that."

"It doesn't mean anything. It means Richard got busy and forgot to tell Jeannette." Pamela spread her hands in apology. "But for what it's worth, I'm sorry."

"It's not worth much." The undisguised rudeness set Pamela back on her heels. "I flew here from Tokyo."

"My brother has so much he's trying to handle."

"I am sympathetic to that. But where *is* he?"

"In California," Grenier said, joining the conversation. He levered himself out of the chair and extended his hand. "I don't believe we've met. Mark Grenier."

Fujasaki stared down at the artificial hand. His discomfort was evident by the way he barely touched fingertips to the fingers of Grenier's prosthesis. "Kenzo Fujasaki. And why is he in California?"

"He's trying to prevent an incursion," Pamela said. "It's taking longer than he anticipated."

"When is he returning to New Mexico?"

"We're not exactly sure."

"Then I must go to California to see him."

"That might be faster. He's working out of the California office," Pamela said. "Or perhaps there is something I might help with?"

"The way the company is constructed, there are certain actions that can only be taken by the CEO. Mr. Kenntnis was eccentric that way." Fujasaki's brow furrowed in a Jovian frown. "He should not have given his successor the same power and privileges."

Pamela stiffened at that. Despite their issues, the siblings were very loyal to each other.

"And just what do you mean by that?" she demanded.

"It was not directed at Richard. I would feel that way toward any person not Kenntnis in the position. The point is we have a dilemma. There is a company to be run, and the head of the company is off playing policeman. Apparently to the world." The disdain was clear.

"Just as there are things that only the CEO can do, there are tasks that only Richard can perform as the paladin," Pamela said. Anger clipped the edges of her words.

"Ah, yes, this . . . weapon." One didn't have to be a master of subtlety to hear the sneer in the final word.

Pamela bristled at Fujasaki's tone. "Yes, the weapon. It's the reason Lumina exists—to support the man with the weapon. Not the other way around."

That did not go down well. "This is not a video game. Lumina is a massive enterprise employing thousands of people. Mismanagement has consequences for their well-being and security."

"And monsters ravening through the world wouldn't make their day any better either!"

Grenier stepped in before the situation deteriorated further. "You both have a point, but chief financial officers are about bottom lines, not greater societal issues. It's not fair to browbeat Mr. Fujasaki for doing his job, Pamela. And you yourself have been warning Richard that financial problems will hinder his efforts as the paladin."

She gave him a blistering and accusatory look at what she saw as betrayal. Grenier didn't care because of what he'd seen in Fujasaki's expression. Even beneath the Asian reticence, Grenier read approval at what he'd said. Perhaps Mr. Fujasaki would like to talk with an adult. Grenier began planning how to make that happen as the CFO said, "It seems I must arrange for a flight to California. We should call Richard and inform him."

Pamela checked the time on her computer. "I'll call and make sure he's at the office when you do arrive."

She picked up her phone. "I'll have my assistant make you a reservation."

"If I can't fly today, please have her arrange for a hotel as well."

"There are guest rooms in the penthouse," Pamela said.

"Mr. Kenntnis did not have us to stay."

"Richard does."

There was no give in the rigid profile. "I would prefer a hotel."

"Okay, but . . . okay." She capitulated, realizing that further argument was futile.

There was a quick conversation with her assistant. When Pamela was finished, Fujasaki cleared his throat. "I would like to see Mr. Kenntnis."

"He's not here."

"All indications were that he was not competent. Are you saying that has changed since last we saw him?"

"No. He's at one of our scientific facilities being studi—" She broke off, and when she resumed it was with a more diplomatic word. "Examined."

"Why a laboratory and not a hospital?"

Long fingers moved nervously through the papers on her desk. "Richard was honest with all of you about Kenntnis. He told you Kenntnis isn't human. Because of that, our doctors were baffled. Richard thought maybe our scientists would have a better shot at restoring his mind. And believe me, nobody wants Kenntnis restored to us more than my brother."

"Your brother showed us photographs of that thing he claimed was Mr. Kenntnis."

Pamela drilled Grenier with a look. "Tell him. You're the one who captured Kenntnis."

"Well, we're never quite certain what these multidimensional creatures might be," Grenier temporized.

Pamela's glare deepened. "Based on everything Kenntnis told Richard, he wasn't . . . isn't one of those things. He's from our dimension."

"According to Richard," Kenzo said. Pamela wisely let that one go past without comment.

There was a tap on the door, and Pamela's assistant entered carrying a handful of papers.

"We have you flying out tomorrow morning at six thirty, and I got you a room at the Tamaya Resort."

"Is that near the airport?"

"Not really," the assistant answered.

"I would prefer—"

"No," Grenier interrupted, "you really wouldn't. The dining choices at the airport are limited at best and horrible at worst. There are three excellent restaurants at Tamaya, and it's quiet and beautiful. You had a long trip already, you should rest and relax before you travel again."

"I confess to some jet lag." And in a final salvo of passive-aggressive, Fujasaki added, "It's a long way from Tokyo."

"I'll have one of our security officers drive you," the assistant said, and she escorted Fujasaki out of the office.

Pamela collapsed into her chair with a whoof. "Okay, that could have gone better." Her expression tightened. "I'm going to kill Richard."

⟨⬥⬥⬦⟩

Sick of L.A. traffic and actually physically sick from nerves and lack of sleep, Richard had opted to hire a driver. Johnny had texted his location. It was another unfinished road on the east side of the subdivision. There were five cars parked on the edge of the dirt road, one of them a limo. Calderón's old pickup truck squatted in the middle. It seemed surrounded and almost threatened by the grilles of the new, expensive cars. The driver parked, and Richard stepped out of his limo. His phone vibrated in his coat pocket, but he ignored it.

Johnny and the old man stood on one side of a pair of sad-looking rocks maybe a foot wide by a couple of feet long, their red sandstone surfaces pitted and cracked. They thrust up out of the dust like basking crocodiles. To Richard's mind they didn't look like much.

On the other side of the rocks were six men in business suits. The contrast with the Indians in their jeans, T-shirts, and work boots could not have been more striking. Richard studied the Anglo faces. Three of them looked both pissed and nervous. One just looked really nervous and kept grabbing at his shirt collar. Another was taking notes and looked calculating. Richard guessed he was a lawyer. The final man seemed aloof and unmoved, and Richard recognized him. It was Alexander Titchen himself. He met Richard's gaze, and Richard was surprised at the calculating pleasure in those brown eyes.

Richard drew close enough to hear Johnny say, "This is a holy place. A place where the spirits live." The Native American folded his arms across his barrel chest and stared at the men.

There was a long silence, then one of the suits asked, "And just how do you know that?"

The old man said something in a language Richard assumed to be Chumash. Johnny listened and then answered, "Grandfather says he sees the signs."

"And what signs are those?" asked another Anglo.

There was more conversation, and again Johnny answered. "Grandfather says white people can't see them." It so closely lined up with what the archaeologist had told Richard, that Richard had to look away and produce a cough to cover his overwhelming desire to laugh. Once again he felt his phone vibrate.

"Then how do we know any of this crap is real? You're just looking to hold us up for money or something, aren't you?" one of the reps said.

Richard bristled on Johnny's behalf, though the Indian didn't react, just said in a flat, dull tone, "We don't want nothing from you. We just want you to move this road. Leave the spirits safe and in peace."

The extremely nervous man looked very relieved. "Oh, well, if that's all, we can *easily* do that," he gushed.

Titchen had a reaction to that. He again looked over at Richard, and this time he added a thin smile. It was starting to give Richard the creeps. His phone went off again, and this time Richard reached into his pocket and turned it off. Whoever was calling could wait.

"And if we say no?" one of the subdivision reps blustered.

Richard stepped in. "Then you can see us in court."

"And before that we'll make sure every magazine, newspaper, and online outlet does an article about us and this subdivision and how you are fucking us," Calderón said.

"I'm not getting my construction company dragged into that," said the nervous man who Richard now realized must be the developer tasked with building the subdivision. "We'll move the road. It's only a couple of feet."

Johnny glanced at Richard. It struck Richard that Cross hadn't said how much of a change to the rune was necessary. He decided more was better. Richard gave an almost imperceptible head shake.

"No, we do not wish the dust and rain splashed on the spirits."

"So how far should we move it?" the developer asked.

"At least . . ." Richard quickly flared his fingers three times to indicate fifteen. "Fifteen feet," Johnny said.

Once again Titchen looked over at Richard, then abruptly turned and walked back toward the limo. Everyone looked after him in confusion. "I . . . I guess that means it's okay?" the developer said uncertainly. There were nods from the remaining men. The reps and the contractor and developer climbed back into their cars and drove away. Johnny and Richard stood by the pickup. The Indian studied the limo.

"Guess you really are rich," he said laconically.

"Yeah," Richard said. He held out his hand. "I'll get my lawyers— the real ones—started on buying that acreage, and you pick an architect for your health center. Have him or her bill us. And thank you."

A shrug was all he got in response. Johnny and the old man got into their truck. Richard got back into the limo. The driver executed an awkward K-turn on the dirt track, and they bounced down the road toward the pavement. Dust rose up behind them in pale plumes. They were winding back out of the subdivision when suddenly Titchen's limo pulled out of a side street and blocked them. Richard's driver let out a yell and a curse, and slammed on his brakes.

Richard leaned forward and peered through the front windshield.

"Uh, mister, you got a fix for this? 'Cause I sure don't. I'm just hired to drive," the driver said.

Touching the hilt of the sword for reassurance, Richard climbed out of his car. Walking toward the other limo, Richard reflected on how truly vulnerable he was. Vulnerable to someone with a high-powered rifle in his or her hand. Vulnerable to a sprinkle of strontium in a salad at a restaurant. Which brought his thoughts back to Mosi. Pamela had to find a way. There had to be a replacement for him. He drew the hilt and kept his right hand against the base. Suddenly Johnny was at his side. He was carrying a shotgun. Richard gave him a sideways glance.

"Looked like you might need some help," Calderón said.

The passenger window whined down and Titchen leaned out. "Well, I guess this round goes to you, Rich."

Richard was taken aback. He had expected a clipped East Coast accent but instead Titchen's Cajun accent poured out like warm molasses. "It's Richard, or Mr. Oort, but yes, I'd say this round goes to me" was Richard's response.

Titchen smiled and studied the hilt. "Why don't you just use it? You know I'm a threat."

"Because I expect you have a guard dog with a gun trained on me right now."

Titchen's smile broadened and he glanced at Calderón. "Like you."

"We're cautious men," Richard replied.

"I am, but I don't think that applies to you. You got out of the car." Titchen paused, scratched the side of his nose. "You're really not at all what I expected."

"Glad I could confound you," Richard said.

The smile snapped off. "I'll be watching," Titchen warned.

"Back at you."

The window rolled up, and the limo backed up, turned, and drove away. Richard slumped with relief, sucked in a deep breath.

"That guy's gonna fuck you over unless you fuck him over first," Johnny said. And he walked back to the pickup. Richard returned to his car.

They were halfway back to L.A. when Richard remembered he'd turned off his phone. It flickered back to life, and he saw he had ten messages. Seven of them were from Pamela and three were from Dagmar. Making like a small, frightened animal, Richard's stomach closed down into a hard, aching ball and ran for cover against his spine. Something terrible must have happened. New Mexico was easy. It was an hour ahead of California. Richard spent several minutes calculating the time difference between L.A. and London. It was early evening in London. Start with Dagmar or start with Pamela? The higher number of calls indicated that his sister was upset, to put it mildly. Richard admitted to cowardice and called the woman who was less likely to yell at him.

Dagmar's assistant answered. "Is she still in?" Richard asked, hoping she had gone home, which would indicate the crises had been averted.

"Oh, yes," Craig said. "I'll ring you through."

Dagmar picked up instantly.

"Hi, what's up?" Richard asked in a breezy tone.

"You had a meeting with Kenzo in Albuquerque, and you were not there." His COO's German accent was more pronounced than usual, and she wasn't using contractions, a sure sign she was upset.

And then he remembered. "Oh, shit."

"I could not have put it better."

"Shit, shit, shit, shit, shit. I'll call him."

"It is likely to be a most unpleasant conversation."

"Even if I grovel?"

"That would probably make it worse. Even when you fuck up, you must fuck up with assurance."

"Well, those are some words to live by," Richard muttered.

"Richard, you must get control of things," Dagmar said. "Now I am going home. If you want, we'll do a conference call with Kenzo, and I'll try to help mollify him."

"Thanks. I appreciate it."

Richard had barely hung up when his phone rang again. He looked at the caller ID. It was Pamela.

He closed his eyes and braced himself.

"You are a certifiable idiot!"

"Yes, yes I am."

Agreement didn't stop the tirade. "How on earth could you forget about a meeting with Kenzo?"

"Because I'm an idiot?"

"Don't smart off to me. He was angry. I mean *really* angry and deeply offended."

"I know. It was terrible of me, but I don't have a time machine. I can't go back and change it now."

"You just don't treat people that way."

Now Richard was starting to get pissed. "I know that and I've said I'm sorry, so maybe it's time for you to stop beating me up and figure out what we do now. What's Kenzo going to do?"

"He's heading to California tomorrow to see you."

"Lovely. Just what I need."

"You run this company! You have obligations!"

"I know that too." Richard realized he was getting louder and louder. He rolled up the privacy screen between himself and the driver. "I also had an obligation to keep a tear from opening in Orange County."

"Did you get it done?"

"Yes."

"Good, but somebody has to manage this company," Pamela added.

"I keep offering it to you, and you keep refusing. But keep pushing and I'll do it. And I can too. I can do anything I want with Lumina and every other company Lumina owns." He'd expected another explosion, but what he got was a long silence. He felt his heart lightening at the thought she might seriously be considering the offer.

When Pamela finally spoke again, her tone was deadly serious. "No. I couldn't do it. Oh, I'd manage to count the pennies very effectively, but just like I don't have a sense of humor, I don't have . . . well, call it that vision thing. You do, and that's what's needed for Lumina. Look, I've got to go. Another call's coming in."

Richard had a feeling it was a dodge, but he didn't argue. It was so unexpected to have that kind of praise and support from his sister, especially on a day when he'd fucked up so badly. "Thank you," he whispered, but he was talking to a dead line.

Then he realized he didn't know when Kenzo was arriving. Jeannette would be able to tell him, and she wouldn't yell at him. Probably. Maybe. He made the call and learned that Kenzo was flying the next morning on a six thirty flight, and he would be at the L.A. office at ten sharp. Richard had a feeling the *sharp* was a direct message from his CFO. Only at the end did Jeannette's professional demeanor slip.

"So, are you going to let me keep your calendar and make *all* your calls now?"

"Yeah," Richard said, and he suspected he sounded about six years old.

Grenier left the seven-story Lumina building before five o'clock and went to his town house complex, but not to the actual town house. Instead he went to the association clubhouse, where there was a holdover from an earlier, pre-cell-phone era—a pay phone. The television was on in the commons room, the flat screen showing a baseball game while sports commentators commented on the plays. Grenier's interest in sports was nonexistent, so he had no idea who was playing. A couple of young men played pool. The sharp *clack* of the balls formed an odd syncopation with the voices from the television and the cheers and groans from the spectators.

At the pay phone, Grenier balanced the phone book on the mound of his belly and flipped through the yellow pages to restaurants. He made a reservation at the Prairie Star for two at seven. Then he called the Hyatt Regency Tamaya and asked for Mr. Fujasaki. The CFO agreed to dine with him. Grenier had known he would. Thirty years of ministry had taught Grenier how to read people's desires. Fujasaki wanted to vent. Grenier would be the sympathetic listener.

He then went home, showered, and changed into a loose linen shirt that he could leave untucked. In the garage he removed the magnetic tracking device from his car and left it on the top of the hot-water heater. Richard and his watchdogs would assume Grenier was safely ensconced at home for the night. He climbed back into his car and headed north.

Bernalillo originally had been a sleepy little town some twenty miles north of Albuquerque. Predominantly Hispanic and rural, it had suddenly exploded as a bedroom community for both Albuquerque and Santa Fe. It now touted two coffee shops, a great diner, and a ring of expensive subdivisions selling adobe McMansions. The trailer parks and older houses were hanging on, fighting a rear-guard action, and the locals were dining at the Denny's or the Taco Express and wondering what had happened.

Grenier drove west through the main intersection, air-conditioning going full blast to try and counter the glare of the westering sun. The tires thrummed on the bridge over the Rio Grande. Summer heat, upstream dams, and farmers and ranchers irrigating had reduced it to a few exhausted trickles of water meandering among mud flats.

Coronado had written that the river was a mile across and the grasses had brushed the bellies of his horses. The conquistador had founded Bernalillo when he wintered over during his search for the Cities of Gold. *He probably wouldn't recognize it now, and not just because of the buildings*, Grenier thought as he studied the sandy hills dotted with scrub brush and a few piñon and juniper trees. He looked down at the glutinous mud and the tangle of plastic pop bottles and beer cans snagged in the river willows. Thus had man wrought. Unlike many of his televangelist ilk, he had known that man-made climate change was real, but he had pushed the party line that it was a myth. Partly because that was what was expected by his listeners and viewers, and partly because once the Old Ones returned, none of it would matter. The world would have changed profoundly. As long as Grenier could finish out the remainder of his life in comfort and wielding power, he didn't particularly care what came after.

Just over the river and on his right loomed the massive bulk of the Santa Ana Star Casino, one of the many Indian gambling palaces that had popped up on nearly every pueblo. Why they hadn't had the sense to build three casinos and pool the moneys was a mystery to Grenier. They could have minimized initial outlay and maximized profits, but that was Indians for you.

He headed north and left the ugly, crass world of fast-food restaurants and casinos behind. The narrow road wound through scrub and sagebrush. Suddenly lush green appeared, the golf course that surrounded the Tamaya resort. It was jarring against the beige of the sand and the blue of the Sandia Mountains rising in the east, and in this drought-prone desert it seemed the height of folly.

The hotel was large and sprawling, built in the pueblo style and actually quite attractive. Fujasaki was waiting for him in the cathedral-like lobby. The space was anchored by a giant fireplace built of sandstone blocks. Mercifully, it stood cold at this time of year. Around it were sofas, comfortable chairs, and checkers and chess tables. The Japanese man was seated in a massive overstuffed chair, fingering a bishop and staring down at the board with a frown between his dark brows. Grenier's footfalls were loud on the stone floor. Fujasaki turned and studied him. The frown didn't fade.

"Mr. Grenier."

"My car is out front."

"We don't dine here?"

"The Corn Maiden is good if what you crave is vast amounts of meat from various animals. The Prairie Star has a more eclectic menu and the best wine cellar in New Mexico."

"That sounds excellent."

They drove the short distance to the old adobe building on the edge of the golf course. Grenier was a bit of a regular and Greg took him to his favorite table, which offered a view of the mountains off to the east.

"Mr. Grenier, would you care to see the wine list?" the maître d' asked as he whisked the napkin onto his lap.

He cocked a brow at Fujasaki. "Do you drink red wine or do you prefer white? They have an excellent Turnbull Merlot 2008."

"That will be fine."

Greg nodded and vanished. Fujasaki picked up the large leather menu and studied it. He seemed in no haste to break the silence. It was a powerful trick. Americans hated silence and often rushed to fill it, thus losing their advantage. Grenier, however, knew the game and knew how to play it. He also had no desire to offend his guest's Japanese sensibilities. It was a culture that required that one move slowly to business.

Greg returned with the wine and a fresh-faced young woman who took their orders. Grenier ordered the cold cucumber-and-almond soup special, the cold beet salad, and the pork loin in cherries. Fujasaki ordered a green salad and the sea bass.

"Have you come often to New Mexico?" Grenier asked as they sipped wine and Grenier devoured the bread that had arrived.

"A fair bit. But often Mr. Kenntnis and I would meet in London."

"Why did he settle here? Do you have any idea?"

"None." The word was accompanied by a head shake that nicely indicated bafflement and frustration. Fujasaki paused for another sip of wine, then added, "I have tried to convince Richard to move operations to London. He would have Dagmar at hand, and she could advise him more easily, and it's more convenient for me."

Grenier noted that Richard was not referred to as Mr. Oort. "I take it the boy's not having any of it?"

The dark eyes flickered at the use of the diminutive, but there was no objection. "No. He says there must be a reason Kenntnis chose New Mexico and Albuquerque, and he's not going to second-guess Kenntnis." Fujasaki took a slow sip of wine, his eyes locked on Grenier's over the rim of the glass. "He takes the most outlandish actions, but over something so sensible and trivial he is equally—"

"Headstrong?" Grenier suggested. "Stubborn?"

"Granted the company has always run at the whim of the man in control, but I thought someone young and inexperienced would be guided by the officers who have worked for Lumina for decades." Complaint and outrage danced on every word.

"Richard's agenda is different from the normal ones that dictate how a company is run," Grenier said, but he had elicited as much mutiny from Fujasaki as was going to occur this early in their dealings. He merely gave a grunt. Grenier gestured with the bottle, and Fujasaki indicated to refill his glass.

"I've only been to Japan once," Grenier said, "but I found it a beautiful, elegant, and very civilized country."

"Yes, you led a crusade there back when we had a Christian prime minister. It caused quite a controversy."

Grenier shrugged. "It's what I did."

"And now you do public relations for Lumina Enterprises and earn a modest salary. Quite a comedown."

"It beat the alternative."

"Which was?"

"Imprisonment or, more likely, death."

It was a bit of a conversation stopper. Fortunately, Grenier's soup arrived. He used it as a way to let the conversation cool down. The Sandia Mountains slowly turning brilliant pink offered a distraction.

"Sandia means watermelon," he remarked in between sips. "At sunset you see why."

Fujasaki followed the head nod and looked at the mountains. "Very pretty" was the dry response.

Grenier selected another topic, the latest exhibit of Tokugawa art at the Denver Art Museum. While he spoke and finished his soup, Fujasaki just watched him. The salads arrived. Grenier took special notice of how Fujasaki ate. In Grenier's experience, you could tell a lot about a man by his eating habits.

Fujasaki ate with quick, economical bites. He chewed carefully and swallowed slowly. A cautious man. Richard was like a hummingbird. He darted at his food, tore it into small pieces so no one would notice how little he was actually eating. A restless spirit. Grenier stopped, the fork halfway to his mouth, and subjected himself to the same analysis. How did he eat? He shoveled, cramming in every bite. Savoring the food, yes, but eager for the taste of the next bite. Did that make him a greedy man? He contemplated his reasons for meeting with Fujasaki and had the answer.

Art having proved to be uninspiring, Grenier launched into a third topic. He tried politics.

Fujasaki stopped him with an upraised hand. "Mr. Grenier, while I admire your attention to what you perceive as cultural sensitivities, I am a modern Japanese. You don't have to circle the subject. You asked for this dinner, so please, just get to the point."

He leaned as far forward as the bulge of his belly would allow. "You're worried about the financial health of the company under its present leadership." Grenier gave Fujasaki an opening, but the CFO was a good negotiator—he gave back nothing. "With your knowledge of this company and its assets, we could possibly—probably—arrange things so the other officers would be willing to push for a change at the top."

"The documents are very clear. The company is Richard's. It can't be taken from him," Fujasaki said.

"But he can give it up," Grenier answered softly.

Fujasaki leaned back. The dark eyes regarded him with a hawk's stare. "And just how would that come about?"

"I know Richard's mind. I know how to manipulate him." Grenier spread his hands.

"Interesting." Fujasaki took another bite of fish. His face was impassive.

Grenier finished his pork loin and scraped up the remains with a last piece of bread. Popped it into his mouth. Chewed, swallowed, and waited.

Fujasaki pushed aside his plate, then stood up, "I will speak to my officers. I think they might be open to the conversation. We'll be in touch." He tossed his napkin onto the table. "There is a shuttle that will take me back to the hotel. Thank you for dinner."

Grenier watched him walk out and seethed a bit. He didn't like being treated like an underling. He waved over Greg.

"I'll take a tiramisu and a cappuccino."

Lacing his fingers on his stomach, he leaned back and contemplated a future when Kenzo Fujasaki would be picking up the check and bowing him out of the restaurant.

Chapter

EIGHT

RICHARD swam laps, the water sluicing down his arm with each stroke. It was seven A.M., and Richard had the pool at the Sofitel to himself. Kenzo's plane was probably taxiing onto the runway in Albuquerque, or it might already be in the air. Richard ran through scenarios as he drove through the water and debated how best to mollify his CFO. He realized he actually didn't know the man well enough to make a plan. Forty minutes later, the final lap completed, he rested his hands on the tiled edge and boosted himself out of the water. Richard was years away from his days as a gymnast, and he was starting to note the difference in his upper-body strength. *Almost thirty*, he thought and found it depressing.

He was in the bathroom shaving when his phone rang. It was

Calderón's number, and he was surprised. He'd assumed their business was concluded.

"Hey, what's up?" he asked in lieu of a standard greeting.

The voice that replied was old and whispering. "This is Joe." It was the old man who had accompanied Johnny the day before. The old man who had worked on archaeological digs. "That man. He's here. With others."

That man. Richard didn't have to ask for his identity. It could only be Titchen. "I'm on my way."

No time to make the drive to Orange County. Richard brought up a listing of helipads on his phone. There was one literally across the street at the Beverly Center. He quickly arranged for a pickup, then threw on clothes, grabbed his pistol and the sword, and headed across the street.

Wind from the rotors tugged at his tie and blew his hair. His loosened forelock tickled his left eyebrow as he climbed into the cockpit. The pilot was a young Asian American. He had the coordinates for Tecolote, and with a lurch and a sway the helicopter waddled into the air.

It took forty minutes, and Richard quivered through every one of them. Willing the chopper to go faster, resisting saying anything to the pilot. He knew that the drive would have taken three if not four hours, but not being in control was driving him mad. Eventually Tecolote came into view through the windshield. There was no limo, but a large Cadillac Escalade was parked among the pickups and inexpensive and aged cars. Was Titchen still there? Richard felt his gorge rise and swallowed hard.

"Can you put us down there?" Richard asked, and pointed at the dusty open area between the trailers and the stone house.

The wind off the rotors was whipping the water in the kiddie pool into frothing waves. Dogs stared up at the helicopter, their jaws working. Richard presumed they were barking madly. People were spilling out of the trailers. Johnny was standing near the SUV with a white-haired, pudgy man in a suit. They both stared up at the helicopter.

The pilot nodded and lowered them swaying to the ground. Dust rose up to dance around the sides of the chopper. A bump and they had landed. The engine was cut and the rotors sang their way to silence. Richard jumped out and pulled the hilt out of its holster. This time the dogs kept their distance.

The door of the main house was thrown open, and another Anglo man appeared in the doorway. He was in his early forties with a hard body that was just starting to lose tone. His brown eyes raked Richard with a cold glance.

Richard strode toward Johnny, who moved to meet him. The older man trailed after, and now that he was closer, Richard could see the man's rosy cheeks and tooth-blinding smile that appeared only on toothpaste commercials, infomercials, and television preachers. Richard recognized him from when he'd researched Gilead. This was Pastor Jacobs, who led the only church in Gilead. A third man appeared from inside the house. He was big, really, really big. His T-shirt hugged his torso, and the bare arms it revealed were heavily muscled.

No wider than a beer truck, no taller than a lamppost, Richard thought. All five of them met near the door of the house.

"You sure know how to make an entrance," Johnny said in his laconic way.

Johnny made the introductions. "Pastor Jacobs," he said, indicating the pudgy man. He nodded at the cold-eyed man, "Deacon Medford." The last was Brother Sutherland.

Jacobs thrust out his hand.

Richard almost reflexively took it but then noticed that Medford was staring intently at the hilt with recognition in his eyes, and Richard realized moving his right hand away from the hilt was not a good idea. The toothy smile on Jacobs's face slipped, and he eventually dropped his hand.

"Mr. Titchen was inspired by your actions," Jacobs said. "He's offered to fund a private school here."

Richard glanced at Johnny. "Don't do it."

"Who are you to tell these good people what they can and cannot accept?" Medford snapped.

Richard ignored them and kept talking to Calderón. "They're tied in with Titchen." He looked back at Jacobs. "Where is he?"

Johnny answered, "He's left, but not before he upped your ante. He'll do everything you said you'd do, and build us a school and buy us a fire truck—"

"Don't be a greedy fool!"

Richard whirled at the remark. The old man, Joe, stood behind him. He was glaring at Johnny. Calderón looked pissed.

"What do we care which of these rich assholes pays us off?"

"Because Titchen is an evil asshole," Richard argued.

"I got something to show from Titchen. With you it's just been talk so far. He brought us computers for the kids—"

Ice water seemed to run down Richard's spine. None of the kids outside playing . . . All of them in the main house . . .

"They're in the main house, aren't they?"

Johnny's expression was all the answer he needed. "Get out of my way." Richard was startled by the sound of his own voice. He was practically growling.

The four other men exchanged glances. There was a small amount of space between Medford and the gorilla. Richard darted through it and felt the goon's hand clutch at the back of his suit coat.

"Hey!" Calderón shouted.

Richard was inside. The brightly colored Gaia computers were on the battered sofa and the table, a few were on chairs, all abandoned when the helicopter had arrived. The kids were grouped at the windows. Medford, Jacobs, the goon, Johnny, and Joe were right behind him. Richard drew the sword.

"He knows!" Medford yelled as Richard lunged at the nearest

computer. A wild discordant screeching mixed with the humming chord of the drawn sword.

"Jesus Christ! Jesus Christ!" Johnny was gabbling.

The tip of the sword tapped at the computer, and it dissolved into stinking sludge. The inhuman sounds became deafening. The kids were screaming.

"Jimmy, why have you got a gun?" Jacobs babbled at the big man, Sutherland.

The preacher looked confused and terrified, and Richard realized Jacobs had been a dupe. The minister moved toward the goon, effectively blocking his shot. Richard seized the opportunity and threw himself into a shoulder roll that brought him almost to Sutherland's feet. He flipped up the blade of the sword, hitting the big man in the groin. He collapsed convulsing to the floor, his finger tightening spasmodically on the trigger. The gun roared, and Jacobs let out a startled little cough. Blood bloomed on his white shirt where it was pulled taut over his round belly.

"Get out of here!" Johnny screamed at the kids. They bolted through the front door in a mad stampede.

Joe hobbled toward a cabinet. Medford shot him in the back. The Chumash man collapsed with a cry, hands clawing, trying to reach the source of pain. Medford had Johnny by the throat and was holding the pistol to the man's temple.

"Drop the sword, paladin," he said.

Calderón's eyes made it clear he wanted Richard to ignore that command. But Richard held up his free hand in a placating gesture and dropped onto one knee to lay the sword on the floor.

"And the gun in your shoulder rig." Richard complied. "Now kick them over to me."

Richard started to rise. As he did, he drew the .38 from its ankle holster, jerked it up, hoped luck was with him, and fired. A dark hole appeared in Medford's forehead. He toppled backward as blood began to trace a pattern down his face.

Thirty. I'm getting way too good at this.

Johnny ran to the old man. Looked up at Richard, shook his head.

Rage took him. Richard strode over to where Jacobs lay gasping on the floor. The preacher whimpered as he stared at the blade.

"Don't kill me. Don't hurt me. Don't kill me. I didn't—" Jacobs started to cry.

Richard stared down into Jacobs's frightened, pleading brown eyes, tears running over his cheeks and snot glistening on his upper lip. His rage dissolved into sick shame. Kneeling, Richard pulled out his handkerchief, ripped open the minister's shirt, and jammed the makeshift bandage into the bullet hole. Jacobs screamed. It trickled away into agonized moans.

"I'm sorry," Richard said softly to Jacobs, "but I have to." He laid the sword on Jacobs's shoulder. The preacher went into violent convulsions that almost bent his back into a circle.

Richard began moving through the room, touching and destroying each of the computers. The stink was becoming unbearable, and he tried breathing through his mouth. He jerked his chin at the unconscious thug. "Get him restrained, and here's your story," he said to Calderón. "These crazy white eyes came down because they were angry at you about the subdivision. They started shooting. You shot back." He tossed his .38 snubby to Calderón. "This is yours in case they run ballistics, but I bet they won't. The cops will have a story that works." Richard destroyed the final computer. He sheathed the sword and returned the hilt to its holster. "Now I'm out of here." Richard headed for the door.

"Wait. What the fuck is that thing? What the fuck is going on? Who are you?"

"You know who I am—"

Calderón threw out his arms in a frantic, frustrated gesture. "I mean *what* the fuck *are* you?"

"Look, I'll explain everything later. Right now you need to call for an ambulance and then call the cops. In fact somebody probably already has, with all the gunfire."

"You want to not have been here," Calderón said.

"You got it in one."

Johnny nudged the unconscious goon's wrists with his toe. "He isn't gonna support the story, or the preacher, and you landed a helicopter."

"I expect you have enough clout to make sure that doesn't get mentioned, and I'm going to have an alibi." Richard looked down at the unconscious men. "Also, often when the reaction is violent, they experience memory loss. We can hope that will happen here. They're going to have worse problems when they wake up. Like a murder rap. Oh, and fire the snubby once so you'll have residue on your hand. Just in case they check."

"You're putting a lot of faith in things breaking just right."

"Sometimes that's all we've got. Now I've got to go." Richard opened the door, and he could hear the distant wail of sirens.

Johnny's hand fell heavy and warm onto his shoulder. "Thanks."

Richard just nodded and ran down the steps and toward the helicopter.

The old woman had the gaggle of kids gathered close around her near the wall of a trailer. Adults were milling around in confusion. Behind him, Richard heard the sharp retort of another shot being fired. He reached the helicopter and stared up into the alarmed eyes of his pilot.

"Get us in the air," Richard ordered.

"There was shooting, shouldn't we wait for—" Richard fished his badge out of his suit jacket pocket and flashed it at the pilot. "Oh."

Scrambling into the passenger seat, Richard buckled in and pulled on the helmet, and they rose into the sky on a pillar of dust. As they headed north, Richard wondered if Johnny was a good liar. Would the community pull together and follow his lead? Would Jacobs and Brother Sutherland remember and finger him? Richard had one thing going for him—police departments tended not to care what happened in marginalized communities. On the other hand, white men had been shot by a minority. Richard feared that Johnny might need very good representation. He'd call Pamela as soon as they landed. His wandering thoughts had brought him around to Lumina . . . and *Kenzo*.

Richard jerked up his wrist to check his watch. It was quarter to ten, and they were forty minutes from L.A. Sick with anxiety, Richard watched the roofs of the suburban sprawl that extended from Orange County almost to Santa Barbara go crawling past.

⬦⬦⬦

It was ten forty-five by the time he pulled into the parking lot at the office building. Richard had called Amy from the road, told her to tell Kenzo, *"I'm on my way. Hang on, I'll be there soon."*

"He's really pissed" had been the whispered response.

Richard never made it to the office. He met Kenzo in the lobby. The Japanese man stood at the glass doors, staring out at Wilshire Boulevard, tapping his foot and checking his watch.

"Kenzo," Richard panted.

"I have a taxi coming" was the terse reply. The words were a thin veneer over bubbling anger.

Normally Richard would have wilted at that tone, but he had been through a firefight, killed a man and seen another killed, and his impulse control had taken a hike. He turned to face the security guard and said, "When the cab arrives, tell the driver he's not needed. Give him this for his trouble." Richard handed the bemused guard a twenty.

"How dare you!" Kenzo said, crossing the room in three agitated steps.

"Yes, sir," the guard said. "Is that . . . blood, sir?"

The guard's hesitant question jolted Richard. He looked down and realized his left cuff was stained with blood. Kenzo was staring at the knee of his gray trousers. There was more blood there. He must have knelt in it when he did first aid on Jacobs.

"I will second the question! Is it blood?" Kenzo demanded.

"Yes."

A complex mix of emotions made up of both repulsion and fascination flickered across the CFO's thin face. "What have you done?"

Richard was damned if he was going to justify himself or his actions. "My job," he snapped. "Shall we go up to the office?" He gestured at the elevators.

The rent-a-cop was staring at him, wide-eyed. Richard pulled out his shield, flipped back the cover, and showed it to him. The guard stepped back behind his little desk.

It was only after they were in the elevator that Kenzo spoke. "Has anyone died?"

"Yes, two people."

"Killed by you."

"I only shot one, and if it makes you feel better, he was a bad guy."

"You are the head of Lumina Enterprises." The words came out as an explosion.

"Yes. _I_ am the head of Lumina Enterprises."

They measured looks that were matched in hostility and determination. The elevator doors opened before either had backed down. Richard stalked out and led the way to the office.

"Amy, hold my calls," he ordered as they passed her desk and went into the inner office. Richard held the door for Kenzo, then firmly closed it behind him.

"Okay, get it off your chest," Richard said.

"You owe me an apology," Kenzo said. He then folded his arms across his chest and stared at Richard, his gaze dark and implacable.

"That's it?"

"What more do you wish me to say? The onus is on you for your heedless and immature behavior."

An ever-tightening band of pain closed on Richard's forehead, and he heard another male voice, this one unaccented, the timbre deeper, which had always given it the ring of authority. His father's voice. Offering critique in words almost identical to Fujasaki's. Reaction to the shoot-out had weakened the bonds of control. Fury tore them to shreds.

"I saved a man's life this morning. Yesterday I ended a threat that could have brought monsters into this world. Your time and, frankly, your wounded pride are immaterial when measured against those acts. You are a bean counter. Your *only* purpose is to crunch numbers so *I* can do *my* job. Now say you're sorry and get the fuck out of my face because I have things to do." Richard stood, listening to the blood pounding in his ears, feeling the rage-induced tremors begin to subside.

The older man had blanched, but he recovered his composure and said stiffly, "I will tender my resignation."

"No. Not right now. I'm too stressed and pissed, and you're too pissed for either of us to make a reasoned decision. Now let's get back to New Mexico. I've had enough of California."

Grenier didn't think a direct call to Alexander Titchen was the way to go. He could have, because once upon a time they had been allies in an attempt at world domination. Titchen had donated to Grenier's church and his broadcast company. Grenier had reciprocated with instruction in how to contact the Old Ones and all matters magical. On a more mundane level, Grenier had helped provide the names of senators and representatives who would be open to the legal form of bribery that existed in modern American politics.

Those days were long past, and since he technically worked for the other side now, Grenier knew he wouldn't be trusted by Titchen, and he bloody well knew he couldn't trust Titchen. But he needed to erode Richard's support among his officers. The best way to do that was to make him spend a king's ransom acquiring Gaia.

Richard had a soft spot for children. Despite his sexual proclivities, Grenier fully expected him to marry at some point just so he could have kids. The fact that these computers had been put into the hands of poor children around the world would incline Richard to spend any amount. Grenier's plan was to ensure that Richard spent a fortune.

He pulled nervously at his lower lip. His belly rumbled and he rubbed it distractedly. Of course, he had to be sure that he brought Lumina merely to the edge of collapse and not past it. He had to be able to bring it back. Grenier shook off the worries. He believed he could, but for now the focus had to be on increasing the company's cash flow problems.

No fingerprints. That was the key. Good thing he was the media manager for Lumina Enterprises. It gave him so much access. So many ways to start a rumor.

Grenier pulled out his cell phone, then changed his mind and put it slowly back in his pocket. Richard was a trained investigator and a damned good one. Once the leak happened, he would start digging. He needed to hit something . . . someone before he hit Grenier.

Jorge bounced into the office with his iPad in one hand and a cup of coffee with a donut balanced on the rim in the other.

"Hey," he said.

Grenier looked up into that aquiline face and smiled.

At LAX, Richard showed his ID to the TSA and got waved through the line. Since he wasn't wearing an airline uniform, glares from the other travelers, penned like cattle in a slaughterhouse chute, accompanied him. On the plus side, he got to leave Kenzo behind in the slowly snaking line. Once at the gate area, he called his sister.

"You know that meeting of the officers you recommended? Let's do it, but let's do it in Rochester at the research facility. Let them see Kenntnis, see what we're trying to do with both him and the sword. And how are you coming on that other issue?"

"Your package is ready for you to pick up," she said, surprising him.

"Really?"

"Yes. I thought you wouldn't want it delivered."

"No, no, you're right. How did you do it?"

"It wasn't easy, but I had an unexpected ally. It seems the little girl wants to be with you."

"Really? Mosi is turning out to be even more interesting than I thought."

"The aunt is still her guardian, but she's agreed that you'll have custodial rights, and be allowed to house, educate, and provide for the girl. They do insist that you bring her back once a year to connect with her culture."

"Sure, we can do that, and Pamela, thank you. You're amazing."

"Whatever. How did it go with Kenzo?"

Richard saw the CFO approaching down the concourse. "I'll tell you when I'm back, and would you pick me up? I don't want to ride with Kenzo."

"Went that well, huh? Okay." He couldn't tell from her tone if she was amused, weary, or frustrated. Maybe all three.

He remembered Johnny's likely predicament. "Oh, and I may need you to find a good lawyer for someone out here."

"Oh, God, what now?"

"It's complicated."

"It always is with you," she said sourly, and hung up.

He then called Weber. "Wha . . . ?" Belatedly Richard realized it was dark o'clock in Kenya.

"Sorry to wake you."

"Yeah, Richard, what's up?" Weber now sounded instantly alert. Like most cops, he awakened quickly.

"I need you back at Lumina. Right away."

"Okay. The plane is off—"

"Charter one. I need your expertise."

"Okay. See you soon."

Richard turned off his phone and felt a growing tension in his chest. He had just acquired a child.

Now he had to keep her safe.

Southwest got them back to Albuquerque in the late afternoon. On the plane, Richard had picked a middle seat between a tired-looking businessman and a young guy with earbuds thrust deep into his ears—not the most comfortable, but a sure way to keep Kenzo from sitting with him. Joseph and Estevan were at the airport to pick up Kenzo, and the CFO gave Richard a look when he saw Pamela in a separate car. Richard knew he was being rude, but the waves of disapproval and anger coming off the man had him shivering now that his own anger had faded.

Back at Lumina, Cross had left a message that he wanted to deliver a briefing. The homeless god requested that Richard come to his box because, as he put it, *They're beatin' on me and I might fly apart.*

As Richard walked toward the large shipping crate, he heard the hiss of a camp stove. The sound took Richard back to Boy Scout camping trips. He pushed aside the blanket. Cross had a pan of beans heating on one burner, and he was toasting bread over the other.

"Want some? Beans on toast."

"No, thanks."

Cross piled the toast with baked beans and finished it in five slurping bites. He began toasting another slice of bread. "They're gathering," he said. "The minute your sis started the legal moves, they zeroed in on the kid."

"Well, we knew that would happen. They monitor everything we do," Richard said.

"Which is why you wisely sent me to that shit hole known as Shiprock. They weren't going to try and snatch her from her aunt with me there, 'cause unless they send another of my kind, no human can take me. Well, you could, though you won't, you bastard."

"I know, I suck, and no, I won't kill you." Richard frowned. "And why wouldn't they send an Old One to counter you?"

"Because we don't take orders from monkeys."

"You do."

"Yeah, well, I'm a special case. I made a deal." For an instant he looked old and not terribly human. Cross gave a shake of his head. "Anyway, they don't want to send human numbnuts or even a human sorcerer into Shiprock 'cause that's an insular and suspicious community with lots and lots of guns, and a worldview that takes monsters in stride. The bad guys would get their asses handed to them. No, better to try the snatch or the murder when you're isolated."

Richard swallowed several times to try and ease the hollow feeling in his gut.

"If it's any comfort," Cross continued, "I don't think they'll send a magic user. Too risky for them to go up against a paladin, and goons with guns are cheaper to train and replace." Another slice of bread and beans disappeared into his maw.

"Anything else?" Richard asked as he stood.

"Of course, problems everywhere, and those damn computers aren't helping, but nothing you have to deal with right this minute." Cross abruptly switched topics. "Sure is gonna be weird having two paladins around at the same time." Cross perked up. "Hey, she's an impressionable kid. Maybe I can convince *her* to kill me."

"I still have the sword. And don't you dare lay that burden on a child."

"Okay, fine, just thinkin' out loud. Okay, I'm outta here. Better get back up there." And Cross vanished.

Richard turned off the propane and carried the pan back into the building. He recognized it as one of Franz's and figured there would be an explosion in French and German when the Alsatian chef discovered the theft.

———◦✦◦———

He woke after too few hours of sleep and slipped down to the pool in the basement for a swim. Richard knew that Joseph had informed Franz of his return because after his swim, he found chafing dishes waiting in the kitchen with a selection of breakfast choices. The French toast prepared with orange juice and Grand Marnier tempted him. Richard added a few slices of bacon and settled in to read the e-mail that had piled up during his absence. Periodically, he tried Weber's cell. The man wasn't answering. Good news. It meant he was on a plane.

Two hours later Pamela arrived at work and came immediately upstairs. "I've got your dog and pony science show set up for next week," she said. "I'll send e-mails to Gold and Dagmar today. Kenzo we can just tell."

"Assuming I keep him on," Richard replied.

"So you haven't decided yet?"

"Truthfully, I haven't had time to think about it."

"Richard, this is one situation where I think keeping him inside the tent is the smarter choice," his sister said as she helped herself to eggs and ham. "He's got—"

The hum of the elevator had Richard holding up a finger to silence her. Weber walked into the kitchen and nodded at the siblings. "Okay, I'm here. What's going on?"

Richard outlined the situation.

Weber piled food onto a plate. "Explain to me why having the only known paladins in the world, in a car, driving back to Albuquerque together is a good plan."

Richard paced. "Because I need time to start getting to know the girl. I thought a helicopter ride might scare her, and if someone fires a Stinger missile at us, the chances of our surviving a crash in a chopper are poor."

Pamela's jaw clenched and she looked away. Richard realized she was frightened by his words.

"And they're better in a car?" Weber asked.

"I'd have a chance to react."

"So would your pilot, but I understand the need to at least *think* you're in control." Weber softened the comment with a smile. "What are you driving?"

"The armored SUV."

Weber ate for a few minutes, then knuckled his chin. "Okay, here's what we do. We get four identical SUVs—"

"That's going to cost a fortune," Pamela objected.

"I think I see where he's going," Richard said. "And the decoys don't have to be armored. They just all have to look alike." He looked to Weber. "Right?"

Weber gave him a thumbs-up and a nod. "We place them so they can all head off in different directions. I'll be in my four-by-four pickup following you, and we'll get a light plane to pace us."

"Somebody armed in that plane?" Richard asked.

"Of course, but let's hope it doesn't come to that. I can get away with commanding a small, personal army in Mexico, Africa, or the Middle East. They tend to frown on it here in the States."

"I should have had you bring people from overseas. This is going to deplete our security at the building."

"They're more interested in hurting you than us," Pamela said heavily.

"True, but they know they can hurt me through all of you." Richard stepped to the bay window in the breakfast nook and looked out at a murder of crows whirling between the building and the mountains. "We spiked them in Mexico, and I poked them hard in California. They are not happy with me, and Cross says they're watching us very closely."

"Is there likely to be a magical attack?" Weber asked. He rubbed a hand across his brow. "I know how to counter violence, but that unnatural shit . . ."

"Cross doesn't think they'll risk a sorcerer or an Old One, but just in case I'd suggest packing a knife . . . or three." Richard turned back to face them with a grim smile. "Let's hope they'll be smart. They know what happens if I get to them. Goons with guns are easier to replace."

"Well, all righty, then, let's do it . . . says the goon with a gun."

Richard flushed and threw out a hand. "I'm sorry, I didn't mean it that way—"

Weber cuffed him on the chin. "Would you stop it? I was joking."

"Sorry."

"And stop apologizing," Weber said. He briefly cupped Richard's cheek, then gave it a pat. Richard moved away.

"How soon can we be set up?"

"I should have everything in place by tomorrow morning."

The house phone rang. Pamela answered the extension in the kitchen, listened, and held it out to Richard. "It's Jeannette."

"Yes?"

"Mr. Fujasaki has arrived. May I send him up?"

"No, I'm too busy. Give him an office and tell him I'll see him"— Richard did mental counting—"day after tomorrow. No, better make it the day after that." He hung up. "Well, let's get to it."

Weber polished off the last bite of his breakfast, and he and Pamela left. Richard stacked the dishes in the dishwasher, packed a small overnight case, and rode the elevator down to the subbasement, where he grabbed a shotgun and several boxes of shells from the armory. He added a few boxes of ammo for the Browning.

He got off the elevator in the lobby, intending to go to the security office and talk to Joseph. Kenzo was seated on one of the modern black-and-silver sofas, flipping through a copy of *Forbes*. Paulette, the receptionist, gave Richard a helpless look and shrugged her shoulders.

Kenzo stood and took in the shotgun Richard held in one hand and the stack of ammo boxes in the other. "We must speak."

"I don't have time for you right now."

"Why? What are you doing?" The CFO nodded toward the gun. "More to the point, what are you doing that requires weapons?"

"You don't need to know."

The nostrils thinned, and the lips tightened. "Meaning you don't trust me."

"Meaning that it's not personal. It's following security protocols. Now, if you'll excuse me." Richard pushed past Kenzo and went into Joseph's office.

RICHARD stood on the balcony of his room at the River Front Marriott hotel and looked down at the San Juan River churning below. The white manes of the rapids and the deep blue water set an odd counterpoint to the red rock cliffs that enfolded the river and the town of Farmington. Nervous, he checked his watch. He was due to pick up Mosi in forty minutes. Acid churned in his gut. He wouldn't wait any longer.

He tossed a ten on the bed as a tip for the maids and grabbed his case. As he passed Weber's room, he tapped on the door.

"Yeah?"

"Let's go."

Weber emerged and fell into step with him. "You're going to be early."

"They can live with it," Richard replied.

Out in the parking lot, Weber got on the radio to his team. Richard made his preparations at the SUV, removing the shotgun from its case and stashing it between the front seats. He and Weber exchanged tense nods. Richard started to climb into the car, but Weber caught him around the shoulders and gave him a hard squeeze.

"Be careful." The big man abruptly released him and strode off to his pickup. Richard watched him for a long moment, then got in the car.

A mere twenty-two miles separated Farmington from Shiprock. The bright morning sun splashed on the rocky outcroppings like the spine of a fossilized dragon and pointed up the shabbiness of the human buildings that seemed to huddle precariously in the harshly beautiful landscape. Richard glanced into the rearview mirror. Weber was a few cars back. The small plane whined overhead.

He made the twisting turns up to the house and climbed out. The aunt opened the door and motioned for him to come in. Today the house smelled of frying onions and macaroni and cheese, a lingering memory of last night's dinner. Mosi was waiting in the living room, a small pink suitcase placed precisely in front of her feet. Richard picked it up.

"Is this all you have?" Richard asked. Mosi's face was tight, closed in, her eyes shadowed by her lowered lashes.

"What else would she have?" the aunt asked in a pugnacious tone.

Richard was taken aback. "I just thought there might be toys . . . or something," he stammered. Silence met his remark. He cleared his throat. "Well, we better get going."

The stony expression faltered, and Mrs. Yazzi gazed desperately down at her niece. "You're all that's left of my brother," she said. "You don't have to go with this *belegana*."

The little girl answered in Navajo. A spirited discussion broke out in a language he didn't know. Richard stood by awkwardly. Mosi wrapped her arms around her aunt's waist and hugged her hard. She knelt and opened up her little suitcase and took out a bracelet and a lovely seed pot. She handed them to her aunt. She then looked up at Richard and said, "I'm ready. Let's go."

They headed for the front door. "Mosi! You call. Be good."

"Good-bye, *ma yaashi*," the little girl said huskily, and followed Richard out to the big Toyota Land Cruiser.

Richard placed the suitcase in the back and made sure Mosi was belted in. She noticed the shotgun and gave him a quizzical look.

As he turned the key and the engine began to growl, he asked, "Your aunt doesn't want you to come with me?"

"No."

"But you do."

"Yes."

"Why?

The girl's head snapped around, her long black hair swirling like a shadow. "You'll keep me safe. And if I stay, the devils will come here too. Better they come after you."

It struck Richard as funny and he gave a sharp laugh. "You're probably right. The bracelet and the pot. Why did you give them to your aunt?"

"She needs them more."

"Did your dad make them?" Richard asked as they bumped across the potholes in the road heading for the highway.

A nod. "He'd make them and sell them in Gallup or to the tourists."

"It was good of you to share them with your aunt. Maybe we can find some things your dad made and buy them for you." He glanced over at her and smiled, but it died at the sight of her brows drawn into a hard frown.

"Why do you white people think money can fix everything? My daddy is *dead*. I don't care about his bracelets. They won't bring him back." Beneath the rage, tears lingered like the whispered cry of a wailing violin. Shame at his own glibness and thoughtlessness kept

Richard silent for several long minutes. He was not going to buy this child's trust or affection with calculated kindness and trinkets.

They made the turn onto Highway 64. Only then did Richard say quietly, "You're right, Mosi. I apologize."

This time it was sincere and she knew it. She gave a curt nod and hunched down deeper in the big bucket seat.

Richard shifted, reached behind his back, and pulled the hilt out of its holster and put it in the cup holder in easy reach. He slipped on the radio headset and said, "Heading out now."

"Copy that," came Weber's voice.

They drove back to Farmington. Near the center of town they reached a large, complex intersection with multiple roads branching off in different directions. The four other identical Land Cruisers waited in various parking lots as Richard and Mosi cruised through. They pulled out, and Richard and the other drivers began an intricate shell game weaving in and out, switching positions. Then they all sped off.

One headed east and south toward Bloomfield and Albuquerque, another toward Durango, and two cars and Richard headed back toward Shiprock. In Shiprock, one car headed north on Highway 491 toward Cortez, Colorado, and the other headed south on the same highway toward Gallup, New Mexico, and I-40, while Richard headed west into Arizona. The plan was for him to go until Highway 64 met up with Highway 160, then he would double back east and north, enter Colorado, drive past Mesa Verde, through Cortez and Durango, and continue east until they reached Pagosa Springs, where they would finally head south for Santa Fe and Albuquerque. He hoped that by then any pursuers would be completely confused.

It was going to be a long drive, and it would probably be ten or later before they reached Lumina headquarters. Assuming there were no problems. He glanced over at the profile of the silent child. "I brought some audiobooks, and there's music too. We can also listen to the radio or play white horse bingo."

"What's that?"

"Every time you see a white horse and call it first, you get a point. Whoever sees more white horses at the end of a trip wins."

She wrinkled her nose. "That sounds silly. I'll look at the books."

"They're in the armrest," Richard said. He had picked a selection, everything from *The Wind in the Willows* and *The Little Princess* to *Men of Iron* and Harry Potter. Mosi studied the covers intently, focusing very closely on E. H. Shepard's charming illustrations for *The Wind in the Willows*.

"Do the animals talk?" Mosi asked.

"Yes, they do."

"Then I'd like to listen to this." He nodded and helped her load the disks into the six-CD changer.

"*The Mole had been working very hard all the morning, spring-cleaning his little home. First with brooms, then with dusters; then on ladders and steps and chairs . . .* " The voice of the male reader filled the car.

Richard remembered another voice reading those words, a soft, light soprano. He tensed, expecting the memory of his mother to make him sad, but instead he found comfort. He wondered what she would have made of Mosi. He had a feeling she would have liked the girl.

It was tough trying to listen to the reports from the other drivers with the audiobook playing, but keeping Mosi entertained was also a priority, so he tried to block out the adventures of Mole and Rat and Toad while he listened to the other drivers and the miles unrolled beneath the tires.

Richard and Mosi were just outside of Mancos, Colorado, when Steve, the driver heading south on Highway 550 toward Cuba, New Mexico, reported there was a jackknifed semi blocking the road. "Looks like a concerned citizen is waving down traffic. Hang on."

Richard heard the whir of a window being rolled down, then murmuring voices. Then the whir of a window again and the purr of an engine returning to highway speed. Steve's voice came back over the headset. "Asking if I was a doctor, but checking out the car pretty thoroughly. Also, he was packing." Richard released a held breath.

"They've divided their forces," Weber's voice came in. "At least that part of the plan is working."

"Wonder when it's our turn?" Richard murmured back.

Several hours later they reached Durango. Richard's stomach reminded him that he had skipped breakfast. If his belly felt this empty, he was sure Mosi was hungry too. "How about some lunch?" he asked. She nodded. "What do you like?"

There was again that nose wrinkle. He was beginning to identify it as an expression of deep thought and consideration. "Taco Bell. I like hamburgers too." She looked out the car window at the passing buildings, all brick and late-nineteenth-century quaint. Richard sighed and resigned himself to at least seven years of fast food.

He shifted and pulled out his iPhone. "Here, look up restaurants on this." She gave him a questioning look. "It's safe. There are no monsters inside."

She took the phone, and he walked her through how to get online. She read off the names of various restaurants and even some reviews. The childish tones were flutelike.

"Zia Taqueria, good nu . . . nutritious food," she read, stumbling a bit over the word. "Best Mex ever. Good, healthy food."

"That sounds like the place," Richard said. "Read off the address for me." She did and surprised him by going to the map function and giving him very concise directions. "You're good at that," he said.

"I was Daddy's navigator. That's what he always said."

Richard didn't know how to respond to that, so he didn't. They found the restaurant and were soon inside placing their orders. Mosi had rolled taquitos. Richard went with fish tacos. Mosi made a face.

"That's not real Mexican food," she said.

"It is in Mexico, where they have ocean."

"There's no ocean here, so you shouldn't have fish," she said.

Thinking about all the frozen seafood he had eaten since he'd moved to New Mexico, Richard had to concur. "Okay, you got me there."

"So why are you going to have them?" she asked.

"Because it seems . . . healthier?" His own hesitancy turned it into a question.

Mosi began wiggling in her chair. "Do you need to go to the bathroom?" Richard asked. She nodded.

"Okay." He stood up.

"I can go by myself. I'm not a baby." The childish outrage made him want to chuckle.

"I know that. I just want to walk you to the door," he said.

"You're scared," she accused.

"No, just cautious. Come on."

While he loitered in the small hallway, he realized his bladder was full too. From behind the door to the women's restroom he heard a toilet flush, then the sound of running water. Mosi emerged. She was using her hair as a veil.

"My turn. Wait for me right here," he said, and ducked into the men's room.

Back in the dining room, Richard took a fast look to see if anyone new had arrived. He spotted Weber already wolfing down a giant burrito. They exchanged almost imperceptible nods. A few minutes later their food arrived. Mosi ate with quick dainty bites, dipping the rolled taquitos first in guacamole, then in salsa, and then nipping off the end with her front teeth. While they were eating, Richard's earpiece buzzed. It was Hank, the driver heading south toward Gallup.

"I hit a spike strip. All four tires are flat. I've steered onto the shoulder, and there are some Staties approaching. Though I'll lay money they're not Staties."

Richard left the table and moved away from Mosi. Weber was hearing the same report, and they exchanged a glance. Richard sensed

that he looked as grim as Damon. "You're just an honest businessman driving to Gallup," he told Hank. "Don't offer any resistance.
Once they realize you don't have the package . . . Be careful. Check
back as soon as you can."

"Will do." The radio contact went dead.

Richard returned to the table, but he'd lost his appetite. Mosi finished the last bite of her taquito. "You ready?" Richard asked her.

She nodded. "But you didn't finish."

"I decided maybe you were right about the fish."

She gave him a look from beneath lowering brows. "You look
funny."

"We're fine" was his temporizing answer.

Richard tossed money onto the table. They made another bathroom stop, and then they were back in the car and on the road.

"Jerry took this opportunity to gas up the plane," Weber reported
over the headset. "He'll catch up with us."

"Okay," Richard replied.

Forty minutes later, Hank still hadn't checked back in. Richard
keyed the headset. "Hank? Hank, come in."

An unknown female voice came on the radio. It sounded young
and unsure. "Uh . . . who is this?"

"Identify yourself," Richard said authoritatively. It didn't have the
desired effect.

"You first, *pendejo*!"

It wasn't worth lying. Everything was going to lead back to him
and to Lumina. "Lieutenant Richard Oort, APD."

"Oh . . . uh . . . Patrolman Tina Gallegos, State Police."

"What's your situation?" Richard asked.

"I've got a dead guy in an SUV just south of Tohatchi near Navajo Service Road 37. Somebody spiked his car and shot him in the
head." Richard closed his eyes briefly. "Is this guy a cop?" Patrolman
Gallegos asked.

"Not exactly," Richard said.

Weber intervened. "Richard, let me handle this from here. Patrolman, I'm Damon Weber, head of security for Lumina Enterprises. Hank Lundkvist worked for me. Whatever we can do to assist in capturing his killers—"

Richard cut the radio. He didn't want to hear any more. His palms were slick on the steering wheel. He removed one and then the other to wipe them dry on his trouser leg. It was just a matter of time before their enemies reached the right car.

⸎

Grenier, riding the elevator up to the sixth floor, reflected with no small amount of satisfaction on how Kenzo had come striding into his office yesterday afternoon. The executive had demanded without any preamble, "Do you know where Richard has gone?"

"I thought he was here. He just got back from California—"

"Yes, and now he's gone again." Grenier felt again that flash of irritation that he had once again been shut out. Kenzo wasn't finished. "This situation cannot continue. I'm setting up a conference call with Gold and Dagmar. I'd like you to be part of it."

"I'd be delighted. Does Pamela—"

"She is not an officer of this company."

"I might point out that neither am I."

"She is also his sister."

"Ah, I see."

The elevator arrived, and Grenier went into the conference room. The fountain in the corner chuckled and murmured to itself. Kenzo was seated at the table checking e-mail on his phone while Jorge put the finishing touches on the AV equipment.

Jorge reacted to Grenier's entrance. "Look, Mr. Fujasaki, I'm still not real sure about this. Shouldn't Pamela be here? And Richard didn't authorize this."

"I did," Kenzo said. "And as an officer of this company I have that right."

"Yeah, well, then why is *he* here?" Jorge asked with a jerk of the thumb toward Grenier.

Anger washed through the former televangelist, but he just smiled. "Mr. Fujasaki wanted me to be here." *And you're so going to get yours, boy.*

Jorge shrugged. "Okay, New York and London are on the line. Just hit Play on your computer, and you'll all be connected."

"Thank you. You may leave," Kenzo ordered.

Jorge slouched out in that way of youth that expressed disdain, offense, and indifference. Kenzo keyed the computer, and the big wall screen sprang to life. It divided in half, with Dagmar on one side, and George Gold on the other. Satisfaction flowed warm and sweet through his chest. Savoring the moment, Grenier took his place among the chief financial officer, the chief operating officer, and chief counsel of Lumina Enterprises.

"Okay, what is this about? And what's so urgent that you call a meeting when it's past nine o'clock here?" Dagmar asked. She scanned the table in Albuquerque. "And where's Richard?"

"Not here, and no one has any idea what he's doing," Kenzo said.

Grenier decided to cement his position. He murmured, "As is so often the case."

"You heard about the events in California?" Kenzo asked.

"Yes, I was informed," Dagmar said.

"What do you think?" Gold pushed.

Dagmar shrugged. "It's Richard's job."

"His job is managing Lumina Enterprises," Kenzo countered.

"It's both," Dagmar shot back.

"And that is precisely the problem," Kenzo said. "These events in California have us once more back in the public eye. We have a CEO who swaggers about the world shooting off guns and assaulting people."

"And this one is going to be harder to sweep aside because it occurred on American soil," Gold jumped in. "Somebody's going to sue."

Grenier stirred. "Perhaps the solution is to separate the two positions—"

The big double doors were flung open and Pamela stormed in. Jorge was a step behind her, looking defiant and scared. Pamela's rather narrow nostrils were compressed, and blotches of color bloomed on her pale face. "What in the hell is going on here?" she demanded.

"Ah, so the boys didn't tell you about this little party," Dagmar said.

"No." Pamela turned on Kenzo. "And how dare you hold a meeting of the officers and not include Richard?"

"Because we are, in fact, discussing Richard," Kenzo said.

"By what right? And what is *he* doing here?" Pamela indicated Grenier.

"Mr. Grenier has experience managing a large commercial enterprise—" Kenzo said.

"Don't you mean large *criminal* enterprise?" Pamela retorted.

Kenzo continued speaking as if there hadn't been an interruption. "He's been a businessman. You're not. Richard is not. The company is approaching a crisis. I'll use any asset to avert it."

"My brother is the head of Lumina and he should be present for these discussions."

"That's the problem. Richard is so rarely present," Kenzo said, his tone cold.

"You're just angry because Richard told you to wait here for him, and then when he got back from California he took off again. Well, he's on his way back. He'll be in later tonight," Pamela said.

Grenier held up a restraining hand. "The point is that the officers are beginning to think that folding both the task of managing Lumina and serving as the paladin into a single individual is not in the best interests of the company."

Dagmar reacted. "No, the officers never said that. You started to say that. We've only got one paladin, and Kenntnis made Richard the head of Lumina. Apparently Kenntnis didn't think it was a problem with having a single individual hold both positions."

Pamela hesitated. "That's not exactly accurate," she said slowly.

"Which part?" Dagmar asked.

"The paladin part."

There was reaction around the table and on the screen. Fury at having this information kept from him had Grenier's teeth clenching and jaw aching. In his mind's eye he watched his careful plans collapsing.

Pamela continued. "We've found another one. Richard's getting her now. That's why he's not here."

"So this woman could take over and leave Richard free to deal with the company," Gold said, relieved to have an out.

"Not . . . yet. She's only nine."

"Nine!" Kenzo exploded.

"How did you . . . ? Did you take her from her family?" Dagmar asked, angry and suspicious.

"Her family was killed . . . Look, it's a long story. For her own safety, Richard wanted it kept very quiet."

Kenzo made a dismissive gesture. "This is interesting but not relevant. It's our job to ensure the viability of the company. Someone needs to manage Lumina. You can't argue with that, Dagmar."

The woman hesitated but finally spoke. "No, I can't, and we've got cash flow problems. Purchasing Gaia is . . . well, let's just say it's an expense we didn't need right now." The words were reluctant, but they were spoken.

Pamela stared at the screen, her expression haunted. She seemed a forlorn figure whose thin shoulders seemed too fragile to bear the weight of what was happening. "What is it you want?" she demanded. "For Richard to step aside? Let someone else run Lumina?"

"Would he consider that?" Gold asked rather too eagerly.

"I have no idea. You'll have to ask him," Pamela snapped back. "Which is why this meeting should never have been called without including Richard. And I'm going to make sure he hears my opinion of this . . . this . . . insurrection."

Grenier cleared his throat. "Given my background and experience, if I can offer Richard any help or advice I'd be happy to do so."

Pamela turned on him. "What's your angle, Mark? Richard took you in, protected you—"

The reminder of his fall and his vulnerable position caused his affable mask to slip. "And I've given good service in return. But if Richard runs this company into the ground, none of us will be safe. There won't be security teams operating in shit holes around the world, funding for secure locations where scientists can work, a plane to fly Richard and his toy sword to the latest problem spot."

"Don't you be dismissive. Don't you *dare* be dismissive!" Her hands were clenched at her sides, and her breasts rose and fell in time to her rapid pants. "He's . . . he's . . ." She turned away and shook her head.

Grenier heard the husky rasp of unshed tears in her voice. Kenzo looked away, discomforted by the naked emotions now swirling in the room. Grenier saw a way to recover his position. He stepped in close to Pamela and laid gentle hands on her shoulders.

"What is it, Pamela? How can I help?"

She dashed the back of her hand across her cheeks and turned to face him. "He's going to get killed. He came back from Mexico with twenty-seven stitches. This thing in California could have gone bad, really bad, and . . . and . . ."

"So wouldn't it be better to lift one burden off his shoulders?" Gold asked, infusing a wealth of concern into his voice.

Pamela stepped away from Grenier's chaste embrace and faced the screen. He watched the mane of brown hair sweep across her shoulders as she shook her head. "No, because then he'll just have more time to go to these . . . openings . . . invasions, and at some point he won't come back."

The attack he'd been expecting for hours came south of Chama in the midst of the Carson National Forest. *How clever of them to wait until I've been driving for hours and I'm tired*, Richard thought. There was no time to brake or even swerve, as knives, like crystal and ice, erupted from the asphalt. They glittered, malevolent and unnatural, in the honey trickles of sunlight through the boughs of the dark pines.

Cross had been wrong. They had brought a sorcerer.

THE magically summoned blades did their job, slashing all four tires of the big SUV, but technology and keeping up with the advances of same wasn't a high priority with the Old Ones or the traitors who served them. This car had been built to Lumina specifications and possessed Roll On inserts in the tires. Richard could keep going at sixty miles an hour for sixty miles on the ceramic inserts. Unfortunately, someone was warping the laws of physics in their reality, and so machines tended to stop working. The car's engine died.

But then it caught. Apparently the magic wielder had shot his wad. The car leaped forward again, and Richard flipped a finger at the unknown and unseen sorcerer, but then his eyes dilated at a flare of fire vomiting from the trees. Fear closed his throat and dug like claws into his shoulders as the bed of Weber's truck was hit by a rocket-propelled grenade. The truck spun out, and flames erupted from the gas tank. The passenger-side door was flung open and Weber rolled out, clutching his rifle and a satchel that Richard knew contained grenades and ammo. Weber was trying to keep the body of the truck between him and the attackers on the east.

Unfortunately, the bad guys weren't stupid. Small-arms fire spat from the trees on the west. Weber dove head-first into the shallow ditch that ran next to the road. Dirt clods kicked up at the edge, driven skyward by the hail of bullets. To Richard, time stretched, and the dirt seemed to fall back to earth in slow motion.

Go on! Go on, one part of his mind was commanding, but another impulse was to rescue. This was Weber. Sharp pings sang against the skin of the SUV. They were coming under attack, and on this particular stretch of road the trees formed a canopy overhead, effectively cutting them off from their guardians in the sky.

Richard placed his hand on the back of Mosi's head, and pushed her down. "Stay low!" he ordered. She did more. Unhooking her seatbelt, Mosi slid down into the foot well of the car, wrapped her arms around her knees, and braced herself.

Grateful for her quick thinking, Richard turned his attention back to Weber's predicament, and spotted the figure in the trees lifting the rocket launcher back onto his shoulder. Another hit on the pickup and it would detonate, with dire consequences for the man in the ditch next to it. Richard spun the wheel and made a sharp U-turn to the right.

"Hang on really tight," he yelled to Mosi and took them off the road, jounced through the ditch and onto the steep verge. He was driving back toward Weber.

"Hunker down!" he yelled into his headset. Weber threw himself flat in the ditch.

As he drew alongside the burning truck, Richard turned straight into it. Weber was prone in the ditch. Richard aimed carefully to keep the Roll On inserts from clipping Weber and drove the front of the SUV into the side of the pickup. Metal shrieked as he pushed the burning vehicle across the road and wedged it against the trees near the man with the rocket launcher.

The truck was nearly engulfed in flames now, and the fire was spreading to the drought-distressed trees. The dry pine needles went up like Roman candles. Richard threw the SUV in reverse and accelerated away from the truck just as it exploded.

Burning pieces of truck rained down all around them, and there were hollow crashes as some debris fell onto the roof of the car. A man-shaped figure, wreathed in flames, ran out of the trees. Mosi popped up trying to see. Richard shoved her back down into the foot well. His ears were ringing, so he couldn't hear the screams from the burning man. He hoped it was the same for Mosi.

Seconds later, there was another explosion, as the missile in its launcher also exploded. Men in faux military garb moved into the road, advancing on their car. They took careful shots aimed only at the driver's-side window. Then the guns stopped firing.

A strange groaning penetrated the ringing in Richard's ears. The car's engine died again. Mosi gave a cry of fear and pointed at the tops of the massive Ponderosa pine trees. They were shaking, swaying, then they began to fall. Dark green limbs beat the ground like wrestlers tapping out. A fence was being built all around them, hemming them in.

Richard spotted a woman farther down the road, making sweeping gestures with her arms. "I have to stop her," he told Mosi, as he grabbed up the sword. "Stay in the car. Lock the doors. Keep your head down."

She climbed onto the passenger seat and grabbed his arm. "I can shoot," she said. She was pale and her lips were bloodless, but there was a martial light in those dark eyes.

"Guns won't work right now. And you're only nine. No."

"My middle name is Dezba, it means 'goes to war.' And I have my brother's wrist rocket. It's in the suitcase." She was panting, her voice jumping with fear, but her dark eyes burned with determination.

Richard stared down at her. *She lost her family to this war. She's a paladin. Her life isn't going to be easy or normal, and nothing I do can change that.*

And in a flash of insight he realized that the goal of their enemies was probably to capture her. Otherwise that missile would have been launched at the car carrying the paladins. If the Old Ones and their minions could capture a child paladin and twist her, shape her to their own purposes, they would have an enormous advantage. Which meant she could probably shoot at them with impunity.

"You got anything to put in that slingshot?" he asked.

Mosi nodded. "Marbles."

"Get it!"

She scrambled back over the seats and returned moments later with the slingshot clasped to her wrist and a soft velvet bag clutched in her hand.

"You can't open the windows on this car, but there are weapons slits you can fire through." He indicated the catch. Mosi nodded, fished out a marble, opened the slit, and fitted the marble into the slingshot. An attacker was approaching. Mosi drew back, took careful aim, and let fly. The marble took the man in the center of his forehead. His head snapped back at the impact, and he collapsed. Richard nodded, rolled over the seats, and crawled over her suitcase in the cargo area to the back hatch. He wrestled it open and jumped out.

The moment his feet hit pavement, he drew the sword. With his free hand, he pulled down the back hatch, though he could feel his wrist creaking and the muscles in his biceps quivering from the weight. The tree fence was enough to block a car, but a man on foot could easily run through them. He couldn't so easily run through the mercenaries. Fortunately, most of them were focused on the marbles flying from the SUV and didn't seem to have noticed his exit from the rear of the vehicle.

One of the mercs had come around to the driver's side and pulled a hammer off his belt. He swung it against the window, and the glass starred. If he succeeded in breaking through and unlocked the doors, he would capture Mosi. Richard spun around to the side of the car and charged the man, point of the sword outstretched. The merc turned and tried to parry with his hammer. Richard turned the rapier-like sword and let the metal of the hammer scrape along the blade, then he drove the sword deep into the man's chest. He wasn't going to rely on a tap and a hope the reaction took the man down.

Blood bubbled from between the man's lips, and he dropped slowly to his knees. Richard pulled the sword free as the man fell forward onto his face. *Thirty-one*. Richard kept the count. He suspected that these men were mercenaries. They had been hired to do a job, and now they were dying without ever knowing they were fighting for monsters.

Hunkering down, he scuttled toward shielding branches of the fallen pines and dove into their painful camouflage. Needles bit at his hands, face, and neck, and he felt sap matting his hair. Richard found a gap and slipped through, eyes flicking in all directions looking for the sorceress, and trying to keep the bowel-loosening terror at bay. She stood, face contorted, body hunched with concentration, panting with exhaustion. She was using an extendable pointer as a focusing device. Not as subtle as Grenier's reading glasses had been. Much more wandlike, implying the woman didn't have as much control over the magic as Grenier. *Or she'd just read too much Harry Potter*, Richard thought. Here was the woman who'd hired the mercs, who was prepared to sell out her own species. Rage killed his fear, and he charged out of the trees.

The sorceress reacted to Richard's footfalls on the asphalt as he made his flanking approach. She whirled and her mouth moved, though Richard couldn't hear. An arc of coiling, lurid red burst from the end of the pointer and raced toward Richard.

Richard made no effort to dodge the spell, just let it hit and wash over him. It accomplished nothing besides a singed stink. The woman threw another blast of pure magic at him. This time Richard casually lifted the sword and parried the incoming spell. The red was swallowed by the deep black of the sword blade. The woman blanched.

Richard's fear retreated a bit and cockiness took its place. This girl clearly was a second-stringer. Richard continued to advance. "That's it? That's all you've got?" Richard yelled, his words echoing weirdly in his ringing ears. "What are you? A moron? Hello, paladin." He tapped his chest. "Magic can't hurt me." His anger was growing with each step he took toward her. What kind of monsters would take a little girl and use her—?

His righteousness stuttered and died. How was what he was doing any different? His focus and concentration shattered, so he missed the movement when the woman bent and laid the tip of her pointer on the asphalt. And then he was falling as the ground vanished beneath his feet. Magic might not affect him, but gravity sure as hell did.

Richard clawed at the edge of the hole with his right hand. The paving and the ground were rough, as if an invisible monster had taken a bite from the earth. Between his scrabbling feet and his now torn and bloody right hand, he managed to keep from sliding to the bottom of the deep hole, but the tired muscles in his arm were starting to tremble. Maybe he should just drop to the bottom and figure out how to climb back out? He risked a glance over his shoulder. The hole looked to be about ten feet deep, and the same knives that had destroyed the SUV's tires extruded from the soil at the bottom. Even if he controlled his slide to the bottom, he was going to get skewered. He dared not drop the sword, but he needed both hands to pull himself out.

Maybe she would walk over to check her handiwork. Or stomp on his fingers so he'd fall. Then she'd be in range of the sword. But the toes of her boots didn't appear. She was waiting for fatigue and gravity to do their jobs. Maybe not such a second-stringer after all. Richard knew he couldn't hold on much longer. Desperately, he cast about for a solution. He studied the hilt. There was one part of the curving Klein-bottle shape that was thinner than the rest. He raised the hilt to his mouth and closed his teeth around the section. The sword wasn't exactly light, especially when the blade was drawn. Richard clamped down hard and worked his fingers free of the hilt. His teeth felt like they were being pulled from his jaw, but once he released the hilt, the blade vanished and it got a bit lighter. The blood pounded in his ears, his breaths were harsh gasps, and there was a faint sound like the buzzing of an angry bee that he couldn't identify. It formed a counterpoint to his body's desperate efforts to survive.

He grabbed the hilt and thrust it into the holster at the small of his back just as his right hand gave way. Gathering all his strength, Richard pushed up from the wall with his feet and grabbed the edge with his left hand. Got the right hand back in place, pulled himself up, and found a knife blade thrusting at his face. He jerked his head to the side, and fire flared along the side of his head as the knife cut his scalp. Blood was running over his ear and down his neck. She brought the point of the knife down and pierced his right hand. Richard screamed.

Please, Damon, get Mosi away, he thought as she aimed at his left hand. The angry bee sound was much louder now, and he realized it was the engine of a small plane. It coughed and cut out as the plane came into the area affected by the magic and went into a stall. Richard saw something hurtling down from above. The object wasn't large, but it hit the woman in the back of the head, and she went down like a poleaxed cow. Gritting his teeth against the pain, Richard used his injured hand to pull himself over the lip of the hole.

A box of ammo lay off to one side, top partly off, bullets spilling like silver and gold treasure onto the pavement. There was an indentation in the back of the woman's skull, and blood oozed sluggishly through her hair. Richard rolled onto his back and looked up as the belly of the plane passed overhead, gliding impossibly low. The side door was open, and Richard could see Estevan, shoulders braced against the door to keep it open, one foot resting on the wing, and only the harness to hold him in place. *Of course!* Richard thought. *She knocked down the trees.* Thus allowing his crazy pilot to go into a dive and come barreling down the road. Richard could not imagine the skill required to drop that plane into the narrow opening that had been created. And then Estevan had made the throw of a lifetime and proved that gravity won every time. The engine coughed again, then roared to life and the plane lifted, nearly brushing the tops of the trees farther down the road.

As he lay there, Richard realized it had gone quiet. Mosi! He staggered to his feet. The woman was still breathing. Richard drew the sword and laid it on her back. She went into violent convulsions. Then cradling his wounded hand against his chest, he ran back through the fallen trees. On the right side of the highway, the exploding truck had started a forest fire. Bodies littered the road and the verges to either side. Richard glanced down at an unconscious mercenary, a marble lying nearby. Mosi had definitely given a good account of herself. While he ran, Richard keyed his headset and called the plane.

"Jerry, you crazy bastard. Thank you."

"It was pretty boss, wasn't it?"

"Hang close for a minute, okay?"

"No prob. We're your eyes in the sky."

Weber was already at the SUV when Richard joined him. Weber threw his arms around Richard, pulling him into a bear hug. "Jesus Christ! That was close," the ex-cop gasped. "God, your hand."

"Didn't hit a bone. Hurts like hell, though," Richard panted. Weber pulled a handkerchief out of his pocket and gently wrapped Richard's hand. The blood made a Rorschach pattern on the white cotton.

Mosi pushed open the door and climbed out. The eyebrows were drawn into a fierce frown, and her lips compressed into a thin line. Richard acted without thought. He hugged her close. She stiffened, and he quickly released her.

"Good job, kiddo," he said, trying to cover the awkward moment.

"Is the *adilgashii* dead?" Her voice was high and shaky, reaction setting in.

Richard knew his expression was as confounded as Weber's. He temporized. "Uh . . . yeah. Yeah, definitely."

"Who is *he?*" Mosi thrust a finger at Weber.

"This is Damon. He's been following us, protecting us."

"Didn't work."

Weber gave a shout of laughter. "Well, you're not entirely wrong there, but we won and that's what counts."

"How are we going to get to Albuquerque?" she asked.

Weber looked around at the burning truck, the battered SUV, the massive, fallen Ponderosa pines, enough dropped guns to arm a revolution, and finally the bodies. "And how are we going to explain all this?"

Richard considered. "Attempted kidnapping foiled by my elite bodyguard?" He gave Weber a wan smile.

Weber surveyed the carnage. "I must be one hell of a guy." The ex-cop sucked on his teeth and stared at the crystal knives protruding from the road. "But what about those?" He pointed again.

"The *adilgashii* made them," Mosi said with the air of a mother talking to a particularly dim child.

Weber dropped down on one knee in front of the little girl and asked, "Okay, what's an *adilgashii?*"

"You white people say witch. It's much more complicated. It's things and people that disrupt *hózhó.*" Her stance and expression had changed, and Richard realized she was once again quoting an authority figure. She had an uncanny ability to evoke that other person. "You just have to explain that."

"Well, we can't tell the cops it was witchcraft." Weber paused and rubbed a thumb across his forehead. "Even if it was witchcraft."

"So why can't we tell—"

"Enough, we've got to get Mosi out of here. I don't want her pulled into this," Richard said. He keyed his headset. "Jerry, can you take Mosi? She's small."

"We'll wallow a bit, but we'll manage."

"Good. Can you set down on the road?"

"There's an opening about a half mile ahead. Meet you there?"

"Yes."

They ran and found the Cessna waiting. The little girl's face was set, her mouth grim as Richard helped her into the cockpit. He gave her hand a squeeze with his uninjured hand. "Don't worry. I'll be there soon. My sister is there. Pamela. She's nice. She'll look after you until I arrive."

The door closed. Weber and Richard stepped back, and the plane went taxiing away and lifted into the clear August sky.

"*Nice*. That isn't how I'd describe Pamela," Weber drawled. "She's never been nice to me."

"She'll be nice to Mosi." Richard glanced up at his former boss and smiled. "It's just reactionary jackbooted thugs she doesn't like." He paused. "And me."

They jogged back toward the scene of the fight. The fire had really taken hold. They weren't going to be able to wait for too long without risking immolation. *Talk about out of the frying pan*, Richard thought. Faint and in the distance they heard the ululating cry of approaching sirens.

"And speaking of reactionary jackbooted thugs . . . What, exactly, is our story going to be once the cops arrive?" Weber asked.

"I think we go with the kidnapping story. I'm very wealthy. It's plausible," Richard said between pants. Now that the adrenaline had faded, he felt sick and exhausted. The wounds on his head and his hand hurt like blazes, and the imperfectly healed wound on his side had decided to comment as well.

"And all the shit caused by the magic?"

"We've been cops. You know how we think. We always want the simplest explanation. We'll just say it's some kind of high-tech road-side . . . device."

"You know, that was my personal truck," Weber said.

"Lumina will replace it."

They were back at the SUV. Richard pulled out a handkerchief and wiped his streaming face. It came away bloodstained. "Can't wait to tell my officers about this."

"Look on the bright side. It'll make some wounded guys and one dead guy in California seem like small potatoes," Weber offered.

ELEVEN

RICHARD and Weber rode the elevator to the Lumina penthouse shortly after eleven P.M. The effluvia in the enclosed space was half stale man sweat and the rest divided between woodsmoke and gunpowder. Richard could also smell pine sap where it had shellacked his hair. The two men had been taken to Española to be interviewed, and it went better than Richard had expected. Turned out Weber knew several of the cops. That connection and Richard's still active badge had kept the questioning cursory and friendly. A doctor had been called and a half inch of hair around his head wound was shaved. Richard winced, more from pained vanity than actual pain. The wound was stitched, and the doctor said they could come out in a week. His hand was cleaned and bandaged. The most comforting thing was the doctor's calm assertion that he wouldn't lose any mobility. He would still be able to play the piano. A few hours later, Jerry had returned with a helicopter and whisked them back to Albuquerque. The pilot had even gotten permission to drop them in the parking lot of the Lumina building.

The doors opened, and new smells overcame their stink. Roasted potatoes and grilled steak. Franz had been busy. There was a crowd in the living room: Pamela, Grenier, Kenzo, Franz, Cross, and Mosi. The little girl was huddled in a corner of the couch, clutching a throw pillow to her chest. The pillow went flying, and she came bouncing off the sofa and rushed up to Richard. He opened his arms, then dropped them awkwardly when no hug followed. She stared intently into his face, then gave one emphatic nod.

He hid his discomfort with a false growled comment, "What are you still doing up?"

"She wouldn't go to bed until she was sure you were all right," Pamela said, and sighs seemed to hang on every word.

"What the hell happened?" Kenzo demanded.

"Are you okay?" Grenier asked.

"Have you eaten?" Cross asked far too casually and with a covetous glance toward the dining room.

"No, we haven't. And yes, we're starving," Weber said. "So don't bogart my food!"

"May we shower first?" Richard asked. He was met with a chorus of nos. He decided if they could stand his stink, he could too. They settled at the dining room table. The light from the chandelier glittered in the glass of the buffets and off the china stored inside.

Pamela repeated Kenzo's question. "Okay, what happened?"

Richard kept his eyes down, focused on cutting off another bite of steak. The blood from his preferred rare preparation flowed toward the potatoes. It brought back memories of the blood staining the pavement and his gut-fluttering fear. He set aside his knife and fork, and forced back the nausea that threatened to overcome him.

Franz, watching from the kitchen door, darted forward and snatched up Richard's plate. "I took the liberty of also preparing an egg custard. Perhaps you'd prefer that, sir?" Richard nodded.

"I'll finish that," Grenier said before Cross could speak up. The homeless god slumped back in his chair. Franz looked at Richard, who nodded his assent. Franz set the plate down in front of the former preacher and took away Grenier's now-empty plate.

Weber gave Richard another look, but when he saw no evidence that Richard was about to speak, he began the tale. Partway through, Mosi abruptly spoke up.

"I got two of them. The others stayed back after that."

Pamela rounded on Richard. "You gave this child a gun?"

Richard spooned up another bite of custard. "Actually, she had a wrist rocket, and she was damn handy with it. And if guns had been working, and I had one I thought she could safely handle, then yes, Pamela, I would have given her a gun. She had a right to defend herself."

"You white people act like guns and knives and things are snakes," Mosi said, scorn evident in every word. "They don't turn in your hand and bite you. My father taught me to shoot, and he said . . . he said . . ." The girl's lower lip started to tremble. She abruptly left the table.

"Do you think she's finished?" Cross asked, and glared at Grenier like a dog warning another away from his dish. When no one answered, Cross pulled over the abandoned plate.

"Are you just going to sit there?" Pamela demanded. "Go after her."

"Sometimes people just want to be left alone," Richard said.

Franz brought out dessert, a delicate raspberry soufflé. Richard found that it went down without too much rebellion from his stomach. He waited until the coffee cups had been emptied a couple of times, and Cross and Grenier had each had thirds on the dessert, then he stood. "Some of us have had a long day."

"We're meeting tomorrow, correct?" the CFO asked.

"Yes, Kenzo. I'll see you in the morning. Let's say ten."

They all moved into the living room and one by one said good night to him. Pamela actually kissed his cheek. "Try to get some sleep," she whispered.

"I don't have an apartment in town any longer," Weber said. "You got crash space for me here?"

"Of course," Richard said, and led him to a guest room.

The door to Mosi's room was closed. Richard hesitated outside, then walked on. In the master suite, he stripped out of his clothes and stuffed them into the laundry basket, even the suit coat and slacks. Maybe dry cleaning would pull out the stink. He then stood in the shower, letting the hot water pound on his neck and shoulders. It hurt when the water hit his head, but he needed to get clean. Slowly, tense muscles released.

He went through the bedtime rituals—water pick, toothbrush—and slid into bed. He tried to make a dent in the stack of reports on the bedside table, but it was no use. He couldn't concentrate and he couldn't sleep. Anxiety shivered along his nerves. What if the computers that filled Lumina were compromised? What if they were inside? He touched the hilt of the sword where it rested beneath his pillow. Rising, he put on a bathrobe over his pajamas, and put the hilt in his pocket. He would check on them. No harm in that. Richard pulled a flashlight out of the drawer and flicked it on. The bright halogen glare was a scar in the darkness. He switched it off and put it away. His eyes fell on the candlestick and candle on the dresser. He lit it and stepped out into the hall. Richard recalled that Kenntnis had done this the first night he'd slept at Lumina. So when had Richard become the guardian? And truthfully it wasn't a role he felt he could fill.

He went first to Weber's room. Muffled snores could be heard through the closed door. Clearly the man was all right. But Richard couldn't fight the need to see. To be sure. Richard softly opened the door and stepped into the room. Weber lay on his back, one foot free of the covers and hanging off the side of the twin bed. Richard had slept in this room. He'd fit in the narrow bed better than the big former cop.

Shielding the light of the candle with a cupped hand, Richard stepped closer and studied the square, tanned face. At the acne scars along the jawline, the sharp line where the tan on his neck abruptly stopped and the pale chest began. Richard wanted to touch Weber's tousled brown hair, now tipped with gray. Fortunately, the need to hide the light of the candle made that impossible. Richard backed out of the room.

Next Mosi. She was in the same room where Rhiana had once slept. A shudder ran through him as if somehow Mosi's fate would be the same as Rhiana's. *You humans and your silly superstitions.* Richard could almost hear Kenntnis's deep basso voice and the laughter at the edge of the words. He opened the door to her room and moved quietly to the side of the pretty canopied bed. The candlelight glittered in Mosi's wide-open eyes.

He had to say something. Various responses occurred and were rejected. *Are you all right?* Of course she wasn't all right. Her family had been butchered and she'd been through a terrifying firefight. *Can't sleep?* Duh, obviously.

"I wanted to be sure you were safe."

"No place is safe. They came into our hogan."

"They can't come in here," Richard said.

The arching brows drew sharply together. "Then why are you checking on me?"

"Fair point. I *know* they aren't here, but I worry they might be."

"That's how I felt about Auntie's computer," Mosi said. She stared up at him with the neutral expression that looked so alien on a child's face. The silence stretched between them, then she said, "Why did you want me?"

"I want to keep you safe."

"But you'll want me to do stuff. What do you want me to do?"

"Study." Richard smiled at the sudden frown on the childish face. "Grow up."

"When do I get to fight?"

Richard sat down on the edge of the bed. "When you grow up."

"Why is that always what adults say?" The frown became even fiercer. "And I fought today!"

"You did indeed. And very well too."

"Will I get a sword?"

"Maybe you'll get the one I use," Richard said.

"But that would mean you were dead. You don't get to die."

"I'll try not to. And we are trying to make more swords. Maybe even make it so it's not a sword."

"That would be good. Swords are kind of stupid when there are guns," Mosi said authoritatively.

Richard chuckled. "Yes, you're quite right, but this was made a long time ago when people only had swords." He stood up. "Now go to sleep."

He started to leave, but Mosi asked, "Where will I go to school?"

"We haven't decided about that yet. Maybe you'll study here with tutors. We've got some time to decide. Now go to sleep."

"You go to sleep too," she ordered.

Richard left, shaking his head over this precocious, interesting little person who had entered his life.

***

The three of them ate breakfast in the dining nook in the aggressively modern kitchen. Franz had sent up a bewildering array of chafing dishes that rested on the island buffet like silver treasure chests. They were filled with eggs, ham, sausage, and bacon, and blueberry pancakes. Sunlight through the bay windows glanced off the flecks of opalescent blue that veined the stone. Mosi was fascinated with the big stainless steel toaster, and she browned nearly half a loaf of bread before Richard called a halt to it. Richard ate a slice of bacon, but then contented himself with a cup of yogurt and berries. Weber dug in cheerfully, heaping his plate with several poached eggs, every variety of meat, and stack of pancakes. Mosi also had a good appetite and did justice to the feast Franz had prepared.

Weber chatted with the little girl and even drew out a few cautious smiles. Richard kept quiet and watched. He felt awkward and uncertain about how to interact with the child. He hadn't had a lot of experience with kids, particularly one from a very different culture. Fortunately, Mosi took the conversational lead.

"What are we going to do today?" she asked in a tone that made it far more of a demand than a query.

"I'm going to show you around Lumina."

She gave a one-shoulder shrug. "What's to see? It's an office building. And why do you live in an office building? That's weird."

Richard chuckled. "Well, I guess that's true, but there's something in the basement I think you'll like."

Mosi jumped up. "I'm done now. Can we go see?"

"*May* we go see."

"That's what I said."

Richard shook his head. "Not exactly. The word 'can' indicates ability. I know you can walk. 'May' indicates permission. You're asking me if it's okay to go downstairs."

"Still seems the same to me."

"It's more polite to say 'may' when you're asking for something."

The child was fast losing patience. "Does this, like, matter?"

"In certain circumstances, yes, it matters very much. And yes, we will go in just a minute." Richard turned to Weber. "What are your plans?"

"Thought I'd say hi to the ex while I'm in town. Catch up with a few folks at the APD. If that's okay? Or do you want me heading back to Kenya right away?"

Not ever was the rather desperate wish. Richard pushed it away. "Take a few days." Richard smiled and cringed when he found himself adding, "It's nice having you around."

Mosi skipped a few steps as they walked through the dining room, living room, and over to the elevator. Richard hit the button for the basement, one level below the parking garage. As they rode down, Mosi leaned against the far wall, hands thrust into her pockets, staring at him.

"What do I call you?"

"Richard's fine."

"Auntie said you were going to be my guard . . . guardian."

"That's right."

"What's a guardian? What does that mean?"

"I'm going to look out for you."

A flash of the fear showed. "Protect me?"

"Yes. Always."

She nodded. The elevator came to rest with a sigh and gentle bounce. Mosi stepped out. She cocked her head, looked up at Richard. "That makes you my *na sha dii.*"

"What does that mean?"

"Protector."

"I like that. And you can still call me Richard."

They walked through the blue-tiled archway, and Mosi gasped when she saw the swimming pool. The soft lights in the water cast an aqua hue over the beautiful tilework. The fluted columns supporting the roof and the decorated tiles gave it the feel of a Roman bath. Steam waved in a white pennant over the hot tub.

She turned back to Richard. "This is yours?"

"Yes . . . well, Lumina's."

"Can I swim in it?"

"May I," he corrected. "And yes, you may."

"I don't have a swimsuit."

"We'll go shopping and get you one."

"It would be funner if it was outside in the sun," Mosi said.

"But then you wouldn't be able to swim in the winter," Richard countered.

"Okay, I guess that's true. What are through those doors?" She pointed at the doors at opposite ends of the room.

Richard pointed to the one on his left. "Food storage and a water purification system. The other holds fuel, replacement solar panels.

"But come on, there's more to see," Richard said, and beckoned her back to the elevator. He pulled the key from beneath his shirt, inserted it in the control panel, and sent them down to the subbasement. Here was Lumina's armory, shooting range, and gym. Mosi moved down the long line of weapons, ranging from various types of guns to spears and swords and bows and arrows.

"I can come down here?"

"With an adult," Richard said. "Either me or Joseph."

"*I* or Joseph," Mosi corrected with a militant look.

"Sorry, but you use 'me' rather than 'I' in this case."

"Why?" she demanded.

Richard chuckled, thought about it. "Damned if I know. We'll ask Pamela, she'll know."

"But why do I have to be with you or Joseph?"

"Because weapons are dangerous, and you're"—he almost said *a kid* but stopped himself and said more diplomatically—"not quite grown up yet, and I'd get in trouble for letting you use them without supervision."

"My daddy would have let me," Mosi countered.

Richard leaned back against the table that held the reload equipment and folded his arms across his chest. "Now, that's a fib, and I know it is because I know from meeting you and seeing the kind of person you are that your father must have been a very smart and wise man, and a very smart and wise man would not let his nine-year-old daughter handle weapons without him watching over her." He paused, then added, "Or do you want to tell me I'm wrong about your daddy?"

The stony expression softened, and tears glittered in her dark eyes. She ducked her head and looked away. "No. My daddy was very smart." She turned and headed for the door. Richard followed. "You're going to get those computers and wreck them, aren't you?"

"Yes."

"You promise?"

"I promise."

Later that morning it was time to confront the Kenzo problem. Hoping to make the meeting seem less fraught, Richard sat down at the piano and, though it hurt, he began playing a Chopin étude. Kenzo entered before he'd finished. Richard lifted his hands quickly off the keys.

"It should be illegal to stop midmeasure like that," the Japanese man said.

"I didn't want to seem rude," Richard said.

"May I point out that that doesn't seem to have stopped you before," Kenzo said dryly.

They locked eyes for a long moment, then Richard dropped his hands back onto the keys and finished the étude.

Kenzo waited until the last chord faded from the air, then asked, "So, what is your decision?"

For some reason the blunt delivery and the crack about his rudeness irritated Richard, and he replied too quickly. "You stay . . . mostly because it's too damn much work to replace you." The moment the words emerged, Richard knew it had been a mistake. He had managed to seem lazy and to disrespect Kenzo all in one careless statement. "What I mean is that I have no idea how to find someone with your skills and qualifications to act as a CFO to a company of this size and magnitude." Richard ran a hand through his hair and winced when he hit the bare patch and the stitches. "Look, I'm sorry. Please, I do need your help and I respect your knowledge and your advice. Please stay."

"For the time being I will remain . . . in memory of Mr. Kenntnis. Pamela mentioned something about allowing us to see Mr. Kenntnis and ascertain for ourselves his condition."

"Yes, we're arranging for that."

"Good. How quickly will that occur? Should I return to Tokyo?"

Wary of touching his head again, Richard tried clasping his fingers and found that hurt too. He gave up and dropped his hands to his sides. "I don't know yet. I've called Rochester, and I think we can set it up in the next few days."

"Then may I have an office here so I can work?"

"Oh, of course. Jeannette will handle that."

Jeannette, ever competent, had Kenzo settled into a fourth-floor office within minutes. When she returned, he beckoned her into the office.

"Yes, sir?"

"Mr. Fujasaki's cell phone is a Lumina issue, right?"

"Yes." She cocked her head and gave him a measuring glance.

"As is Mr. Gold's."

"Correct."

Richard clasped his hands behind his back and paced over to the window. "I'm concerned about the security on those phones. Perhaps you could monitor the numbers called and calls received. Make sure they're . . . secure." He turned back to face her.

There was a twinkle in her brown eyes. "I can do that, sir. We can't be too careful. Anything else?"

"Please get Eddie on the phone."

Within moments, Jeannette had connected him with Rochester. Eddie, never one for social niceties, launched right in. "So we're trying to get ready for this big confab, but then the guys in the energy division find out, and now they want to make a presentation to the officers about orbiting solar collectors."

"Hello to you too, Eddie."

"Huh? Oh, right, hi."

Richard smothered a chuckle. "I don't see how that's a bad thing."

"Have you ever *met* the energy team?" Eddie asked.

"No."

"They're a bunch of geeks." Richard forbore stating the obvious. "And there's something you have to know—when a bunch of scientists get together and try to talk to normal people, they always fuck it up."

"Why?"

"Because they're not normal, and there are different types. There's the guy who gets sidetracked into some really obscure piece of technical minutia and bores the snot out of people. Then there's the guy who hasn't been at any of the meetings but has to tell everybody how they're fucking it up, which makes the normal people think there's a problem with the project. If you're really lucky there'll be the schmoozemeister, the guy who probably isn't all that good on the science, but he's a great salesman, and he might be able to pull the meeting back from the edge of disaster. Oh, and expect a couple of them to start having a conversation on some *completely* different topic while the presenter is talking—"

"Is there a point in here somewhere?" Richard asked, amused, but also aware of the time ticking away.

"Oh, yeah, right. Okay, point being all scientists do this, but the guys on the energy team are the *worst*."

"Eddie, you do realize this is sort of the pot calling the kettle black, right?"

There was a squawk of outrage. "I don't do that."

"You totally do."

"Well, okay, maybe I do, but at least I'm *aware* of it."

"Look, I want the officers to see what you're up to, and why the work we do costs so much money. Let the energy team present. Then we'll let the officers interact with Kenntnis and discuss what you're doing to try to restore him, and we'll end with the work to create another sword. Or swordlike thing . . . weapon."

"Okay, but don't say I didn't warn you," Eddie said in tones of deep foreboding. He hung up.

Richard went back to work. An hour later Pamela walked in. She didn't have to speak for Richard to know something was wrong. "What's happened?"

"Gaia has figured out that Global Computing is a front for Lumina. There's an article in the *Wall Street Journal*. As a result, the price of Gaia stock has shot through the roof."

"*I'll be watching.*" Titchen's final words to him.

Richard drummed his pen on the desk, and the sharp *tink* of metal against stone seemed harsh in the silence. "We have to get control of Gaia. No matter the cost."

"Richard, we're low on cash."

"Then we take out a loan. The computers are out there. Destroying children and their families. Enough of them in one place might even open a tear. We have no choice." He paused and pushed away the papers. "How was the link between Global and Lumina discovered? Assuming the most charitable conclusion—did somebody screw up?"

"I don't think so," Pamela said slowly.

"So we go to door number two—that this was deliberate. Somebody leaked the connection," Richard said grimly.

"I'd put my money on Grenier," Pamela said. "He's been making like Iago for days."

"Not sure I follow that," Richard said. "Am I Othello?"

"More Desdemona with Kenzo as the stand-in for Othello."

Richard wasn't sure how he felt about that. "Okay, I'll play detective. Which means you have to do my paperwork."

Her expression was sour, but she held out her hand for the sheaf of papers.

The boy's expression was half defiant, half devastated. Grenier savored the satisfaction, it was almost as good as a meal at Tamaya.

"I didn't do it. I didn't tell anybody. I didn't even *know* about it."

Richard looked at the paper in front of him. "Records indicate your sister bought one hundred shares, then sold them the minute the stock price shot up. You should have gone a bit farther afield to find your front." Richard's tone was implacable.

"How would we have the money for something like that? I'm a starving student. She works as a waitress at Olive Garden. I have student loans."

"At the time, the stock price was at eleven. It's not hard to come up with twelve hundred dollars. Especially when it netted you well over five thousand."

"Then where's this money I supposedly got?" Jorge challenged.

"The brokerage firm indicates it was paid directly into your sister's checking account."

Jorge spat out, "This is bullshit! And you were snooping in my sister's bank account?"

"I'm still a police officer. It wasn't real hard to get the authorization."

"I don't fucking believe this!"

"Let me show you." Richard turned the big screen of his desktop computer. Jorge leaned in, and Grenier watched as the color drained out of his face. The boy's lips were white, and he could barely force out the words. They emerged as a whisper. "But I didn't do it. We didn't do it. Somebody else put it there. I'll give it back. I didn't . . ." Outrage had given way to fear and grief. There was the burr of unshed tears on the words.

Richard stood, indicating the meeting was over. "It's not the money. Well, it is, but not this tiny amount. It's the damage this revelation did to Lumina's bottom line."

"Please, Mr. Oort, please believe me."

"I'm sorry, Jorge. I can tolerate many things, but not disloyalty. You're fired. Your office has been cleared. You'll find your things boxed and waiting for you in the lobby."

"Please, please, Mr. Oort. Take another look. Somebody set me up." The boy's eyes slid toward Grenier.

Grenier watched Richard closely. The man had a soft spot for the desperate and afraid, and an especially soft spot when the person happened to be an attractive young man. For an instant Richard hesitated, indecision flickering across his face. Then he regretfully shook his head. "I don't have any more time to spend on this, Jorge. Frankly, you're a minor irritant among a number of major crises."

The grief morphed into bitter anger. "Yeah, what's one spic kid when you're saving the fucking world? Except what's the point if you don't give a shit about individual people? You're no different from any other rich asshole!" The boy stormed out.

Richard pressed a hand to his face. Grenier moved ponderously to his side and laid a hand on the younger man's shoulder. "You going to be all right?"

There was a hint of moisture swimming in the blue eyes. "I hate to fire people."

"With luck, you won't have to again," Grenier said, enjoying the moment.

Richard stared at the computer screen. "I have a feeling that the Richard who existed a few years ago, who had never heard of Old Ones, or Lumina, or paladins, would have taken another look," he said quietly.

However much he might despise Richard in other areas, Grenier had an abiding respect for his abilities as a detective. A deeper investigation would ultimately reveal Grenier's cyber fingerprints. Grenier said, "You're leaving for Rochester tomorrow. Let it rest until you get back. I'll let the boy know you're going to take another look. And bluntly, you can't be that man any longer. You have responsibilities that far transcend the needs of any single individual."

"With apologies to *Casablanca* . . ." Richard gave a grim smile. "The problems of one little person don't amount to a hill of beans in this crazy world?"

"Yes, that's it exactly."

Chapter TWELVE

ROCHESTER wasn't known for its fine hotels. Jeannette had done her best and booked them all into the Edward Harris House Inn. They had basically taken over the place, with Dagmar, Kenzo, Gold, Brook—Lumina's second pilot—Cross, Pamela, and Mosi. Weber had also come along, saying he wanted to see exactly what the scientist and aid workers he protected were actually doing. He would depart out of JFK to return to his troops in Africa. Pamela had argued against bringing Mosi, but Richard didn't want her out of his sight. The girl, in a show of studied nonchalance, had pronounced the Gulfstream to be vastly superior to the Cessna.

Richard had confidence in his scientific staff, but a lot was riding on these presentations, so as usual he found it nearly impossible to sleep. He had packed his best suits and selected the blue pinstripe with a deeper blue shirt and a silver-and-blue tie. The hilt was arranged in the holster at his back, and he slung on his shoulder rig. The tailor had done a good job. The fact he was armed would be obvious only to another law enforcement professional. The damn shaved spot and angry cut was annoying, but wounds healed and hair grew. He just had to be patient. Richard knew that was vain, but he also needed all the confidence he could muster.

He headed downstairs to find the owners had laid out an impressive breakfast including old-fashioned johnnycakes. As a native of Rhode Island, Richard took johnnycakes very seriously and had missed the crisp cornmeal cakes since his move to New Mexico. He made a mental note to ask Franz to add them to the breakfast menu back at Lumina headquarters.

Dagmar was next downstairs. He stood and hugged the older woman. Her brown hair was expertly highlighted, and she was dressed in businesswoman chic.

She held him at arm's length and looked him up and down. "You look good. You've gained some weight. But did you sleep?" she added severely.

"No, but the stress will be off after today," Richard said.

"Famous last words. This is Lumina."

One by one the others joined them. Gold had become paunchier and balder since Richard had last seen him some six months ago. When Pamela and Mosi came downstairs, Mosi ran to take the seat next to Richard. Her long hair was shimmering blue-black, and she wore a cute short set. Pamela went off to join Gold, the other lawyer in the mix. Kenzo sat with Dagmar, and Weber took the chair to Richard's left, but it was a singularly silent breakfast. Only Cross seemed to have any appetite, and the B and B staff seemed stunned by the amount of food he consumed. Or perhaps the ratty jeans and T-shirt were what really put them off.

At nine, the cars arrived. "Ride with me, Pamela," Richard said. She cast him a questioning look but joined him and Mosi in the armored Lincoln Town Car. Richard plugged a set of headphones into his phone and handed to it to Mosi. "Listen to some music."

"You don't want me to hear stuff," she said, her tone accusatory.

"That's right."

"I want to hear."

"Okay," Richard said. *"Je vous remercie de vous joindre à moi,"* he said to Pamela.

Mosi glared at him. "That is no fair! You wouldn't understand if I spoke Navajo!"

"No, I wouldn't, but I'm hoping you will teach me so it can be our own private language."

She glared at him. "It's real hard," she warned.

"Then you'll really have to help me."

Mosi huffed and settled the earbuds into her ears. Richard still continued in French, which he and all of his siblings spoke fluently. "You sent me a text regarding Jorge," he said.

"Yes. Are you sure about terminating him? We could be opening ourselves up to a lawsuit."

"Don't worry. He'll be reinstated just as soon as I deal with . . ."

"What? What are you up to?"

"You ever hear of the Greek Gift Sacrifice?"

"Vaguely."

"It's a chess move. You deliberately lose a piece in the hope of gaining a tactical or positional advantage. Kenzo and Grenier are actively working against me. I want to draw them out. Lull them into making a move."

"You know this how?"

"I've become a paranoid bastard, and I have levels of surveillance on Grenier he can only guess at."

"Like what?" Pamela was eyeing him with both fascination and revulsion.

"The usual, we monitor his phone calls, there's a tracer on his car. That one he found. He leaves it in his garage when he doesn't want me to know where he's going, but there's a tracking device built into his prosthesis."

"Jesus God. That's . . . such an incredible violation of privacy. Are you spying on everyone? On me?"

"We're playing for life-and-death stakes here, Pam. There are certain niceties I just can't afford. And yes, I have surveillance on you and Amelia and her family, on a lot of people. We're dealing with monsters, Pamela. Would you prefer I leave you unprotected?"

His sister sat with that for a moment. "All right. I guess I can see that. So what are you going to do?"

"Here's the first step." Richard opened his briefcase, pulled out a sheaf of papers, and handed them to Pamela.

She frowned at the top page, then flipped through a few more pages. "Richard, they'll kill you for this."

"One hopes not literally. And if it happens—well, it's all on you, sis. There's no one else I would trust. I'll leave you the company . . . companies, and you'll have Mosi."

Pamela put the papers in her briefcase. Her jaw was tight. She cleared her throat. "I guess you did learn a few things from that brief time as a stockbroker," Pamela said gruffly.

"More than you'll ever know," Richard replied.

The cars pulled through the gates and down the long driveway to the Lumina research facility. Dr. Eddie Tanaka met them at the front doors. Amazingly, the Japanese American was in a suit and tie. Richard had a hard time reconciling the young T-shirt-and-jeans-wearing scientist with this professional look. Two years ago, Eddie had nearly been killed when Old Ones and human fanatics had attacked a Lumina facility. Now he oversaw Lumina's science division. Richard wondered if he'd done the right thing moving Eddie into administration. Had Richard cost the world a physics breakthrough by doing that? He comforted himself with the knowledge that Eddie still managed a few research projects on the side.

Introductions were made and Eddie handed them all badges.

Kenzo stared at his. "Is this really necessary? We're officers of the company, not casual visitors."

"These are personnel dosimeter film badges. We have an accelerator here," Eddie replied.

The confusion on the older Japanese man's face was evident. Cross slapped Kenzo on the shoulder as he walked past. "Meaning there's radiation and you might want to know if your nuts are glowing."

Kenzo blanched. He then snapped a question in Japanese to Eddie. The scientist shrugged and said, "Not a clue, dude. No hablo Japanese-o." Kenzo looked annoyed.

Eddie led them to a conference room where the scientists had already assembled. Richard hung back. Eddie made a face and gave Richard a fingers-crossed gesture. Richard gave him an encouraging nod, and they entered.

More introductions. Dr. George Driscoll stood by a laptop at one end of the table. On the far wall was a white screen. There was Dr. Milind Ranjan, a round-faced East Indian with a degree in high-energy physics from IIT Bangalore. Dr. Dieter Helman, a German they'd recruited last year. Dr. Brad Delany, formerly of Lawrence/Berkeley. He wasn't much taller than Richard, and his shaggy brown hair and youthful features made him look about twelve. Finally, Dr. Ron Trout, a heavyset man with graying hair and a face pitted with ancient acne scars. He had his feet up on the table and was busily inspecting his toenails revealed by a pair of battered sandals. The scientists were all attired in T-shirts and jeans or khakis, and they didn't look much like a crack scientific team, but then Richard supposed that he didn't look much like a CEO. The smell of coffee and donuts was carried on the current of cool air from the vents.

They took their seats and the presentation began. The energy team hadn't gone so far as to provide the "Blue Danube Waltz" as background, but it was all very reminiscent of the iconic twentieth-century movie *2001: A Space Odyssey*. Richard had feared that Mosi would be bored, but her gaze was riveted on the screen.

"Using robots will substantially reduce the cost of construction because we won't need any kind of base or station that can support and protect humans," Driscoll said, while on the screen a vast solar array was being constructed by energetic boxy robots. Off to the left, Earth hung like a green-blue marble, clouds swirling across the continents. Behind the array hung the sun. It looked like the graphic designer had tweaked the colors to make the sun an even richer shade of gold.

Richard knew he shouldn't be snowed by incredible graphics, but damn, the images scrolling across the wall screen were breathtaking. He noticed that the scientists were watching his reactions, with the expressions of dogs hoping for a treat, rather than the screen.

Trout, the toenail inspector, looked up, his mouth twisted sourly, and he said, "I keep telling you this rigid construction is the wrong approach. Streamers of material would be—"

"Damn it, Ron!" Ranjan burst out. "Would you shut up about your damn streamers? You've missed most of the meetings on this project, and you don't know what the hell you're talking about!" The deep brown eyes first flicked toward Mosi and then Richard. He ducked his head in embarrassment. "Sorry, sir, pardon my French."

Richard waved it off and nodded at the stricken presenter. "Go on, Dr. Driscoll."

Eddie shot him an I-told-you-so look. Richard just shrugged. Driscoll cleared his throat and muttered some of the sentences they'd already heard, then picked it up again. "Meanwhile on Earth, ground-based construction crews will be erecting the dipole antenna arrays and bringing the grid out to the energy farm. This will provide employment in our targeted country."

The screen obligingly showed a graphic of hard-hatted men pouring concrete and erecting antennas. Sand dunes flowed away, and on the horizon hung the golden sun. It concluded with an image of the array completed. A forest of antennas like silver anemones connected by glittering webs of thin wire in a garden of sand. Driscoll snapped off the computer and jumped up to turn on the lights. They all turned to look at Richard.

Richard steepled his hands. "Are any of these targeted countries likely to nationalize our energy farms?" he asked. He noted that Kenzo looked surprised at the question and felt a bitter sense of vindication.

Driscoll gaped at him and stuttered a bit as if surprised by the question. "I . . . I guess that might be an issue. I just thought if we bought the land—"

Dagmar interrupted. "You're talking about constructing this in parts of the world where the rule of law, and the sanctity of personal property, aren't well regarded," she said.

Richard stepped back in. "There's a lot of ugly empty in the U.S.— Texas, for example, and southeastern New Mexico. We should look at purchasing property there too, and other countries that won't seize the asset. Spain, maybe."

"Siberia," Delany piped up

"That whole nationalizing thing," Richard said gently, "sort of started in Russia." Delany blushed.

"The beauty of this is that we can just change the target from the satellites. The country might seize the farm, but we don't have to give them the energy," Ranjan said.

"I have a question," Gold said. "We're going to be sending laser or microwave pulses down to Earth from space—"

"Lasers are more likely with nanophotonic antennas receiving," Helman interrupted. His German accent lay thick on the words. The entire exchange was starting to make Richard feel like a moron. He noticed that once the picture show was over, Mosi had pulled out the iPad mini he had given her and was reading.

Gold looked as confused as Richard felt, but he plowed on. "Whatever. So how do we handle issues of air traffic? It would sort of wreck your day to have a laser punch through your airplane. The lawsuits would be a nightmare."

Dagmar jumped in. "And what about birds? No one will love us if we start incinerating birds."

"At the planet's surface, the beam we're contemplating would have a maximum intensity at its center of twenty-three mW/cm—" Ron began.

"Damn it, Ron! Remember what we said. No numbers! No formula," Eddie yelped.

"Yes, please, no numbers," Richard echoed.

"Just one number," Kenzo said in his dry, precise way. "How much is this going to cost?"

They sank back into the chairs, and looks shot around the table as fast as their little laser pointers. Richard didn't need voices to supply the words.

You?

How about you?

You want to answer that?

Oh, crap! He would ask that!

Finally, Ranjan slid a piece of paper across the table toward Richard. Kenzo intercepted it, and Richard suppressed a flare of annoyance. Kenzo's normally expressionless face registered shock. "Absurd. Utterly absurd."

Richard gestured, quick and angry. Kenzo handed over the paper. Richard looked at the figure, blanched, and collapsed against the back of his chair. "Wow. That's . . . that's a lot of money. Okay." He pulled his voice out of the soprano range and back to its normal tenor. "The world needs clean energy. Whoever can deliver is going to get rich, very rich, and do a little good along the way. I'd like it to be Lumina, but we need to know when we'd hit the break-even point. And does this"—he gave the paper a shake—"include launch costs?"

"No." Helman, ever the laconic German.

"It would be great if we had our own lift capacity," Driscoll said wistfully, and Richard remembered from his file that he'd tried to join NASA as a payload specialist before they'd shut down the shuttle program.

Richard shook his head. "We looked into this last year, and there is no way we have the money to start our own space program. So how do we launch these robots and the materials to build these platforms?"

Ron spoke up. "We shouldn't be launching materials. Use the moon for the resources."

"Yeah, Ron, but then we've got to have a permanent base on the moon *first*," Ranjan pointed out.

"Not to mention the power to process the raw material," Delany added.

Ron swelled up like an angry lizard. Richard rushed in before scientific mayhem could ensue. "It's pretty clear that the federal government and NASA aren't going to offer delivery services. Especially with the Air Force taking more and more control over NASA. So who else has launch capabilities?"

"The Europeans," Eddie suggested.

"Yeah, but that means dealing primarily with the French," Delany said and punctuated it with a shudder.

"The Indians," Ranjan offered hesitantly.

"And the Chinese," said Driscoll. "They're farther along with their program than India. No offense," he hastened to add. Ranjan nodded.

"Word is that the space program is firmly under the control of the Red Army," said Helman. "I think that's worse than the French."

Richard could see another squabble starting. He averted it by rolling back his chair and standing up.

Eddie hurried to offer another suggestion. "There are a number of private firms that have real promise. Space X, Blue Origin, Orbital Science. We could talk with them about partnering up."

"I like that idea better," Richard said. "Thank you all. This really has been enlightening and exciting, but I need to do some research and talk with my officers"—he indicated Kenzo, Dagmar, and Gold with a nod—"before I can give you a definitive answer." Richard forced a smile. "Gold, can you check out the airspace issue?" The lawyer nodded.

Richard looked up and found eyes focused on him in total anticipation. He held up a restraining hand. "Just because I'm having legal look into something doesn't mean I'm going to agree to fund this."

A blizzard of incomprehensible conversation began as Richard and his officers left. Richard picked a route that would take him past the tray with its few remaining donuts, but the scientists were quicker than the cop. The cinnamon crumb Richard had been eyeing was grabbed by Ron.

———◇◆◇———

Kenzo fell into step with Richard. "You're not seriously considering this?"

"Sooner or later it's got to be considered. For the sake of the planet. Maybe we could form a consortium, bring in some other companies as Eddie suggested."

"Mr. Kenntnis liked to avoid such entanglements. We have subsidiaries, but we own them outright."

Richard hoped he masked any sort of reaction when Kenzo mentioned the subsidiaries. "This might be too big for a single company to handle. Let's discuss it further."

"Speaking of Mr. Kenntnis . . ." Kenzo's voice trailed away significantly.

"We're going to take you there now," Richard said, and nodded to Eddie.

Eddie had a sheaf of photographs that showed satellite images of Kenntnis when he was in his light form and trapped in spin glass at Grenier's compound. Kenzo gave them a cursory glance. "Yes, yes, you've shown these to us before, but with digital magic this could have been fabricated, and why should we believe that this thing was Kenntnis?"

"Why would we make up a story like that?" Eddie demanded.

Kenzo gave Richard a pointed look. "So he could take over the company."

"Trust me, if that's what I wanted I would have made up a better story than something that sounds this crazy," Richard said dryly. It was an effort. Rage was a twisting pain in his chest. "Let's examine the facts. Kenntnis disappeared when he entered Grenier's compound in Virginia to rescue me. He was trying to flee when he was captured. When Kenntnis was freed, he finished the action he was taking, which was to return to New Mexico. But it happened almost instantly, which implies he was still in his light form," Richard said.

"One hundred eighty-six thousand two hundred and eighty-two miles per second. It's not just a good idea, it's the law," Eddie intoned. The officers looked blank, not recognizing this as a geek's attempt at humor.

"Once he reached Lumina headquarters, he reverted to his human form," Richard concluded.

"And if he was . . . is this light creature as you claim . . . well, how do you capture that?" Gold asked.

Eddie opened his mouth, and Richard hurried to forestall a barrage of science babble. "The scientists"—he nodded toward Eddie—"described it to me as spin glass, which is a way to make light stand still. And there was magic involved. It was a mix of physics and magic," Richard concluded lamely.

"Both seem to be pretty much the same for laymen like us," Gold said.

Kenzo broke in, "Assuming for the moment this is true—"

"Look, stupid guy." Everyone jumped because Cross was suddenly with them. "Could you maybe stop and reflect that almost every name he's taken has some reference to light or knowledge. He was Prometheus to the Greeks, Scientius and Lucifer to the Romans, Loki to the Norse, and by the way, people think Loki means 'breaker of shit' or 'trickster,' but the earliest word that gave rise to the name was *white light*. Think Kenntnis was maybe trying to tell us something? You know, sort of literalizing the metaphor."

"Hush," Richard said. Cross looked rebellious, but he pressed his lips together and made the zipper motion.

"When did he become Kenntnis?" Pamela asked.

Cross tried to answer while keeping his lips tightly shut. A series of grunts and *mmm*'s emerged. Mosi giggled. Richard cast his eyes heavenward in a plea for patience. "You can answer. Just don't be rude."

"Around 1780." Cross looked down at Mosi. "You're going to meet Coyote, little one."

Gold was looking puzzled. "Why Kenntnis?"

"Because, moron, Mr. Lumina, or Mr. Light, or Mr. Fire sounds stupid," Cross said. Richard cleared his throat. "Was that rude?"

"Yes."

"Sorry," Cross tossed offhandedly to Gold.

Dagmar intervened. "Kenntnis means 'knowledge' in German." Her German accent was very much in evidence.

"Oh," Gold said.

"I'm sorry, Kenzo, you were saying?" Richard prompted.

"I wanted to know how did Mr. Kenntnis get free."

"I removed the magical part of the equation," Richard said.

"That tells me nothing."

"There was a girl—a human–Old One hybrid—trained in physics, but also a powerful sorceress. She was powering the spin glass trap. I used the sword on her. Stripped away her ability to do magic. She's a vegetable now in a long-term care facility in California." Richard delivered the recitation in a flat, emotionless tone. Inwardly, guilt and doubt churned into acid in his gut because he had promised he would never harm Rhiana. The best he could do to alleviate that guilt was have Lumina pay for her care. He didn't mention that to Kenzo. He wasn't sure how it would be received.

"So you were his rescuer. Convenient."

Richard again let the sneer pass. "I didn't know it would have that effect. I did it because Rhiana was a threat." He didn't add that he feared he had done it because Rhiana's actions had led directly to a dear friend's murder. Had it been vengeance or justice? Perhaps it had been a bit of both.

Eddie led them down several flights of stairs to a basement apartment. Gold reacted to the layers of security from cameras, motion detectors, infrared, and guards with guns.

"What? Is he dangerous now?" Gold asked.

"No, this is to protect him," Richard said. "I don't know if the Old Ones could actually kill Kenntnis, but I never want him to fall into their hands again. While he was trapped, the world went crazy. I don't want to risk that happening again." He paused, not sure whether to go on with his deeper analysis of Kenntnis, but decided candor was the best policy. "I think he's like an ur-creature, an avatar of rationality, if you will. When he's not present, bad things happen." They reached the door to Kenntnis's quarters. "I know you all knew him as a man, but he is an alien. Somehow he can manipulate matter and build himself a physical form."

Cross jerked a thumb at his chest. "Like me. Only he's got control over how he looks. Me, not so much. My form gets warped by all the good little Christians. Hell, you don't think I'd willingly look like this, do you? The wimpy Jesus thing is a real drag."

Richard turned to the door's control panel and underwent fingerprint and retinal scans. The big door swung open, and they entered the apartment. Richard had sent some of the furniture and objets d'art from Kenntnis's penthouse atop the Lumina building here. He had hoped that the familiar items might help restore Kenntnis's mind.

The room smelled of sandalwood incense, and Bach played in the background. Kenntnis sat in a large armchair. The more you studied the man, the greater was the sense that his form encompassed all races and all types. His age was indeterminate. He could have been anywhere between thirty and sixty. He looked up as they entered the room, but there was no other reaction. In the past year plus, he had regained most of his bulk and was again six foot six and more than three hundred pounds. His skin was a rich ebony, which made the swirling silver and gold lights in his eye sockets all the more startling. It was the one place where he no longer matched the human norm.

"When *we* come in," Eddie said, "he doesn't react at all. It's only when you're here," he said to Richard.

"I don't think it's me. I think it's the sword. I think that's what he senses." Then Kenntnis promptly blew that theory out of the water by switching his focus from Richard to Mosi. The little girl met his gaze without any sign of discomfort.

"No," Cross said. "It's paladins. Maybe it's because you're more akin to him than you are to other humans."

Richard found that conclusion faintly disturbing. He also hated talking about Kenntnis as if he weren't present, so he walked over to him and took his hand. "Hello, sir. How are you? The officers have come to see you."

Kenzo moved forward. "Mr. Kenntnis, it's Kenzo Fujasaki." There was no reaction. Kenzo might have been invisible.

Gold pushed forward. "Mr. Kenntnis, your instructions were to turn Lumina over to Richard if you failed to check in once every twenty-four hours. You're back now, but you haven't checked in, so does that directive still apply?" Nothing.

They really do want me out bad, Richard thought, but he kept silent. From the corner of his eye he saw Mosi investigating the bookcases. She took down an illustrated copy of *Peter Pan* and began looking at the pictures.

"Does he ever speak?" Dagmar asked.

"No," Eddie said.

Kenzo snapped at Eddie, "What is wrong with him?"

"Best guess, the time he spent in the spin glass damaged his cognitive abilities. Light degrades when it's in the glass. He probably suffered dispersion," Eddie said. "It would help if we could get him to turn back into the light-dust thingy. Maybe then we could figure out what part of him was his brain and figure out how it was damaged. We're stumped because we don't know whether to treat this as a medical problem or a physics problem."

"I can think of a simpler explanation," Gold said.

"Yeah, what's that?"

"He's been drugged."

Richard stiffened, and his inchoate anger now focused. "If you're accusing me of stealing this company, George, then fucking do it. Let's have it out."

Pamela cast an agonized glance at Mosi, who had looked up from her book. "But maybe not right now . . . and not right here." She turned on Gold and in an undertone hissed, "And frankly, how *dare* you accuse my brother? I've never seen anybody who wanted a job less!" Pamela's face twisted into that sudden *uh-oh* look.

Kenzo, quick as a shark, leaped in. "Then perhaps he should step aside."

All of Richard's fantasies of walking away from the burden burned off in the possessive white-hot rage that swept through him. "Not a chance!"

He strode over to Mosi. "Would you mind staying here and reading? Or maybe read aloud to Mr. Kenntnis? He'd probably like that." She studied the big, silent figure for a long moment. "Are you afraid of him? You don't have to be."

"His eyes are all funny."

"That's because he's an alien."

Pamela and Dagmar both reacted. Pamela's mouth became an O of surprise, and Dagmar took a step toward him, but Richard was undeterred. He raised a hand to hold them back.

"A good alien?" Mosi asked.

"Yes, a very good alien. He came here to help humans."

"Like Superman."

Richard found it interesting that she thought first of Superman as an alien rather than a superhero. Was that because she felt like an alien in the white culture? Which was ironic—her people had been on the North American continent first. Or maybe it was being with him in a new life. He just hoped he could be as wise as Pa Kent.

Richard nodded. "Yes, like that, but he didn't have superpowers. He was just really smart."

Mosi twisted her mouth around for a few moments, then nodded.

Richard turned to go and was surprised when she caught the hem of his jacket as he turned away. She motioned to him to come close. He leaned down and she put her lips to his ear. "Everybody's really mad," she whispered.

"Yes, but it's going to be all right," he whispered back and touched her hair lightly.

Chapter

THIRTEEN

THEY returned to ground level. "We need a conference room," Richard said to Eddie.

"Um, we're all set up for the sword experiment."

"It can wait," Kenzo said.

"Mr. Oort. Mr. Oort!" A voice calling, loudly. Richard turned to see a tall Chinese man rushing toward them. Richard drew back reflexively and his hand slipped to the Browning. The years he'd spent as a cop made him wary of people getting too close too fast.

Eddie hurried into speech, "Richard, this is Dr. Chen. He's the guy we brought in on the sword project after the crystallography test didn't give us much. We realized we needed to step up to Big Hammer Tech, and Chen man is the best for that."

"Ah, yes, Dr. Chen, welcome." Richard held out his hand.

"You have it? You have brought the object? We have theories and would love to start the next round of testing."

"Yes, that's one of the reasons we're here."

"Excellent. Excellent. Well, shall we begin?"

Richard glanced at his officers. It was clear from Kenzo and Gold's expressions that they wanted to have the fight. Richard was torn. His anger had faded, and now he had that aching, oily feeling in his gut that had always happened whenever his father had been about to lecture him. He decided on cowardice.

He nodded to Dr. Chen. "Lead on."

"We will have this conversation," Kenzo said in an undertone.

"Yes, but not right now."

They went down hallways into another wing of the building and into an elevator and descended several floors. "We have a small accelerator here," Eddie explained. "It's nothing compared to Fermilab, Berkeley, Oak Ridge, or Cern, but what we learn from this initial test will . . . might tell us what kinds of tests will give us the most bang once we get on one of the big machines so we're not wasting time." Eddie's excitement had created a babble of word salad.

"So this test today won't tell us anything?" Richard asked.

Chen stepped in. "Probably not, but it will indicate the direction we should go. We'll then petition to run an experiment on one of the larger machines."

"So what are you planning to do?" Richard asked.

They had entered a white-tiled control room. Wires snaked in all directions, some bound together with duct tape, and computer screens were festooned with sticky notes. The initial design might have suggested high-tech competence, but the scientists had turned it into controlled chaos. Richard's earlier feeling of cocky confidence had faded. All he could think about was the upcoming confrontation with his officers.

"First, I would very much like to see the object," Dr. Chen said.

"Its behavior has been described to me, but I find it rather fantastical. Perhaps a demonstration? That might affect the parameters of the experiment." He sounded less like a Nobel Prize–winning physicist and more like an eager teenager. "And Eddie . . . Dr. Tanaka says you should inoculate me. I'm eager to experience that."

"It's often painful," Richard warned. "I don't want you incapacitated right now. We'll do it after the experiment."

Eddie jumped in. "You've said yourself it's usually not as hard on us science types since we're a bunch of Commie pinko atheists."

Dr. Chen flinched. Richard gave Eddie an exasperated look at the gauche reminder that Dr. Chen was from China. "What? Oh, shit, I was rude again, wasn't I?"

"Yes," Richard said.

"I didn't mean because he was Chinese. I mean, some people think all of us scientists are like that." Eddie paused and considered. "And I guess that's sort of true. At least about the atheist part."

The three technicians in the room were laughing. Dr. Chen unbent and also chuckled. Richard pulled the hilt from its holster and drew the sword. The overtones from the sword blended rather unpleasantly with the room's hum. Chen moved from one side of the blade to the other, peered closely at the space-black metal, jumped a bit when the silver lights washed through like a retreating galaxy. He reached out a cautious finger.

Richard pulled the blade away. "Best let me do it, with someone close by to catch you."

Alarmed by the implication of what he'd heard, Chen stepped back. "Well, perhaps we should postpone the inoculation."

"So I ask again," Richard said, "what is it that you're planning to do?"

From the corner of his eye, Richard noted that Kenzo and Gold were in a huddle on the far side of the sterile room. Pamela and Dagmar were talking. Richard caught Weber's eye and cocked his head toward the two men. Weber nodded and drifted that way. Richard brought himself back to the scientific discussion.

"I think the blade goes into a pocket universe when it's sheathed. I'm thinking a neutron-scattering experiment that would have an H+proton beam slam into a target to generate neutrons that would directly probe the nuclear structure of the sword," Chen said.

"Will all of this make it possible for you to do what I want?" Richard asked.

"Which is . . . ?" Dr. Chen asked.

Richard sheathed the sword and lightly bounced the hilt on his palm. "Make more of these. Well, not exactly this. I'd really love a more up-to-date shape. I'm sure this worked out great for Charlemagne, but I'd like something more appropriate to our era. A gun. A Taser. Something."

"Well, let us see what it is and how it works." Chen reached for the hilt.

Richard pulled it back. "I don't let it out of my hands. I'll take it wherever it needs to go."

Eddie was suddenly frowning. He rubbed a hand on his head, causing the thick black hair to stand up like a rooster's comb. "Oh, shit. What we really need to bombard is the blade."

"But there's no blade unless I'm holding it," Richard said. "Can I stay inside the accelerator?"

"No, the beams are running in a vacuum, and there's a shit load of radiation generated. The hilt's going to need to cool down for at least twenty-four hours, and we'll still check with a Geiger counter just to be sure." Eddie chewed at his lower lip. "If there was just some way—" He sighed. "But I guess there isn't."

"No," Pamela said firmly. "There's not."

"I don't like this. Not having the sword available for a day," Richard said. "Is there any other way?"

"Not if you want more of these."

Chen and Eddie watched as Richard wrestled with the decision. He finally sighed and nodded. "Okay. Just be careful, all right?"

"We're always careful." Eddie turned to Chen. "So let's start by bombarding the hilt. It might agitate something, cause something to happen."

"That doesn't sound careful," Richard said as Weber, who had just walked up, added, "Is this the throw-shit-against-the-wall-and-see-if-any-of-it-sticks method?"

"Well, we usually have a calculation that tells us how sticky the shit might be," Eddie shot back.

The decision having been made, one of the technicians led Richard through a set of big metal doors, down stairs and catwalks, until they reached an access panel. There was an adjustable pedestal inside. Richard set the hilt in the center. The gray curves, beautiful and enigmatic, echoed the curving metal walls of the accelerator. The hilt looked like a piece of abstract art on display in a gallery of the distant future. The tech closed the panel, and Richard hesitated, staring at that blank metal. He had literally not been parted from the blade for years. It felt like he was not only naked but also skinless. Finally, he followed the waiting tech.

Back in the control room, a completely unintelligible conversation was taking place among the scientists and techs. Richard and his officers retreated to the back wall so they would be out of the way.

Weber sidled up to Richard. "They clammed up when they noticed me. What I did manage to hear was all about cash flow worries and that you aren't a businessman."

"Well, they're not wrong if by that they mean that I don't put money over people," Richard whispered back.

The techs and scientists were exchanging cryptic commands, buttons were pushed, commands were typed onto keyboards with a sound like robot chickens pecking. Richard had expected to hear something—a rising hum, the crackle of electricity, *something*—but it was just human voices and keyboards in the control room. The computer screens were filled with scrolling numbers and oscillating lines like a heart monitor for the universe.

One screen showed the hilt in its lonely isolation far below them. "Why do you have cameras on it?" Dagmar asked.

"Because it's in vacuum, things can get really hot, and we don't have a cooling line to bleed off the heat. We want to be able to monitor the target and make sure it hasn't shifted, or isn't getting degraded," Chen explained.

"Could this damage the sword?" Richard asked. Anxiety coiled in his chest. "Maybe we should hold off—"

But things were happening. The screens with their lines of scrolling numbers and oscillating lines went wild. Richard's gaze flew to the camera screen. The hilt was surrounded by color, strange purples, orange, and a burning white center. There was a blinding flash that had everyone yelling. And then it was gone.

The colors.

The flash of light.

And the sword.

————◇◆◇————

For several heartbeats, Richard's mind seemed empty of any and all thoughts. Horror gripped him. It felt like the world should have gone silent over this catastrophe, but instead the scientists were yammering about how the beam had vanished with the sword.

"Well, that ain't good," Cross said.

Richard blinked as if that could bring back the sword. The pedestal remained empty. Then Richard frantically clawed at the holster at the small of his back though he knew the familiar weight of the hilt was not there, yet somehow hoping it would be. *Empty.* Like the pedestal. Like his heart. Guilt slammed down. Kenntnis had entrusted him with the sword. With Lumina. With the world. He had betrayed that trust. Richard met Kenzo's gaze and saw the bitter pleasure in the man's dark eyes. Resolve stiffened his spine and set-tled the sick pain in his gut. There was no time for guilt or despair. He had feared that this moment would come. What he had not an-ticipated was that the sword—or the loss of it—would be the pre-cipitating event. But whatever the reason, it was time to act.

"Well, it seems your role as paladin is at an end. So perhaps it is time to discuss your other role."

Richard ignored Kenzo and went over to Eddie, who was in a hud-dle with Dr. Chen and several other scientists. Richard pulled him out.

Eddie was babbling. "I'm sorry, I'm so sorry. We'll figure it out. We'll get it back. I promise—"

Richard cut off the agonized words. "Is there a room in this build-ing, other than Kenntnis's quarters, that locks from the outside?"

Eddie blinked at the intensity of Richard's whisper, then said, "Huh?"

"Yes or no." Richard's urgency seemed to penetrate.

"Uh . . . yes. But—"

"Take us there. *Now*."

Richard turned back to his officers. Gold and Kenzo were again in a huddle. Dagmar looked devastated. Pamela just seemed stunned. "Let's let the scientists work, figure out what happened. We'll ad-journ to another room," he said.

Richard gave Eddie a shove to get him moving. They all trooped out. Dagmar fell into step with him. "Richard, this is a disaster. What are—"

"Not now."

"If not now, when?"

Eddie led them upstairs and down several hallways. Kenzo walked directly behind the young scientist, with Gold at his side. The march order indicated their contempt for Richard. He was irrelevant. For-gotten. He didn't mind. He welcomed it.

Richard dropped even farther back to Weber's side. "Richard, what—" the ex-cop began.

In an undertone Richard said, "Be ready."

Eddie had stopped in front of a door with a keypad lock. He typed in the code, pushed open the door. Richard realized it was a storeroom at the same time Gold and Kenzo reacted. Richard rushed them, grabbed Kenzo's arm up behind his back with one hand, slammed his other hand into the financial officer's back, and shoved. Weber, only a half step behind him, grabbed Gold in a wrestling lift and flung him into the small room. Richard pulled the Browning out of his shoulder rig and drew down on the goggling executives as they struggled to regain their balance and turn to face him.

"Get their cell phones," he ordered Weber.

"Richard! Have you gone mad?" his sister demanded.

"This is false imprisonment!" Gold shrilled.

Kenzo glared at Richard. "You're finished." The Japanese man grabbed Weber's wrist and turned it in a tricky maneuver that Richard recognized as jujitsu. "You will not take my phone. This is an outrage!"

Richard calmly fired a shot past Kenzo's ear. The man jumped, yelled out in Japanese, and inadvertently released Weber. The big cop quickly rammed Kenzo face-first into the wall and took the cell phone from his pocket. Gold clawed at his pocket and practically threw his phone at Weber. He alternated between looking nervously at Richard, at the gun, and at Weber. The former cop backed into the hall.

"Okay. What now?"

Richard pulled the door closed and heard the lock snap shut. "We get out of here." He started walking.

"What? Who? Where? What do you mean?" Dagmar was almost wailing as she trotted after him.

"Kenzo and Gold think they're going to take control of the company. And they may, for a little while, but they've gotten in bed with

Grenier, and he'll outplay them and then stab them. And I sure as hell don't want to place myself and Mosi in Grenier's power."

Richard increased his fast walk to a jog. It was hard on the two women in their high heels, and they quickly shed their shoes, carrying them as they all ran downstairs to Kenntnis's quarters. At the door, Richard turned to the young scientist. "Eddie, who do you most need to *get the goddamn sword back?*"

"Uh . . ."

"Well, figure it out and get them! Meet us at the cars." Richard checked his watch. "You've got fifteen minutes. Go!"

Richard keyed in the code on Kenntnis's door.

"Richard, would you have shot them?" Pamela asked, her tone low, hesitant. He glanced over at her and saw the deep discomfort and almost fear on her face.

"If necessary I would have made my point, but fortunately I didn't have to because Kenzo thought I would," Richard said with a grim smile. "That's all that mattered."

The door swung open.

Mosi's piping child's voice floated out to him. "'She dreamt that the Neverland had come too near and that a strange boy had broken through from it.'"

Mosi looked up from the book as they entered, as did Kenntnis. "Come, Mosi. We have to go. You can bring the book." Richard bent over Kenntnis and offered his hand. "Sir, we're going." The big man slipped his hand into Richard's and was gently pulled to his feet.

"Clothes?" Dagmar asked.

"No time."

Back upstairs and through the front doors. Blinking in the hot September sun, Richard impatiently checked his watch. Eddie, trailed by Chen and Ranjan and Ron Trout from the energy meeting, ran through the front doors. The four scientists skidded to a halt in front of Richard.

"Okay," Eddie panted.

"I feel responsible, Mr. Oort," said Chen. "So anything I can do to help."

"Is this a most exciting escape?" Ranjan asked, and he seemed thrilled at the prospect.

"It is an escape, but with luck it will be rather mundane." The East Indian scientist looked disappointed. Trout just looked impassive, and Richard wondered if the man had any sense of what was happening. What had happened.

"All right. We're going first to the B and B to collect our things. Then we head to the airport, making stops at ATMs as we go. Pull as much cash as you can," Richard instructed. He gave mental thanks that he'd made it mandatory that all Lumina personnel carried their passports at all times. Of course that didn't help with Mosi. There hadn't been time to procure a passport for her. Acid churned through his gut. He pressed a hand against his stomach and took several deep breaths.

"And where is the airplane going?" Pamela asked.

"I haven't worked that out yet," Richard admitted. "We could hook up with our forces in Kenya."

"I expect that's the first place they'll look," Weber said.

Tension and East Coast heat and humidity had a trickle of sweat running down his sides and tickling his sideburns. His mind jumped from country to country where Lumina had facilities. Which of course put them completely off-limits.

"Want some advice?" Cross asked.

"Please."

"Turkey. Ankara," the homeless god said.

"Why there?"

"Kenntnis was really tight with Atatürk. 'Course we knew him when he was still Mustafa Kemal, but there's a cadre of generals, sort of a secret cabal, who have sworn to support Lumina. You turn up with Kenntnis in tow, and they'll take us in. Do anything we need." Cross considered for a moment. "Probably even wax some people for us."

"Well, let's hope that's not necessary. History wasn't my strong suit. Remind me who was Atatürk?"

"Military officer. Beat the British at Gallipoli. Became a national hero. Turned politician. He oversaw the dismantling of the Ottoman Empire, passed a new constitution, secularized and Westernized the country, granted women more rights than they had in most other countries in that era. Not a paladin, but close. He was a hell of a guy. Too bad he was also an alcoholic. Liver cirrhosis killed him before his time."

"And Kenntnis advised him on all these changes?"

"Yep."

Richard pulled out his phone and called Brook. "Is the plane fueled?" he asked the pilot.

"Yes, sir."

"Can we get to Ankara, Turkey, from here?"

"Lemme check." There was silence for a few moments. "Yes. Since we upgraded to the Gulfstream G650 we've got a range of eight thousand miles. Shall I file a flight plan?"

"Is there some way to hide where we're actually going?"

"Not a chance," came the disheartening reply. "Not after nine/eleven. And am I going to end up in jail again?" Brook asked, and despite the joking tone Richard could hear the concern.

"No."

"Just checking. When do we leave?"

"Within the hour."

He hung up the phone. Everyone was huddled around him. It seemed strange to be planning a desperate escape on a bright September afternoon while standing on oil-stained concrete in a parking lot. In the distance he heard the hum of tires on a nearby road. A plane flew overhead. There was the monotonous drone of cicadas. Normal life. Except it wasn't.

Dagmar touched his arm, drawing him out of his reverie. "Richard, I'm not coming with you," she said. "You'll need somebody on the inside. Someone who can report back to you."

"Dagmar, you have a family."

"Which is another reason I really can't go. I can't leave them."

"If they figure out you're two-timing them, your family will be in danger," Weber warned.

"I know, but you can't be on the run with an entourage of kids and spouses and parents," Dagmar argued. "Peter and I will work something out. Now *go*. When do you want me to release Kenzo and George?"

"You've got to buy us time to get clear. We can't land and find cops or Interpol waiting for us."

"So, hours."

Richard nodded. "Tell them I locked you up too."

"I hope they believe me." Dagmar went back into the building.

"We meet you at the airport?" Eddie asked.

"Yes. And on the way be sure to hit ATMs and get money. Pull out as much as you can," Richard said.

Eddie nodded and led Chen, Trout, and Ranjan to his Audi. Richard climbed into a car with Kenntnis and Mosi. Weber slid behind the wheel, and Pamela joined them in the backseat.

"And what about *our* family?" Pamela asked.

Richard considered his sister Amelia, her husband, Brent, and son, Paul. He had offered them protection in New Mexico, but Amelia couldn't accept the truth about the world or life in Albuquerque, and they had soon returned home to Boston. Then there was his father, also in Boston. If his enemies took the elder Oort, Richard knew he probably wouldn't much care. The memory of his father's hand cracking against his face had not faded. He didn't much care about his brother-in-law either, but Amelia and Paul . . . he would bend if they were in danger.

"Can you get them? Take them into hiding until this is resolved?" he asked his sister. "Amelia may listen to you."

Pamela gave a tense nod. "Okay."

Back at the B and B, it didn't take long to pack. Richard handed over his Lumina credit card and took care of the bill, and then they were heading toward the airport. They stopped several times for people to draw out cash. Richard spotted a branch of the interstate bank where Lumina had an account. He went in and withdrew $9,999 in cash to avoid the large-currency transaction report. By the time Pamela and Weber had withdrawn funds, they had $29,997.

At the airport, they pulled up to the front and dropped off Pamela. She leaned into the car and frowned at her brother. "Try to find some way to contact me. Let me know you're all right."

"That may not be easy. You all need to dump your phones."

"So how the hell will I know when it's safe for us to come home?" The profanity was unusual in his sister.

"I'll put an ad in the *New York Times*."

"Okay, I guess that will work. Which section?"

He gave her a grin to mask all his doubt, worry, and regret. "Personals, of course."

"You're an ass." She turned away, then suddenly whirled, leaned into the car, and grabbed him in a fierce hug. "You be careful," she whispered.

"You too." He forced another smile. "Sorry about your bank account."

She shrugged. "It's okay. I'll put the touch on Amelia. She's a doc."

They drove to the private aircraft section of the Rochester airport, where Brook, Jerry, Eddie, Trout, Ranjan, and Chen were waiting. Richard hurried them up the stairs and into the plane. Just inside, Kenntnis paused, and there was a flicker of a frown. Richard realized the man hadn't seen this new plane, and Richard was somewhat heartened at even this small reaction. Richard got Mosi and Kenntnis buckled in, settled into a seat, and checked his watch. They were doing well. After they were in the air, Richard opened the pouch containing the money. Eddie and Talbot added their funds—another $4,000. Mosi's eyes were wide as she watched him distribute bundles of money to the companions.

That's when he looked around and realized that he had a young child in the company of only men. He began to wish he had kept either Pamela or Dagmar with him. Preferably Dagmar. She at least had children. *Yes, children of her own that she wants to care for. Mosi is my responsibility now.*

Richard brought up the entertainment center, and they scanned the selection of movies. There was a clash of wills when she wanted to watch a particularly violent action movie. "No."

She glared up at Richard. "My daddy—"

"No." He brought up the PG selections. "You can watch any movie listed here."

"Those are baby movies."

"Harry Potter is pretty scary."

The lower lip was thrust out, she crossed her arms over her chest, but finally nodded. "Okay, I'll watch that."

Richard cued up the first film. He walked away, reflecting that as a paladin her job would be to rob Harry and his friends of their magical powers. Which brought him to the real issue. The child had endured the butchery of her family and only a few days before had witnessed violent death. What was he really accomplishing by censoring her movies? She might be only nine, but her childhood was irrevocably over. Yet as a parental figure he needed to set and maintain boundaries for her behavior. What had happened to her was real, but he could mitigate it by giving her life structure.

"I can try to keep it as normal as possible," he muttered aloud as he brewed a cup of tea in the galley.

"It is never a good sign when you are talking to yourself," Weber said. "What's up?"

"Worrying about Mosi. What have I done to this child by taking her?"

"Probably saved her life. Or at the very least prevented her falling into the hands of those sons of bitches."

"They might never have found her if I hadn't . . . hadn't . . ."

"Cared enough to tell a child she wasn't crazy and that her brother wasn't himself when he committed murder?" His hand gripped Richard's shoulder. "You can only do the best you can. You can't anticipate every outcome."

It was unconscious, driven by the sense of isolation that lay on him like a smothering cloak. Richard leaned into Weber.

Surprisingly, the older man didn't withdraw, but Richard realized he was out of line and straightened abruptly. "Sorry."

Surprise became shock when Weber dropped an arm over his shoulders and held him in place close against his side. "You're lonely."

Richard started to deny it, then hung his head. "Yes. I don't mean to make you uncomfortable."

"You're not." Richard's gaze flew up to Weber's face, but the man was carefully looking the other way and had not released him. Richard felt disoriented. In another circumstance he would have found the embrace tender, even affectionate, but this was Weber. Richard stepped away.

Weber jammed his hands into his pockets. "So how do we get in touch with these generals?"

"Turn up in Turkey without visas for a start." Richard removed the tea bag, tossed it, and tipped half-and-half into his cup. "Though what then . . ." He folded his lips together but couldn't hold back the words. "I lost the sword. How do I protect us? Protect the world?"

Weber drew in a preparatory breath, then slumped.

"Yeah, you've got no idea either," Richard concluded.

Cross ambled up to them. "What are we talking about?"

"Contacting the generals," Richard said.

"Wish you could just whammy us to Turkey the way you do yourself. Then nobody could trace us," Weber said.

"No, you don't," Cross said. "When I travel, I cross realms that would fry your little monkey brains."

The two humans exchanged a glance, and Weber shuddered. Richard didn't blame him. They had rescued a child from one of those realms, and looked through far too many gates and tears in the intervening years. The worlds revealed were scary and most were inimical to human life.

"Don't pick up any hitchhikers," Richard said dryly. "We currently have no way to dispatch them."

"Don't think they won't try. And yeah, that's a problem. Makes me start to wonder if I hitched my wagon to the wrong star" was Cross's snide reply, and there was again that glitter in his eyes that Richard had seen before and that disturbed him more each time he saw it.

"But back to the generals and this cabal . . . fraternity . . . secret society . . . what the hell do I call it? How do I contact them?"

"You announce this plane belongs to Lumina, and someone from the group will show up," Cross said authoritatively. "It's been a long time since we were here, so the people will have changed."

"How long is long?"

"Nineteen twenties."

"So how do we know this group still exists?"

"Guess we'll find out" was the comfortless reply.

FOURTEEN

A touch to his shoulder brought Richard awake. He had reclined his seat to full horizontal and had been deep in a dream where he was trying to explain to Weber why they needed ice cream, and Pamela and Mosi kept walking out a door but never seemed to actually leave. He was instantly awake and looking up into Brook's face.

"Sir, we've got a engine light," the pilot whispered. "I don't think it's anything real serious, but Jerry and I would like to set down at Istanbul rather than Ankara and get it checked."

Richard took the seat back up. "Okay."

"We're about forty minutes out."

Standing, Richard tried to generate a little saliva in his dry mouth. He tasted stale coffee and the ham sandwich he'd made hours before, and his bladder was urgently suggesting he find a toilet. He paused to check on Mosi, who was deeply asleep, one hand tucked under her chin and the blanket pulled up around her ears.

After relieving the pressure, he washed his face and hands, brushed his teeth, and studied himself in the mirror. A razor would be in order. Whatever he was going to face in Istanbul, he'd better not face it looking like a bum. He pulled his garment bag out of the overhead and retreated to the small office at the back of the plane. The electric razor vibrated against his chin and cheeks and forced him to concentrate on something other than the lost sword, the lost company, his lost way. He hoped a splash of aftershave and a clean, pressed suit in an elegant Prince of Wales windowpane in shades of blue, lavender, and gray would make him seem less like a fugitive and more like a man in charge to whomever he was going to meet. And maybe his kempt outward appearance would convince even himself that he wasn't frantically creating plans on the fly.

He had managed to transfer the subsidiaries, but since he had no money to operate them he was going to have to shutter the buildings and furlough the staffs. Which meant they weren't really viable companies; they were just chits in the game he was playing with his rebellious officers, and mostly with Grenier. A game he didn't, as yet, see any way to win.

He shot his sleeves, straightened the pocket handkerchief, and stepped out of the office.

He went up to the cockpit, where Jerry was on the radio with the tower while Brook manned the controls. A voice on the radio: "Say again?"

"This is N zero zero four three nine GA, registered to Lumina Enterprises."

"State your position, aircraft type, and souls on board."

"Nancy zero zero four three nine Gold Apple is a G650 out of Rochester, New York, en route Ankara, eleven on board. Currently twenty miles out from Istanbul Atatürk Airport. We have an engine light."

There was a long silence, then the voice, "State your passengers by name, please."

Jerry shot Richard a look. Richard nodded his assent. "We have Mr. Kenntnis, Mr. Oort, Mr. Cross, Dr.—"

"That's sufficient, GA, you are positively identified. Be advised there is a military helicopter to your west. You are cleared to land on runway . . ."

Richard left to be sure that Mosi was securely buckled up and belted himself in.

As the wheels kissed the runway, Richard saw the military helicopter out his window. It also seemed to be landing, and quite near to them. "The welcome wagon," he muttered to Weber, seated at his side.

"Let's hope they're actually . . . uh . . . welcoming."

They taxied to a stop just outside a private hangar. By the time they had the doors open and the steps down, a man dressed in military uniform, liberally decorated with braid, pins, and badges, was already waiting on the tarmac. From the top step, Richard surveyed him. He looked to be in his late thirties with dark hair tinged faintly with red. Richard said over his shoulder, "Lot of cabbage on that coat."

"Somehow I don't think he's a first lieutenant," Weber muttered back.

Richard pulled himself to his full height, lifted his chin, and descended the stairs. He extended his hand. "Richard Oort, my security chief, Damon Weber."

"General Zafer Marangoz," said the man. "Welcome."

The handshakes concluded, Marangoz asked, "You have Mr. Kenntnis?"

"Yes. He's still aboard. Unfortunately he's . . . unwell. I take it you're . . . ah . . . a representative of the organization we were told to approach?"

"Yes, I am with the Işık. Light," Marangoz added helpfully at Richard's expression.

"Ah," Richard said. "Look, General Marangoz, there's no graceful way to say this. We're in trouble. We're on the run and need a place to go to ground. Can you help us?"

"We know of your troubles. There was a move to have you arrested." He held up a reassuring hand at Richard's expression. "We have handled that. The military still has certain prerogatives in this country. It is probably best you stay in Istanbul tonight while we make arrangements for your travel to Ankara. Cars will be arriving shortly." Marangoz paused, then added in tones of awe, "May I see Mr. Kenntnis?"

"Yes, of course, come aboard."

They reentered the plane. Marangoz gave Mosi a curious but kindly glance, then froze when he saw Kenntnis. "Unchanged," he whispered.

"Excuse me?" Richard asked.

"There are photos of him with Kemal. He is unchanged."

"Yes, well, it's rather hard to explain," Richard began.

The young general gave him a blazing smile. "Do not worry, Mr. Oort, we, more than others, understand he is something more than human. You see, there is a mosaic of him in a villa in Hierapolis, a Roman city next to the modern city of Pamukkale. Perhaps we will stop there en route to Ankara. It is worth seeing."

Richard gazed at Kenntnis. "Yeah," he said slowly. "I'd very much like to see that." He wondered if Kenntnis saw an early image of himself, if it would stir some memory or reaction. It was worth the chance.

There was the sound of car engines outside. "Come, let us be away," Marangoz said.

Brook and Jerry caught them. "What do we do with the plane?" Brook asked.

"I can't afford to refuel it and send you back."

"Who said anything about wanting to go back?" Jerry asked. "I'm sticking with you." Brook nodded.

"Okay, then. Lock it and leave it."

There was bustle and confusion as they prepared to debark. Richard found Brook at his side. "Um . . . my name. It's Knadjian."

"Yes, I know."

"That's Armenian."

"Ah . . . oh," Richard added as the very unpleasant history between Turkey and Armenia came forcibly to mind. "Is this going to be a problem?"

"Not unless they make it one. It's probably a good thing my grandfather isn't here. He wouldn't be polite."

"How about you?"

"I've never been to Armenia. I've been inoculated." He paused for a moment. "And isn't that an example of what we're fighting against anyway?"

"Yeah, I guess that's true." Richard added in an undertone just to himself, "I just wish I felt like we were winning."

It was an unconscionably early hour when Grenier's phone rang. He heaved himself to the side of the bed, groping for the receiver, and knocked it to the floor. Cursing, he rolled out of bed and tried to bend down for the fallen phone. His distended belly made that impossible, and he had to drop to his knees to be able to pick it up. He fumbled with the buttons but got back the buzz of a disconnected line. Grunting with effort, he used the edge of the mattress to return to his feet and checked the time: 3:40 A.M. Then he noticed the red light flashing on the phone, indicating a message.

It was Kenzo, and even with only two words—*Call me*—he sounded extremely put out. Grenier called him. "Should you be calling me at home?" Grenier asked when the CFO answered.

"It doesn't matter now. Richard is out as head of Lumina. He has taken actions that Gold and I believe to be actionable if not criminal." Anger crackled around the words. "In the meantime, we wish you to take over management of the building and personnel in New Mexico."

"What's happened? What has he done?"

"There is no need for you to know the details." The tone was arrogant and dismissive.

"To borrow a phrase of Richard's, I refuse to be treated like a mushroom." Grenier broke the connection.

Smiling, Grenier walked to the kitchen, pulled out a carton of milk, and took a long drink. He mentally kept count. At about the two-minute mark, the phone rang again.

"You hung up on me."

"Yes. I will not assume responsibility without authority."

"And I will only accord you the responsibility appropriate to your level of authority. Accept or don't, but those are the terms."

It wasn't in Grenier's best interests to alienate the CFO. He changed tacks. Suffusing his voice with sympathy, Grenier said, "Richard must have humiliated you rather profoundly for you to be this angry. I've never before heard you lose control. It's not your style."

A sigh gusted across the phone line. "Forgive me, it has been a trying period. I spent part of yesterday and most of the night locked in a storeroom."

"Good God!"

"Richard seems to have been planning this for some time. He's transferred all the subsidiary companies into a new sole proprietorship he created. He didn't attempt to move Lumina. We would have been alerted to that."

"My understanding is that Lumina subsidizes most of those companies," Grenier said.

"Quite true. He will find himself financially underwater in short order, but meanwhile we have lost control of the feeder companies actually doing R&D work." Kenzo paused, then grudgingly continued. "I never thought Oort was terribly bright. What I hadn't realized is that he's cunning."

Oddly, the criticism rankled. "Oh, he's bright." Grenier almost went on to say, *"He played me brilliantly,"* but in the last second he realized such a reminder of his perfidy and his past was perhaps not the wisest move. "It's Richard's insecurities that make him seem vapid."

"So you'll take over governance of the main headquarters?" Kenzo asked, returning to the pressing issue.

"Yes, but you'll need to inform key personnel. They won't take my say-so," Grenier warned Kenzo.

"It will be handled," Kenzo said.

"Quickly?"

"Immediately."

"How are you going to proceed?"

"We're filing suit against Richard, both civilly and criminally, but he's taken the plane and is on his way to Ankara. We've contacted law enforcement in Ankara. They'll be waiting when they touch down. And there is an extradition treaty between the U.S. and Turkey. On a more mundane level, we're withdrawing the offer to purchase Gaia. We simply can't afford it until we get our financial house in order. We'll be in touch. Call me with any problems," Kenzo concluded, and the connection was broken.

Tapping a finger against his front teeth, Grenier considered, then dialed Richard's cell number. "This number is no longer in service," the robot woman informed him. Grenier had a sudden image of an expensive iPhone in a garbage can somewhere in Rochester. He should have expected this. Richard was a policeman. He knew that phones could be used to trace and to locate.

He tried to go back to sleep, but after an hour of tossing and turning, he rose, showered, dressed, and made waffles from scratch, liberally mounding them with blueberries and whipped cream. It was still only six o'clock. He paced, checked the clock. There would be no one at Lumina beyond security and the chef, Franz, until eight, and they needed to get the word. By seven, he couldn't contain his tension and anxiety. He drove to the Range Cafe, where he treated himself to a second breakfast of eggs con queso. The cheese and green chili sat heavy in his gut, so he ate some oatmeal as a stomach settler.

By then two hours had passed, and he felt he could safely assume that word had been given to the Lumina staff. He was certain of it when he entered the lobby and Paulette glared at him. Joseph opened the door to the security office and stared at him with the expression of a man contemplating dog shit on his shoe. Joseph shut the door without uttering a word. Grenier moved to the elevator.

In his office, he gathered up his files and the few personal items that adorned his desk—the crystal paperweight, a pair of antique bookends in the form of an old man seated in an armchair with a book on his knee that supported his reference books.

Grenier still persisted in using a dead tree dictionary and thesaurus over going online. There was just something about the feel and smell of actual books. Some of that was personal preference, some dictated by his role as televangelist. Fundamentalism feared change and advancement and celebrated a golden age embodied by the past, so he had continually attacked technological advancement and atheist science on his show. At its base, though, there was a very mundane reason why he chose paper books over electronic readers—magic played holy hell with high-tech items, so there wasn't much point keeping them around if you were a sorcerer.

He lifted the stack of books, then decided it was beneath his dignity to lug them. He would send someone to pick them up. When he stepped off the elevator on the sixth floor, Jeannette's expression was stiff, frozen. "Mr. Grenier," she said formally, but her eyes revealed her despair, resentment, and contempt for him. Grenier decided in that moment whom he would assign as pack mule.

"Jeannette, please go down to my office and bring up my books.

And I'd like Chinese for lunch. Bring me a menu from Chow's. In fact, I'd like you to start a menu book for the office." Issuing orders to the haughty personal assistant felt very good.

She ducked her head and momentarily pressed her lips together. "Very good, Mr. Grenier. Are you planning on firing Franz?"

"No, and while I enjoy haute cuisine, I have an eclectic palate, and I want variety."

He went into the office. The faint scent of Richard's aftershave, Stefano Ricci Classic, still lingered in the room. He moved to the piano, folded back the lid, and gently touched a key. *Where are you?* he wondered.

He moved to the broad granite desk, placed his paperweight and the bookends, then took the chair. Because of Richard's rather diminutive height, it was set too high, and his stomach pressed against the edge of the desk. He grabbed the handle and lowered the chair, adjusted the back, laced his fingers on his belly, and surveyed the room. Contentment washed through him.

FIFTEEN

THEY were taken to a hotel in the old city. It was a four-story sandstone building that wore its age like a dowager wears jewels and dignity. There was no elevator, just worn stone stairs. The mullioned windows held thick glass, and magnificent carpets covered the floors. On one wood-paneled wall there was a fireplace with a hood of beaten copper and set all around with magnificent painted tiles in shades of blue and green like peacock tails. The desk clerk, a young woman whose head scarf was a frame for the perfect oval of her face and her pale green eyes, greeted them and handed out keys. "There will be tea in the breakfast room on the upper floor. Once you are refreshed, please come and be welcome."

Richard counted keys and realized there wasn't one for Mosi. "My ward will also need a room. Next to mine," Richard said. More than ever Richard wished he had a woman in the party. He hated to leave the child alone, but his sister's warning hung ominously in his mind. "And Mr. Kenntnis will share a room with me."

"Hey, Mr. Oort, can Mr. Kenntnis bunk in with me?" Ron Trout asked abruptly. "I've been monitoring something, and I'd like to keep watching it."

"Uh . . . sure." He turned to the receptionist. "Then I guess we don't need another room."

Only Richard, Mosi, Weber, and the two pilots actually had luggage. The four scientists, Cross, and Kenntnis went right to the breakfast room, while a couple of young men in bellmen's uniforms carried the bags up to the rooms. Weber quickly intervened before one of the men could pick up his big duffel bag o' guns as he called it. They didn't need that problem in addition to all their other problems.

Richard noted that Mosi's brows were drawn tight together. He fell into step with her as they went up the final flight of stairs to the topmost floor. "How are you doing, kiddo?" Richard asked softly. "I know things have been kinda crazy for the past week."

Mosi looked up at him. "Where are we?"

He started to reach for his phone, then realized it was in a Dumpster outside the bank in Rochester, and the burner phone he had bought didn't have Internet access. "There's a computer in the lobby. After we have some tea I'll get online and show you. We're in a very large country called Turkey that is the crossroads between Europe and Asia."

"Okay." She paused, then glanced up at him. "We're a long way from home, aren't we?"

"Yes. Yes, we are." He risked it. He put an arm around her shoulders and hugged her briefly against his side. He was gratified when her arm slipped around his waist and hugged him back.

"It is bad for Navajo people to travel beyond the edges of the four sacred mountains without protection." She had once again taken on the cadence of a different person. Someone older and rigid.

"Who told you that?" Richard asked.

"Grandfather. We didn't go to a singer and get me special turquoise to protect me."

"Weber and I can do that."

"You're not a mountain."

"No, I'm a man. That's more useful than a mountain . . . or turquoise."

Her nose wrinkled and she twisted her mouth a bit, then a small smile broke out. "I think my daddy would think that too. Sometimes he got mad at Grandfather over the old ways. Grandfather didn't want Abel to have a computer." Her expression became bleak. "But he was right about that, wasn't he? So maybe he was right about the turquoise too?"

Richard caught her hands. "No, Mosi, rocks and mountains don't have minds. They can't think or do things. Men did things to those computers so they became like windows, and it will be people who stop them. We'll talk more about this later, okay?"

She nodded and ran away up the stairs. Richard followed, suddenly a lot more worried about cultural differences and how what Mosi would learn at Lumina would challenge her beliefs.

The breakfast room was basically a sunroom with windows on three sides. Richard looked out at the graceful minarets and the dome of the famous Blue Mosque. Beyond it bulked Hagia Sophia. Through another window, sunlight danced on the rich blue of the Bosphorus. Richard noted the small mosque nestled right next to the hotel. He thought he'd better warn Mosi about the *adhān*, which would likely ring through their rooms at various times of day. A plate of cookies and baklava, already seriously depleted, was set out on a table, and the receptionist was pouring a pale golden tea into clear glasses. Richard accepted his and took a sip. It was apple flavored and delicious.

Mosi sniffed hers suspiciously, then tried a sip, and gave him another brief smile. "It's good."

"Yes, it is." Richard thanked the young woman, then turned back to Mosi. "Why don't you try one of those pastries? The one with the honey on it. You'll like it." She went off to the table, and the scientists made room for her. Richard noticed that she chose to sit next to Kenntnis.

He moved to a window and stared out over the city. Weber and Cross joined him. "So what now, boss?" the homeless god asked.

"We wait for our general to turn back up, and head for Ankara tomorrow. I want you to do some recon. Since we filed a flight plan, they know where we are. See if there's activity near to us."

"I'm thinking we better pull watches," Weber said.

"Agreed. Brook and Jerry can help. They're both ex-military."

"That'll make the night a bit easier."

Richard looked at Cross. "Without the sword, we're depending on you for protection. Guns can handle human followers, but if something else shows up . . ." Richard's voice trailed away.

"I'll do my best. But I've always viewed self-sacrifice as overrated." And with that Cross walked out of the breakfast room.

Richard studied Weber's grim expression. "So, you found that rather disturbing too?" he asked.

"Oh, yeah."

"I don't want to leave Mosi alone, but for obvious reasons I can't put her in a room with . . . well, you understand. You have anything that can help with that?"

"Yeah, gotta small camera that links back to a handheld monitor."

"Are we sure that is any less creepy than having a nine-year-old girl sleeping in a room with any of us?"

"No, but what's our alternative?"

Richard sighed and rubbed at his forehead. "Okay, set it up."

Weber's eyes scanned the table with the scientists, pilots, one little girl, and an alien gathered around a now-empty plate. "One last thing. How are we going to feed this mob? Not sure I want to have us all troop off to dinner."

"We'll order takeout. Have some of the hotel staff bring it back. Eat dinner up here. Why don't you find out if anybody has food allergies or any particular dislikes?"

"Having heard these guys talk in that meeting . . . that should only take an hour or two," Weber said grumpily, but he moved off to the group.

Richard desperately wanted to slip away. To have a few minutes of privacy in his hotel room. To try and mentally prepare for what might come, and try to plan. But he couldn't walk out on Mosi and leave her with strangers. Not that he was all that familiar to her, but she knew him better than any of the others. For one moment he wondered if some nemesis had seized the sword because there were now two paladins. If somehow the universe had a perverted sense of fair play and decided two paladins and the weapon gave an unfair advantage to Lumina. He studied Kenntnis's dark face, the eyes alight with those whirling lights. He could imagine the man's scornful rejoinder to such a suggestion.

Eddie sidled up to Richard. "We gotta go buy some underwear and socks at least or ain't gonna be pretty in another day." Eddie rolled an eye toward Trout.

Richard pressed a hand against his brow. "Yeah, okay, but make it fast. And for God's sake stay together." Eddie nodded and returned to the table.

The receptionist proved to be as helpful as she was beautiful. She marked on a map where there was a shopping district. It was near the famous Grand Bazaar, and Chen looked wistful as he studied the tourist map. "That would be a sight to see," he said.

"Maybe when we're not running for our lives," Richard said dryly.

"Ah, I take your point."

And indeed the scientists surprised him by returning in record time. While they were gone, Richard talked with the receptionist about dinner plans, and she recommended a restaurant that specialized in Anatolian cuisine. Even better, she ordered for them and sent one of the bellmen off to collect the food. There was an amazing lamb stew and a kind of bread that looked like a puffed-up pillow, a seafood chowder, also a selection of salads consisting of shredded tomatoes, cucumbers, and spices Richard couldn't identify. Dessert was again a honeyed pastry. The staff had thrown open the windows in the breakfast area to catch the evening breezes. They carried the scent of the sea and the cry of gulls. While they were eating, there was a burst of static from the loudspeakers on the mosque next door, and then the muezzin's call blasted through the room.

"Gonna be fun to try and sleep through that," Trout grumbled.

Mosi leaned in close to Richard. "That was pretty."

"Yes. It is."

"What was it?"

"The Islamic call to prayer."

The straight nose wrinkled. "Islamic, that's like Muslim, right?"

"Yes."

"Aren't they bad people?"

"No worse than any other people."

"Who's their god again?"

"Allah."

"There are a lot of gods, aren't there? Navajo gods and white people's gods." She looked over at Chen. "Are there Chinese people's gods too?" Richard felt himself stiffening. Eventually he and the girl had to have the conversation about the true nature of so-called gods, but not when she was nine, and not when her life had been so utterly disrupted.

"Not as you would describe it," the scientist said with a soft laugh.

She looked at Richard. "Which white god do you pray to?"

"I don't, Mosi."

"Pray?"

"Believe in gods."

She surprised him by looking pleased. "Does that mean we don't have to go to church?" The men gathered around the table chuck-led, and Richard gave a shout of laughter.

"That's exactly what it means."

"Oh, good."

Eddie leaned in to the little girl. "And just so you don't think he's weird—none of us believe in God."

"Why not?"

Eddie opened his mouth, but Richard intervened. "Maybe this isn't quite the time for a theological discussion."

"Oh. Right. Yeah."

After dinner, people began to drift off to their rooms. Mosi was yawning. Richard took her to her room.

"I'm right next door. Call me if you need me." He waved at the small monitor. "And one of us will be watching to make sure you're okay."

"Okay."

"Don't forget to brush your teeth."

"Okay."

"Sleep tight, and there's going to be that call . . . song . . . again, only really early in the morning, okay?"

He started to leave, but Mosi grabbed his hand. "Are the monsters coming?"

Richard hesitated and decided against lying. "Not right away. Go to sleep now. And lock your door."

———— ⊱⋅⊰ ————

Gold showed up that afternoon. Grenier had not been told, did not expect him, and he immediately saw it for what it was.

"Checking up on me already?" Grenier made no effort to hide his annoyance, and it threw the chubby lawyer off balance.

"No, no, just wanting to see how you're settling in. Everybody treating you well?" Gold took a surreptitious glance around the office.

"Richard was too familiar with underlings. They resent the fact I'm exerting appropriate authority, but they'll come around." He paused, then asked, "I'm curious, did Dagmar go with Richard?"

"No, apparently he locked her up too."

"Really? I find that strange. She's always been very devoted and loyal to Richard," Grenier said.

"Well, maybe she realized that he was destroying the company."

"Perhaps, but I would strongly recommend that you keep a somewhat closer eye on her going forward."

"Thank you for you input, but we've worked with Dagmar for a long time. I think we know her a little better than you."

"Would you like a cup of coffee?" Grenier asked.

"Please."

Grenier keyed the intercom. "Jeannette, do come in and prepare a coffee for Mr. Gold." The woman marched in, her lips set in a tight line. "What would you like?" Grenier asked Gold. "We're trying to get Jeannette up to speed as a barista, though I may have to pull in one of the younger girls. Jeannette just doesn't seem to be catching on."

"If you'd like my resignation, Mr. Grenier . . ."

"No, no. I quite enjoy having you working for me." He knew she got the barbed reply and enjoyed the hurt that flared briefly in her eyes. There had always been an undercurrent of contempt in her dealings with him. Payback was so sweet.

Gold asked for a latte with a double shot. It took longer than it should, but eventually Jeannette brought him the cup topped with frothing milk. As she handed it over, she blurted out, "Do we know anything about Mr. Oort?"

"That it's none of your concern," Grenier snapped.

Jeannette cast him an absolutely poisonous look and stalked out of the office.

Gold reacted to the look. "Maybe you ought to fire her."

"No, the younger employees look to Jeannette and Joseph for

guidance. Once I bring those two to heel, the rest will fall in line." Grenier's prosthetic hand clenched.

"I wonder why she isn't quitting," Gold mused.

Grenier decided Gold really had little understanding of human nature. "She thinks she can spy on me and limit my influence. It makes her feel important to defend the office until Richard's return. Eventually she'll realize he's gone for good, despair will set in, and then I'll have her."

"Damn, you sound like a shrink."

"There's not a lot of difference between a therapist and a minister," Grenier replied. He paused, then added, "Kenzo didn't give me much detail about what happened in Rochester. You do have the little girl, right?"

"No, Richard took her," Gold replied. He blew noisily across the top of his coffee and took a sip. "Mmm, that's good."

"We've lost control of *both* paladins?"

The lawyer shrugged. "It doesn't really matter since the sword is gone."

"You mean Richard took it."

"No, I mean it's gone. As in poof, vanished."

The lawyer's tone was matter-of-fact, almost blasé. Grenier jerked upright, his breath going short, rage at the man's denseness settling like a choking weight in his chest. But more than rage was the bone-numbing fear that gripped him. "Gone? Do you have any idea . . . This is a disaster."

Two years ago, he had promised to deliver the sword to his masters. He had failed, and rather than face the judgment of the Old Ones, Grenier had fled to Richard for protection. Protection afforded by the sword, the only weapon that could kill an Old One. And now it was gone. Grenier felt the cold chill of vulnerability. Agitation pulled him to his feet, and he came around from behind the desk to loom over the other man.

"We have no weapon! No paladin to wield the weapon! No defense!" His voice rose with each word.

"Against what? The gate *you* opened is closed—"

"And many, many things came through. Many are still here. Richard didn't kill them all. Tears are still opening. We need the sword and a paladin."

"Well, we don't have either." Gold's tone was testy.

"We've got to make another weapon. Weren't people working on that?"

"Yes, and Richard took them too."

"Then we need to locate Richard! Now!"

"We're working on it, but the Turkish authorities are proving to be . . . elusive."

"Why?"

"Fuck if I know."

"Do we know why he went to Turkey?" Grenier asked.

"Not a clue." Gold finished his coffee. "Look, I just came to check on you. See if you needed anything—"

"I need the sword and that child!"

"This is getting really tiresome. What part of *we don't have them* aren't you getting? Your job is to help us put this company back on its feet financially. That's it. That's all."

Grenier paced. His gut hurt and he realized it was terror, bowel-loosening terror. "We need a way to compel Richard to return. Get those scientists working again. Is Pamela with him?"

"No, not according to flight records."

"We need to seize his family. And Weber too—"

Gold was on his feet, blocking Grenier's perambulations. "Now just a minute. Do you know how crazy you're sounding right now? We're not thugs or criminals. Richard is filling that role quite nicely. Imprisoning us, stealing the plane, transferring companies in secret. We're requesting he be extradited. It will take a while—"

"We don't have a while."

Gold stepped back, glared at Grenier. "You can be replaced just as quickly as we put you in place."

Grenier forced himself to breathe. He closed his eyes, plans churning through his mind. It would almost choke him to do it, but he needed to mollify the other man. Play the supplicant. "Yes, yes, you're right. Sorry. I've allowed my own fears to take control. Please, forgive me."

"Sure. Okay." Gold headed for the office door. "Well, glad we had a chance to talk. We'll be in touch. Let us know if you need anything."

The heavy wood-and-glass door whispered closed behind him. Grenier sat down on the padded piano bench. It was clear that the Lumina lawyer was going to immediately report to Kenzo that Grenier was unstable and needed to be replaced. Grenier had to move against them before that happened, and he had only one play left—throw himself on the mercy of his former masters and their acolytes. Mercy wasn't their long suit, but he had something to trade. The knowledge that the paladin had been disarmed.

Heaving himself to his feet, he waddled quickly to the desk, grabbed up the phone, and started to dial. He then looked at the door. Pictured Jeannette spying, reporting back to Richard. He hung up the phone and left the office. He would call Alexander Titchen, but from the safety of a pay phone.

Chapter SIXTEEN

RICHARD handed off Mosi's monitor to Jerry, who was on first watch, then went to his room, but he was unable to settle. Finally he changed out of his suit and into jeans with a leather jacket over his button-down shirt to hide the pistol. He then slipped out the door. Jerry was just making a sweep down the hall. Richard pressed himself against a wall until the pilot had moved on. He then hurried down the stairs to the lobby. A shadowy figure rose out of an armchair near the elaborately tiled fireplace. Reflexively Richard reached for his gun, then relaxed when he recognized the big form.

"Thought you might be restless," Weber said.

"You know me too well."

"You're not going out—"

Desperate, Richard interrupted. "I've got to. I feel like I can't breathe—"

And was in turn interrupted when Weber held up a restraining hand and said, "*Not alone.* Come on. I'll go with you. Wouldn't mind a look at this city, however briefly."

They stepped through the front door and tensed when a figure moved out of the shadows. It was a young man in the green uniform of the Turkish army and carrying a machine gun. He smiled and nodded. Richard glanced around and realized there were more soldiers lurking at points all around the hotel and even several on the roof.

The young man saluted. "Lieutenant Kartal. General Marangoz had the hotel cleared of all guests save your party and thought it best to provide security."

Weber and Richard exchanged glances. "I'll go tell Jerry we've got security outside so nobody panics and shoots somebody," Weber said, and reentered the building.

"Please thank the general and tell him how much I appreciate his actions and having you here," Richard said.

The young man leaned in and lowered his voice. "These others," he indicated the guards. "Just soldiers. But me . . . I am a member of Işık." The pride was evident in his voice. "During the troubles two years ago, we had more than a few incursions. Djinns, *nasnas*, demons. We know what's at stake. We will allow no harm to come to Kenntnis."

Weber returned.

"You are going for a walk?" asked Kartal.

"Yes. If you think it's safe," Richard answered.

"Stay in the central area, and you should be fine. But you should go and look. This is a beautiful city. It's a shame you must leave tomorrow."

The two men walked off. The air smelled of exotic spices, jasmine, and the sea. Windows were open on this warm September night, and there was the sound of voices, televisions, and from one apartment jazzy and upbeat music with a Middle Eastern tonal structure.

They walked through an oval-shaped park and came upon an Egyptian obelisk. Richard stopped and studied the red stone with its bas-relief pedestal. There was a plaque explaining that this was the Obelisk of Theodosius and that it stood in the center of what had been the Hippodrome built by Emperor Septimius Severus. Richard slowly turned in place, trying to picture the track, the racing chariots, pounding hooves, the screaming crowds.

"Damn. Shit load of history here," Weber said as he finished reading. "Makes you realize how young America really is."

They walked on. Weber asked, "Are you one of those people who reads every bit of info in a museum?"

"Guilty."

"Thought you might be."

"Why?"

"Always thought you were too bright to be a cop."

"I'm the dumb bunny of the family," Richard said, trying to keep it light. He hunched a shoulder. "I loved it," he added quietly.

"Being a cop or being a dumb bunny?" Weber teased.

Richard cast him a mock frown. "Being a cop. I wish—" He broke off. "But it does no good to repine."

"Repine," Weber repeated. He shot Richard a quick smile. "Yeah, real dumb."

They had to wait to cross the street until an electric trolley had gone sparking and rattling past. At this hour of the night, car traffic was sparse. They found themselves in the gardens in front of the Blue Mosque. Behind them and across another street was Hagia Sophia. The massive dome dominated the night sky, and the four minarets that surrounded the enormous building seemed oddly out of place, built as they were out of nonmatching stone. Standing between the two monumental buildings, Richard felt even smaller than usual.

Which had probably been the intent of the builders—to stress the insignificance of man.

"Is that a mosque too?" Weber asked, nodding toward the looming bulk.

"No, not anymore. It began as a church, then became a mosque when Constantinople fell to the Muslims; now it's a museum by order of Atatürk. He didn't want it to become a source for religious conflict."

"Huh," Weber grunted. "Yeah, he does sound like he was one of ours."

"Of course, the current government is talking about turning it back into a mosque."

"One step forward, two steps back."

"Sometimes it feels hopeless," Richard said with a sigh.

Weber slapped him on the back. "Come on, leave it. Drop the worry. At least for tonight."

They moved deeper into the garden. There were a few people about, and Richard and Weber gave them a careful look, but they appeared to be just tourists doing exactly what Richard and Weber were doing.

A large reflecting pool lay between them and the exquisite building with its six minarets and the innumerable domes climaxing in the massive dome at the back of the building. Colored lights played across the gray stone exterior, creating the illusion it was actually blue.

"Wow," Weber said.

Richard just nodded. Abruptly, fountains in the pool shot water high into the air. Lights hit the cascading water, turning it to frothing lace, and they were viewing the mosque through a gauzy veil. Droplets of water dampened Richard's face. It felt wonderful in the sultry heat.

"I wish I could visit this city in a time of peace," Richard said quietly.

"Pretty romantic place, isn't it?" Weber's voice came from behind him, and there was an odd husky catch on the words.

Richard glanced back. "Yes. It is." He stepped away from the edge of the pool and walked down a pathway lined with flower beds. Weber fell into step with him. His hands were thrust deep into his pockets, and he frowned down at the pathway. "What's wrong?" Richard asked.

"I'm working up to something. Just bear with me, okay?" The tone was testy.

"Okay."

They made their way along the side of the building and came upon an entrance leading into the courtyard. The gates were open. "It's our only chance. Shall we risk it?" Richard asked.

"Sure, what's the worst that can happen? We get thrown out."

"Or arrested."

"You've got a general in your pocket."

"True."

They hurried through the archway and found themselves in a enormous space with stone tiles underfoot and a breathtaking view of the domes and four of the minarets. In the center of the courtyard stood the hexagonal ablution fountain. The splash of falling water echoed off the walls and the colonnaded walkways, sounding almost like bells. Seagulls, crying like lost women, soared around the spires of the minarets, splashes of white against a star-studded sky.

"So strange . . . how much magnificent architecture, music, art has been created in celebration of something that, at its core, is a lie," Richard said softly.

"The world would have been a poorer place if we didn't have this," Weber said, indicating the building. "Or Notre-Dame."

"And Mozart oratorios and Bach cantatas. But then there's the flip side. Wouldn't we have been better off without the Crusades, and jihad, and the Inquisition, and al Qaeda?"

"And Pat Robertson being wrong about every prediction he ever made," Weber added with a chuckle.

"Comic relief has its place."

They left the courtyard, their footsteps echoing off the stone. They walked down the opposite side of the street and came across a hookah café that was still open. There was one table with bright young things of both sexes, but mostly it was men drinking and taking hits off the water pipes. The room buzzed with low-voiced conversations, and gurgles and bubbles as smoke was drawn through the water. Competing scents of flavored tobaccos intertwined with the velvet smell of Turkish coffee. It should have been horrible, but instead it was rich and exotic.

"I could use a beer," Weber confessed. "And I still smoke. When I'm not around you."

"Oh, what the hell. This may be my last chance to go wild."

"Hope not," Weber threw back over his shoulder as he led the way into the café. "If you do decide to let your hair down, I'll have your back."

"You always have."

The café appeared to be populated almost entirely by locals. There was one young punk couple sporting tattoos, speaking German, and trading kisses in a corner. Both male and female eyes lingered on Richard as they were led to a corner table.

"Does it ever get to you? The way people look at you?" Weber asked.

"Yes, but in this case it's because of my coloring."

"And your looks. You have to know how handsome you are," Weber said.

Richard was startled by Weber's words. Weber had always teased him about how Richard broke hearts just by existing, but Weber had never said anything quite so overt. He was saved from answering— an answer that could only make him appear insincerely humble or a coxcomb—when a waiter brought over a hookah. The base was made of stained glass covered with flowing script and feather patterns. Weber selected an apple-flavored tobacco and ordered a beer. Richard ordered a gin and tonic.

"I've never seen you drink before," Weber remarked.

"Booze gets me into trouble," Richard answered, but didn't elaborate. He didn't really want to admit to Weber that when he got drunk he usually ended up in somebody's bed, and worse.

"So why risk it?"

"Because after this fabulously crapstatic few days I could use one."

They sat in silence while Weber drew in slow hits on the hookah and downed his beer. He ordered another. Richard sipped his drink. By the time he'd finished, Weber had downed a third beer. Richard indicated the hose. Weber handed it over, and Richard inhaled a lungful of smoke while the bubbles grumbled and mumbled. Coughing, his eyes streaming, Richard croaked out, "I thought the water would make it smoother."

Weber pounded him on the back and chuckled.

Another sip of the g&t soothed Richard's throat. "Okay, not trying that again."

Weber indicated his empty glass. "Another?" he asked while he waved down the waiter and ordered a fourth beer.

"Better not. Booze and I have had a rocky relationship."

"You said that before." He pushed. "What does that mean?"

"That I'm likely to wake up wondering why my shorts are in the freezer—"

Weber chuckled. "That sounds kind of fun."

"It was. Until it . . . wasn't," Richard said. He stared down at the bottom of his glass and tried not to remember a night of pain and humiliation. Richard eyed Weber's fallen soldiers and added, "And maybe you should slow down if you're going to watch my back."

"I can do that and still gather a little liquid courage."

"Okay. What does that mean?"

Richard was presented with Weber's profile. "I ever tell you why my marriage ended?"

"No, and it wasn't any of my business so I didn't ask." Richard shrugged. "I assumed the usual reasons cops' marriages go bad—long hours, stress, bringing the job home while being unable to talk about the job once you bring it home."

"That was part of it." Weber paused, chewed on his lower lip, then added, "We also had a really shitty sex life. She said I was like a fucking rodeo rider. Nine seconds and off."

"Okay," Richard said slowly. "A little TMI. And you're telling me this, why? Maybe I *better* have another drink." He waved down the waiter.

"Carol was my second wife. I got married for the first time right after I went into the army. Partly because it's what you do when you get out of college, right? And partly because it made it easy to avoid going off whoring when we were on leave. Came home on leave to discover she'd been screwing the lawyer preparing the divorce papers. Then I got to avoid whoring 'cause I could say I was depressed over the divorce. I did one more tour after my ROTC obligation was over, then I got out, joined APD, got married again. Life goes on. Another marriage bites the dust. Then you fucking turn up."

"I didn't think I was that much trouble."

"Oh, you were, and not just because of Lumina and monsters and all the rest of the shit." Weber sucked down another lungful of smoke and exhaled slowly, watching the streamers of smoke undulate in the air in front of his face. Finally he asked, "You want to know why I asked for that transfer to the Mesa del Sol substation after that actor came by the precinct looking for you?"

The drinks arrived before Richard could answer. He gulped down a mouthful and said harshly, "Because you found out I'm a fag and that disgusted you."

"No, and don't talk like that." Weber drained half his glass.

"Because once I knew . . . how you were—" He broke off and looked away. Took a deep breath. "It was too much of a temptation."

Richard couldn't tell if his head was spinning from the gin or what he'd just heard. "Excuse me?" He shook his head, took another mouthful of gin. Swallowed. "But you never. . . . Are you saying . . . ?"

Weber finally looked at him. He didn't look happy. He looked like a man in emotional agony. "Yeah," he said shortly.

Richard stood, tossed money on the table. "Let's get out of here."

They returned to the street. They walked side by side, not looking at each other.

"I have really good gaydar. How could I . . . did I . . . miss this?"

"'Cause I spent years in the army developing my gay camo."

"Oh." Hesitantly, Richard asked, "Did you . . . Have you . . . ever?"

Fortunately Weber understood without Richard having to elaborate. "Maybe."

"That's not something you're usually unsure about." Richard risked a quick glance at Weber's profile. The older man's jaw was set.

"It is if you're blind drunk."

"Oh. The old so-how-drunk-was-I-last-night? dodge."

"You gotta understand. When I was in the service, Don't Ask, Don't Tell hadn't been repealed, and you hear the taunts. You join in for protection. Eventually it gets buried so deep that you almost convince yourself you're not really . . . like that."

They were back at the obelisk. A late moon was starting to rise. Half of Weber's face was in high relief, the other side in shadow. Tentatively, Richard reached out and touched Weber's jaw. His hand was grabbed, fingers crushed between Weber's.

"I'm sorry," he started to say, but Weber pressed his lips against Richard's palm. "Damon, not here," Richard said warningly.

His hand was dropped and they resumed their walk back to the hotel. "Let's go to your room," Richard said when they were in the lobby.

"You need to get some sleep," Weber said, reverting to his protective role.

"No. In the midst of what have been a monumentally horrible few days . . . well, right now I'm happy. And I'm going to spend a few hours enjoying the feeling." He twined his fingers through Weber's.

"Are we . . . ?"

"Maybe." Richard gave him a fond smile. "Depends on how drunk you are."

Weber glared down at him. "If you think four beers has me more than just pleasantly buzzed—"

"Brag, brag." He couldn't control the impulse. He lightly touched Weber's lips with his fingertips. "Come on."

Up the stairs and into the room. "I'll be right back. I just need to check on Mosi."

He tapped on Jerry's door. The grizzled pilot came to the door dressed in boxers and already holding the monitor. "All quiet. You know everything on the TV is in Turkish?"

"Fancy that."

Richard checked the camera. It showed the child soundly asleep in her bed.

Richard went to Weber's room and found the door slightly ajar. Inside, he shrugged out of his jacket and shed the shoulder rig and Browning. "Now, where were we?"

"At the point where I'm scared shitless." Weber folded his arms across his chest, the ultimate protective stance.

Richard almost said *me too*, but he bit back the words. Weber was scared enough without Richard laying his emotional baggage on him. Almost six years before, Richard had been raped. His injuries, coupled with his humiliation and fear it would happen again, had left him impotent. Just thinking about sex with someone of either gender left him with the shakes. Rhiana's beauty and his fleeting arousal had opened a physical gate, and then Angela's love had begun to ease the psychological block, but Richard had wondered if he would ever again be able to contemplate true intimacy with anyone, much less a man. Weber had aroused Richard's interest from the moment they had met, but now they were at the moment of truth. Would his demons rise up and wreck everything?

And of course there was a ghost hovering over the moment. *Angela.* She had loved him, but Richard couldn't reciprocate. Ultimately they had fought, and he had sent her away to meet her death. Richard rubbed at his jaw, remembering when Weber's fist had crashed against it in blame and anger. Would Weber also think of Angela this night? Relationships were concentric, interlocking circles constantly jostling and affecting each other.

He studied Weber's face even though he knew every feature by heart. Richard had imagined it would take someone calm and assertive, probably older, to calm his fears. Now he was faced with Weber, who was definitely older but also horribly nervous and unsure. The older man's trepidation gave Richard confidence. Richard drew in a long, shuddering breath. Right now only one relationship lay before him. It deserved his total focus. *No doubts, no regrets, no fears.* At least not tonight.

"Why are you looking at me like that?" Weber asked.

"Because up till now I've always had to sneak my looks, and because you're handsome." He laid a hand on Weber's cheek, felt the prickle of stubble against his palm, and the acne scars.

"No, I'm not."

Richard kicked off his shoes. Weber awkwardly pulled off his cowboy boots, then Richard took Weber's hand and tugged him until they were sitting side by side on the bed. He gently caressed the nape of Weber's neck.

Then Richard kissed him. There was that inevitable moment of awkwardness where noses bump, and nobody's quite sure which direction to tilt his head. Weber clutched at Richard's shoulders, mouth hard, lips closed. Richard lightly outlined Weber's lips with the tip of his tongue, testing the boundaries. The man made a sound that was part moan, part sob, and part curse, and then Weber gripped Richard hard enough to crack his ribs, send pain flaring through his stitches and then his mouth softened. Their tongues met, and the back of Richard's head exploded.

They lingered, just kissing. Weber tasted of beer and tobacco and a rich taste that was all his own. They were definitely going to have to talk about the smoking, because that was not a taste Richard loved. Weber's hand was pressed hard against Richard's back. Eventually the older man found the courage to slide his hand down, pull Richard's shirttail out of his jeans, and slip his hand beneath the material. The heat off Weber's skin was an ember against Richard's flesh. His sigh became a moan.

He judged it was time, so Richard laid a firm hand in the middle of Weber's chest and pushed him down on the bed. Richard slowly unbuttoned Weber's shirt and ran his fingers through the hair on his chest. There were a few gray hairs among the brown, and it was appropriately masculine. Crisp and curly against his fingertips and not too sparse, but without enough fur to qualify as a bear. Richard was glad. He wasn't all that fond of the new aesthetic in gay culture.

Since he was fair to the point of albinism, Richard's chest was almost bare, and what hair he had was virtually invisible. He hoped Weber wouldn't mind. Richard bent and slowly kissed his way from the hollow at the base of Weber's throat, finding the musky smell and salty taste of the man's sweat intoxicating as he moved down to the waistband of Weber's trousers. Weber's back arched and he gave a sharp gasp. An erection urgent and painfully hard pressed against Richard's jeans. He also wasn't all that well endowed, another area of insecurity, and Richard paused.

The security chief grabbed the front of Richard's shirt and worked with clumsy, desperate fingers at the buttons, and succeeded only in tearing one off in his awkward haste. Richard's breath caught in the back of his throat and he felt his erection softening. Richard fought down the panic. This was Weber. He was scared too. Richard's heartbeat slowed, his breath steadied, and he caught Weber's hands between his.

"Hey, hey," Richard said softly. "Slow down. We've got all the time in the world."

"That's a bit of a lie, isn't it?" Weber grunted.

"Okay, but we've got tonight." He loosened Weber's belt. "And I'm reputed to be pretty good at this. Or at least I used to be."

"I'm told it's sort of like riding a bicycle."

"That's a terrible analogy."

"Well, I could have come up with worse, like falling off a log or . . . or . . ." Weber's voice was jumping with tension and arousal as Richard slid the older man's pants down over his hips.

"You're babbling." Richard sat back on his heels. "Yep, boxers. I had you pegged right." Weber's erection was powerfully evident, and Richard's body responded.

"What's wrong with boxers?"

"Nothing. They're the conventional, conservative choice."

"They're comfortable. I like to let the boys breathe. You brief snobs."

"And how would you know?"

"'Cause I've had to cut clothes off you how many times when you've been shot, stabbed, clawed—"

"So why are you taking so long now?"

After that they pretty much stopped talking. And Richard discovered that Weber was right—some things really did just come back to you.

⋄━◈━⋄

Much later, Richard leaned on an elbow and watched Weber sleep. He started to slip out of bed, but the movement woke Weber. The older man scrubbed at his face. "Hey. Must have fallen asleep. Sorry."

"It's okay. Thought I better get back to my own room."

Weber grabbed his wrist and pulled him close. "Don't go."

"It'll be dawn soon."

"Are you ashamed?"

"Oh, hell no," Richard said. "I just want to make sure you have time to . . . well, process all . . . this before other people . . . know."

"I've processed it just fine."

"And?"

"It's nicer when you're not so drunk that you can't remember much." The corners of Weber's eyes crinkled.

Richard leaned down and kissed him gently. "I've always loved the way you can smile with just your eyes."

"Before you go, I want to ask you something."

"Okay." Richard settled back, his head on Weber's shoulder.

"There was one point . . . last night when you seemed . . . scared. Did I do—"

Richard laid a hand across the older man's mouth. "No, you didn't do anything, and yes, I was afraid, but only for a moment because it was you and I knew I didn't have to be afraid."

"Something happened. What?"

So Richard told him because he didn't want any lies or secrets between them. It was all laid out, about how sex had been his drug of choice, about Drew and the Russians, the rape and the aftermath.

"You're looking quite fierce," Richard said softly.

"Yeah," Weber growled. "I want to find that asshole and kill him."

"I've had a lot of time to think about that night. I've come to realize that Drew was probably freaked out by what had happened. So he panicked and handled it badly. If he'd taken care of me, gotten me to a doctor instead of dumping me like so much trash, I probably would have ended up feeling pathetically grateful to him. And I wouldn't have met Sergeant McGowan. I wouldn't have become a cop . . ." Richard paused. "And I wouldn't have met you."

"Okay, I won't kill him, but I still want to punch him out."

"I took care of Drew. I wrecked his company."

"Good." Weber touched him between the brows. "What? You're looking upset."

"I've discovered I can be a very vengeful person, Damon. It's a side of me that I don't particularly like."

"Sometimes the assholes just deserve it."

"Maybe. But I don't want to become one too while I dish out their deserts—justified or otherwise."

Richard slipped out of bed and pulled on his jeans, slipped his feet into his loafers. He stuffed his socks into his jacket pockets, inspected the abused shirt, and settled for just carrying it along with the holstered gun. He headed for the door.

"Hey," Weber called. Richard paused, looked back inquiringly. "You were right."

"About what?"

"You are pretty damn good at this."

The muezzin's call began. The haunting sound stabbed him to the heart, and Richard suddenly felt very lonely and, like Mosi, very far from home. He longed to climb back into the bed with Weber and forget about Lumina, the sword, Old Ones, everything but this man and this moment. But Mosi deserved better, so he squared his shoulders. "You're not so bad yourself."

"I just need to practice more."

"That can be arranged. See you at breakfast."

Chapter SEVENTEEN

RICHARD tapped on Mosi's door at seven thirty. She opened it. "Good morning," he said, then added as gently as he could, "Next time ask me to identify myself before you open the door. Make sure it's someone you recognize before you open it." He tried not to make it seem like criticism, but he obviously failed because the child wilted. Richard fought back the urge to hug her; instead he knelt so he was looking up at Mosi. "I'm sorry, honey, I wasn't trying to be mean." He hesitated, then went on. "We are in danger, and I want you to keep safe."

"Okay, I won't mess up again. Can I have a gun?"

"We have to find you one that will fit your hand." Richard could just imagine Pamela, and Amelia, for that matter, swelling with outrage at the very suggestion he would arm a nine-year-old child. It wasn't making him all that comfortable either, but their situation was bad, maybe even desperate. "Shall we get breakfast?"

"Uh-huh. I'm hungry."

They climbed the stairs to the breakfast room. The day was clear and beautiful, with a few puffy white clouds to offer contrast to the deep blue of the sky. The scientists were already there and eating like starving Cossacks, but still managing to talk an incomprehensible mélange of scientific jargon. Occasionally, a word would float by that Richard recognized. *Quantum, mass, light speed.* Kenntnis, an unblinking and enigmatic figure, sat silently in their midst. Occasionally, Trout or Chen would put a slice of bread or a piece of cucumber in his hand, which he would hold for a few moments, then drop back onto the table.

Richard led Mosi over to the buffet table laid out with loaves of crusty bread to be sliced, platters of cheese and cold cuts, fresh tomatoes and cucumbers, hard-boiled eggs, a bowl of muesli, hot water for instant coffee and tea, and three pitchers: one with milk, another with clear golden apple juice, and another containing an orange liquid that was no color known in nature. The young man on duty saw Richard frowning at the bright orange fluid and said with obvious pride, "We serve genuine Tang."

"Huh, really. How interesting. I didn't know anybody used Tang anymore," Richard replied.

"The astronauts use Tang," the young man said with no small amount of disapproval at Richard's lack of respect.

Richard, trying to correct the misstep, hurriedly said, "Yes, you're right, and that makes it very . . . cool."

He turned to Mosi. "What would you like?"

"I want the astronaut stuff."

"Okay."

He poured a glass of Tang for the girl, then helped himself to a glass of apple juice. She took a sip and made a face. She motioned to him urgently. He leaned down and she whispered in his ear, "This is awful."

Richard chuckled and traded glasses with her. "What do you want to eat?"

"I don't know. This is kinda weird."

"How about some cereal?"

"Okay."

He helped her get a bowl prepared and saw her settled at a table, then Richard went back to the buffet and got a slice of bread and butter. A now even more familiar presence loomed up next to him. "You need some protein. Have an egg, or put some meat on that bread."

Richard glanced up at Weber from beneath his lashes and gave him a crooked smile. "Do you have any idea how suggestive that sounds?" he asked softly. Damon's cheeks reddened, and he gave a cough that was both embarrassed and pleased.

"Doesn't diminish my point. Eat something."

"Okay." He picked up a hard-boiled egg, and they joined Musi at her table.

"What are we doing today?" she asked.

"We're going to another city."

"Will we be safer there?"

"Yes." Richard hoped it was true.

Lieutenant Kartal marched in a few minutes later. He looked incredibly rested for someone who had been up all night. Richard suddenly felt thirty rushing at him as he contemplated the younger man. "The cars are here."

They didn't return to the commercial airport but instead were driven to a nearby military base. A large helicopter squatted on the tarmac like a prehistoric beast with skin of tan and green. General Marangoz stood by the steps, along with four heavily armed soldiers. The Lumina refugees piled out of the cars.

Jerry contemplated the chopper, sucked at his cheek, and spat out a glob of phlegm. "Never thought I'd be riding in one of these fuckers again."

"I hear you," Weber said.

"Well, at least nobody will be shooting at us," Brook said as he joined them.

"You hope," Cross said cheerily as he walked past.

"You're a real asshole. You know that, don't you?" Jerry said to the homeless god.

"Guys, ixnay on the ursingcay, okay?" Richard said, and glanced down at Mosi.

The men shuffled and looked embarrassed. "Uh, yeah, right," Jerry said. "Forget sometimes."

Lieutenant Kartal saluted the general and bid them farewell. Richard helped Mosi up the steps and surveyed the interior of the craft. He'd flown on a lot of helicopters, but only commercial passenger models. The seats looked functional and utilitarian rather than comfortable, and the interior seemed cavernous despite the presence of a large tank that looked rather like a hot-water heater that was taking up the back half of the cabin.

"What's that?" Richard asked.

"Extra fuel," Brook answered. "That's why the Mi-17 has the range it's got."

"We will be able to reach Pamukkale and then on to Ankara without needing to refuel," General Marangoz explained. "We wish to give your enemies no chance to anticipate your location."

"Makes sense," Weber said.

Richard was not reassured. "So there's a load of gas in that thing?"

"Yes," the general answered.

"Then I really hope nobody shoots at us."

Brook and Jerry sat as close to the cockpit as they could manage. Richard wondered if pilots were terrible backseat drivers. The door was closed, and the rotors began beating. The whine and roar of the turbines was like a fist beating on his chest and set Richard's ears to ringing. There was a lurch, and the helicopter started to lift.

Mosi stared out the round window. Her lips were slightly parted and she looked down at the receding runway with an expression of wonder. She continued to stare, rapt, until they had left Istanbul behind them and the ground below was indistinct and less interesting. Then she turned to Richard. He could see her mouth moving and had a vague sense of sound.

He leaned in close and yelled, "What?"

Mosi put her lips to his ear and shouted, "This is cool. I've been on a little plane, and a fancy plane, and now a helicopter. I've never done any of those things before." Richard watched as the pleasure faded and her eyes seemed to go flat. "Abel would have really liked this."

Once again he had the urge to hug her, but he pulled his arm back down. He was starting to have a better sense of how to read her body language. This was not a moment where she would welcome comfort. He settled for a nod, then leaned his head against the armored wall of the cabin and tried to sleep. He failed.

A few hours later, Marangoz stood and lurched over to Richard. He pointed at a window. "Pamukkale," he yelled.

Richard cranked around to look out. Below was a small town, and ahead were high white cliffs. Within moments they were over the cliffs and the true beauty and form were revealed. What from a distance had appeared to be just white cliffs was in fact a series of blindingly white terrace pools holding shimmering aquamarine water. Water cascaded from pool to pool. On the topmost level of the cliffs, icicles appeared to be hanging off the rocks. On one edge of the cliffs, a weathered stone building was half buried in what looked like glittering snow. Richard couldn't help it. He gasped.

"Cotton castle. That's what Pamukkale means in Turkish," Marangoz shouted.

By now all the Lumina people were huddled at windows, staring at the wonder below. "What made it?" Richard yelled over the beat of the rotors and the rumble of the engine.

Eddie spoke up. "It's travertine forming the pools. There must be hot springs that are precipitating calcium carbonate."

"Exactly correct," General Marangoz said approvingly.

Then the pools were behind them, and the chopper was sweeping over tumbled ruins, all that remained of the Greek and Roman spa town of Hierapolis. An enormous Roman amphitheater swept past beneath them, the stone seats forming a horseshoe and falling steeply to a stage that still held a few broken columns. On all sides of the helicopter, there were half walls of long fallen and forgotten buildings. Marble columns thrust up like broken teeth from brown and green gums. In an area of open ground, the helicopter dropped slowly and settled with a sway and a bump. The engine shut down. The silence was almost shocking after the constant noise.

Richard unhooked his seat belt, stood up, and groaned. "Shi—" He broke off abruptly. "I feel like somebody's been punching me in the kidneys."

The former soldiers laughed, and Weber slapped him on the back. "Too many rides in limos and flights on G5s or G8s or whatever you've got now. Getting a little soft there, Oort."

"Yeah, feel free to give the macho bullshit a rest," he shot back, then winced at the profanity after he'd just lectured the others.

They all clambered down and stood in a field of grass. Richard wondered what sort of picture they would have presented. Sixteen men if you counted the crew of the helicopter and one young girl. And what a disparate group they were. Eddie still had on the suit he'd worn for the tour. The other scientists were dressed very casually. Cross looked like a derelict. Kenntnis was a massive figure dressed in a black suit. There were armed soldiers. Richard realized that he didn't see any people moving through the ruins.

"Did you close it off?" he asked Marangoz, and swept his arm in a wide arc.

"Of course. We wanted no disturbance." Marangoz left two of the guards with the pilots and helicopter, and headed off at a brisk pace in the direction of the cliffs. "The mosaic you want to see is in a building near the theater." They all trailed after him. Mosi was at

Richard's side, her head turning from side to side as she surveyed the ruined city.

"This is like Chaco, but . . . more. Who made this?"

"Lots of people. Greeks and Romans, Byzantines and Turks."

"We're very small, aren't we?"

"I suppose when you measure us against the sweep of history . . . yes, we are."

"Recently archaeologists discovered the Gates of Hell at this site," Marangoz said cheerfully.

Mosi shrank against Richard's side, and a small hand was slipped into his.

"It's not really the gate to hell. There is no such thing as hell," Richard said quickly. *Although I suppose some of those worlds I've seen through the tears would qualify.* That was information that Mosi did not need, not until she was much older.

The general seemed to realize the misstep and explained, "Mr. Oort is right. In the olden days it was known as Pluto's Gate."

Mosi's nose wrinkled. "Pluto? He's Mickey's dog. In the cartoons."

Richard choked back a laugh. Eddie and Ranjan weren't as successful. Their laughter echoed off the ruins. Mosi drew herself up stiffly, angry at the laughter.

"Pluto was what the Romans called the god of the underworld," Richard explained to Mosi. "It wasn't hell exactly. It was just the place where the dead went." While he was talking, he noticed Kenntnis beginning to crane his head. The skin between his brows wrinkled.

Mosi's lower lip was outthrust, and she had folded her arms, presenting a picture of offended dignity.

"I apologize," Richard said softly. "We shouldn't have laughed at you."

"No, you shouldn't have." She unbent a bit and asked, "So, what is it if it's not really a gate to hell?" She still sounded grumpy.

"It's a cave that has ruined columns and an altar, a bathing pool. There is a lot of vulcanism here. That's what makes the water hot, but it can also release toxic fumes. They are concentrated in this cave. Anything that went inside died, so the ancients decided it was the route to the underworld," Marangoz explained.

"What's vul . . . vulcanism?" Mosi asked.

"Why don't you walk with our scientists for a minute and they can explain more?" Richard suggested. She nodded and moved to join Eddie, Chen, Rangan, and Trout.

Richard dropped back to Kenntnis's side and looked up into that dark face. The man seemed more present than he had in a long time. "Do you remember this place, sir?" Richard asked softly. He didn't get an answer, but for a brief moment it felt like his words might have been more than mere sound to the alien.

They skirted the edge of the gigantic amphitheater. Wind sighed in pine trees that stood like sentries on the horizon and bent the grass. Unfamiliar birdsong danced in the air. Marangoz led them down a path and toward a building that was reasonably intact. A modern metal roof had been placed over one part of what had clearly once been a Roman villa. They entered and were on an elevated walkway suspended a few feet above the floor. Each room had an elaborate mosaic floor, and many of the walls still held painted designs of flowers, Greek keys, landscapes. The work was beautiful.

"They understood perspective," Chen said in wonder.

"Yep, invented concrete, glass windows, had hydraulics. Then you monkeys got really stupid and gave us the Dark Ages, the Black Death, and the Crusades. To which my kind all said, *Why, thank you very much*." Cross's sarcasm was acid on the words.

"Not my people," Chen shot back. "We were block-printing books and founding the Sung Dynasty and inventing gunpowder."

"And *my* people invented chess, and the concept of zero, the decimal, the square root and the cube root, and algebra," Ranjan broke in.

"Well, I'm sure not going to thank you for *that* one," Weber said.

Richard felt a headache coming on, but he just couldn't muster the energy to shut them all up. Then he didn't have to because Eddie jumped in.

"Hey, dudes, isn't this the kind of shit that Lumina was founded to combat? That whole xenophobic my-shit's-better-than-your-shit stuff?"

"Perhaps a few too many 'shits,'" Richard said with a significant look down at Mosi. "But we get your drift. Thank you, Ed—" Richard broke off, stammering his way into silence.

They had entered a large room. The walls were painted to resemble a summer sky. Despite the fading of centuries, the blue and the clouds conjured a sense of peace and ease. In this room, the elaborate floor mural had been covered with a layer of protective glass—it truly was remarkable.

It showed a banqueting scene. Men and women dressed in togas and stolas lounged on couches; one man wore a laurel wreath. The table was covered with trays of delicacies, and slaves were dotted around the table forever frozen at their tasks. In one corner, musicians played. Standing at the end of the table was a Roman soldier, his helmet beneath his arm, the other hand resting on the hilt of his sword—a series of interlocking gray curves. A Klein bottle at a time when such a thing shouldn't have existed. Richard knew that hilt. He had carried it, fitted it to his hand for the past three years of his life.

And standing behind the Roman officer and towering over him was Kenntnis. He was dressed in a plain tunic and sandals. The long-dead artist had captured some of the unique qualities of Kenntnis's face, and obsidian had been used for his skin. Seeing even a representation of the sword brought back to Richard the desperateness of their situation and his own culpability in the disaster. He had to grip the rail on the walkway to keep from dropping to his knees. The exhaustion he had been holding at bay fell on him like an avalanche.

Weber was suddenly there, catching him around the waist, keeping him on his feet. Richard groped for Weber's shoulder, clung for a moment, then straightened. Eddie and Chen had recognized the hilt. Eddie gripped Richard's arm hard enough to make him wince.

"He was a paladin!"

"Yes," Richard said.

"Paladin, what does that mean?" Marangoz asked.

Richard shot Cross a look. The Old One looked back blandly, and Richard realized Kenntnis and Cross had been advising Atatürk in the late 1920s and early '30s. A period when there had been no paladin, no one to carry the sword.

"Mr. Kenntnis needs people in the field. A paladin leads those efforts," Richard said. He stepped in close to Cross and said quietly, "What became of him?"

"Couldn't say. Before my time. Well, I was around, but just barely. Nose in the trough, lapping it up. Despite their engineering accomplishments, the Romans were real brutal motherfuckers. It was a movable feast following their legions."

Kenntnis was behind the gawking crowd. The two soldiers Marangoz had brought for security were looking from Kenntnis to the mosaic and back again and talking rapidly in Turkish among themselves. Richard pushed through them all and went up to Kenntnis. He gently touched the alien's sleeve.

"Sir, I'd like to show you something." There was no response. Richard took Kenntnis's hand and led him through the crowd. He pointed at the mosaic. For a long moment nothing happened, then the silver lights flared in Kenntnis's eyes bright enough to illuminate the floor, and then for a fraction of a second the room was filled with blinding light as if the world's largest flashbulb had just gone off. Everyone shouted in alarm and stumbled back. Ranjan lost his footing and fell off the walkway. Richard blinked away the halos of the afterimage. Ranjan was trying to climb off the glass and back onto the walkway. Fortunately, the glass was thick enough to bear his weight. Trout had pulled out a calculator, and the stubby fingers were flying across the small keys. Weber had Mosi wrapped in his arms.

Richard cautiously approached Kenntnis, who was once again standing with that faraway look. "Okay. Well. That got a reaction. Not exactly what I was expecting."

"What were you expecting?" Weber asked.

"I don't know. A miracle?" He gave a twisted smile.

"Oh, you don't want one of those," Cross said. "That would be bad. That would mean magic was at work. And we got no way to shut it down."

Anxiety had his belly in an uproar as Grenier stepped out of the office and checked on the threshold when he saw Jeannette at her desk. "Why are you still here?"

The woman looked up at him, her expression cold and distant. "I had work I needed to finish."

"Well, go home. It's seven o'clock."

"I know Mr. Gold is on his way. I can stay—"

"No!" Grenier forced a smile and moderated his tone. "Really not necessary. I know I came on a bit tough in the beginning, but I really do value your knowledge and insights, Jeannette."

The tone that had always worked on the older ladies in his congregation wasn't cutting it with the executive assistant. Her upper lip curled, and she swept him with a cold glance. She stood, gathered up her things, and said in a tone so neutral that it was in itself an insult, "Thank you." She walked to the elevator.

Yes, he thought, *she'll have to be fired once I'm past tonight*. Grenier waited to make certain she didn't return for some reason, nervously checking his watch. He was running out of time. He tried to jog to the conference room but was soon winded, and the jiggling of his gut was uncomfortable. He walked to the cabinet at the far end of the room, opened the lower section, knelt down with a grunt, and pulled out a large and elaborate first aid kit. Flipping open the snaps, he pushed back the top and surveyed the contents. The portable defibrillator was in the center slot.

He pulled it out, returned the case to the cabinet and hurried to the office. The granite desk didn't have a front so he couldn't hide the defibrillator underneath. He looked around frantically and finally settled on just tucking it in the trash can beneath his desk. He went to the bookcase and took down the cut-crystal decanter containing single-malt scotch and two cut-crystal highball glasses. He arranged everything on the desk and poured two fingers of scotch into his glass. He left the decanter unstoppered. It had to look as if he was just finishing pouring when Gold entered.

And what if he doesn't want a drink?

Unwelcome thought, that. Grenier pushed it aside and fingered the vial in his coat pocket. Somehow he had to get Gold to ingest the gamma hydroxybutyrate, known on the street as EZ Lay or Liquid Ecstasy. At higher dosages it caused unconsciousness. He hoped he had bought enough.

Grenier's frenzied preparations had kept him from having to actually contemplate what he was about to do. Now in the few moments he had, he sank down in the chair and replayed the conversation with Alexander Titchen. The billionaire's nasal voice with its syrupy Louisiana accent had held a gloating tone, making Grenier wish he had been less condescending to the man back in the day. Titchen had clearly enjoyed lording it over Grenier, laying out the conditions for Grenier's return.

"You need to prove your sincerity, Mark."

"I already told you the sword was lost. Richard is vulnerable. You can take him down now."

"It was a nice start, but we need a bit more. We'd like y'all to remove the Lumina officers. Clear the way for our people."

"Remove?"

"Don't be dense, Mark."

"You mean kill . . . ? I'm a fat fifty-four-year-old man!" he had objected.

"But cunning. You were always real cunning. Get back to us when you're done."

"They're scattered all over the world. I can't get at them, and if I travel there and then they die . . . " He had known he was whining but had been unable to stop.

"Well, now, that's a fair point. I'll tell you what. Kill one of them, and we'll handle the rest. We just want you to have some skin in this game."

Kill one of them. Could he do it? Grenier had done hideous and frightful things. He had ordered people killed, he'd ordered Richard beaten, he had even personally tortured the young man, but he had never killed anyone. Well, not with his own hands. But he had to if he was going to have any hope of surviving. He had picked Gold because he knew he could get the lawyer to come, and he figured the portly fifty-something lawyer would be an easier mark than the spare and fit Kenzo or the equally fit Dagmar.

Don't think about the end result. Just think about the process.

He heard the elevator arriving. Grenier surged to his feet, pulled out the vial, and tipped the GHB into the glass. Vial back into his pocket. He missed and it fell to the floor. No time to bend down. Actually couldn't bend over the bulge of his belly. Really no time to kneel. It was small, Gold probably wouldn't notice. He snatched up the decanter and splashed in scotch just as Gold bustled through the office door.

"You said there was a problem. What's happened?" the lawyer demanded.

"There's been a hacking attempt against our company computers. I think someone inside has been providing information to that kid that Richard fired." Grenier smoothly handed Gold the glass while he was talking. The lawyer automatically took it.

"Jesus. Any idea who?"

"I have my suspicions." Grenier picked up his own glass and clinked it against Gold's. He took a sip and mentally held his breath, waiting, hoping, watching.

Gold followed suit, and Grenier's gut felt suddenly loose with relief. Grenier waved Gold into the high-backed chair across the desk from him and took another encouraging sip from his glass. Gold took another sip.

"Well," Gold nudged, "who is it?"

"I suspect my assistant."

Gold gulped down a large swallow of scotch. "Jeannette? I find that hard to believe."

"She's become very attached to Richard. As women often do," Grenier said. "I think she feels more loyalty to him now than to Lumina." Grenier drew out the words, taking his time, letting the seconds crawl by.

"She won't be easy to replace," Gold said, and took another swallow of scotch. "As I recall, Kenntnis hired her when she was in her twenties."

"If we fire her, I expect we will lose Joseph too," Grenier said. "And that's worrisome. He knows this building, its weak points. They might get up to something. In fact, he's been very insubordinate."

Gold took another drink. There was only a small amount of scotch left in his glass.

"There's clearly another floor below the pool level," Grenier continued. "Joseph claims the only key to send the elevator down to that level is with Richard, there isn't a duplicate. I don't believe him. Do you know what's at the lowest level?"

The lawyer shook his head. "Not a clue." The words were slurred. Gold frowned down into his glass. "I don't feel . . ." His eyes widened, and he looked up at Grenier with dawning understanding and sudden fear. "Wha . . . Wha . . ." He slumped, and the glass fell out of his hand, the last of the scotch wetting the Oriental rug. Grenier cursed. He hadn't anticipated that any would spill. He would have to blot it before the EMTs arrived.

Moving as swiftly as possible, Grenier pulled the portable defibrillator out of the trash can. Gold wasn't completely unconscious. His mouth worked, and a bit of drool ran down his chin. His eyes were filled with fear and desperation as he stared up at Grenier.

"I'm sorry," Grenier said softly as he unbuttoned the lawyer's shirt. "You seem like a decent enough man, but you've never seen what I've seen. You don't know them and fear them as I do. And you can't keep me safe." He was relieved to see that the man didn't wear an undershirt. That made it easier.

He applied gel to the paddles and laid one in the center of Gold's chest. The other he slipped onto Gold's back just to the left of his spine at shoulder-blade level. There was a whine as the charge built. Gold's eyes closed as the drug overcame him and he slipped into unconsciousness. Grenier triggered the defibrillator, sending the charge through the lawyer's body. The current hit the healthy heart and threw it into defib. Grenier stepped back and watched Gold groan and struggle to breathe as his heart failed. Grenier had stood at the bedside of dying parishioners. He knew what death looked like. He had just never before been its midwife.

He examined his emotions. Waited for the moment of guilt or horror. And felt only a weary emptiness. He noticed his hands were steady as he repacked the defibrillator in the first aid kit in the conference room. Back in his office, he picked up the vial and placed it carefully in his pocket. He took a washcloth from the bathroom, wet it, and wiped away the traces of gel on the man's chest and back. Grenier decided to leave the glass, which had fallen from Gold's hand, and even the wet place on the carpet. It was a heart attack. No one would question that, and it added to the sense that the lawyer had been suddenly struck down by a massive coronary. No one was going to blot up the spilled liquor and test it.

Closing his eyes, Grenier summoned the grief, fear, and sadness. He felt his breath grow short and the sting of tears in his eyes. He picked up the phone. Dialed.

"Nine one one. What is your emergency?"

It was showtime.

Chapter

EIGHTEEN

By the time the second long helicopter ride was over, all Richard wanted was a hot shower and a chance to collapse on any kind of bed. Actually, he would have settled for space on a floor. He was paying for the almost sleepless night and the shock over what he had seen at Hierapolis. At the airport, there were cars waiting, ready to drive them through the maddening traffic of Ankara. The city was situated in a valley surrounded by almost vegetation-free brown hills and high ridges. Modern buildings occupied the valley, while the barren hills were covered with squatters' houses built out of scrap wood, concrete blocks, and tin. On the highest two ridges loomed walled fortresses built from red stone.

Their cavalcade turned onto a large boulevard, and after a sharp right turn they drove up a steep hill. Flower beds filled with red and white flowers forming the Turkish flag dotted the thick green grass.

A checkpoint manned by heavily armed soldiers lay ahead. They were waved through. Apparently they were expected. The road dead-ended in a circular cul-de-sac. The cars were parked, the engines shut off. The Lumina refugees climbed out.

Weber surveyed the view from the hilltop and looked toward the massive stone buildings that loomed off to their right. "Impressive, but I'd rather have checked into a hotel and gone sightseeing later," he said quietly to Richard.

"Since we're fugitives, I think we should probably be grateful and go along with anything our hosts want us to do."

"Within reason," Weber replied.

General Marangoz gestured toward a long walkway formed by bricks with grass growing between the stones. "The Road of Lions," he said proudly. The entrance to this walkway was flanked by stone buildings with statues out front. One showed a group of three women in traditional Turkish garb; the other grouping was a soldier, a peasant, and man in a suit holding a book. They were stylized and reminded Richard of Fascist art. Dr. Trout gave voice to his thought.

"Very Stalinistic," he grunted.

Chen, studying a placard, said, "Considering when they were sculpted, I'm not surprised."

They headed down the walkway between stylized statues of crouching lions. There were very reminiscent of Assyrian art. The walkway ultimately debouched into a ceremonial stone-flagged plaza. The gigantic space could probably have accommodated more than ten thousand people. On this late September afternoon, there were only a handful of tourists and a number of heavily armed soldiers marching with slow goose steps through the plaza. At various points, soldiers stood stiffly erect and unmoving before sentry stands. Underfoot, multicolored travertine pieces formed elaborate patterns that made Richard think of the Oriental rug back in his office in Albuquerque.

Straight ahead and up an impressive stone staircase was a colossal square building surrounded by massive colonnades, the Atatürk

Mausoleum. Opposite the building was another colonnade through which they could see the skyscrapers of modern Ankara. The other sides of the plaza were delineated by buildings constructed from the same stone and marked by colonnades.

"Damn," Eddie muttered as he joined Richard. "All this to bury one guy?"

"He was their George Washington. The father of his country," Cross said.

"Yeah, but *damn*."

Marangoz pointed at the massive building. "The Hall of Honor. There is a symbolic sarcophagus inside, but Atatürk's actual tomb is beneath the building. Come, my comrades are eager to meet you, and you must wish to rest after the journey. I must also report on what happened at Pamukkale."

Instead of returning to the cars, Marangoz led them into a building on their right. Richard was startled to find himself in a museum gift shop. Any item that could possibly hold an image of the founder of modern Turkey was for sale. Kemal Mustafa's intense blue-eyed gaze stared at Richard from mugs and rugs and key chains and refrigerator magnets, even ashtrays. Three young women, their faces framed by head scarves, stood behind various counters ready to assist any customers. Marangoz nodded at the eldest and led them through a doorway and down a set of stairs.

"The museum commemorates Atatürk's life and legacy. Perhaps you will tour it after the mausoleum has closed," Marangoz said to Richard.

"I look forward to that," Richard said.

They moved through several rooms filled with portraits of Mustafa Kemal and portraits after he became Atatürk, and depictions of famous battles. They entered a room filled with furniture and a set of evening clothes laid out on a bed as if waiting for the imminent arrival of the man himself. There were numerous black-and-white photos of Atatürk at various public events. Richard's attention was caught by faces in a crowd at a school dedication. Both Kenntnis and Cross were there. Well to the back and tucked in among others, but it was indisputably them. The date on the photo was 1936.

There was a small door off to one side. Marangoz unlocked it and gestured them inside. They found themselves in a mechanical room filled with the hum from the heating and cooling units and the faint smell of machine oil. Marangoz approached an open area on one wall and pressed several stones in a particular order. A portion of the wall swung open. They quickly stepped through to find a pair of soldiers, one male and one female, at stiff attention on either side of the wall panel. Directly in front of them stood two older men who, judging by their uniforms, were also generals. The soldiers snapped off salutes to Marangoz and pushed closed the wall.

Marangoz made the introductions. "Mr. Oort, please meet General Hasak Çelik, and General Karamat Sözer. We three are the coterie that at present leads Işık."

Richard shook hands with the men. Çelik was white-haired, and his face was a net of wrinkles. Sözer seemed to fall in age somewhere between Marangoz and Çelik. "Thank you for offering us refuge," Richard said. "May I introduce my companions. Doctors Tanaka, Ranjan, Trout, and Chen, part of my scientific team. Brook Kna—" He remembered and held back the Armenian name at the last second. Brook looked relieved and grateful. "And Jerry, my pilots. Damon Weber, head of overseas security, my ward Mosi Tsosie."

"It is our pleasure," Çelik said, but he sounded distracted, and both he and Sözer were staring only at Kenntnis and Cross.

"You're obviously familiar with Kenntnis and Cross," Richard said dryly. *We might as well not even be present*, he thought. *And maybe that's a good thing. If they knew just how useless I am.* He shook off the bleak thought and said, "Generals, perhaps if we could retire to someplace more private?"

"Yes," said Çelik. "Let us show you to your quarters and then we can talk."

Richard found himself suddenly flanked by Mosi on one side and Weber on the other. The little girl pressed herself against his side. The man allowed his hand to brush briefly across Richard's.

"Are we going to live here? Underground?" the child whispered.

"For a little while," he said soothingly.

Then it was Weber's turn. "Can we trust these guys?" he asked in an undertone.

"I don't think we've got a choice right now."

The underground facility forcefully reminded Richard of the lowest floor of Lumina's headquarters. Armories, a communications center, mess hall and kitchen, dormitories. Kenntnis and Cross were offered a private room, but Richard quickly stepped in. "I would prefer that we all remain together."

The generals looked to Cross, who shrugged. "He's the boss," the homeless god said.

They were shown into a room with ten bunk beds. Richard led Mosi to a bed at the far end of the room and in a corner. "We're going to make you a little tent, okay?" She nodded. Her features were pinched and tired. She grabbed his sleeve. "I'm hungry," she whispered.

Richard felt like a fool and a brute. "Of course you are. Let's take care of that right now." He turned back to the three generals. "My ward hasn't had anything to eat since breakfast. Can we get her something?"

Cross perked up at the mention of food. "Yeah, chow! I'm good with that."

"Of course," Sözer said. He said something in Turkish to a young woman guard. "Tamay will take her."

Eddie saved Richard from rudeness by stepping in before Richard could object. "Hey, we're scientists, which means we're a lot like starving locusts. How about we all go and find some chow while you go off and have the big boss confab?"

Tamay looked to Sözer, her expression questioning. The general nodded. The four scientists, the pilots, and Mosi followed the woman. Both Tamay and Mosi had matching ponytails of long black hair.

Richard caught Cross by the back of his T-shirt as he tried to join the parade. "Uh-uh. I think we need both you and Mr. Kenntnis."

"Fuck. Oh, okay."

Richard glanced at Weber. "Damon, you should get something to eat." Weber gave him an exasperated, disbelieving, and affectionate look that left Richard with a warm glow in the center of his chest. "Not happenin'. I'll eat when you do."

The generals led the foursome to a high-tech conference room. Richard guided Kenntnis to a chair, and the big man sank down obediently.

"What is wrong with him?" Marangoz asked.

Richard, realizing he needed to command this situation, moved to the head of the table. He remained standing as he swept the three uniformed men with a glance. "He's been mentally damaged. But let me brief you on the situation."

It took a while. Walking them through the events that had led to the opening of a full gate between the dimensions, the spin glass trap, the activities of Lumina after the gate had collapsed, the insurrection of his officers. "So here we are, and we appreciate you granting us asylum while we regroup."

Çelik steepled his knotted and age-spotted hands and leaned forward. "When we agreed to shelter you, we were under the impression we were doing this for Mr. Kenntnis. We were unaware of the seriousness of his condition." He glanced at the hulking, silent figure in the chair.

Cross started to respond but subsided when Richard held up a hand. "General, with respect, *I* lead Lumina. Mr. Kenntnis placed the company in my hands prior to the time he was injured. What my team requires is access to high-level scientific facilities. It is our understanding that Ankara University can supply what we need."

"For what purpose?" Sözer asked.

Since they didn't know about the sword, Richard saw no reason to enlighten them, but he had to give them some reason for that access. "They are searching for a way to reverse the damage to Mr. Kenntnis. Surely a worthy goal." He gave them a thin smile.

The three men exchanged glances and nodded. "It will be arranged," Çelik said.

"Excellent."

Weber stepped in. "Next point. He," Weber indicated Richard, "needs a secure way to communicate with his staff back in New Mexico, and I need a way to talk to my team in Africa."

Richard nodded in agreement. "And it needs to be airtight. Our enemies knew we were headed to Ankara, but I'd rather not pinpoint our exact location."

"Not a problem," Marangoz said. "Our computers are not linked to any outside computers, and we have primitive landline phone service that is under constant guard so no one can place a tap. We also have encrypted satellite phones. For e-mail we put messages on a flash drive and take them off-site. We have a van with a burst transmitter built in. Messages are returned to us the same way."

"How do you monitor for incursions?" Weber asked.

"That we can do from normal military facilities, and we have our people scattered throughout the various branches of the service," Sözer said.

"Smart."

"And paranoid. We know what we're facing," Çelik said.

"There have been reports in the press of arrests of top military officers by the Islamist government. Is that just the normal tensions between civilian and military control, or are these moves really designed to get at Işık?" Richard asked.

"We have begun to suspect the latter," Sözer said grimly.

"Democracy advocates in the EU and editorial writers present this as a positive. They have no understanding of what is actually at stake," Marangoz said.

"I sincerely hope that you and Mr. Kenntnis are not going to be some kind of precipitating event," Çelik concluded.

The old man's eyes were hooded and cold, and with his wrinkled neck and wattles, he reminded Richard of an ancient turtle. "And I sincerely hope that you aren't thinking about using us as a bargaining chip in your struggle with the government," Richard said softly. They held the stare for a long moment, black eyes locked on blue. The dark eyes dropped first. Richard stepped back from the table. "If that's all, I'd like to make some calls. And if Mr. Weber, Mr. Cross, or I can be of any service to you, please feel free to call upon us."

"We saw from the Lumina Web site that you specialize in closing tears," Sözer said.

"Yes. Yes, we do," Richard said with a level of certainty and bravado that he hoped they couldn't see through.

"That is good to know."

Cross spoke up suddenly. "Good, confab done? *Now* can we get some chow?" Richard shot him a quick and grateful glance. The homeless god quirked an eyebrow and gave him a small nod.

The meeting broke up. Marangoz sidled up to Richard. "Please believe that we are very pleased to have you here," the youngest of the generals said with a sharp glance at Çelik.

Weber fell into step with Richard and said in an undertone, "Goddamn. That took some brass balls. Remind me not to play poker with you."

"Let's just hope to hell there's no reason for them to cash in on the offer until . . ."

"Yeah."

"I better get on this. I need to talk to Joseph and Jeannette—"

"No, you're going to eat something and sleep for a bit."

"Damon—"

"Look, you don't want to call them at the office. Wait until they're home. Use the nine-hour time difference to give yourself a break."

"And what if there are taps on their home phones too?" Richard asked with sudden anxiety.

"There might be, but you can't become so paranoid that you end up freezing, and at some point us having intel is worth the risk."

"You're very wise."

"No, just older and a bit more experienced than you," he said, and gave the nape of Richard's neck a brief rub.

It had been a whirlwind of activity since George Gold's tragic coronary. Grenier had called Kenzo immediately after the EMTs had departed with the body to give the CFO the sad news. Kenzo was momentarily shocked, said he would inform the family, and then moved to end the conversation, saying he had to find a replacement.

Grenier had cleared his throat, "Might I suggest—"

"No," Kenzo had snapped, "you may not." And hung up.

Grenier had stared at the receiver for a long moment, choking on rage, feeling blood pound in his ears. *You're next* was the vicious thought, and he hoped that however Kenzo died, it would be painful.

Late that night he had reported to Titchen. The man had listened without comment and then said, "Well done, Mark. And did you enjoy your first taste of hands-on murder? When you have permission, it's usually mighty exhilarating."

"I'm not a killer." It was an instinctive response, uttered automatically, and the moment the words were spoken Grenier realized he had forever made himself subordinate to Alexander.

Titchen's laughter was a wild howl. "That's adorable."

"So how soon until I have—"

"There's just *one* last little task."

"That wasn't our agree—"

"Uh-uh, don't argue now. You need leverage to negotiate, and you don't have any." The amusement in Titchen's voice was palpable.

Grenier's gut roiled with acid. "What do you want me to do?"

"Lead the team that will be going to Turkey to recover the child and Kenntnis. You know Oort very well. Your insights will be useful."

"The child and Kenntnis? What about Richard?"

"I expect he'll have to be killed."

"What if I can capture him?"

"Little ambivalence there? And where Oort is concerned, your track record isn't great. First he tricked you, and then he made you his bitch. A lot of people view you as a traitor, and they're nowhere near as forgiving as I am. But not to worry, I'll keep you safe, Mark. Just remember your place."

"As *your* bitch?" Grenier said coldly.

"Why . . . yes. Best make your travel plans. We'll have a team assembled. They'll meet you in London."

The next morning, Grenier broke the news of Gold's death to Jeannette, who was unfazed. "There was a message waiting from Mr. Fujasaki when I got in, and also a message from Rachel, George's wife. She and the three girls will be arriving at one twenty. I've already talked with the hospital about releasing the body to French's Mortuary and arranging for transport back to New York."

"Ah . . . well . . . very good." The display of competence and composure had Grenier off balance. He'd hoped for a reaction and a chance to play the comforter. It aggravated him that she hadn't given him that opportunity. "And I need to get to London. When will the plane be returned?"

"The Turkish authorities have been difficult to deal with, and we don't have pilots right now. In order to fly the plane back, once it's released, we need a crew of two."

"I need to go now."

"Then might I suggest booking a commercial flight," she said in that same flat, cold tone she always used with him.

"Fine," Grenier snapped. "First class."

A few hours later, she had him booked on a flight that afternoon out of Albuquerque to Dallas, and from Dallas to London Heathrow.

The timing actually worked for him to have the limo deliver him to the airport at the time Rachel Gold and the daughters were arriving. It made him seem incredibly thoughtful, and he was at last able to apply his pastoral skills as he comforted the grieving widow. Patting Rachel Gold's hand, he told her that it had been quick and that he didn't think George had suffered. He just wished he had been able to do more. Rachel gratefully pressed his hand as he eased her into the limo and thanked him breathlessly for his kindness at this difficult time.

As the car pulled away, Grenier stood awash in conflicting emotions. He had a warm sense of satisfaction from Rachel's gratitude, but there was the dissonance of knowing that gratitude was due only to her grief. Grief caused by him. *You murdered her husband.* What kind of man could do that and then face his wife? A desperate one, Grenier concluded.

<hr />

The repeater on his Breguet wristwatch went off at three A.M. He had taken Weber's advice to reach his people at home, hence the ungodly hour. Richard had tucked the watch under his pillow so as not to disturb the rest of his crew, but over the snores of seven sleeping human males, the gentle bell was hardly noticeable. Richard could see the sag in the mattress over his head where Weber slept in the top bunk. Richard slipped out of the bottom bunk, pulled on trousers and a shirt, picked up his shoes and socks, and moved quietly to the door. Kenntnis's eyes were a silver glow in the darkness as he watched Richard tiptoe past his bunk. The creature didn't seem to sleep in any way that was understandable to humans. Richard noticed as he passed Cross's bunk that it was empty. He wondered what the homeless god was up to.

Stepping into the main rooms of the Işık headquarters, he was met by a young lieutenant, who handed over a satellite phone. It was far bulkier than the razor-thin cell phones that were the mark of a sophisticated and absolutely insecure future.

"We'll drop the scrambler once you're in position," the young man said, while Richard put on his socks and shoes. Then the soldier led Richard out of the bunker and through the portrait room toward the stairs. On every side, Atatürk frowned down at Richard. The piercing blue eyes reminded Richard rather forcibly of his father's eyes, and they seemed equally as disapproving.

"I know. I know. You don't have to tell me," Richard muttered to one of the portraits. "I fucked up."

Though he longed to go outside, Richard knew it would be foolish so he made the call from the gift shop while the soldier kept watch. Fortunately, he had the kind of mind that retained phone numbers. He dialed Jeannette. She answered on the third ring and he could hear a television in the background.

"Hello?"

"Jeannette, it's Richard—"

"Oh, thank heavens."

"What's wrong? What's happened?" He knew her voice too well not to be aware of the agitation clipping each word.

"So much and none of it good. Mr. Fujasaki put Grenier in charge of the office here—"

"Well, I expected that—"

"And George Gold is dead."

"What? How?"

"He had a heart attack."

Richard's first thought was for the family. Gold's wife was a vivacious five-foot-nothing woman with a great and exuberant laugh. Gold, while not as short as Richard, was not a particularly tall man, but in a mysterious twist of genetic fate, all three daughters towered over their parents. "How are Rachel and the girls?"

"They arrived this afternoon."

"Wait. He died in New Mexico?"

"Yes, he was meeting with Grenier."

"We have an EMT on staff," Richard said.

There was a pause on the other end of the line. "It was after hours," Jeannette said slowly. "Everyone but security had gone home for the day."

Richard groped for support. His hand found the edge of a counter, and he leaned against it. "Where's the body?"

"At French's Mortuary. The hospital released it late this afternoon."

"We need to get Jeff from the coroner's officer over there right away to examine the body," Richard ordered. "Can you get me his number?"

"Just a minute. I'll see if he's listed." Richard waited as the television sound receded. He heard the click of the keys on a keyboard. "Here it is."

Richard committed it to memory. "Thanks," he said.

"You'll tell me what he finds?" Jeannette asked.

"Of course."

Richard didn't know Jeff well. The man had taken over as coroner after Angela was murdered, and Richard had always felt the doctor blamed him for her death. It was irrational, just Richard projecting because of course Jeff didn't know the events that had led up to Angela's death, but it put an edge on all their dealings.

A child answered the phone. "Walker residence."

"Is your daddy home?"

"Daddy!"

A few moments and Jeff's voice came over the line. "Hello?"

"Jeff, this is Richard Oort. I need a favor. A big one."

"It's eight thirty—"

"I know, and I apologize, but I wouldn't ask if it wasn't important."

"Is this police business?"

"Potentially." Richard outlined the situation.

"Okay, I know the staff at most of the mortuaries. Are you at APD headquarters?"

"No, I'll call you back in . . . well, how long do you think it will take?"

"Few hours."

"Shall we say three?"

"Sounds good, but call my cell." He provided that number.

Richard handed the phone back to the young soldier, who murmured in Turkish into his radio. They returned to the bunker, and Richard went at once to the bunk bed, climbed up, and shook Weber gently awake.

For a brief instant he enjoyed the feel of the man's warm skin against his palm. Weber blinked and rubbed a hand across his face. "What? What time is it?"

"Ugh o'clock," Richard whispered. "Damon, something's happened."

Weber slid down from his bunk. He was wearing only his boxers, and shadows played across the arch of his rib cage and his pectoral muscles. Richard stole looks while Weber threw on clothes and followed Richard out of the sleeping quarters. Once the door closed, Richard outlined the situation.

"So you think it's more than just a simple heart attack?"

"I think I want to be sure." Richard looked around. "I wonder if we can get coffee or tea."

"This is a military operation," Weber said. "There's going to be food and caffeine available day and night."

He was right. There were cold cuts, cheese, bread, tomatoes, and cucumbers available. Richard asked for coffee. It arrived in a tiny cup with a thick foam on top. He carefully sipped the hot, sweet brew, feeling the texture of fine grounds, gritty and rich, against his teeth. Weber made them each a sandwich.

"How you doing?" the older man asked.

"Honestly . . . I don't know. If I stop and actually think about . . . well . . . everything, then I just want to curl up and suck my thumb. As long as I can keep doing something, I can hold it at bay."

"Hold what at bay?"

"The knowledge of how badly I messed up."

Reaching out, Weber gripped his hand and gave it a hard squeeze. "Richard, I know you don't believe this, but you're a hell of a leader. Shit, we followed you into that compound in Virginia and faced fucking monsters—"

"We were only there because I'd lost my temper with Angela and sent her away, and got her kidnapped . . ." He stared down into the dregs of his coffee. "And I couldn't even save her. I got her killed."

"No, a psychopath killed her. You don't get to take the blame for every shitty thing that happens. That's arrogance to think you have that much control and power. And bluntly, you've got to put what happened to Angela aside. It's past. You've got to take care of the living, and right now you're doing fine. Those scientists are here because they trust and believe in you. You had a plan ready for when things went south . . . Look, we're gonna figure this out."

"Well, the scientists will."

"Don't sell yourself short."

Richard glanced up and gave him a smile. "But I am . . . very."

"Ah, shut up."

After that they chatted about inconsequential matters while Richard obsessively checked his watch. It seemed like years before the three hours were up. Once again he and the soldier headed up to the gift shop with the satellite phone. Weber insisted on coming too. The sun was rising, burnishing the stone of the mausoleum compound with golden fire. In Albuquerque it was late night.

Jeff picked up on the first ring. "It was murder," he said, without greeting or preamble.

"Tell me."

"I found gel on the victim's chest and back, indicating somebody had used a defibrillator on him."

"He'd had a heart attack, wouldn't that be—"

"I checked with the EMTs. They said he was cooling when they arrived and they knew there was no point in taking extraordinary measures. They never used a defibrillator. Nor did the hospital. But if you shock a healthy heart, you'll throw someone into arrest, and the placement of the paddles indicates that's what happened."

"How did you figure it out?"

"The gel. You have to use gel on the paddles or the skin will be burned, but the only way to remove the gel is with soap and water. Just wiping it away will leave a residue. Your killer didn't know that. You got a suspect?"

"Yeah, the last person who was with him. Mark Grenier."

R ICHARD, Grenier's on his way to London. He's in the air now." There was a brief pause. Richard could hear Jeannette typing on her keyboard. "Actually, he's landed. Oh, God, I'm so sorry. I should have suspected—"

For the first time in all the years he'd known her, Richard heard the thread of panic and hysteria in his assistant's voice. "Jeannette, stop it. This isn't your fault. If anyone should be apologizing, it's me for trusting him even a little."

Her heard her take a deep, steadying breath. "Okay. What can I do?" she asked, sounding much more like herself.

"Deal with Rachel and the girls. I've got to call Dagmar and Kenzo. Warn them."

"You think—"

"Yeah, I do."

He called Dagmar first and discovered from her husband, Peter, that she had gone into the city for an early breakfast with Grenier. Richard's hand was trembling so badly he had to start over punching in the number for her cell phone. It was now nine thirty A.M. in Ankara. Soon the visitors would be arriving, and he'd have to retreat back to the Işık bunker. "Come on, come on," he muttered as the phone rang. It went to voice mail. He called back. Again she didn't answer. He called again. The fourth time, she took the call.

"Whoever you are I don't know you, so stop—"

"Dagmar, it's Richard. Just listen. Gold was murdered." There was a sharp intake of breath on the other end of the line. "I suspect Grenier. Are you with him now?"

"Yes."

"Make an excuse. Leave. Go home. Get your family. Run."

"Okay."

She broke the connection, and Richard offered up thanks that his people were smart and didn't waste time dithering. Next he dialed Kenzo's number. He had no idea of the time or the day in Tokyo. The CFO answered quickly. "Fujasaki."

"Kenzo, it's Richard. *Don't hang up!* Hear me out. Gold's dead—"

"Yes, I know. You need to come—"

"It was murder."

"Nonsense."

"It's been verified by the coroner. You're in danger."

"And you are demented."

"Grenier is in London with Dagmar right now. I just warned her." That seemed to give the man pause. "That trip was not cleared."

"Even if I'm wrong—and I'm not—what would it hurt to get someplace safe? You and your family." Over the line, Richard began to hear a rising sound like a growl. Then he heard screams. "Where are you? What's happening?" he demanded. A pulse was hammering in his throat and head.

"The subway. I don't—" Kenzo broke off with a choking sound.

A voice yelling in Japanese came over a loudspeaker. "Kenzo!" Richard shouted. There was no response, just an animalistic grunting sound. The clunk of a phone falling. Screaming. Then nothing.

After Dagmar's abrupt departure, Grenier sat in the Delaunay's posh surroundings trying to decide if he could trust the woman's excuse. Dark wood, brass, and marble art deco flooring created a sense of a bygone era, but he suddenly felt isolated by the screens that discreetly separated the tables. It felt like danger was approaching and he couldn't see it coming. The hollandaise sauce on his eggs Benedict was congealing. He took a sip of coffee. It tasted bitter and added to his sense of unease. She had said her son had become ill at school, but something felt off.

The message from Titchen to "draw her out" had come by way of a limo driver who had met Grenier at Heathrow. Grenier had called Dagmar from the car, suggesting an early breakfast meeting. Then the call, and she'd bolted like a pheasant flushed from cover.

There was a growing murmur from patrons in the restaurant spilling over to the usually unflappable waitstaff. Someone had a video playing on a smart phone. Grenier heard "Tokyo" and "terrorist." He pulled out his own phone and brought up the browser. It was breaking news and it was everywhere. There had been a terrorist attack on the Tokyo subway. Dozens were dead, and it was feared the death count would rise. A cold knot settled in Grenier's belly. He pushed away his half-eaten breakfast. He might have felt no guilt over Gold. But *this*? Was this Titchen's way of removing Kenzo? It was like swatting an ant with a sledgehammer.

He waved over a waiter and asked for the check. Tossed down the Lumina credit card. A few moments later the man returned, leaned down, and said in low tones, "So sorry, sir, but the card has been denied."

"What? That's not possible—"

"They say the card has been canceled, sir. Perhaps another card or cash . . ."

Grenier was a man who liked to keep wrapped in cash, and he had changed money at Heathrow. He counted out bills, stiffed the waiter on the tip, and hurried from the restaurant. He stood on the sidewalk and dithered. Something had happened. But what? Should he call Lumina? But it was the middle of the night in New Mexico, and would that superior bitch give him any information?

He started walking blindly up Drury Lane. Within a few blocks he was panting, his lower back aching, and he was becoming footsore. He had checked into the Claridge hotel before going to meet Dagmar, but with the card canceled he had no way to pay that bill. The rooms at the venerable old hotel were very pricey. Panic clogged his chest. He stepped into a small grocery so he was out of the bustle of people heading to work. After aimlessly wandering aisles and trying to decide if he was nauseated or starving, he realized there was no alternative. He pulled out his phone and called Titchen.

"Something's gone wrong," he said without preamble. "Dagmar took off like a frightened hare, and my credit card has been canceled."

"Well, that's unfortunate," Titchen said.

"Were you . . . did you . . . Tokyo?" It was so unlike him to be inarticulate. Grenier tried again. "Am I to assume that Kenzo has been dealt with?"

"Oh, yes."

"It seems . . . excessive."

"It was a juicy treat for one of our . . . friends. Where are you?"

"Some grocery store."

"Find a café and stay there while I make some inquiries."

"I'm still useful to you," Grenier said somewhat shrilly, but he had already been disconnected.

He located a coffee shop and ordered a hot chocolate. His roiling gut couldn't take coffee. Minutes ticked past, became an hour. He made four trips to the john to void his upset bowels. Almost two hours later, his phone rang.

"Well, you really are a fuck-up," Titchen said.

"Wha . . . what?"

"They figured out Gold was murdered. There's a warrant out for your arrest."

"Oh, God." He was shaking so hard the small table where he was seated actually shifted a few inches. "You're not going to . . . You'll help me, won't you?"

"Yes, because you still might be useful as bait to draw out Oort."

"So how—"

"We're creating forged documents for you. You'll be picked up and flown out on a private plane to Turkey. Stay where you are. We will collect your luggage from the hotel. It will take a few more hours."

Grenier hung up. It took several tries before he managed to get the phone back in his coat pocket. Regret was a taste coating his tongue. If he had never plotted, never betrayed Richard, he would be safely in bed back in Albuquerque, he would have a job, a salary, a life. Now he had none of them, and even the chance for a continuing life seemed tenuous at best. He had gone from commanding to being commanded. He had rolled the dice, and they had come up snake eyes.

Tears stung his eyes. He was a fat old man with no friends and no allies. And loneliness tasted even worse than regret.

A few more hours meant six. By the time someone arrived to collect him, Grenier was butt sore from the too-small wooden chairs, humiliated by the manager asking him to leave (a wad of cash had ended that request), and ravenously hungry. The pastries and the limited choice of fresh fruit had not made for a very filling lunch. He had been driven to a private airstrip, where a G5 waited. Grenier had expected the private plane. What he hadn't expected was to find Titchen aboard.

Once in the air, Grenier had been forced to wait yet again while Titchen made phone calls and went over documents with an assistant. Grenier sat in the back of the plane, his belly rumbling and his tongue thick with stale coffee. Finally, Titchen stood, moved to the back of the plane, and settled into the seat across from Grenier. Titchen gave him a tooth-flashing smile and leaned in.

"So, the last report we have of Oort is when he and his merry band landed in Istanbul. But you said they were heading to Ankara. Any idea why the change? And why Turkey?"

"No, no, and no."

"Well, that's not very helpful, Mark. You really need to step it up, start earning your keep around here."

Fury scattered Grenier's caution to the winds. He didn't care what happened, he was going to wipe away that smirk. "And you always were a ham-handed amateur," Grenier said in his most pleasant tone. "Killing over a hundred people to get one man? Forcing me to commit a murder that has now cost me my place? A place, by the way, that could have been very useful to you." Grenier had to hand it to the man, the mask of Southern charm never slipped despite the insults.

"Well, as I always say, you can't grind with water that's already past. So how do we proceed? There's fourteen million folks in Istanbul, and Ankara's got almost five million. We sure can't search the cities. How do we find him?"

"Richard's driven by a need to measure up, and he has a white knight complex. He'll always ride to the rescue."

"So we threaten someone he cares about?"

"Yes, that would work. There are also more subtle things we can try. He has Cross with him. We can use an Old One to track Cross. They can find each other."

Titchen gave him the toothy smile again. "Well, *you* won't be much help with that, seeing as how you're crippled."

"I know things. I know there's a place of power in Turkey. Where the veils are thin. Ask me nicely and I'll tell you."

Titchen stood and looked down at Mark. "Thank you, Mark, for your invaluable suggestions. We'll try 'em all. Nice enough?"

"I'll choose to ignore your rather insincere tone. It's in Hattusas."

"What the hell is that?"

"It was the capital of the Hittite Empire back in the second century B.C. There's a modern village there now, Boğazkale. It's some two hours away from Ankara."

"Well, that's convenient." Titchen started to walk away but turned back and added, "Oh, and I may just stake you out like a goat for a tiger. I expect Mr. Richard Oort isn't real pleased with you right about now. If he finds out you're in Turkey, I expect he'll want to come out and deliver an ass whuppin' to you personally."

And there you'd be wrong, you dimwit, Grenier thought as he watched Titchen walk away toward the front of the plane. Oh, Richard would find a way to punish him, of that Grenier was very certain, but it wouldn't involve a *whuppin'*. It would be far more subtle and terrible than that.

⟡

Two days slipped past. The scientists were taken at eight each night to the university to work and returned to the Işık bunker at six each morning. The first evening, there had been a tense exchange with Trout when Richard absolutely refused to allow Kenntnis to leave the safety of the mausoleum. Eddie had interceded on Trout's behalf.

"Richard, I think he's on to something big."

"That would cure Kenntnis?" Richard had asked.

"No."

"Then what? What's so important that we'd risk him?"

"I don't want to say just yet," Trout growled.

"In case it doesn't pan out," Eddie hastened to add and to soften the rudeness of the older man's response. "But if it does, it's gonna be *huge*—"

"I'll win a Nobel," Trout concluded.

"And Lumina will make a fortune," Eddie added.

"Well, we could certainly use that," Richard said, but still had dithered.

Weber had stepped in. "Look, you can't win by playing it safe."

"And you can also lose big by being reckless."

Richard bowed his head and considered. He turned to General Sözer, who was on-site. "You'll have people guarding them?"

"Absolutely, and despite recent events, the military is still very powerful in this country."

Ultimately Richard had agreed.

He and Mosi had negotiated a bedtime at eight thirty with a thirty-minute reading slot, but lights went out at nine. The first night she had read alone. The second night she asked him to read to her. Richard found that he liked it

Now it was the early hours of their fourth day in Ankara, and Richard was once again in the gift shop at two in the morning, talking with Joseph and Jeannette. This time, though, he had been able to call the office. There was an echoing feedback indicating that Jeannette had them on speakerphone.

"Scotland Yard can't find any trace of Grenier. They think he got out of the country somehow," Joseph said.

"Damn it!"

"What can he do now? He's on the run," Jeannette said, and satisfaction filled her voice.

"The fact he could escape a dragnet means he's got help," Richard said.

"Any theories on who?" Joseph asked.

"My bet is on Titchen after all the shenanigans with the buyout of Gaia. Mark was up to his neck in that."

"So what are their capabilities?" Joseph asked.

"We know this much about their capabilities," Richard replied. "They can arrange to release sarin in the Tokyo subway."

Jeannette sounded subdued when she said, "I hadn't thought of that." She switched topics. "Oh, I had Dagmar's assistant go by the house. The family's gone, and all the cell phones were left."

"That's good," Richard said.

"For them. But Richard, there's nobody running Lumina right now," Jeannette said. "With Grenier gone and Kenzo and Gold dead, can't you come home now?"

A wave of homesickness washed over him. Richard blinked, trying to clear the grit from his burning eyes. He was exhausted from stress and making these phone calls in the dark hours before dawn.

Joseph made the point before Richard could and put their predicament in blunt perspective. "Those sarin gas guys . . . they're still out there."

"Oh, yes, that's true," Jeannette said in a small voice. "I'm sorry, I'm really not being nearly paranoid enough."

That made Richard laugh. "That's okay. Maybe someday we can all stop being paranoid."

"That's not gonna happen until the last of these buggers and their human traitors are killed," Joseph said.

"And I don't have the sword, so I can't kill the buggers. Probably another argument against us coming home. And there's another little wrinkle: I need to get these lawsuits against me handled before I can come back. Put an ad in the *Times* for Pamela so she can get on this for me. And tell her she's now chief counsel for Lumina. I'll call again tomorrow."

"Take care," Joseph and Jeannette said in chorus.

He went back downstairs but didn't bother returning to his bunk. He knew he wouldn't sleep. Weber came into the mess hall at five

A.M., planted his fists on his hips, glared at Richard, and said, "Am I going to have to knock you over the head and put you in bed?"

"The second part of that statement sounds good."

Weber gave a shout of laughter, and Richard felt the blood rising in his face. "Oh, God, Damon, I'm sorry. My internal editor must be out to lunch. I get this way when I'm tired."

Weber took the chair across from him. "Actually saying what you're thinking and stating what you want? I like it." He continued in a more serious tone. "So, what's keeping you awake?"

"What's not? But mostly Mosi. I'm not doing right by her. She's getting very restless, and who can blame her? We can't go on living like Morlocks. She's a kid. She needs to go outside, play, and I've got to get her started with some kind of study regimen."

"So let's go out."

Richard shook his head. "It's too dangero—"

"And so are we . . . dangerous, I mean. We can protect her from most human threats, and if an Old One shows up—well, we've always got feet."

Richard stood up and stretched. "What's that line from *Monty Python and the Holy Grail? 'When danger reared its ugly head, he bravely turned his tail and fled.'*"

"Hey, there's nothing wrong with a strategic retreat."

Richard sighed. "We just seem to be doing a lot of it right now. As for Mosi . . . I'll think about it."

General Çelik came into the mess. The smile of greeting that curved Richard's lips curdled into a grimace when he saw the expression on the old man's face. He came quickly to his feet.

"We have a situation," Çelik said.

TWENTY

ONCE again Richard found himself aboard the Mi-17 chopper as it beat its way east toward the village of Boğazkale. The beams of the rising sun came through the front window like fragments of golden glass to pierce his eyes and set a hammer beating against the inside of his skull. The noise, the movement, and the light combined to have gorge rising up the back of his throat. Richard pulled a bottle of water from his pocket, took a sip, closed his eyes, and swallowed hard. Çelik was aboard with eight soldiers. Lumina was represented by Richard, Weber, and Cross. Richard had left a note for Mosi and woke Brook and Jerry to ask if they would entertain the child until he got back.

"*Is this going to be dangerous?*" Brook had asked.

"*No,*" Richard had replied. He hoped that proved to be true.

Weber, head thrown back against the side of the helicopter, was snoring. His feet were resting on his big bag o' guns. Cross was on the other side of the chopper, matching the security chief snore for snore. Richard looked out the window as they passed over a narrow two-lane highway, a ribbon of black against the green of the grasslands stretching out in all directions. He wondered if it had changed much since long-forgotten conquerors had swept across these lands. Power poles marched along the side of the road. A number of them looked like they were wearing wide sombreros. Richard squinted. A soldier grinned at him and offered binoculars. Richard nodded in thanks and took a closer look.

The telephone pole was topped by an elaborate birds' nest that looked to be at least four feet in diameter. "What the hell?" He nudged Weber with his elbow. "Damon. Wake up. You've got to see this."

"Huh." Richard offered the binoculars and pointed. Weber took a look. "Damn, didn't know there were pterodactyls in Turkey." As they watched, an enormous stork flapped its way beneath the helicopter. Because of its size, the immense wings seemed to beat in slow motion. It came to rest in one of the massive nests, settling down with almost prissy care.

"Well, that was pretty amazing," Richard yelled over the rotors. He leaned across toward Çelik. "What can you tell me about Boğazkale?"

"Kurdish village. They farm, but mostly they are herdsmen. Following the goats and the sheep into the mountains in summer, returning to the village in winter. They make money guiding tourists through the ruins, working as laborers on the archaeological digs." Çelik gave a grim little smile. "And of course they sell rugs. We *all* sell rugs . . . or have relatives who sell rugs."

The helicopter banked hard to the right, throwing Richard against Weber, who placed a steadying arm around his shoulders and left it there as they began their descent. Gray stones formed lines, squares, and rectangles against the grass. Sheep and goats dotted the hillsides, and scrambled through the ruined foundations of what had once been a great city.

Four thousand years ago, Richard thought. They roared past a large building with crenellated walls that seemed to be constructed from adobe. Clearly a reconstruction in the Hittite style. Which looked a lot like Assyrian architecture to Richard. He wondered who had been here first.

Ahead of them, a cluster of buildings with red-tiled roofs and whitewashed walls lay cupped in the folds of the valley. It was probably just his imagination, but Richard felt like the modern village was huddling, trying to pull away from the lowering ruins on the hillsides.

They drew closer. No people rushed out to investigate their arrival, and what had seemed dark spots on the cobbled streets and in the meadows resolved into huddled bodies. Richard looked at Weber and grimaced. There was a coldness in the small of his back where the hilt should have rested. The soldiers were murmuring to each other, and Çelik looked as old as death and just as grim.

The chopper set down with a lean and a sway. Cross woke up when Çelik barked orders, and the soldiers deployed immediately, forming a perimeter around the general and the foreigners. Richard jumped down and drew his gun. There was something about the silence that had the back of his neck prickling. The soldiers maintained discipline, but Richard saw their eyes flicking rapidly in all directions. Cross stretched and sniffed.

"Yep. Old One stink."

"Is it still here?" Richard asked. Cross shook his head.

Çelik gave more orders, and the troops began leap-frogging into the village, which seemed to possess only one actual street. They found bodies almost immediately. Men in rusty black pants and embroidered white shirts. Women in calf-length dresses wearing head scarves. Children, some clutching toys. A dog howled mournfully and thrust his muzzle into the limp hand of a girl near the city square. The thin wrist was encircled by a bracelet of almost abstract blue glass eyes. There was no human sound. Just wind, and howls, and the distant chime of bells. Richard whirled at the sound.

"Bells. On the goats," Çelik said.

Richard and Weber knelt next to a man's body and searched for some indication of the cause of death but found nothing. One pocket held another of the glass eyes hanging beneath an embroidered image of St. George slaying the dragon. Çelik waved to his troops to break order and begin searching the buildings. Many of the buildings had the blue eye hung at the door. Richard touched one that was attached to an elaborately crocheted peacock tail. More of the glass eyes formed the eyes in the bird's tail.

"What are these?" he asked Çelik.

"*Nazar boncuğu.* The blue eye. They're believed to ward off evil."

"Sure didn't work here," Weber said unhappily.

Richard entered building after building and found only death. It was the infant in a crib in an upstairs room that sent him reeling back to lean against a wall, choking on tears, overcome with horror. He gasped for a few moments, mopped at his face, which ran with equal parts tears and sweat. He knew it was stupid, but he wrapped the tiny baby girl in her embroidered blanket and carried her downstairs. He placed her gently on the breast of the young woman whom he guessed was her mother. The woman had been struck down as she stood at her stove. The burner was still on, the contents of the pan burned to an unidentifiable sludge that resembled charcoal. Richard turned off the burner and backed out of the charnel house.

They all rendezvoused back in the main square. The soldiers were muttering, looking in all directions. "What killed them?" Çelik demanded.

"An Old One," Cross said. "We need to find the opening. See if it's still open."

"You can locate it?" Richard asked.

"Oh, yeah, but with its stink all over everything, we're gonna have to get close." Cross glanced at the hills across the valley, the gray stones like broken teeth in the grass. There was something chilling about those enigmatic lines.

"Damn, those ruins have gotta cover five or six square miles," Weber said.

Richard looked around the square. There was a sign in several languages indicating a museum. "Let's see if there's anything about the site that might narrow the search."

They went inside. Past the ticket taker dead in his kiosk. The museum itself was small. Some pottery, tools, clay tablets with cuneiform pressed into their surfaces. There were pictures of sunburned men and women working in test trenches assisted by local citizens, and photos of points of interest in the site. Richard skimmed down the long description. He learned that the site had been discovered in 1834, but no real excavation begun until 1906. The most notable discovery was of a peace treaty between King Hattushili III and Pharaoh Ramses II. The original was in a museum in Istanbul, and a copy was on display at the United Nations. Proof, Richard thought, that diplomacy had a long history. It was recommended that they view the Lion's Gate and the King's Gate, also a temple in the lower city. There were pictures of stairs ascending the city walls and tunnels that ran beneath the royal enclosure.

Çelik, reading the Turkish version over Richard's shoulder, reacted to something. "It was known as the City of a Thousand Gods," the general said softly, as if worried that some of them were still listening.

"Well, that's never a good thing," Cross grunted.

Richard read about the last days of the city when a mysterious illness had swept through, killing almost everyone. He and Çelik exchanged glances. "Rather like what happened last night, yes?" the old man said.

"Yeah." Richard resumed reading, and had just about resigned himself to a long search across the entire ruin when his eye was caught by a small section about the mystery surrounding a strange green rock, almost perfectly square and about two feet high that stood in the temple complex in the lower city. Geologically, the rock matched nothing in the area. The closest analogue was to a quarry in Egypt, but even that was in some doubt. There were also handprints that had been worn into the surface of the stone by thousands of worshipers over decades. The rock was just one of the many enigmas of Hattusas. Richard mutely pointed at the section. Everyone leaned in to read.

"Want to bet that rock really isn't from around here? As in, not even from this world? Or even this universe?" Cross said.

"I don't take sucker bets," Richard replied. "Let's check it out."

"Any idea where it is?" Weber, ever practical, asked.

Richard shrugged. "In the lower city."

They stepped back outside. It was now midmorning and it looked to be a warm September day. Which meant the smell of corruption was rising along with the temperature. Back in Albuquerque, Richard had always kept a small jar of Vicks on hand to try to overpower the smell of a rotting body. Other cops used cigarettes, and as if on cue, a number of the soldiers lit up. The Turkish tobacco was pungent and rough, and Richard was grateful for it. He was trying to hold the horror at bay. *Go back to a cop's clinical analysis.* This was a crime scene. An enormous crime scene, but still a crime scene.

———◇❉◇———

The actual ruins were some distance away. Çelik jerked his chin toward a truck parked nearby whose driver had half fallen from the cab in the act of fleeing death. "It will be faster," he said almost apologetically. Richard nodded in agreement.

The soldiers and Cross climbed into the bed of the truck. Weber pulled the body free and slid behind the wheel. Richard found himself wedged in the middle between Weber and the general. A blue eye swung from the rearview mirror as they jounced down a long dirt road, past the mock Hittite building, and stopped at a pole gate. Çelik ordered his troops to take defensive positions, then he, Richard, Weber, and Cross moved into the ruins. Richard froze at the sound of low moans and realized it was wind through the rocks. He shook off the fear and started walking.

Remembering lessons from Chaco Canyon, Richard at first tried to stay off the gray stone foundations, but the footing was treacherous. The tall grass hid loose stones and holes. The foundations offered a stable walkway. They moved past one deep trench in which enormous pottery jars, buried in the earth almost up to their rims, yawned like screaming mouths. There was one weathered gray rock on a pedestal that resembled a drunken abstract artist's vision of an animal. Richard looked more closely and had the vague sense of eyes and fangs. He remembered the lion statues that lined the entrance to Atatürk's tomb. This weathered stone, like the embryo of a lion, had been the model.

"Let's split up," Richard said. "We'll cover more ground that way." Weber looked like he wanted to object but finally nodded and moved off.

Cross stood tensely erect, his neck stretched, nostrils fluttering. "There are voices on the wind," he said, and walked away.

Richard shuddered, feeling isolated and very vulnerable. Behind him, a man cried out in fear. Richard whirled, drawing his gun. But the soldier was simply kneeling on the ground, arms wrapped around his head, rifle in the dirt in front of him. Keening, he rocked back and forth, and Richard realized they were not inoculated. Richard was a genetic freak immune to magic, and even he felt a soul-crushing dread in this place. How much worse for a young soldier, a normal human sensing an unnatural evil and unable to flee? An older officer ran to the boy and placed a comforting arm over his shoulders.

And I can do nothing to help them.

Setting his jaw, Richard forced himself to walk on. He spotted a body in the midst of the ruins, and just beyond it was the stone. The vivid green was easy to spot. Richard moved first to the body. It was a heavyset man of middle years, and he had been shot in the temple and at close range. The brass shell casing glittered among the rocks. Richard yanked out his handkerchief and picked up the casing, tucked it into his pocket. He then turned to the stone.

It stood near the back of what had once been a rectangular room, and it had clearly been hewn and shaped. On at least two sides the corners were still fairly sharp. Cautiously, Richard approached. The green stone reached to roughly knee height, and the top was stained with dried blood. He circled it, and from one angle the sunlight struck in a way that allowed him to see the shadowed handprints that had been worn into the sides. Some of the blood that had been poured over the stone had caught in the indentations.

"Damon! General! I found it!" Richard yelled. The others made their way quickly to join him. Cross literally came loping up with the air of a hunting cat. He studied the rock, and his eyes went completely black. Even after all this time, it was still disturbing to Richard when he watched it happen. Weber and Çelik arrived.

Weber looked at the stone, then slowly pivoted, studying the gray stone ruins that stretched out in all directions. "Yeah, this baby is clearly not from around here." The drawling tone broke the bubble of tension that had settled in Richard's chest. He gave a short laugh.

He turned to Cross. "Well?"

The creature didn't answer, and then from the corner of his eye Richard caught movement. Çelik was approaching the stone, his hand outstretched. His face had gone slack, and his eyes were unfocused. With a yell of alarm, Richard threw himself at the older man, catching him around the waist and knocking him off his feet. They came down on one of the low walls, and the general gave a grunt of pain as his hip hit hard against a notched stone that looked like it had once carried water. Çelik suddenly seemed aware of Richard, arms locked around Çelik's waist, knee planted on the older man's thigh.

Çelik looked around, then tore his eyes away from the stone. "Thank you," he said simply.

Richard climbed to his feet and offered a hand to assist the general. "Don't look back. Walk away. Let us handle this."

The old man nodded and started limping slowly and painfully back toward his troops. He paused but didn't turn, just called out, "I wanted to touch it. The desire consumed me." He shook his head and resumed his painful progress.

"Yeah, and he would have found himself in a less than fun place," Cross said from behind Richard.

Richard turned. "You back now?"

"Yeah."

"So?" Richard nudged.

"One of your kind did some magic shit, and one of my kind came slithering out."

"So it's a tear?" Weber said. "It's not like any one we've ever seen before."

"That's 'cause it's not a tear. It's more like a portal. I haven't ever seen anything quite like this before either. Pretty cool," Cross answered.

"That wouldn't be my first reaction," Richard said dryly.

"So what can we do about it?" Weber asked.

"Nada since the paladin here lost the sword."

"*He* didn't lose it. It was those scientists' fault."

"Yeah, that's right, defend your sweetie."

"He's not. . . . And how did you . . ."

Richard stood staring thoughtfully at the ground, almost unaware of the bickering behind him. He whirled on Weber and Cross. "I feel like this was a message, or maybe a gauntlet being thrown . . . to me."

"You know, not everything is about you," Cross said.

"I think this one is."

Weber accepted his statement. "So, who?"

"Let's find out. We need to keep looking around."

"What if this was an attempt to draw you out?" Weber asked. "Staying here could be dangerous." He nervously scanned the hills.

"They couldn't be sure"—he ticked off the points on his fingers— "that I was still in Turkey. If I was, that somebody would inform me. That I'd respond. This is chess, Damon, and this is just the opening gambit."

"These people weren't pawns!"

Richard flinched at the tone but realized it wasn't directed at him. It was inchoate fury seeking a target. He understood, he felt it too, but he had to stay detached, analytical, clinical. His enemy wasn't panicked, that was clear. Richard had to match that calm. "I never said they were. But they were used that way. Come on."

He started up a path that led onto the hills. Three young goats with multicolored coats stared at them from devil-slitted eyes, bleated, and leaped away with a ringing of bells. They found the Lion's Gate. Two towering stones formed the stiles on either side of the gate, and the figures of lions seemed to be emerging from the stone. Their forepaws rested on stone platforms set at the base of the uprights. The face of the figure on the left was sheared away, but the lion on the right still snarled, the eye sockets glaring out at the world, and the body sprawled at its feet. An old man lay in the dirt. A carved stone figure of a lion had rolled from his hand. More carvings were arrayed on the stone pedestal at the lion's feet. More lions, bulls, a flat stone carved with bas-relief figures of Hittite warriors. Clearly the old man waited here to sell souvenirs to the tourists. Richard bent and picked up the little lion. The work was exquisite. The tail was a serpent, on the back of the neck was a two-headed eagle, and the mane was suggested by leaf-shaped figures. The creator had even managed to have the mouth open but left the fangs in place.

Richard's fist closed on the figure and he forced back his rage. "I promise you. I'll find them," he whispered, and he closed the old man's staring eyes. He took the little lion as a reminder of that promise.

They moved on, and then, carried on the wind, they heard faint cries. All three men broke into a run along the side of a stone wall built into a hillside. There was another body in front of a stone doorway that led into the hill, but this one was weakly moving. Terrified and suffering dark eyes were raised to Richard's. The young man looked to be in his late teens, with skin like old ivory and his black hair matted with sweat and dirt. His legs were bent at unnatural angles. Just looking at those broken limbs was sickening. His wrist had been cut and was still slowly seeping blood.

Richard knelt at his side and slid an arm beneath the young man's shoulders, levering him up slightly, and cringed when the boy wailed in pain. "I'm sorry, I'm sorry," he muttered. The boy's lips were cracked and bleeding; he had been out here a long time. "Damon, there's water in my coat pocket. Open the bottle for me."

The older man handed him the now open bottle, and Richard held it gently to the boy's mouth. He gulped at the water, but Richard was careful to pull it away periodically. "Easy, easy." The boy coughed and cried out again. Richard looked up at Cross and Weber. "It will be agony for him if we try to carry him. Is there some way to get the helicopter up here?"

Weber backed off, then scrambled up the rock wall set in the hillside. He dropped back down. "It's fairly flat on top. We can do this. Who do you want to go back for the chopper?"

"You."

Weber headed off at a steady ground-covering run.

Richard laid the boy back down on the ground, then shrugged out of his coat, folded it to form a pillow, and slipped it under the young man's head. "Do you speak English?"

"Yes. Some."

"What's your name?" Richard asked as he wrapped his handkerchief around the boy's cut wrist.

"Acabey."

"I'm Richard. Can you tell us what happened?"

295

The boy shivered and closed his eyes, then slowly began to speak. "Three cars arrived. Big cars. Expensive. Grandfather told us to hurry up to the gates and the stone with our carvings. These people had money. I was at the stone."

"The green stone. In the lower city?" Richard clarified. The boy nodded. Richard frowned. "I didn't see any of your beautiful carvings."

"They bought them all. No one had ever bought everything before. They gave me so much money." Acabey glanced down at a pants pocket bulging with lira. "Then the man with all the money nodded to other men who were with him. One of them drew a gun and shot Riza."

"Who's Riza and why was he there?" Richard asked. It probably didn't matter, but he was falling back into cop mode. Get every detail. You never knew what might be important.

"We make the tourists hire a guide. Better for everybody. Riza has worked digs for years and years. He knows . . . knew so much." A few tears leaked from the corners of the boy's eyes and ran down into his sideburns. "Then other men grabbed me. The rich man opened a briefcase and took out a bowl and a knife, and a long crystal like amethyst. He told the fat man with the glass hand to collect blood and gave him the knife and the bowl."

Cross and Richard exchanged looks. "Well, guess we know where Grenier washed up like a fuckin' beached whale," the Old One grunted.

Acabey continued. "One of the men held my arm and the fat man cut my wrist. He almost filled the bowl. It hurt so bad. Then he took it back to the rich man, who began to speak strange words and poured the blood over the stone. He struck it with the amethyst. It shattered, and there was this terrible stink. Then this thing like shadow and blood slithered out of the stone." Richard, his hand on Acabey's shoulder, felt the boy start to shake.

"I know this is hard and terrifying, but can you tell us anything else about this creature?" Richard asked gently.

"Eyes, so many eyes." He flung his head from side to side. "No, no."

"It's okay. It's okay," Richard soothed. He glanced up at Cross. "Ring any bells?"

"Not right offhand. It's not like we're all related or are in a bowling league together or something. Actually, we mostly hate each other."

Richard thought about that. If these creatures posing as gods all hated each other, was it any wonder that religious hatred was such an integral part of human history? In the distance, the *thwap* of helicopter rotors started up.

Looking back at the boy, Richard asked, "How did you get up here?"

"Some men dragged me. Then they . . ." He gulped. "They broke my legs."

The beat of the rotors grew to a roar, and the belly of the Mi-17 swept overhead.

"We're going to get you to a hospital now."

"My grandfather. He was going to the Lion's Gate. People always buy at the Lion's Gate. Can you get him? And my parents and sister are in Boğazkale."

Richard hesitated. He had done only a few grief calls during his time at APD. It was hard enough to tell a family that their loved one had been killed. How could he tell this boy his entire community was gone and that he, however unwillingly, had played a part in those deaths? He decided not to lie, just, for the moment, omit.

"I'm sorry, but I found your grandfather. He's been killed." The boy whipped his head to the side, trying to hold back tears. Richard removed the lion carving from his pocket. "He did beautiful work. May I keep this? As a reminder?"

The boy, his eyes glistening with tears, regarded the little lion. "Of what?"

"That I'm going to find these men and see that they face justice."

"I want to kill them," Acabey said savagely.

"That's just death. I want them punished."

Acabey stared up into Richard's face and gave a taut nod and squeezed Richard's hand. Weber, with soldiers in tow, jumped down next to them.

"My family . . . ?"

"First, hospital."

Four soldiers gently lifted Acabey up to waiting hands of the soldiers on top of the wall. He screamed in pain, but they got him to the helicopter and used the medical kit to give him a shot of morphine.

Çelik said quietly to Richard, "Are we done here?" Richard nodded.

The engines whined, the rotors began slowly turning, and then the ground was receding beneath them, the buildings becoming mere flashes of red tile in the midday sun.

Richard gazed out across the empty grasslands. "I wonder where it's gone."

"I have a feeling we'll be finding out real soon," Cross replied.

Chapter

TWENTY-ONE

DURING the helicopter ride, Çelik had been on the radio constantly. Richard assumed he was informing various government agencies of the deaths in Boğazkale. When they landed at the military base, an ambulance had met them and taken Acabey to the hospital.

Back at Işık headquarters, Richard requested a meeting with all three generals. The expressions on the faces of the men who looked up at him were grim. Richard stood at one end of the oval table, flanked by Weber and Cross.

"What is it after?" Sözer asked.

"Best guess, Mr. Kenntnis and my ward. Maybe me as well."

Marangoz looked at Cross. "You were here with Kenntnis in the thirties, and like him you have not aged. Are you of his kind—"

"Uh . . . short answer . . . no."

"But you are clearly not human, so can you not do something to combat this thing?" Sözer asked.

"Yeah. But whether I can beat it . . ." Cross shrugged. "Well, that's another issue. And it's got little human helpers and it will get more. You gonna be ready to shoot your own citizens?"

The soldiers exchanged glances. "This comes at a difficult time," Çelik said. "There's tension between the civilian government and the military. We had sworn to honor Kemal's vision and keep Turkey secular, but the Islamists have gained in both influence and government authority in recent years. They have been chipping away at our power and prerogatives. If the military is seen as attacking civilians . . ."

"Bottom line. Can they . . . will they find us?" Weber asked.

"I'm here and Kenntnis is here. They'll find us." Cross's tone was flat and implacable. "They can't sense Richard or the kid, but we're like goddamn flares."

Weber blew out a sharp breath. "Well, that's just great. So how secure is this facility if . . . when they do?"

"And is there a back way out?" Richard asked.

"Of course," Marangoz said. "We weren't going to trap ourselves."

"We need to make sure everybody knows how to use it." There were nods of agreement. Richard continued, "We know one of the men present at Boğazkale was Mark Grenier. He would have just arrived on a plane out of Britain. We really need to know who else was with him, and given the timing of the attack on Boğazkale, they probably landed in Ankara. It would have been a private plane. It would be nice to know for certain who we're up against."

"We will make inquiries," Sözer said.

The meeting broke up. Richard checked his watch. Nearly five P.M. He realized his head was light and his legs rubbery. "I need food and sleep. Preferably in that order. Everybody okay with that?" he asked Weber and Cross.

"Huh, maybe it is the End of Days," Weber said, but he was smiling. "First time I've ever heard you reach that conclusion without somebody nagging."

"I can be taught."

"I'm gonna head out. Patrol a little," Cross said. "Sure wish we had that sword."

"Not as much as me," Richard snapped.

"Well, you'd be wrong, it's *my* only hope for an ending." The creature splintered into red-tinged light shards and vanished.

"And our only hope to keep from ending," Richard muttered to the empty space.

The scientists, Kenntnis, and Mosi were in the mess hall. Weber and Richard paused in the doorway for a moment, watching. At this time of day, there were heated chafing dishes, and the room was filled with the aroma of grilled kofta and pilaf. Chen was holding a piece of construction paper, and as he flipped and turned it, various colors and designs appeared. There was an array of colored pens on the table in front of the little girl and the scientist. Mosi was frowning, but suddenly her brow cleared and she gave a bell-like laugh. She grabbed the paper and manipulated it while the scientist nodded and smiled.

"Do we dare let them go and work tonight?" Weber said, speaking aloud Richard's thoughts.

"Let's find out where they're at on recovering the sword."

"I have this horrible vision that it just bounced around that lab in Rochester and is sitting in a janitor's closet or a men's room somewhere."

"If only we could get that lucky."

They walked toward the men and the little girl at the table. When Mosi saw Richard, she jumped up and ran to him, clutching the piece of paper. "Look! We made a hexaflexagon!" Her excitement and the fact she wanted to share it with him filled Richard's heart. He looked down at the folded construction paper and saw a flash of color between the seams. "We made different faces different colors, and then when you fold it you get to see them. Dr. Chen says this is math, but this is fun math."

"That's wonderful. You'll have to show me how to make one."

"Okay, let's do it now."

"Damon and I are really hungry, Mosi. Let us eat first."

She looked mulish for an instant, then she nodded. "Okay. But you promise?"

"I promise." His body ached for sleep, but he thought he could hang on a bit longer for her.

Famished, he ate six of the intricately spiced lamb meatballs and a mound of rice. While he ate, Mosi cut and folded construction paper, colored the sides while keeping up a meandering explanation of how it all worked. Richard met Chen's eyes over the child's head, and they shared a smile.

"You have children?" Richard asked.

"A daughter."

"I'm sorry. I'll try to get you home as soon as possible."

"It is all right. I feel an obligation," Chen said.

"Speaking of, how are you coming on that . . . ah . . . project?"

Chen picked up on Richard's obvious reluctance to speak openly about the sword and was equally vague. Unfortunately, the answer was far more specific. "Alas, not well. I wish I had better news."

Richard and Mosi played with the hexaflexagon for a while. Weber finally intervened. "Hey, Mosi, would you show me how to make one of those things?" Richard threw him a grateful glance and stood up. He bent and kissed the top of Mosi's head. She didn't stiffen or flinch, and he felt a bubble of joy at her acceptance of the embrace.

Richard laid a hand on Weber's shoulder. "I'll grab four hours and then call the office."

"Six."

"Five."

"Deal."

As he walked past, Richard crooked a finger at Eddie, who jumped up and fell into step with him as he headed to the sleeping quarters. "I'm worried about letting you go to the university tonight. There's an Old One loose," he said quietly.

Eddie paled. Unlike the others, Eddie had seen a fully operational gate and faced down Old Ones at Grenier's Virginia compound. "If one of those monsters is around, there is no way I'm going. None of us should. Trout'll be pissed, but we're not going to figure out the sword tonight."

"Will you ever figure it out?" Richard asked.

Eddie's shoulders slumped. "I don't know. We don't even know what it was . . . is, or how it was made."

"So what is Trout working on if not recovering the sword?"

"It has to do with computing" was the cautious answer.

"Using Kenntnis?"

"It's hard to explain. And there's no point trying to explain unless it's going to be real."

"Okay."

They parted. Richard went to his bunk, stripped down to his briefs, set the alarm on his watch, and crawled under the covers. He didn't remember going to sleep. When he woke, Mosi was asleep in her alcove. Gently pulling back the screening blanket, Richard gazed down at the sleeping child. He would not, *could* not, allow her to fall into Grenier's hands. *How far would you go, and what would you be willing to do to prevent that?* He knew the answer, and he spent a long time under very hot water in the shower trying to wash away that knowledge.

The scientists were still up and appeared to be working. Sözer caught Richard as he was heading upstairs with the satellite phone.

"A private plane arrived two days ago. It is owned by the Titchen Group. There were twelve people aboard, among them Alexander Titchen." The general reacted to Richard's expression. "You know him?"

"We had a run-in. I'm not his favorite person."

"We tried to arrange to have him detained, but we are getting resistance from unexpected sources within the government. And there are rumblings from the squatter slums on the hillsides. Police have been sent in, but I don't have specifics yet."

"Thank you. Keep me posted."

Upstairs, Richard nervously spun an Atatürk ashtray displayed on a counter. It didn't seem very respectful to the father of his country to grind out cigarette butts on his face, but maybe he just didn't understand smokers' culture, Richard thought while he listened to the phone ring.

"Lumina Enterprises."

"Hey, Jeannette—"

"Grenier has called. Five times. He left a number and he wants you to call him."

Richard sat with that for a moment. "Okay. Give me the number." He grabbed a sales pad and pen from next to a cash register.

"Are you out of your mind?"

"No more than usual."

"Richard, you can't trust him."

"I don't, but working in the dark doesn't help me."

Jeannette sighed and gave him the number.

"Everything else okay?" Richard asked.

"No, nothing is okay," she snapped. "But at least we're back functioning. Oh, and I talked with Pamela. She's on the job."

"Good. Talk to you soon." He disconnected, looked up, and met Weber's frown. "Are you going to start in on me now too?"

"You call him, and you'll give something away. He knows your buttons, Richard. He can manipulate you."

"And I know his. Maybe we'll just cancel each other out."

Weber turned away and hunched a shoulder. "Why don't you ever listen to me?"

Richard flinched. He reached out and tentatively touched Weber's hand. "I do. But we've got to kick this one way or the other. We can't go on in this limbo. We can't hide here forever."

Weber closed his fingers over Richard's and squeezed hard. Unfortunately, it was his right hand, and Richard winced and gasped. "Sorry, sorry," Weber said, and bestowed a quick kiss on the abused hand. Richard briefly touched the older man's cheek, then keyed in the number he'd been given. Grenier answered on the first ring.

"Richard. We need to meet. I have an offer for you."

Bubbles from the soda floated ghostlike through the amber of the whiskey. Grenier watched as they fizzed and then died. He lifted the highball glass, the ice chiming against the sides, and took a sip. The bar at the Hilton Hotel was nearly deserted at this hour of the night. Despite the elegant furnishings, it seemed sad and depressing. Titchen had mocked Grenier when he'd proposed a meeting with Richard.

"He won't come."

"He will. We have a past."

"And you really think he would quietly place himself, the child, and Kenntnis in our power?"

"He won't want the streets to run with blood."

"It's going to happen. The Old One is hungry."

"He doesn't have to know that. I'll convince him we're in control."

"You just don't want him killed."

Grenier sensed scrutiny, and he ponderously swiveled on the too-small barstool. Richard stood in the doorway. The muted lights glinted on the silver gilt in his hair. He was dressed, for him, very casually—a crisp white shirt, a leather jacket, blue jeans—and he was studying Grenier. There was something in Richard's expression that made Grenier uneasy. Richard crossed to him.

"Let's go to a booth. This stool is killing me. Do you want a drink?"

"You buying?"

Grenier felt off balance. The boy seemed poised, calm, no down-cast eyes or nervous knotting of fingers. Grenier nodded.

"Lagavulin 21," Richard said to the bartender.

It was a very expensive and very fine single-malt scotch. Grenier was startled. "So, your love of the expensive extends beyond clothes, watches, and pianos."

"And cars. Thanks to Kenntnis, I discovered the wonder of cars."

Grenier found himself struggling to slide into the booth. Richard smoothly moved to a table and sat down. Flushing, Grenier followed, pulled back the chair so his belly would have clearance, and sat down. He eyed Richard resentfully. None of this was going as he had ex-pected.

"You wanted to talk to me. I'm here." Richard looked around. "Where's your new boss?"

"We're colleagues."

"Just keep on telling yourself that." The drink arrived, three fin-gers of golden amber liquid in a cut-crystal tumbler. "I assume you're all going to behave. I'm armed, and there's a squad of soldiers in and around this building. They'll react if I don't come out. Or if they hear gunfire."

"We're not stupid. We don't know the location of the little girl or Kenntnis. Yet. I'm giving you an opportunity to end this without casualties on either side. The sword is gone. Kenntnis is damaged. Your company is collapsing."

"Hmm, sounds dire. So, is this the Surrender Dorothy moment? You might want to recall how that worked out for the Wicked Witch." He gave Grenier an ironic grin. "So what's this alternative you're of-fering?" Richard took a sip of his scotch. Rolled it through his mouth before he swallowed.

Grenier folded his hands on the table and leaned forward with that intense, comforting body language he had learned in countless counseling sessions. "Don't force this to a fight, Richard. There's no need for people to die." His voice was gentle, pleading. "Turn over the child and Kenntnis. Work with us. Titchen has resources. He might be able to recover the sword."

"And have Mosi to wield it. He'd never trust me. Wisely." Richard took another sip of scotch.

"He won't kill you. I won't let him."

"Oh, Mark." The weary amusement was very evident. "You have no say in this. You're powerless. You always have been. When are you going to realize that?"

"Not true. *You* took all of it from me. Made me a beggar."

"Yes, I made it impossible for you to perform magic, but the rest of it . . ." Richard shook his head. "You told yourself you were powerful, but you've never been anything but a pawn. Of the Old Ones. Of Titchen. Even of me. And you're too smart and too self-aware not to have known that deep down. That's why you resented me so much, because I made you face it." Richard paused for another sip. "The Old Ones and these guys . . . they're just using you until you cease to be useful. And didn't you learn your lesson last time? You overpromised, failed, and had to run to me for protection. Where and to whom are you going to run this time? I really hope you didn't promise Titchen that you could deliver me, because you're going to fail . . . again." Richard drained the last of the scotch, stood, and looked down at Grenier. "I will never place Mosi in their hands, and no one, and especially not you, will ever have control over me again."

Grenier watched that upright figure walk away, shoulders squared, back straight, head held high. There was an obstruction in his throat equal parts rage and regret. "You're going to die!" he shouted, to the consternation of the bartender and a businessman with a loosened tie slumped in a corner booth.

Richard looked back over his shoulder. The recessed lights highlighted the chiseled planes of that flawless face. "Everybody does, Mark. And there are worse things than dying."

Richard left the bar. Grenier felt like a drowning man watching a distant shoreline recede. Knowing it was only a matter of time until he was overcome, he lurched out of his chair and ran ponderously after the young man.

His heavy footfalls had alerted Richard. He had stopped and stood waiting in the lobby. Their only witness was a sleepy night-desk clerk leaning on the counter.

"Something else? And you're ruining my exit line." The blue eyes glittered coldly.

"Please. Please, I'm begging you. Let me come back. I know what Titchen is planning."

"How many times do you think you can turn coat, Mark?" Richard sounded almost amused.

"You can trust me this time. I won't betray you. I swear. I can help. I know things. You need me."

"No. *You* need *me*. And no. Decisions have consequences. You have to accept them. Live with them . . . or die with them."

To his utter shame, a sob burst from his chest. "Richard, please . . . help me." Tears were coursing down his cheeks. A great weight seemed to have fallen onto his head and shoulders. Grenier sank down to his knees, reached out with that crystalline hand.

For an instant there was a flash of pity in the ice-blue eyes, then it was gone. "Good-bye, Mark."

As Richard slid into the car, Weber pulled off his headset. Richard removed the small microphone from beneath the collar of his shirt and handed it to the older man. "So? Were you afraid I was going to give in?"

Weber took a quick glance around, cupped Richard's cheek, and gave him a quick kiss. "Where did this badass come from?" Then dropping the teasing tone, he added, "You're sure not the insecure rookie I met six years ago." Richard shot him a shy and appreciative glance.

Weber put the car in gear. "You did scare me a little bit with that stuff about Mosi. I mean, what if we can't . . . what would you do?"

Richard stared down at his clasped hands. "I know what I should do."

Weber swallowed audibly, stared intently out the front windshield. "It won't come to that."

It was late, past one, but there was still traffic. Apparently Ankara bustled at all hours. They left the tall buildings of the city center behind, and that's when they spotted the fires high on the hills. The flames scarred the darkness, illuminating the shanties. Sirens were beginning to howl from various points around the city.

"Coincidence or distraction?" Weber asked.

"Let's assume distraction and get the hell back to Işık."

Richard used the mirrors to check for their security while Weber dodged police and fire vehicles. They were constantly forced to pull to the side to let emergency vehicles pass. The fires were gaining in strength and scope. They hit a roadblock. Minutes ticked past with Weber's fingers tapping nervously on the steering wheel keeping count. An urgent knocking on the passenger window made Richard jump and reach for his sidearm. He recognized the guard, Tamay, and rolled down the window.

"We've been ordered to . . ." There was a Turkish word. "To make . . . order and . . . um, fire." The soldier threw out her arms.

"Keep it from spreading?" Richard suggested. The soldier nodded vigorously.

"I go with. Um, make you past . . ." A frown wrinkled the woman's forehead as she searched for the word.

"Guard post?" Weber offered. Another enthusiastic nod. Weber jerked his head toward the backseat. "Climb in. Sounds like we're on our own," he added to Richard. A few minutes later, the police opened the road again.

Despite the language difficulties, Richard couldn't stop himself. He asked, "What are you hearing?"

"Bad . . . crazy."

"Guess we know where the Old One went," Richard said. Rather than task Tamay's limited English, Richard lapsed into silence and watched the fires. The area affected was getting larger.

Up the hill, past the guards, Tamay took the car away and Weber and Richard ran down the long pathway. The lions were hulking shadows on either side. Weber's longer legs had him pulling away. Richard, hands clenched at his sides, ran harder and caught up. The motionless soldier in his guard box didn't twitch as they pounded past. Someone must have called ahead, because Marangoz was waiting for them at the door of the gift shop.

One look at his expression, and Richard knew there was something worse than fires and riots. "What?"

"Çelik has been arrested."

"I got out just before the police arrived. Çelik got off a text. Don't know if Sözer made it," Marangoz said. The words emerged like machine gun fire.

"How long before they find the way into this place?" Richard asked.

"Çelik will resist, but . . ." He shrugged.

Richard remembered the two days of torture at Grenier's hands and nodded. "So, time to move."

They pushed through the hidden door. Boot heels beat staccato rhythms on the concrete floor as soldiers moved briskly through the headquarters. There was the crackle and squawk of radios, and paper shredders whined and growled, gulping down documents. Under a ventilation grate, other soldiers were burning papers in metal trash cans.

All the Lumina refugees were awake. Mosi, eyes wide and lips compressed into a thin line, ran to Richard and wrapped her arms around his waist. She looked up at him, her expression fierce. "Are the monsters coming?"

"Probably. But we're leaving. Go pack, and give me just a few minutes. I have some things I have to do." She nodded, released him, and ran for the sleeping quarters. "Eddie, I need you." Weber started to walk away. "Damon, you too."

Richard sat down at a nearby desk and pulled blank paper out of a printer tray. He began to write:

I, Richard Noel Oort, place Lumina Enterprises LLC solely under the control of Pamela Celeste Oort. All assets are hers to deal with as she sees fit.

He signed and drew two lines beneath his signature and wrote *Witnesses.* He handed the pen to Eddie and nodded at the page. The scientist's mouth twisted as if he were trying to decide between cursing or crying, but he signed. Richard offered the pen to Weber, who glared at him.

"This isn't necessary."

"You know it is."

"Fuckin' son of a bitch." Weber grabbed the pen and scrawled his signature.

"Cross!" Richard yelled.

The homeless god pushed through the controlled chaos. "What?"

Richard dated the makeshift will and handed him the paper. "Take this to Pamela."

Cross glanced at the brief message. "Pretty shitty legalese."

"I'll take that as a compliment."

"Don't you need me here?"

"I do, but I need this more. Paladins come and go. Lumina has to endure. Go."

For a long moment, the Old One with the Jesus face studied Richard. He inclined his head and said, "It has been an honor." The deep tone and the formal delivery told Richard everything. He swallowed hard, pushing back the fear, and gestured. Cross splintered, and the light shards rushed for the ventilation shafts. Soldiers cried out and ducked as the splinters flew past them.

Richard walked briskly toward the sleeping quarters. "Damon, you're going to escort Mosi, Brook, and Jerry and the scientists—"

"No!"

"I won't have this argument. I don't have time for it." Richard gestured at the anxiously milling scientists. "Are you going to leave them with no protection? I'm expendable. They're not."

"Not to me."

"I'll just be . . . over here . . ." Eddie said uncomfortably. He jerked his thumb toward the other scientists. "There . . . waiting . . ."

"Brook and Jerry both served—"

"Jerry is in his sixties, and Brook never saw combat. It has to be you."

"Richard, please . . . I can't—"

Richard closed his hand viselike on Weber's upper arm. "Save me from the decision that I used to threaten Grenier. Take Mosi. Keep her safe."

Weber slumped, resigned now and accepting. An obstruction filled Richard's throat. He coughed, but it didn't clear. Unable to speak, he shook his head and turned away. Mosi was just closing the top on her suitcase as Richard strode into the sleeping quarters. Kenntnis sat still and silent on a bunk. His head slowly pivoted between Mosi and Richard.

"Mosi, you're going to go with Damon, and Eddie, and the others. Mr. Kenntnis and I will catch up with you later."

The little girl looked from Weber's stone face to Richard's too-bright smile. Her eyes narrowed with suspicion. She planted her fists on her hips. "Are you up to something?" The gesture and the tone made it sound like a quote, and Richard sensed she was channeling her mother.

"Yes. We're going to fool the monsters," Richard said as he wrapped a blanket around several pillows until it was about Mosi size. He touched Kenntnis lightly on the elbow. "Come on, sir, we're leaving." Weber took Mosi's suitcase, Richard clasped her hand, and they headed back into the main room.

Eddie was in a huddle with Ranjan, Trout, and Chen. Their expressions ranged from tense to frightened. Richard glanced down at the child walking next to him, long black hair swinging from side to side. He then looked at his pathetic bundle. Steeling himself, Richard lifted scissors off a desk as he walked past.

"Mosi." Her eyes flicked between the bundle and the scissors. "Mosi, I'm sorry, but I need to cut your hair. I need this"—he gestured with the bundle—"to look like you."

Her hands flew to her head, she pulled the waterfall of hair over her shoulder and clutched it tightly. She was trying hard not to cry. Feeling like a brute, Richard set aside the blanket and pillows, took a strand, and placed the scissors at the nape of her neck. There was a gentle touch on his shoulder. Tamay was there. She reached up and pulled pins from her bun. A cascade of black hair fell over her shoulders. She indicated her hair.

"Please. Be welcome."

"Thank you," Richard said fervently, and hoped the woman knew how deeply he meant it. He cut off her hair, and she helped him secure it with clear tape to the top of a pillow.

"It won't pass close inspection, but it should send the hounds after us."

Weber looked away, took a breath. "You'll need more than your Browning." Richard nodded and followed Weber to the duffel bag. He picked up a shotgun, filled his pockets with shells, and added a box of ammunition for the pistol. "Take a few flash-bangs," Weber said, adding the grenades.

The weight of lead dragged down his leather jacket. "You're ruining my coat," Richard complained.

"You ruined my truck."

"Does this make us even?"

"Not even close."

Finally, Richard picked up three Benchmade automatic knives. "For when the guns stop working," he said with a smile. He had a feeling it was not entirely convincing.

Now fully armed, Richard pulled Marangoz, Weber, Eddie, Brook, and Jerry into a huddle. "I'm going out the front with Kenntnis and my fake Mosi. Give us a head start, then the rest of you boot out the tunnel."

"And go where?" Eddie asked.

"And how do we get there?" Weber added.

Richard looked at the general. "Does Işık still have enough authority to get that plane released and refueled?"

"Yes. We will manage."

"Go back to Lumina. The building is a functional fortress. I don't want to know how you're going to get back to Istanbul. Just in case . . ." Everyone looked in opposite directions. Richard sucked in as deep a breath as he could manage. His lungs felt clogged. "Okay, then."

"May I give you a word of advice, Mr. Oort?" Marangoz said.

"Please."

"Head for the old city, and the Ankara Kalesi Fortress. Medieval buildings, small twisting streets, good places to play, how do you say, cat-and-seek?"

"Right, thank you."

They broke from their huddle, and Richard found Mosi glaring at him. Her eyebrows were drawn into a single straight line from her fierce frown. "You and the *Yá Ahiga* are going to fight—"

Richard, puzzled, looked down at her. "*Yá Ahiga*? Do you mean Kenntnis?"

"Yes," she said in the tone of *duh!*

"What does that mean?"

Mosi's mouth twisted in that way she had when deep concentration was required. "In white people talk, I guess it would be Sky War-rior."

"I like that . . . *Yá Ahiga,*" Richard tested out the words in his mouth.

Mosi's hands waved like startled butterflies. Someone had given the little girl nail polish because her nails were rainbow colors. "You can't learn Navajo now! Are you taking me? I'm a warrior too."

"Yes. You are. You will be. But you're not yet, and no, I'm not tak-ing you." He gripped her shoulders hard enough that she winced. He loosened his hold. "Do this for me. And for your brother, and your parents and grandfather. Be safe. Grow up. Fight them." He released her and stepped back.

Mosi's mouth worked as she fought tears. She flung herself against him and hugged him hard. "Don't die too, *na sha dii!*" she said in a choked voice.

He couldn't bring himself to give her the comforting lie, or the cruel truth. He said nothing, just hugged her again. Gathering up the Mosi bundle and taking Kenntnis by the elbow, he headed for the doors out of the bunker.

"The car is being brought," Marangoz said as he walked past. "Go with hope and courage." Richard nodded and reflected that in any other company Marangoz would have told him to *go with God.*

Weber fell into step with him. "I'm walking you out," he said in tones that clearly said, *Don't argue.* Richard nodded.

Out the hidden doors, as they walked up the stairs, Richard placed the blanket-wrapped pillows in Kenntnis's arms and arranged the hair to fall over his shoulder.

Weber gave him a questioning look. Richard shrugged. "Figured it was more believable if the big guy carried the kid."

Weber gave a laugh that held no amusement. They left the gift shop. Their heels echoed off the stone walls as they crossed the giant plaza. The edges of the horizon were pink and gold like a shy dancer lifting her dark skirt to reveal her petticoats. Soon the rising sun would strike fire from the stones of the mausoleum, a fitting tribute to all that Lumina and Kenntnis represented. A light breeze brought the scent of flowers from the gardens that surrounded the mausoleum. Richard paused to drink it in. The caress of the wind against his flushed cheeks, the smells, the birdsong, the growl of traffic as the city shook itself awake, but over it all was the discordant undulating wail of sirens, the rank stench of smoke, and perhaps, just faintly, humans—screaming. There was no peace to be found in this moment.

A car was idling at the edge of the sidewalk. A young soldier stood next to it. Richard faced Weber. "Tell Pamela to buy you that new truck. My orders." They stood in silence for a moment. "Well, this is it, then."

"You come back."

Richard shook his head. "No bullshit between us, Damon. You know that's not likely. Take care of her. Of all of them." He turned away. Weber grabbed him at the waist and gave him one hard kiss. He then released Richard, stepped back, raised a hand in farewell, turned, and walked away. Richard led Kenntnis to the car. He didn't look back. He had a feeling Damon wasn't going to look back either.

TWENTY-TWO

M OSI sat in a chair in the mess hall, knees drawn up to her chin, and watched the frenzied preparations. Her tummy felt like angry birds were pecking at it. She was so angry. And so scared. She hoped a lot of bad things happened to Richard. He'd broken his word. He was a lying white man. He had said he was her *na sha dii* and that he would protect her, and he broke his word. He left her alone and the monsters were coming.

The big man, Damon, who seemed so fond of the *na sha dii*, handed out guns and knives to the men who had flown the big airplane. The scientists were gathering up papers. They all looked scared, except for the man with the big bare feet who spent all his time with the *Yá Ahiga*. He seemed mad.

Mosi slid out of her chair, marched up to Weber, and announced, "I want a gun too."

He blinked down at her. "Uh, I think you're a little young."

"Richard told his sister he would give me a gun."

"He did not."

"He did too. You were there. At dinner. After the *adilgashii* made a hole in the road with knives in it and your truck blew up and all the trees fell down."

"Shit."

"Told you."

"Yeah, well, Richard isn't here, and I'm not giving you a gun." She glared and glared. The man sighed, looked around. "Look, I really don't have anything that would fit your hand. You still have your wrist rocket, right?" She nodded. "Well, put that on. And here." He gave her a knife with a wickedly sharp and thin blade. "Now you be careful and don't cut yourself."

Mosi gave him a pitying look. "I helped Mother butcher our sheep. I know how to use a knife."

"All righty, then." Weber turned to the scientists and pilots. "Okay, this is us going. Everybody ready?"

There were mutters of assent. Marangoz and a soldier led them into the communal bathroom. While the noncom unscrewed and moved aside a toilet, Marangoz gave terse instructions.

"Make your way to Sincan. It's a town to the west and a little north. We will try to have someone meet you with vehicles. If not," Marangoz shrugged and handed over a satchel, "here are lira. Buy what you need, get to Istanbul, but be cunning."

With the toilet removed, Mosi could see there was a ladder leading down.

"Hope nobody availed themselves of that particular commode," Chen said as he turned around and slipped quickly down the ladder.

One by one they descended into a concrete-lined tunnel lit by small LED pin spots. Mosi found herself in the center of the men. The stink of their sweat was strong in the narrow tunnel, and nervous breaths ruffled the top of her hair. Some of them didn't have very good breath. She found herself thinking about her *na sha dii*. How he always smelled clean and nice. Richard was like no one she had ever known. Someone a little in front released a very long, loud, and smelly fart. There was nervous laughter.

"Sorry, sorry, get gas when I'm nervous," Eddie said.

"Just don't alert our enemies with your pungency," Ranjan said with a laugh.

"Or fart more. Use it like a gas attack. Might put 'em down," Trout grunted. There was more laughter.

"Maybe the talking and laughing should stop?" Jerry, the old pilot, said tightly. The silence and the tension returned.

They stopped, and Mosi heard the sound of metal on metal. A gust of air carrying both smoke and the scents of flowers and cut grass rolled down the tunnel. They scrambled out and found themselves in a park. The grass underfoot was deep and lush, tall trees dotted the rolling hill. On all sides there were perfectly manicured flower beds filled with a riot of massed flowers. Off to the left, Mosi saw a small culvert designed to carry water from the mausoleum, now far above them, down to the storm drains in the street below. It went under another hill as a small tunnel, and she could not see where it let out.

They started down the hill toward the iron fence that divided the garden from the road. Traffic was scurrying past even though the sun was barely up. There were still pockets of shadow among the trees and bushes. The three men with the guns were looking in all directions. Eddie's head was swinging wildly from side to side, but Mosi didn't think he was seeing very much.

The young pilot, Brook, stiffened. Mosi followed the direction of his stare. Was there a darker shadow among the trees? It moved and resolved into a man barreling out of the screen of trees. There were shouts, more men were charging at them from all directions. The scientists were milling like terrified sheep. Mosi scrunched down and darted between a pair of legs. There were suddenly a lot of legs stepping and swaying as people struggled. Mosi noticed that the bad men all had black pants. She saw a chance and went between one set of black-clad legs. The man tripped and fell down with a yell.

A gunshot blasted somewhere above her head, and she heard Weber yelling, "Mosi, run!"

She jumped to her feet and started running. There was someone behind her, drawing closer. She jerked to the side as fingers scraped roughly across the back of her blouse. The culvert was at her feet. She jumped down and ran toward the mouth of the pipe. The footsteps of her hunter were loud on the concrete, and she could hear his breaths like a man blowing on coals to make them hot. Clenching her fists at her sides, Mosi ran as hard as she could and flung herself in a dive at the opening where the culvert joined the pipe and went under the hill. Concrete, twigs, and leaves tore along her legs, and she felt her pants tear as she slid into the pipe. It was very dark and tight, but she could fit. Digging her elbows into the mud and trash that lined the bottom of the pipe, she crawled as fast as she could. Behind her she could hear the man yelling and more gunshots.

"Please don't let anybody die," she said aloud, and hated it because she sounded like a whiny baby.

Angrily, she wiped away tears on her shoulder and kept crawling. It was a big street and it took a long time, but she saw growing light ahead of her. She was on the other side of the big street in an empty area between buildings. She looked back and saw one of the black-pants men trying to dodge the lanes of traffic and cross the street while another was just climbing over the iron fence. She couldn't see her own people. Gulping down a sob, Mosi ran toward the buildings and started turning down streets in random directions. There were people on the sidewalks now, and they looked at her, mud-coated with twigs in her hair, and a tear and cut on her leg. One man tried to stop her. She kicked him hard in the shin. He yelled, and she ran down steps between two buildings.

She found herself in a large courtyard. In the center was the statue of a man mounted on a prancing horse. She looked up into the stern face and recognized the features of the man whose pictures lined the walls where they had been staying. The sun was fully up now, and postcard vendors and a man with pigeons in a cage were drifting into the plaza and setting up. Mosi ran to the man with the birds.

"How do I get to the Old City?" she asked.

His skin was the color of old leather and creased with lines. It made her think of Grandfather. She sniffed and defiantly wiped her nose on her sleeve.

"You all right, child?"

"Yes. No. I need my . . ." She hesitated. If the man knew Richard wasn't kin, then maybe he wouldn't help her. Or worse, stop her and then the bad men might find her. It twisted her insides a little, but she said, "I need to find my daddy. He's in the Old City. Something bad's happened."

The old man glanced toward the hills and the fires. "Yes. Something bad has happened," he said quietly. "You see this street on the left?" He walked her over and pointed. "Follow it. Up. Up. Up." In the distance, crowning a high hill, Mosi saw a large building. It seemed red in the early-morning light. "Just below the fortress is the Old City."

"Thank you."

The old man laid a hand briefly on the top of her head. "*Allahaısmarladık.*"

The bad men wouldn't stop looking, so she didn't want to stay on the same street all the way. Now that she knew where she was going and had a landmark, it wouldn't be a problem. Jumping between streets meant she had to walk farther, but she was strong, she could do it. She started toward the distant fortress. She would find Richard, and everything would be okay.

⟨━◆━⟩

The road spiraled around the massive hill as if a giant with a paring knife had peeled a green apple. It was early, so there was little traffic, which made Richard's pursuers very obvious. The Old One clearly wasn't with them, since they were in cars. Richard had Kenntnis in the backseat and his Mosi stand-in buckled into the front seat. On their left, towers built from blocks of red-tinged stone defended the summit. It was an odd design. All the towers were connected with only limited distance between them, and instead of offering the flat side to the enemy, the towers were offset so enemies would approach the point of a corner. The placement made the towers seem like teeth ready to grind invaders to pulp.

They drove past a little restaurant tucked into the side of the hill, where men were unloading supplies from the back of a small truck. Another curve, and now the battlements were draped with rugs either drying or airing in the sun. It was an incongruous sight from stone jaws to stone laundry line.

The silence was adding to Richard's nerves. "So here we are, sir. End of the line. I guess. We did some good stuff together, didn't we?" Richard gave his head a sharp shake. "This is probably really stupid, huh? It's not like you're going to answer. Maybe you don't even understand any longer. Doesn't matter, and if you don't mind I'd like to keep talking. Kind of helps. So, are there any of your kind left? Somewhere . . . out in the universe? If there are, I wish we could tell them what happened to you. Or better yet, one of them turns up to help. But I guess that only happens in stories, huh?"

The road ended at a car park, and a sign in numerous languages stated that only residents' vehicles were permitted from this point. Richard parked, grabbed the shotgun, and opened the back door.

"Come on, sir." He handed the fake Mosi bundle to Kenntnis. Richard saw no point in alerting Titchen and Grenier to the fact the little girl wasn't with him until it was absolutely necessary. They started up the narrow road. Farther down the hill, Richard heard the engines of the approaching cars. "And while we still have the chance . . . I just want to say . . . thank you. For trusting me with your company and for opening my eyes. About the world . . . and about me."

They passed a few gift shops, closed at this early hour, and then hit an archway that had once held the city gates. Beyond were ancient stone, plaster, and wattle houses two and three stories high and lopsided with age. Overhanging balconies yearned toward each other. Power lines and wires snaked above the narrow cobbled street, and wooden signs adorned with the Coca-Cola label swung gently in the breeze.

"We could almost be in the eleventh century, couldn't we?" Richard asked. Kenntnis remained silent.

Five children, three boys and two girls, raced past, flanked by a pair of fat-bellied puppies yapping with excitement. Richard and Kenntnis walked on, and Richard felt the muscles in the back of his thighs and calves starting to pull from the steep climb. They reached a small courtyard with a battered stone fountain in the center. A few men were gathered, smoking cigarettes. They reacted when they saw the shotgun, but no one approached or said a word. Either it wasn't that uncommon or there was something in the smoky air that gave warning that things were amiss. Richard took the next turn to the right, and they climbed higher.

Past shops with enormous white sacks filled with carded wool. Others displayed wooden barrels filled with dried fruit of every description, dried beans and peas, potatoes and dried lemons. Others were heaped with spices. The smell of different kinds of chili and every other imaginable spice was strong enough to overpower even the reek of smoke. It reminded Richard he was hungry. He thought that was maybe a good sign. That his fear wouldn't immobilize him when the time came.

He picked smaller and smaller streets, searching for a place to make a stand. A place where, he hoped, no bystanders would be hurt.

Titchen's cell phone rang. He answered, listened, then drove his fist into the back of the front seat. The guard seated next to the driver jerked but kept his eyes strictly on the curving road ahead.

"Fucker tricked us! He doesn't have the girl. She was with the scientists."

"But the second team got her, yes?" Grenier asked.

"No. She got away." Titchen rolled a choleric eye toward Grenier.

Grenier didn't misinterpret the look. "I misjudged my influence. I'm sorry."

"Sounds like you also misjudged his smarts and his courage."

"So shall we return to the hotel and let your teams search for her? Or I could go back and coordinate the search. Men such as ourselves really have no business trying to be action heroes. Let your experts handle this."

"No. This guy's made a monkey of me one too many times, and we may need our . . . ally. These numbnuts can't handle that." Grenier watched the back of the driver's neck redden. "And you're really useless."

"Then why am I here? Why didn't you leave me behind?"

"Because I want you to be there when we kill Oort."

"Why? Do you think that's going to bother me?"

"Yeah, actually, I do."

Grenier looked out the side window so Titchen wouldn't see the truth.

The stitch in her side hurt enough that Mosi had to stop running. She forced herself to keep walking, but the road seemed to stretch on endlessly, and she kept having to duck off to the side and hide when cars went past. She looked up at the rugs hanging on the stone walls and was startled that one of them looked so much like the rugs her grandmother had made for sale at the Crown Point rug auctions. She wondered why that was. Realizing she was just standing and staring, Mosi pushed herself back into motion. Then she heard the clop of a horse's hooves. Startled, she looked back, and around a curve came a man driving a wagon pulled by a skinny gray horse. The back of the wagon was filled with milk bottles. The man had a nice face, round and jolly. She decided to take a chance. Stepping out into the road, Mosi waved. He pulled up and looked at her.

"Are you going up there?" she asked, and pointed toward the top of the hill. The man nodded. "Can I . . ." Richard's voice filled her memory. *"The word 'can' implies ability. 'May' implies permission."* She corrected herself. "May I have a ride?" Again the nod. Mosi scrambled up into the seat next to the man, and the horse resumed its patient plod.

"We had horses. Me and my family. My daddy taught me how to ride. I like horses."

The man finally spoke. "So do I. The wind of heaven is that which blows between a horse's ears."

Every part of him hurt. Knees, feet, back. Most worrisome was the ache in his chest as Grenier labored after Titchen and the eight guards deeper into the Old City. They had ignored the sign at the car park and driven three cars into the old quarter. Men had approached, prepared to remonstrate with them. Titchen had raised his arms, called, and the Old One had left the burning shantytown where it had been feeding and flung itself across the sky, trailing shadows and terror. Its arrival filled the area with the stink of burned rubber, rust, and blood. The cars had died and the men had fled, wailing in fear.

Once the Old One joined them, they were forced to proceed on foot, and Grenier was beginning to think the walk alone was going to kill him. The creature made no effort to form a body. It oozed through the streets, wormlike and with multiple tentacles. Within the darkness, there was the sense of eyes, hundreds, thousands of them. As they passed, people abandoned their houses, screaming, weeping, turning on each other. Occasionally a tendril would stretch out and enfold a human, and that human would die.

And each time it killed, Titchen laughed. With each death the laugh became more manic, and even his guards, loyal though they might be, were starting to look at him askance.

How on earth did he get this rich when he is clearly barking mad? Grenier wondered with some resentment. He also wondered what power the creature possessed that its touch could kill. And if it could kill a paladin.

They were almost at the crown of the hill. Judging from the screams, something terrible was going on behind them. Richard stopped, looked back, and tried to decide what to do. Go back? Could he actually help? Didn't matter. He had to try. Whatever was happening below was a direct result of his presence.

He started back down the hill. His leather-soled loafers slipped a bit on the cobbles, so steep was the incline. He was startled when Kenntnis caught him by the arm and kept him from falling. He looked up into the man's face, but the distant expression never changed.

An enormous wall loomed up on their right. Richard had noticed it when they'd first passed, heading up the hill. Mixed in among the cut stones were blocks of marble. Many of them bore carvings of Greek and Roman design, and one block in particular sported a bas-relief face, the mouth open as if echoing the screams from the buildings below.

Richard glanced up at it and froze as a viscous black tentacle oozed from the mouth of the carving. Smaller tendrils emerged from the eyes, and the three merged and braided, trailing down the wall and reaching out toward him. The stink of Old One nearly drove him to his knees. Richard dropped the shotgun, pulled loose a knife, and snapped it open.

Powerful arms closed around his waist, and he was flung unceremoniously over Kenntnis's shoulder. The big man whirled and began running up the hill away from the creeping oily shadows. The jolting run slammed Kenntnis's shoulder into Richard's diaphragm, driving the air from his lungs and sending pain lancing through the stitches in his side. The Mosi bundle had been tossed aside, the pillow with the taped-on hair rolling away to come to rest against the side of a building. The sight of that tumbled hair focused all his hopes and fears. If the Old One was here, then the ruse had succeeded and Damon would have gotten Mosi clear.

Richard was sure of it. He had to be.

Screaming people were racing down the road toward Mosi and her companion. The horse gave a snort of alarm at the approaching crowd. The driver called out in his own language. Some of the men answered him. The man looked terrified and began to turn the horse and wagon.

"No! What are you doing? I have to go up there!"

The man ignored her, but the crush of people made the turn almost impossible, and a back wheel lodged on the stone lip at the road's edge. Mosi couldn't understand the words, but it sounded like the man was cursing as he jumped down from the wagon. He reached up to try and lift her down, but Mosi slapped his hands away. He shouted at her in his own language and joined the people running down the hill. Mosi, panting, frightened, and near tears, sat frozen for a few moments in the wagon. The horse was starting to plunge, trying to pull free. Mosi grabbed the knife Damon had given her, jumped down, and sawed at the leather traces, all the while keeping up a gentle conversation with the horse.

"You're a good boy, aren't you? You and I are going to ride to battle together. Much better than pulling a cart. If you do this, my *na sha dii* will take you home and you'll be my horse."

One by one, the traces parted. The gelding's ears flicked back and forth between her, and then up toward the city. Its nostrils were flaring and Mosi could see why. There was a bad stink in the air. Once the horse was free, Mosi led him over to the stone wall that outlined a parking lot, climbed up, and swung onto the horse bareback. Its back dropped as if he resented the sudden weight, but the horse didn't try to buck. Gathering up the cut reins, she nudged with her heel and sent the gelding up the hill.

TWENTY-THREE

K ENNTNIS continued to pound up a se-
ries of stone steps. Richard, hanging over the big man's shoulder, had
an excellent view of the rugs that lay on those steps. They were covered with evil eye wards, some incorporated into jewelry, key chains,
and various other trinkets. All abandoned now. Grabbing a breath,
he yelled, "Mr. Kenntnis! Sir! Please, put me down."

They passed between thick walls of red stone and marble blocks.
Kenntnis slowed and stumbled to a stop. He lifted Richard off his
shoulder and set him gently on his feet. Rubbing his abused diaphragm, Richard turned slowly and surveyed their surroundings.
They stood in the center of the high fortress. Flagged paving stones
were underfoot, and all around were arched entryways, small rooms
and narrow courtyards, and staircases leading to higher and higher
walls. At some points, they loomed at least a hundred feet over the

central circular courtyard. Richard saw a discarded camera and a scarf clinging to the rough stones. A breeze caught the scarf and sent it billowing high over the walls. This early there obviously hadn't been many tourists, and the few that had been present had fled.

Richard ran up one of the sets of stairs and onto two-foot-wide battlements that offered him a view into the Old City. The black tendrils wriggled along the streets and oozed from windows of the wood-and-plaster houses. Walking in the center of the tentacles was Alexander Titchen. Grenier plodded in his wake, mopping at his face with a handkerchief clutched in his real hand. There were eight armed men with them, not that their guns would do them any good. The only sound was an uncanny humming that lifted the hair on the nape of Richard's neck. Then a new sound intruded. Hoofbeats.

Frowning, Richard moved to a vantage point just above another gate into the fortress. A skinny gray horse, lather on its neck and a rider clinging to its mane, came scrambling up the steps. The rider's hair was a pennant of waving black. Richard didn't need to see the outfit to recognize Mosi. He gave a moan of despair.

Racing down the stairs, he arrived in the courtyard simultaneously with Mosi and her steed. She gave a sob and flung herself off the horse and into his arms. He hugged her close, her tears dampening his shirt.

"Mosi, baby, what are you doing here? Oh, God, I thought you were safe."

"The bad men were waiting. There was fighting—"

Anxiety stopped his breath. "Damon? Is Damon all right?"

"I don't know. He told me to run. I got between their legs, they couldn't catch me, and I got in a pipe. They couldn't fit and I got away."

"Why did you come here?"

"Where else could I go?" she said simply, and the answer had tears stinging his eyes.

Richard blinked them away and glanced back over his shoulder at Titchen and his monster, then past him to the laboring Grenier. For a brief instant, Richard's and Grenier's eyes met. The former preacher looked away. Had that been regret? Grief? Richard wasn't sure. It didn't matter. There was so little time left.

"Come on. Up. We're going up," Richard said.

"My pony?"

"They won't hurt him." Richard hoped he was right. The child was barely holding hysterics at bay. If she saw this horse die . . . "They're after us."

The moment the words were uttered, he realized that probably hadn't been the most comforting thing he could say, but maybe it was the right thing. The decision, the action, he had been trying to avoid now seemed inevitable. But could he do it?

Grabbing Kenntnis by the shoulder, Richard propelled him toward a set of stairs. He put Mosi in front of him. "Keep Mr. Kenntnis . . . the Sky Warrior moving, okay?" She gave a tense nod and laid her hands against the small of Kenntnis's back and started shoving. They climbed onto the first set of lower battlements. A quarter way around the circle was another set of stairs heading up to the next level. Richard pushed them all into a run toward those stairs. The arrival of the men and the creature in the courtyard was too much for the horse. It snorted in terror and bolted through a gate.

"Richard, it really is time to call it quits." Titchen was calling from the center of the courtyard, head craned back looking up at them. "Just give us the child and Mr. Kenntnis. We'll deal gently with them, and we'll make it quick for you. You have my word on it."

Richard drove them up the next set of stairs. "That's very kind of you, Mr. Titchen, but I'm going to decline."

The Old One's tentacles boiled up out of the courtyard, reaching for them. Titchen grated out something in a language Richard had heard only a couple of times before, out of Rhiana, Grenier, and Cross. It was guttural, harsh, and utterly inhuman; it also sounded oddly pleading. The oily black tentacles retreated to roil and writhe in the bowl of the courtyard. The guards, up to their waists in the darkness, were shaking, darting wild-eyed glances at the horror all around them.

The trio had reached the uppermost wall. Two feet wide, and no railing, but a person could boost himself up and almost circle the entire fortress on the top of the walls. Richard lifted Mosi onto the wall. She looked down and swayed for an instant. He caught the back of her shirt.

"Don't look down," he ordered. He climbed up and stretched out a hand to Kenntnis. The big man joined them on the narrow walkway.

"Where are we going?" Mosi asked.

"There." He pointed at the part of the wall that was at the tallest edge of the cliff.

They moved toward it, their pace a careful shuffle. Heights had never bothered Richard, perhaps because of years of gymnastics and the times he'd climbed masts on sailboats. Mosi was doing well, but Richard kept a hand on her shoulder as a precaution. From this highest vantage point, Ankara was spread out before them. He gazed out on the slender minaret of a mosque and the red-tiled roofs of the Old City, many topped with satellite dishes. In the city center, skyscrapers were wreathed in smoke, and on a distant sister cliff was another fortress with gleaming cell towers planted around it like silver spears. An odd juxtaposition of ancient technology and modern technology, and below them, writhing and billowing, the antithesis of human creativity and invention—an avatar of raw passion untempered by reason. On the hills across the bowl valley that held Ankara, a shantytown burned. Screams ripped the smoky air as people huddled in the houses below reacted to the presence of the Old One.

Richard was scared, regretting bad decisions he'd made, wishing he could see Pamela and Amelia and Joseph and Jeannette and Sam and Damon, especially Damon, one last time, but the Old One's mind-numbing horror couldn't touch him or Mosi because they were paladins, empty of all magic, beyond its power to beguile or terrorize. It could not freeze him or keep him from his final task.

Titchen started up the stairs. The creature squeezed and compressed itself into a shape vaguely reminiscent of a human form if a human body were made of squirming snakes. Deep within the dark tendrils there were hints of mucus-filled eyes, thousands of them. Was it one creature or a multitude of small ones? Did it matter? It and its human servant were coming.

Kenntnis reached the most distant point of the fort and stopped, blocked by a stone wall. They stood in a line, Richard, Mosi, and Kenntnis, and looked down at a sheer thousand-foot drop to the valley floor. On the other side, a hundred-foot fall to the paving stones of the courtyard, visible again. Only the long fall would be a guarantee of death. Once again, Richard's and Grenier's eyes met. The fat man's mouth worked, and then he called, "Richard, don't."

Richard wrapped his arms around Mosi, took a breath. She tensed in his arms as she realized what he was contemplating.

Titchen also seemed to realize Richard's intention. He stopped his advance and held out his hands in a placating manner. "Okay, okay, let's all just stop a minute. No need for this. And really, you're going to kill that little girl? Everything I've heard tells me you're not that kind of man."

Mosi looked up at him with an expression that held fear and doubt. "*Na sha dii?*"

The betrayal in her voice broke his resolve. *Protector. You promised to be her protector.* Richard slumped. "I'm sorry, Mosi, I failed you."

"Don't give me to them!"

"I can't hurt you either."

"Use the sword. Make everything all right!" Tears blurred the words.

Never had he felt more useless. An utter failure. He forced words past the lump in his throat. "I can't, baby, I lost the sword."

She stared at him in confusion and said, "The Sky Warrior has it."

He gaped at her, and then shadows came writhing out of a carved face on the mountain side of the wall, grasping for them. Mosi screamed. Richard spun and began feverishly patting down Kenntnis.

"No! Inside!" Mosi slipped past him and looked up into Kenntnis's eyes. "*Yá Ahiga*, it is time to fight."

She drove her hand into his torso. There was that flash of light similar to what had happened in Pamukkale. The shadows shied back. Mosi was holding the hilt. Richard was behind her and knew they were out of time. Wrapping his arms around her, he laid his hands over hers, and they drew the sword together. The musical chord was deafening, and the overtones vibrated in his chest. Richard pulled the sword from her grasp and spun to face the Old One. His heel caught on the rough surface of the wall, and he lost his balance. Arms pinwheeling, he tried to keep himself from going over the edge. Mosi shrieked, grabbed his coat, and steadied him. The shadows were retreating. Richard leaped after them, lunged, and fell to one knee as he stretched as far as he could reach. The tip of the sword sheared through a tendril.

A monstrous, discordant sound, part scream, part wet bubbling, echoed off the stone walls, and the infernal stink that seemed to always accompany the death of an Old One had Richard gagging, his eyes streaming. Titchen began to retreat, then turned and ran along the wall. Richard ran after him. He yelled back over his shoulder, "Mosi, you and Kenntnis find some cover. Go! Go!"

Titchen looked back in panic, and his foot caught on the rough stone. He staggered but had no ally to pull him back. With a wail that became a glissando scream, he went off the wall. Unfortunately, as far as Richard was concerned, they were no longer at the highest point of the fortress. It was a mere sixty or so feet. Titchen crashed on the steps leading up to the fortress, his body rolling across a souvenir-covered rug. He lay, a crumpled form, surrounded by the unblinking blue eyes of the wards.

Grenier suddenly emerged from beneath the gate at a waddling run. He lumbered past Titchen and spared him not a glance. Rage exploded in Richard's chest, but he had armed men to worry about. Grenier's turn was coming.

Dropping to one knee, Richard sheathed the sword and jammed the hilt into his pocket. He then pulled out a flash-bang grenade, removed the pin, and tossed it down among the milling guards. Covering his ears, he looked away so as not to be blinded. The grenade went off with a chest-pounding bang. There were screams from the guards. Richard pulled the Browning from his shoulder rig as a bullet skipped and whined off the stone near him.

He aimed and double-tapped at the guard with the drawn gun. The roar of the pistol damped whatever hearing he had left, but he was pleased to see the bullets take the man in the chest. The guard collapsed.

"Throw down your weapons," Richard yelled, and wondered if the remaining men could even hear him. Certainly the four who were crawling feebly across the flagstone were deafened.

Five down, three to go, he thought. Richard risked a glance. Mosi had gotten herself and Kenntnis down a level and were huddled in one of the small rooms out of the line of fire. Richard was exposed on the battlement, but he also held the high ground. It was literally like shooting targets in a barrel as he drew down on another guard, who seemed to be reaching for his sidearm. His aim was a bit off on this one, and it took the man in the low belly rather than the chest. The final two guards threw down their weapons and put their hands behind their heads.

The timing was going to be tight, but Richard needed to incapacitate the prisoners, and handcuffs were not an option. Keeping his pistol leveled on the guards, Richard pulled the hilt out of his pocket and leaped down the steps. He got within a blade's length of the men, dropped the pistol, and drew the sword.

One of the men tried to be a hero, lunged for Richard, and managed to run himself onto the point of the sword. It wasn't a deep wound, and the touch of the sword had its usual effect of sending him into violent convulsions. Richard spun and slapped the flat of the blade against the only guard still standing. He went down. Then for good measure Richard touched the men still trying to recover from the flash-bang. He moved to the men he had wounded and discovered that one man was dead. *Thirty-two.* The man with the belly wound would need a doctor and soon if he wasn't going to be number thirty-three. Richard touched him with the sword, swept up his pistol, and headed for the gate through which Grenier had fled.

Richard imagined the feel as his fist buried itself in that pendulous belly, planned the blow to a jowled cheek, pictured teeth breaking and blood pouring over the multiple chins. Envisioned Grenier prostrate on the cobbles while he kicked the living shit out of him. Each image sent his rage spiraling higher. He was through the gate and drew level with Titchen's broken body. The man was moaning, piteous, animal-like sounds of suffering. Richard contemptuously drew the edge of the sword across Titchen's chest, cutting through material and leaving a shallow, bloody line across his skin. The convulsions took him, and Titchen screamed in agony.

The sound was like a blow, chilling Richard, and his rage faded to bitter ash. Who was he to inflict such pain? What was he becoming? Then he remembered the child. Huddled, frightened, and now—because of Richard's single-minded fury—abandoned. Grenier didn't matter. Vengeance didn't matter. Mosi mattered.

Richard turned, ran back through the gate and into the fortress. Mosi was standing on the battlement, tears staining her face as she stared desperately toward the gate. When she saw Richard, she covered her face with her hands, the slender body shaking. He raced up the stairs, sheathed the sword, and gathered her into his arms. They sank down onto the stone walkway.

She battered at his chest with a fist. "I thought you had left me!"

"Never, Mosi, never."

He pulled her into his lap and rocked her gently while her tears soaked his shirt and her wails echoed off the walls. Kenntnis emerged from the small alcove and loomed over them, staring down with an almost puzzled expression.

The sobs began to die, then Mosi once again slammed a fist against Richard's chest. She lifted her head out of his shoulder and glared at him.

"Why didn't you tell me about the sword? How it was gone."

"I didn't want to worry you."

"If you had, we'd have had the sword back waaay sooner. You were dumb!"

"Yes, I probably was, but why didn't you tell me when the sword appeared and dove into Mr. Kenntnis's body?"

"'Cause you didn't say anything and I thought it was something *you* had done and wanted to keep it secret since everybody was so mad."

Richard sighed and rubbed at his forehead. "That's fair. I guess we need to talk to each other more."

"Okay. And you can't leave me ever again!" she ordered fiercely.

He didn't bother with words. He just hugged her close. That was how the authorities found them.

TWENTY-FOUR

W HY didn't you go after him? You could have caught him easily." Weber's warm breath puffed against Richard's ear.

There was enough city glow that he could make out the older man's features as Richard lay in the circle of Weber's arms. He was pressed against Weber's right side since a bullet had grazed his left hip, gouging a deep channel almost down to the bone.

It had been an insane day. Richard had briefly been detained by the police, but the presence of heavily armed men who had been attacking a child inclined things in Richard's direction, and his badge hadn't hurt either. It had also helped that rumors were swirling over the imminent collapse of the Islamist government. The arrest and torture of General Çelik had not sat well with the military at large, and the civilian government was scrambling to mend

THE EDGE OF DAWN

fences. Holding Richard and his people blameless was one plank in that fence.

Also, many of the men incapacitated by the flash-bang and then the sword had been eager to throw the blame on Titchen. The authorities didn't want to hear talk about a creature summoned by Titchen that had been threatening the city. As was a cop's wont, they went with the simple explanation—Titchen had hired men with guns to try and effect a very hostile takeover of a fellow businessman, and as a distraction, they had set fire to the shantytown. Richard, wearily amused, let it stand.

Titchen was in the same hospital where Weber had been treated and where Ranjan was currently resting after having a bullet dug out of his shoulder. When Richard had visited the Indian scientist, intending to apologize for getting him into this mess, Richard had found himself stunned into silence as Ranjan thanked him fervently for *"this very big adventure. I feel like James Bond."* Richard had been unable to muster up much of a response beyond, *"Happy to oblige."* The word on Titchen was that he would recover but was likely paralyzed from the neck down from the fall.

Since the danger was past, Richard moved his people to the Lugal hotel. He figured everyone would welcome a private room, restaurants, swimming pool, and spa services with in-room massages available. He had been going to maintain the fiction and get separate rooms for himself and Weber, but the security chief had been blunt. *"Save the money, and you know one of them will be empty anyway."*

"Did you hear me?" Weber nudged.

"Yeah. Why didn't I go after him?" Richard repeated slowly. "Mosi, mostly. I started to, but then I remembered her. She's been through so much, to abandon her would have been . . . unforgivable."

Weber kissed him. "Go on, I can tell that's not all."

It was not an admission he relished making, and it was a testament to how much he trusted this man that he felt he could. "I realized I was becoming the thing I was fighting," Richard said softly. "I didn't just touch Titchen with the sword. I cut him, and there was no reason for that. And if I'd caught up with Mark I was going to . . ."

"Kill him?"

"No, I wasn't that far gone, but hurt him, certainly."

"He needs to pay for what he did."

"He will, but in a court of law. Law, like science, is the antithesis of the Old Ones. They push us to give in to the worst of our nature, to shut off our critical faculties, to embrace hate and violence and vengeance. The law is dispassionate, or it tries to be. It makes you wait and not take justice into your own hands. Grenier will be judged and go to prison."

"And if he doesn't? If he gets some slick lawyer and gets off?"

Richard shrugged. "I doubt he'll survive long. He was party to events where another Old One was killed. He worked with me. They'll find him. They might even find him in prison." Richard fell silent, then added softly, "I almost feel sorry for him, Damon."

"Well, I don't. Bastard tortured you, came crawling, then betrayed you. Fuck him."

"I'd rather not," Richard said with a small smile.

"Oh, God, why did you put that picture in my head?" Weber cuffed him lightly on the head.

"Sorry. How about if I distract you?" Richard let his hand slip down.

Weber caught Richard's hand. "I have a question first. You're heading home, right?"

"As soon as Ranjan gets released, and I deal with Boğazkale."

"Okay. So where am I heading? Where do you want me?"

"Wherever I am."

The worried expression in Weber's eyes cleared. "Okay. Good."

"You and Joseph get to switch places."

"And what is the word from home?" Weber asked.

"Pamela's trying to find some way to keep us from losing all the employees in the subsidiaries, and she and Dagmar are juggling money. They're also lining up people for me to interview to replace Kenzo." Richard sighed. "There is one piece of good news—the stock price on Gaia tanked after Titchen's arrest. But I still need to hire people to track down all those computers and destroy them. Being broke sucks."

"We gonna have to sneak out of here in the dead of night?"

"We can pay this bill, but . . ." Richard shook his head.

Weber gently touched him between the brows with an index finger as if erasing the frown. "Worrying won't help. We'll figure something out." A wicked grin appeared. "How about if I distract you?"

"Uh, sure."

As the helicopter passed over Boğazkale, Richard saw that a fleet of ambulances was parked in the village and masked and biosuited medical workers were gathering and identifying the bodies.

"Do you think the village will be abandoned?" Weber asked Sözer, who had accompanied them this time.

The general shook his head. "No, the archaeologists will want to return. Eventually, the tourists will return because most will never hear of these events. Relatives will come. Life endures."

"It does indeed," Richard said. "And fights like hell to endure," he added almost to himself.

The chopper landed, the rotors slowed, and the engine howl died into silence. Richard climbed out and headed for the stone. He had the sword drawn just in case. Clouds were boiling over the distant hills as if fleeing from the flashes of lightning, and the music of the goats' soprano bells was punctuated by basso growls of thunder.

"Do you think they sense you coming and that's why the storm?" Sözer asked as they walked through the ruins of the lower city.

"I think Kenntnis would tell us we're trying to form patterns where none exist." He gave the general a quick smile. "This feels like normal earth weather to me."

Arriving at the stone, Richard pivoted slowly, looking for any indication that something else had emerged from the portal, and didn't see any. He then laid the blade on the top of the stone. There was a deafening *crack*, and the stone split in half. The interior held overlaid imprints that suggested faces.

Weber blew out a nervous breath. "Well, that's not at all creepy. And once again Lumina damages a priceless archaeological artifact. Go, us."

⸻❖⸻

The Atlantic slipped away beneath the wings of the plane. It was very late, so the lights were dimmed in the cabin. Weber was snoring loudly on one side of the plane. On the other, Mosi, wrapped in a blanket, slept in her fold-down seat.

At the child's insistence, Richard had located the gray gelding, purchased the horse, and arranged to have it flown back to Albuquerque. He gazed down at her fondly, tucked the blanket more securely under her chin, and joined the scientific team waiting in the office at the rear of the plane.

There was an air of barely suppressed excitement from the humans. Kenntnis sat in a chair, silent and enigmatic. Richard took a seat behind his desk.

"Okay, you were going to tell me something but were terrified of eavesdropping. We're at thirty-five thousand feet with ocean all around. Is this private enough?"

"Wow, grumpy a little?" Eddie said.

"Eddie," Richard said warningly.

"Okay, sorry. So you know how I said Trout was working on something big. Well, he did it! He figured it out."

"Couldn't have done it without the chance to really study Mr.

Kenntnis here," the heavyset scientist said. It was the first time Richard had ever seen the man with any expression beyond a surly frown. He was grinning.

Ranjan, his arm in a sling, blurted out, "And it is amazing!"

"A world-altering moment," Chen added in almost reverent tones.

"Okay . . . and it is . . . ?" Richard asked.

Trout laid a welter of papers covered with calculations on the desk in front of him. Richard gazed at them and once again had that uncomfortable feeling of being the dummy in a family of geniuses. He looked up at the assembled PhDs.

"Okay, I'm not a brilliant Nobel prize–winning scientist, so tell me what this is."

"Quantum computing," Trout exploded.

"And that's a big fucking deal why?"

Richard saw Eddie react at his unusual use of profanity. He closed his eyes, pinched the bridge of his nose, and reminded himself that none of these men was his father or his sisters, and they weren't trying to make him feel stupid.

"I apologize, I'm tired. I just need this put in simple English."

It defaulted to Eddie probably because he had the longest history with Richard. The young man sucked in a deep breath and began.

"Okay, so computers today work by manipulating bits that have a value of either zero or one, and they can only do one task at a time. They do that task very fast, but it's one task after another serially. But a quantum computer has bits that simultaneously are both zero and one, and because of this parallelism a quantum computer could work on a million computations all at the same time."

Chen couldn't contain himself. "But we can't look at that happening because if we look at subatomic particles, that will bump them—"

Ranjan jumped in. "And that would make the particles fall onto one or the other state—zero or one—"

Eddie again. "And our computer would be back to being just a simple Turing-type computer.

Trout made an expansive gesture with both hands, as if pushing them all aside. "So we fix that using entanglement, and by studying Mr. Kenntnis I saw a way to—"

"Stop!" Richard yelled. "So, basically, what you are telling me is that a quantum computer is *really, really* fast."

Eddie nodded. "Yeah, faster than all the supercomputers on Earth . . . *put together.*"

"Okay, that's fast," Richard said, impressed.

"Able to do multiple computations at the same time," Ranjan said.

"Can it leap tall buildings too?" Richard quipped.

Eddie put on an air of long suffering. "Making other scientific advances that much easier."

Chen gave a tight smile. "Such as figuring out the sword and how to re-create its power."

Trout leaned in on Richard, resting his fists on the table. *"And it will be worth a fortune."*

"And Lumina will control the patent," Eddie said.

"So our financial problems—" Richard began.

"Are over," Eddie concluded.

<hr />

They landed in Albuquerque late at night and found Joseph, Estevan, Pamela, and two limos waiting. As soon as he took the final step onto the tarmac, Pamela grabbed Richard in a fierce hug, then held him at arm's length, looking him up and down.

"Okay, how are you hurt this time?"

"I'm not."

She gave him a look that clearly indicated she thought he was lying.

Weber stepped in. "He's really not."

She went to hug Mosi, and Richard gave a quick head shake. Pamela backed off, nodded to the girl, and said, "I'm so glad you're all home." She turned to the scientists and Weber. "We've made reservations for you at the Marriott."

People started moving toward the cars. "Damon's coming back to Lumina with us," Richard said.

"We don't have enough bedrooms," his sister began.

"We'll manage," Richard said firmly. Weber coughed and looked away.

Eventually they reached the building, and Richard found that most of his staff were still there despite the late hour to welcome them. Everyone from Paulette, the front desk receptionist, to Franz to Jeannette to Dagmar . . . and Jorge. Richard turned to Pamela, and she gave him one of her tight little smiles.

"Once I knew you'd won, I hired him back."

The young man stepped forward and thrust out his hand. "Wish you'd trusted me, Mr. Oort. You could have told me."

"I needed your reaction to be absolutely natural. Grenier would have seen through anything else."

"And speaking of . . . what happened to that *pendejo*?" Jorge asked.

Dagmar was at Richard's side. "Yes, I'd be *very* interested in that bit of information." There were murmurs of assent from the rest of the assembled staff.

"Still at large. The Turkish authorities are searching for him."

"You don't seem concerned," Pamela said.

"I'm not." He turned to the assembled staff. "Thank you all for being here to welcome us home, but it's really late, and I need to get my ward"—he laid a hand on Mosi's back—"and our newest paladin to bed."

There was a sudden babble of voices as people reacted. The assembled crowd started clapping. Mosi hid her face against Richard. He chuckled and stroked her hair.

It still took a while to actually get on the elevator. Hands had to be shaken, thank-yous murmured, backs slapped. Franz gripped

Richard's suit-coat sleeve and said, "There is a small *casse-croûte* waiting upstairs."

Weber looked pleased at the prospect. Richard, knowing that Franz's idea of "small" was relative, hoped that between Weber and Cross, if he turned up, the snack would get eaten. Finally they were deposited in the marble foyer of the penthouse.

Richard exhaled. "Home." He turned to his sister. "You get home too. Business can wait until morning."

She kissed him on the cheek. Looked from Weber to Richard. Richard tensed, waiting for the frown or blush. Instead a little smile curved her lips. She patted Weber on the shoulder and kissed his cheek too.

"Make sure he eats some breakfast, okay?"

Weber, looking poleaxed, watched her enter the elevator. The doors closed on her broad smile.

Richard watched as Mosi and Weber ate some of Franz's *casse-croûte*. He gave Mosi time to brush her teeth and get into her pajamas, then went into the room to bid her good night. Richard sat on the edge of the pretty canopy bed. Mosi sat up and wrapped her arms around his waist. He returned the embrace.

"There are still monsters . . . out there, aren't there?"

"Yes."

She nodded. "We'll fight them."

"Yes, we will. Good night, Mosi."

He returned to the living room. Kenntnis stood at the side of the Bösendorfer grand piano, and Richard realized it was silent. When the alien had been intact, his presence pulled soft chords from musical instruments all around him. Since his capture and illness, the sounds had been discordant. Tonight it was silent. Richard wondered what that might portend.

Weber sat on the couch, arms outstretched along the back. "So, couch for me? Or are we taking the twin beds?"

"Kenntnis will sleep there."

"The master bedroom . . . ?" Weber's voice trailed away.

"Is mine. Ours." Richard held out his hand.

Richard moved to the desk in the office and looked at the books, the paperweight, the bookends. Jeannette, poised at his side, waited for him to speak.

"Grenier's?"

"Yes, sir."

"Get rid of it. All of it. Please."

"Of course, sir. May I throw it away?"

"Be my guest."

Richard fell silent and studied the room, noted the art—one Impressionist painting and a number of Renaissance pieces. The predominantly red-toned geometric-style Oriental rug underfoot.

"Jeannette, I'd like to keep the Degas, but I want to replace the others with some of the modern pieces from my apartment. They're nowhere near as valuable, but they're more to my taste. They're in storage right now. Maybe you could send Estevan?"

"Of course. What would you like done with these pieces?" She indicated the art currently on the walls.

"We have plenty of wall space on the various floors. No reason why other people can't enjoy them."

"Very good."

"Also, do we have any other rugs? Something less dark. You know my taste."

"We have photos of all of Mr. Kenntnis's possessions. I'll narrow it down to a few choices and bring them to you."

"That would be great." He went to his chair and readjusted it back to his height.

Jeannette paused at the door. "It's good to have you back, sir."

"Good to be back."

"May I ask you a question?"

"Certainly."

"Why now?"

"Excuse me?"

"Why are you making changes now?"

Richard met her eyes squarely. "Because Lumina is mine."